The Wonder
of Now

D0169716

ALSO BY JAMIE BECK

In the Cards

The St. James Novels

Worth the Wait
Worth the Trouble
Worth the Risk

The Sterling Canyon Novels

Accidentally Hers
Secretly Hers
Unexpectedly Hers
Joyfully His

The Cabot Novels

Before I Knew
All We Knew
When You Knew

The Sanctuary Sound Novels

The Memory of You
The Promise of Us

"Jamie Beck's deeply felt novel hits all the right notes, celebrating the power of forgiveness, the sweetness of second chances, and the heady joy of reaching for a dream. Don't miss this one!"
—Susan Wiggs, #1 *New York Times* bestselling author

"*Before I Knew* kept me totally enthralled as two compassionate, relatable characters, each in search of forgiveness and fulfillment, turn a recipe for heartache into a story of love, hope, and some really good menus!"
—Shelley Noble, *New York Times* bestselling author of *Whisper Beach*

PRAISE FOR *ALL WE KNEW*

"A moving story about the flux of life and the steadfastness of family."
—*Publishers Weekly*

"An impressively crafted and deftly entertaining read from first page to last."
—*Midwest Book Review*

"*All We Knew* is compelling, heartbreaking, and emotional."
—*Harlequin Junkie*

PRAISE FOR *JOYFULLY HIS*

"A quick and sweet read that is perfect for the holidays."
—*Harlequin Junkie*

PRAISE FOR *WHEN YOU KNEW*

"[A]n opposites-attract romance with heart."
—*Harlequin Junkie*

PRAISE FOR *THE MEMORY OF YOU*

"[Beck] deepens a typical story about first loves reuniting by exploring the aftermath of a violent act. Readers will root for an ending that repairs this couple's past hurt."

—*Booklist*

"Beck's portrayals of divorce and trauma are keen . . . Readers will be caught up in their journey toward healing and romance."

—*Publishers Weekly*

"*The Memory of You* is heartbreaking, emotional, entertaining, and a unique second-chance romance."

—*Harlequin Junkie*

PRAISE FOR *THE PROMISE OF US*

"Beck's depiction of trauma, loss, friendship, and family resonates deeply. A low-key small-town romance unflinching in its portrayal of the complexities of friendship and family, and the joys and sorrows they bring."

—*Kirkus Reviews*

"A fully absorbing and unfailingly entertaining read from an author with a genuine flair for originality and an engaging narrative storytelling style, Jamie Beck's *The Promise of Us* is an extraordinary and highly recommended addition to community library Contemporary Romance Fiction collections."

—*Midwest Book Review*

The Wonder of Now

A Sanctuary Sound Novel

JAMIE BECK

This is a work of fiction. Names, characters, organizations, places, events, and incidents are either products of the author's imagination or are used fictitiously.

Text copyright © 2019 by Jamie Beck
All rights reserved.

No part of this book may be reproduced, or stored in a retrieval system, or transmitted in any form or by any means, electronic, mechanical, photocopying, recording, or otherwise, without express written permission of the publisher.

Published by Montlake Romance, Seattle

www.apub.com

Amazon, the Amazon logo, and Montlake Romance are trademarks of Amazon.com, Inc., or its affiliates.

ISBN-13: 9781542044325
ISBN-10: 1542044324

Cover design by Emily Mahon

Cover photography by Regina Wamba of MaelDesign.com

Printed in the United States of America

This one is for my Fiction From The Heart sisters: Tracy Brogan, Sonali Dev, K. M. Jackson, Virginia Kantra, Donna Kauffman, Sally Kilpatrick, Falguni Kothari, Priscilla Oliveras, Barbara O'Neal, Hope Ramsay, and Liz Talley, for the friendship, support, and advice that flow from their generous hearts.

Chapter One

Om Namah Shivaya.
   "Let me photograph the treatment," he'd begged.
Om Namah Shivaya.
   "We'll make art, raise money," he'd promised.
Om Namah Shivaya.
   Dammit.
   Peyton opened one eye and stared across the undulating surface of Long Island Sound, which glittered all the way to the horizon. Six hundred thirty-two attempts at meditation in as many days and she *still* couldn't master her own mind.

   Dwelling for months in a decaying body had forced an existential dread that produced few answers, but she'd never been a quitter. In her darkest moments, she'd habitually forced herself to look for silver linings. By thirty-one, she'd mastered *that* ritual. Last year, she'd even found two for chemo, like the way she could blame it for all kinds of personal failings. Its other plus? A handy excuse for opting out of her mother's endless list of social and philanthropic invitations. Of course, those benefits didn't outweigh the weight gain, skin discoloration, nausea, mouth ulcers, and hair loss she'd experienced while undergoing breast cancer treatment.

   Peyton curled a jaw-length strand of newly wavy hair around her finger. Still short, but progress nonetheless.

She uncrossed her legs while taking a deep breath of briny air and then stretched them out, digging her toes into the warm sand. Growing up, she and her brother, Logan, and their friends had played tag here, built sandcastles, lit bonfires while camping out. They'd drifted on rafts and sailed around the Sound, carefree and certain of a future that would always be easy and full of adventure. Now her gaze fixed on the line where earth met sky. These past few months, she'd often stared at that distant place, contemplating her life and purpose and other things she'd never before given much thought to.

Those lazy hours, bookended by the rush of midday and the lonesome stretches of night, had become her favorite part of each day. Stolen moments of peace and presence were probably the closest she'd ever get to nirvana or zen or wherever one is supposed to arrive through meditation.

"Peyton!" Logan called from the flagstone patio. When she glanced over her shoulder, he waved her toward their family's historic shingle-style mansion. Sunlight and water reflected in its dozens of windows, making them look as if they were winking. "They're here. Come see!"

A day or so after her initial diagnosis nearly two years ago, Logan had cornered her with his camera and his big idea. He'd always been able to talk her into anything, and until now, she'd relished his schemes. If she didn't love him so much, she'd seriously consider lining his shower with shaving cream later.

Logan turned and disappeared through the french doors without waiting for her. She hugged her legs to her chest, pressing her forehead to her knees. Why bother with meditation? She had no time for serenity. Not with her brother and Mitchell Mathis—PR pain in the butt—always coming at her with to-do lists.

Peyton pushed herself up and brushed the sand from her bottom, slipped on her sandals, and strolled up the lawn of the rambling estate. Only recently had she come to understand why her great-grandfather had built Arcadia House, and why he'd hidden here—away from most of the world—to write. She barely remembered Duck, as Logan had nicknamed him, but his legendary literature and name lived on—not just here, but all around the world.

She hadn't even closed the doors before Logan bellowed from the vicinity of their father's office, "Back here."

She found him standing at Duck's antique walnut writing desk, surrounded by overstuffed bookshelves that emitted the faintest hint of tobacco, with his hands gripping a sizable cardboard box. When Peyton was a child, this room had been off-limits and, consequently, a place she'd snuck into time and again, tempting fate. Funny how, back then, she'd perceived fate and consequence as a game. *Checkmate.*

"Aren't you blown away?" His smile, warmer and more promising than a summer sunrise on the Sound, settled her. Then he lifted a copy of *A Journey through Shadows* from the open carton.

Her gaze skittered away from the cover image and landed on her metallic-toned Birkenstocks. Before cancer, she wouldn't have been caught dead in such footwear or without a pedicure. Lots had changed since her Joie-sandal days. Some for the better and—she wiggled her unpainted toes—some for the worse.

"Yes," came her dry reply. Blown away, all right, just not the way he meant it.

But like any little sister who ever worshipped her older brother would, she'd agreed to his plan. After all, she'd had little to lose when she thought she was dying.

The result? The memoir in his hands. A combination of his work—including the austere black-and-white midchemo cover photo she now avoided—alongside her most personal fears and naked emotions. The sight of it reminded her that, in a matter of days, people around the world would have access to every nook and cranny of her soul.

And to think, just before her diagnosis, few had believed she still had one.

"Come on." He waved the book in front of her. "Have a look."

She reluctantly accepted the hardcover tome and then sat in a well-worn leather chair opposite the desk. Duck's framed Pulitzer hung on the paneled wall beside her, in its antique walnut frame with blackened edges and ripple moldings, mocking the hubris of his great-grandkids' latest undertaking.

In contrast to her desire to hide from the spotlight, soft light filtered through the large open windows behind Logan, setting him aglow. He removed another copy from the box while shaking his head in amazement.

"This image was totally the right choice for the cover." His green eyes twinkled, no longer burdened by the alarm they'd reflected when first learning of her illness. "Talk about arresting."

He began leafing through the pages, pausing to stare at his own work. She couldn't blame him. Every person she knew, including herself, became self-absorbed from time to time. But while he marveled at his work, she shivered at the memory of the morning he'd caught her crying in private and shot the cover image.

His palpable excitement about their work stopped her from explaining how much she dreaded revisiting the most terrifying, sickly moments of her life. Or describing how rereading the passages and seeing his photos of her double mastectomy and the patient friends who'd since died made her stomach cramp.

If she had her choice, she'd never again look at their book. She'd even give up her share of the proceeds if others would promote it and leave her free to focus on looking forward instead of backward.

It took two minutes for him to notice her utter stillness.

Logan placed his copy back in the box and then pressed his fingertips on the desk, bowing forward a bit—a pose he struck often, putting his lean build and casual elegance on full display. "What's wrong? We should be celebrating, but you look like you want to kill somebody. Me, in fact."

Peyton shifted beneath the weight of the book on her thighs. "Nothing you'd understand."

He pushed away from the desk and came to sit in the chair beside her, running one hand through his hair. His burnished-gold locks would take another few months to grow back to the eight-inch length he'd sported before shearing it off last year in a show of moral support. She still had the gorgeous wig made from his hair in her closet.

"Is it the public response? Don't worry. Early reviews have been stellar." He offered a reassuring nod. "You're a fantastic writer."

Travel writer, she thought wryly. Not an author. Not like Duck.

She'd never aspired, nor could she ever hope, to live up to her great-grandfather's legacy. Writing witty pieces about hotels, restaurants, and tourist spots around the world had never forced a comparison to his contemplative body of work. Venturing into true author territory would invite it, though. Especially after she let the publisher talk her into playing off her great-grandfather's most famous book, *A Shadow on Sand*, with her memoir's title. Not that *that* was her biggest concern.

"Thanks, but this isn't fiction. It's my life—my heart—on display for others to judge." She pressed her hand to her stomach and drew a yoga breath. This sick pit in her gut was trepidation, not self-pity. Until her diagnosis, she'd relied on her beauty, money, and wit as weapons used to disarm and charm. To entertain and seduce. To explore. The mental, physical, and emotional mutations she'd undergone had upended everything she'd understood about herself and her place in the world. The book's release would erase the last vestiges of her former self, which, while she was still figuring out how to be the "new" Peyton, felt like being tossed from a plane without a parachute.

Her brother shot her a wry look. "A quick scroll through your Insta posts proves you've never been shy."

He didn't get it. To him and others, she was better now. Time to move on and celebrate. No one had noticed how she'd yet to share the collective sigh of relief that allowed her family and friends to return to normal. Cancer cells could be sneaky bitches—traveling, hiding, and replicating like bunnies. Her once playful journal now cataloged every cough, ache, rash, and other symptom so she wouldn't forget to report anything to the doctor. She had no idea if or when she would relax and celebrate, but it wouldn't be today.

"I *never* flashed my boobs—or lack thereof—before." Joking kept the onslaught of panic at bay, but Logan's silence proved her attempt had fallen flat. *No pun intended.* Social media accounts gave the public an illusion of her life, but her memoir described personal things she'd never before shared—nor particularly wanted to.

When most people learn of another's misfortune, they offer a quick thanks to God for their own safety and then ponder what they would do if handed a worst-case scenario. She'd drawn the short straw and now knew exactly how *she* would respond—with motionlessness caused by the bitter combination of disbelief, panic, and prayer that had pushed through her veins like arctic slush.

Chances were good that the frigid sensation would remain her occasional companion until—*if*—she reached the five-year cancer-free milestone. As it stood, her next exam was less than a month away.

Peyton knew another truth about bad news. After getting one bit, she could no longer skirt the fray. No longer feel safe. She expected more bad news at every turn and shuddered anytime she projected ahead to that appointment. Knowing that she could be handed another round of bad news made her resent having to spend time doing anything she didn't *want* to do, and she couldn't think of anything she'd rather do less than chase after book sales.

This whole thing had snowballed too far, too fast. The process of writing and working with her brother had been cathartic, but publishing? She honestly could not recall what she'd been thinking when she agreed to sign that contract. Now she couldn't let Logan down, or abandon the pledge they'd made to donate half the proceeds to the

National Breast Cancer Foundation, or piss all over the big advance they'd received.

She was alive, so she shouldn't complain. That's what everyone said, anyhow. This presumption—the forfeiting of the right to voice common complaints—was a side effect of survival that no one talked about for fear of sounding ungrateful.

"I get that this is hard, but you have courage. Focus on the money we'll be donating to research. And the hope that your story might give other women in your shoes." He reached for her hand and squeezed it, as if he could transfer his enthusiasm by mere touch. "You're my hero, sis. I've never been prouder of you than while watching you go through treatment and work on this project."

He'd stood by her always, even when she'd made terrible decisions, like when she hurt her childhood friend Claire over that idiot Todd, who'd made off like the Road Runner the minute she got sick. Logan had then moved Peyton into his home and taken months off work to be there, day and night, so that she wouldn't be alone during chemo. And without him she would've been utterly alone.

Her parents had offered to hire all the best nurses and aides, but they hadn't altered their work or philanthropic commitments to focus their attention on her. That had neither surprised nor troubled her. Life with unsentimental parents didn't mean you weren't loved; it merely meant you weren't the center of anyone's universe. That might explain why Todd's initial pretense that she was the center of *his* world had captivated her. But in truth, her parents' attitude had otherwise prepared her not to expect much genuine affection in the real world.

"Thank you." She raised his hand to her cheek and held tight. For most of their lives, he'd been *her* hero. "But you need higher standards."

Logan tugged at her earlobe. "Are you sure I can't take you to JFK tomorrow?"

"No thanks." She hugged the book to her stomach, which fluttered every time she thought of taking off on the weeks-long European promotional tour that seemed to have materialized out of nowhere. "Unlike you, an Uber driver gets paid for sitting in hours' worth of traffic. Besides, I'll need some downtime before I meet Mitchell and take off for Rome."

She'd looked Mitchell up on LinkedIn and then banged her forehead on her desk a few times. Just her luck to be tethered to a guy who was not only great at his job but also good-looking. Like, *wow*-level handsome, with gobs of gorgeous hair, which was the first thing she noticed about other people ever since she'd lost all hers.

Her prechemo hair—the long, silky blonde curtain that she'd used to flirt or hide or distract—had gone the way of the dinosaurs. Baldness had been a special kind of hell and, in some ways, made her a stranger to herself. Vanity was another of her flaws; she knew this. But having been born with her father's cheekbones and blue eyes and her mother's lean figure, she'd been turning heads since puberty. These days, not so much.

A few unwanted pounds of postchemo bloat remained, and her still-too-short, wavy baby-fine hair didn't fit her, somehow. It wasn't terrible, just wrong. And there was no hiding . . . or flirting. But, hey, she was still breathing.

On the other hand, Mitchell's hair fit *him* perfectly. A rich chestnut mane that had to have a natural wave or cowlick in order to achieve that kind of high flow in his bangs. And those deep-set, beautiful hazel eyes with their disconcerting alertness. They looked as if they could see right through her, and that was from a mere photograph. She couldn't imagine how she'd avoid their scrutiny in person.

His brows were thick like his hair; his lips, full yet firm-looking. The serious expression in his profile photo matched her all-business impression of him, which she'd based on what little email communication they'd had to date.

Hallelujah for that, though. The absence of friendly banter was what made her willing to take this trip with him. At this point in her recovery, she couldn't cope with, much less encourage, the tingly feelings of desire.

Chemo hair aside, even if she were ready to dip her toes back in the dating world, Mitchell Mathis would have far better options than someone with her particular scars and attic full of baggage. After reading her memoir—which showcased her erratic mental state and graphic images of her double mastectomy, ulcers, and more—he couldn't possibly find her attractive.

"If I weren't going to Peru next week for that *National Geographic* piece on Inti Raymi, I'd come with you." Logan sighed.

"It's fine." She stroked the book jacket. "This is our collaboration, but it's my story. Only I can answer reader questions about what I've written. I'll be okay."

"Still, I'm sorry I couldn't get out of my other commitment, although maybe it's best that I'll be back here in time to help with the last-minute details of my engagement party." He pulled his right foot up over his left knee.

The conflict did stink, but she couldn't keep relying on him. He'd already rearranged his life for her and played a pivotal role in helping her begin to mend fences with Claire. She'd agreed to this crazy project, and these author copies sealed her fate, putting her desire to live more mindfully on hold while she pimped the dang book.

"At least I'll be able to participate in the US tour dates," he said.

"Yes, so enjoy this special time with Claire." She pushed his foot. "Consider yourself fired from this babysitting job."

He smiled again, a content smile particular to his feelings for Claire. Peyton wouldn't have bet on that opposites-attract relationship, but her brother had fallen hard. Proof that dreams can come true, given Claire's long-standing crush on him.

Dreams made life brim with excited possibility—or, at least, that's what she remembered. Given her recent travails, she'd forgotten how to dream of anything other than survival. Then again, while dreams generated a delicious buzz, they could also make a person too focused on some goal, which detracted from being "present." These days, Peyton was all about being present, because tomorrow was no longer a given.

"And you'll be back for the party, right?" he asked.

"I wouldn't miss it." Not that long ago, she worried she'd miss so many celebrations with the people she loved. Now she didn't even mind her mom's tedious parties. Much.

He winked. "I'm relieved things between you and Claire are improved."

Peyton nodded, although recollecting her behavior felt a bit like waking up with a massive hangover. "It's still a work in progress."

"At least I'm no longer caught in the middle of two women I love." Logan then craned his neck in the direction of their father's Michter's twenty-year-old single-barrel bourbon. Its unbroken silver wax seal stared back at them. "Shall we break into Dad's stash and toast to our success?"

She welcomed a change of subject. "Sure."

"No reason to wait for him and Mom." He pushed himself out of the chair and poured the amber liquid two-fingers deep into the tumblers before handing one to her.

"What? You don't want to hear the umpteenth lecture about our airing 'dirty laundry' to the world?" She snickered. Never mind the philanthropic mission or the excruciating hours of work invested in the project. She doubted her mom had even bothered to read the advance copy. On the other hand, her mom *had* made one good point: promoting this book would force Peyton to relive everything over again, and further delay her return to "a normal life."

Logan stared at Duck's Pulitzer and then looked back at her while raising his glass. "To keeping the Prescott lit rep alive. Cheers."

She sniffed the bourbon's toffee scent before the liquid burned its way down her throat.

She hadn't drunk alcohol for so long its effect instantly grabbed hold of her, loosening her muscles one by one until her limbs felt soft and heavy and her mood pleasantly fuzzy. Then her phone pinged. She glanced at the text. *Mitchell.*

Checking in. Any last-minute questions or problems?

"My taskmaster." She chuckled, flashing the screen at her brother. She didn't know much about Mitchell, but he didn't seem the type to encourage her to go on a lark while in Europe. His tome-length list of goals began and ended with hitting all the bestseller lists, so side trips to browse the street art in the Quadraro area of Rome or peruse the antiques along Nieuwe Spiegelstraat in Amsterdam hadn't made the agenda.

Thinking of those places made her smile. She'd loved her former career as a travel writer but doubted she'd regain the stamina to return to that lifestyle. Not anytime soon, anyway. This book and her recovery had consumed her thoughts this past year, leaving her little time to plan for life beyond the book release. What fit was there for a former psych major with a bunch of old passports and a semipopular blog?

Logan patted her shoulder. "I'll let you deal with that. Need to get back to Claire for dinner." He finished his drink and stood. "Can I take a few copies?"

"Of course. They're half yours." She didn't need twenty-four copies of that bleak image staring at her, nor was she in a hurry to distribute them to anyone she knew.

It wasn't a lack of pride that stopped her. She'd worked her ass off on the book. Bled onto those pages. It was her best work and she knew it. But the thought of friends, neighbors, and strangers picking over her thoughts and feelings made her want to vomit. This venture had better raise a ton of money to make up for what she'd exposed.

Logan smiled and snagged five books. "If you want to grab lunch tomorrow before you head down to the airport, shoot me a text." Before breezing out of the office, he kissed her head. "Love you. Good luck."

"Bye." She waited until he left and then set her book on the desk and sighed. Looking at the screen of her phone, she pictured Mitchell's intense gaze and imagined him tapping his foot while awaiting her response. That made her smile.

Chemo might've killed a lot of stuff, but the part of her that had always enjoyed keeping a man on the edge of his seat had survived. After counting to ten "just because," she replied.

All set here. Not to brag, but I've been known to be a pretty good traveler. No need for hand-holding. ;-)

Not that, in another lifetime, she wouldn't enjoy holding his hand. She caught her lower lip between her teeth while waiting for the little dots to start dancing on the screen. They lit up almost immediately—confirmation of his workaholic status. She grinned, assuming he got the reference to her former career. Might he respond with something clever this time?

Thanks for the reminder. Always enjoy working with a pro. See you tomorrow.

She frowned, doubting he intended any kind of double entendre with that "pro" remark. Just as well. She really could not abide falling in lust with her publicist.

That said, there was no reason not to dig into her old wardrobe and ditch the Birkenstocks for a couple of weeks. She had less than twenty-four hours to convince herself that this trip across Europe—a return to her natural habitat—might be exactly what she needed to start to feel like her old self again.

Chapter Two

Mitch hit "Send" on a detailed, lengthy email to his new assistant, Rebecca. His blood pressure spiked each minute it took her to respond. These next two and a half weeks could kill him—literally. Delegating his workload to his first employee felt as prudent as handing his credit card to a teenage girl. In his experience, no one ever did anything quite as he expected. Not even when he mapped out explicit instructions.

He glanced out the airline gate's plate glass window, but the behemoth plane blocked the view of the runway. His mouth filled with a sour taste. He'd have to board it—and several more—to accompany Peyton on her European book tour. Her publisher, Savant Press—also his former employer—had pushed the US release date back to avoid competing with the launch of other notable memoirs and biographies, but its European launch kicked off today.

When Mitch first got the call for help from Logan Prescott after Savant had recommended him, he'd popped champagne. After clawing his way into college and then New York publishing, he'd been derailed by an ill-fated office romance. He'd spent the rest of his career at Savant repairing that damage and also fighting the old-guard PR team with then-fresh ideas about how to create buzz through digital and social media. Seven months ago, he'd taken the plunge and founded his own PR firm, List Launch. Now he had full autonomy and the potential for much more income—or utter failure.

Savant's faith in him was vindicating, but he'd have to perform well to keep that pipeline open. Wrangling multiple international publishers and having them apprise him of their plans was always a challenge, but he'd nailed it all down as usual. It was unfortunate, of course, that Logan's schedule was too rigid to work around, but Peyton was the primary draw for this book. The hardest part of this particular job would be motivating his unenthusiastic author.

To date, he'd leveraged the Prescott legacy to get wide media coverage and help secure several major media endorsements for the memoir despite Peyton's reluctance to exploit her name—a position that made no sense. He would've relished having had *any* advantages in life. In any case, this trip meant Peyton could no longer avoid him. Thank God, because they had work to do.

A quick glance at his watch and then at the airline personnel at the check-in desk had his knee jiggling. Boarding would begin in ten minutes, yet there was no sign of his client.

When he turned off his iPad and slipped it into his leather backpack, he caught sight of Peyton's haunting book-cover image peering up at him. Those eyes. That mouth. Her despondent face washed a whirlpool of acid around his stomach and up into his chest.

He closed his eyes, but the memories of his father's losing battle with glioblastoma surfaced anyway. Memories that had convinced him to rely on Rebecca's summary of Peyton's memoir rather than read it cover to cover as he should have. Atypical of him, but he'd do *anything* to avoid revisiting that grief.

If Peyton hadn't been a client who could garner major visibility for his young firm, he might've declined the job altogether. But her memoir could make her *the* success story that took his business to the next level.

Unlike with his dad, he planned to maintain a polite but distant professional relationship with her to protect himself from the sorrow he'd feel if her cancer returned. But to date, she'd survived *and* written a book. By now he assumed she must be well enough to endure the grueling schedule of media events and interviews, signings, and parties. First, however, she'd have to show up.

After fishing his phone out of his pocket, he typed:

Are you in the airport yet?

Fifteen seconds passed before she read the message and responded.

Of course. I'm familiar with TSA requirements. Waiting for my bar tab. See you soon.

He felt his eyes bulge. She'd been relaxing while he fretted at the gate? If she made a habit of last-minute appearances, he'd need blood pressure meds.

Mitch's research had revealed her to be gorgeous, funny, and daring . . . a killer combo. He'd developed a little crush by the time he'd read several blog posts and surfed her social media. Of course, that cover photo exposed the ravages of cancer treatment.

Her physical scars would heal, but if watching his father suffer had permanently changed Mitch, he could only imagine what cancer had done to Peyton's psyche. He then quieted the voice that reminded him he wouldn't have to imagine anything if he'd read the book.

His phone pinged.

P.S. I noticed we had a free evening on Thursday, so I took the liberty of making reservations for dinner in the Trastevere neighborhood of Rome at Enoteca Ferrara. They have the best amatriciana, and the sommelier will pair some nice wines for us.

When another passenger bumped into him, he started breathing again. Turning his attention back to the screen, he only had to picture Danielle's face and remember her duplicity in order to resist the temptation of Peyton's spirited messages. He thought up a dry response to ensure that she'd never find him interesting.

> That's thoughtful, thank you. Let's play it by ear, though. We have a lot to accomplish on this trip and shouldn't risk wearing ourselves out.

He hit "Send" with a heavy sigh. God, he sounded so boring. Three dots pulsed on his screen, followed by her reply.

> I can't accomplish anything if I'm malnourished. Are you sure you want to risk letting me cozy up to the locals for dinner company? Roman men can be very persuasive. Rumor has it that I've been talked into doing crazy things on the Spanish Steps. I need a chaperone. Tag—you're it.

He fought a smile, imagining her being the center of attention and dashing off on any adventure that came her way. Maybe he'd been wrong and cancer hadn't killed her spirit.

He put his thumbs to work.

> You win.

More dots.

> Oh, good. Always my preferred outcome. Signing my check now. See you soon.

He tucked his phone in his pocket, too aware of the pleasant flutter in his heart.

Hadn't he learned his lesson? Years of hard work and careful planning should not be put at risk over an infatuation. His savings had taken a hit after helping pay for his baby sister's college tuition and updating his mom's old kitchen. It'd be another decade or longer until he attained financial security. No missteps now, not even for someone as charming as Peyton Prescott.

Savant knew there weren't any guarantees when it came to publishing, but that wouldn't stop it from expecting him to deliver. This unspoken expectation was what drove him to accompany Peyton on her first book tour—an act that hadn't been necessary when he'd handled more-experienced authors. He had one and *only* one goal for this trip, though—getting Peyton's book as much buzz as it deserved to push it up the bestseller lists.

He stood and looped his backpack over one shoulder, shuffling to the priority-boarding lane with one more glance at his watch. In the distance, Peyton was making her way down the hallway, pulling a tiny carry-on behind her with a travel pillow tucked under her arm.

Taller and thinner than he'd expected, she moved with a grace he hadn't been prepared for. Her lightweight ice-blue top billowed with each step, brushing against leggings that showed off shapely legs. It almost seemed as if her spirit raced ahead to part the crowd for her. "Breathtaking" sounded so trite, but he literally had to think about breathing while watching her move toward him.

After weeks of glimpsing her bald-headed photo on his desk corner, he was now surprised by the blonde locks that brushed her jaw with the kind of natural waves that his sister, Lauren, would call "beach hair."

Peyton's face lit with recognition when she caught sight of him. She must've looked him up, too.

Her quick smile heated something inside him. Something that made him dizzy and feverish.

When she drew near, he extended his hand, his gaze drifting away from the enticing blaze of light in her eyes. "Peyton, it's nice to finally meet you."

"Mitchell."

The brief but firm contact left his hand warm and tingly. He wiggled his fingers at his side. "Please call me Mitch."

Thank God she wasn't a hugger like his sister or he might've melted on the spot. Lauren had hugged almost everyone she'd met since she'd seen *My Big Fat Greek Wedding* on cable, in a determined effort not to be like its Waspy Miller family.

"Okay, Mitch. Thank you for everything you've done to support this launch. I know my editor has big expectations, although they're nothing compared with my brother's." When she teased, her blue eyes twinkled like aquamarines. Stunning.

His heart beat harder, having no defense against the onslaught of desire she inspired. His plan to keep a distance had already faltered and they'd yet to leave New York.

He cleared his throat as the passenger line began moving past the ticket counter. "We've got our work cut out for us. Glad you made it on time."

She motioned "voilà" with her hands. "My timing is perfect. I completely avoided a long wait in those awful gate seats."

Fair point, although he preferred to be early for appointments.

"In the future, I'd appreciate being kept apprised of your plans." If he sounded like a school principal or annoying great-aunt, so be it. Anything that helped draw a line between them might save him from himself.

"Sorry." She patted his shoulder while shooting him a solemn look. "I'll share a secret with you, though. Something I've learned these past eighteen months or so. Don't waste time stressing over things you can't control, especially things that *might've* gone wrong. I'm here on time. It's all good."

"I suppose I can't argue with that," he conceded, distracted by a whiff of the citrusy scent of her hair—a sassy, short hairstyle as free and easy as she seemed. He waved her ahead of him in line. "Ladies first."

"Thank you." She handed the ticket agent her boarding pass and passport and then stepped aside and waited for him to be checked through, too. The man who went ahead of them glanced back at her for a second look, although she seemed oblivious to the guy's interest. "So tell me, have you been to any of our destinations before?"

"No." *God no.* Even if he'd had the spare money to blow on trips to Europe, he detested flying. "But I've planned many events there and have ongoing relationships with the booksellers and publishers we'll be meeting with."

They started down the humid gangway. Each step they drew closer to the entrance of the airplane, the tunnel seemed to narrow and recede. The sickening taste of bile filled his throat.

Conversely, her smile broadened. "Well, then, I'll be your tour guide in each city. I know we have a busy schedule, but I know a million little detours. Tell me all your favorite things to do and I'll come up with some plans."

Handing her information about his favorite anything would be tantamount to arming her for his own undoing.

"You might prefer to rest or be alone during your downtime. Being 'on' in front of journalists, bloggers, and readers for days at a time is very draining." He hesitated to say more. Given her lack of enthusiasm for discussing promotion these past few months, a frank discussion about the toll this tour would take on her might send her running.

She stiffened, making him wish he hadn't said anything. Before he could recant, his phone rang. *Lauren.*

"Excuse me," he said before answering the call. "Hey, Bug, what's up?"

Silence.

Oh yeah. She'd taken a stance against that old nickname ever since graduating from college this past spring.

"Sorry. Old habits." Being eleven years his junior had made Lauren more like a daughter than a sister at times.

"Same old excuse." Her words carried no real heat.

He sensed Peyton listening, so he tucked his chin and lowered his voice. "I assume you called for some reason?"

"I'm having trouble with something . . . a guy."

He whipped his hand up like a stop sign even though she couldn't see it. "Talk to Mom about men unless you need me to publicly destroy someone. Then I'm your guy."

He'd use every weapon at his disposal to go after any man who hurt his sister. From the look on Peyton's face, she approved.

Lauren replied, "A—I can't talk to Mom about men. She's still try-ing to sell *her* mom's 1950s version of life. B—no one needs to suffer public humiliation. This is a work thing."

"Steer clear. Nothing's worse for you or your career than mixing personal and work relationships." A reminder he'd need to repeat to himself every day in Europe. He turned away from Peyton.

After a three-second silence, Lauren said, "There's something wrong with you that the first thing you think about is sex. Trust me, I love you, but I don't want to talk about my sex life with you. I've got girlfriends for that."

He could practically hear her eyes crossing. In any case, he released a thankful sigh. "So then I'm confused. What's the problem? And be quick. I'm boarding my flight."

"There's another paralegal in my department—Joe—with barely more seniority than I have, but he acts like he's my boss. If he mans-plains one more thing to me, I might punch him. But the partner we work for—Gary—*loves* him. I'm talking serious office bromance, with lame fist bumps and everything. I can't complain about Joe to Gary, yet I'm doing more than my fair share of the work, while Joe acts like he's 'supervising' me."

Office politics. Another reason he'd left Savant Press, although he'd had the reverse situation from his sister's. A majority of that office had been female, making him the odd man out, so to speak, which got worse after the mess with Danielle. To nurse heartache at work had sucked, but then to realize she'd used him all along—acting enthralled by his ideas when she'd actually been using them to get ahead herself—had been an unexpected blow that he'd never quite forgotten.

"Establish your own relationship with Gary. Figure out how to make his life easier. If he sees you—and only you—doing that, you won't have to worry about Joe taking credit."

"But *how*?"

"Thought you didn't want any mansplaining?" He smiled, but she didn't chuckle. "Stop moaning and make a list of things you can do to go above and beyond. Things that don't involve Joe."

She sighed. "I was hoping you'd be more specific."

"I can't be. I don't know your job. But I know you, and I know you're able to handle yourself."

"Thanks, I guess." A quiet bell sounded in the background, like she'd unbuckled a seat belt or opened a car door. "How long will you be away?"

"Seventeen days."

"Peyton Prescott." She clucked her tongue. "I looked her up. Her Insta is amazing. She's been everywhere."

He'd noted that as well. In fact, he'd consulted her for some hotel recommendations for their trip, suspecting she'd have definite preferences. Her road warrior status aside, he'd bet her recent journey inward had been her most harrowing.

He glanced over his shoulder at Peyton, who openly studied him while he spoke. "She'll be a good travel companion."

Peyton nodded her approval at that remark—eyes twinkling—setting off another round of flutters. *Again?* God, he had to get control of himself.

Lauren's voice dipped, ribbing him. "Does she know how much you hate to fly?"

He tensed, hoping Peyton couldn't hear his sister. "No."

"Guess she'll find out soon enough," Lauren teased.

"Doubtful. I'll be too busy working."

She huffed. "Why don't you try something different? Knock back some drinks and play cards or *talk* to her."

"This is a business trip, not a vacation. Weren't you listening to my first piece of advice? Never mix work and pleasure, Lauren. Not unless you want to sidetrack your career." He averted his eyes now. Lord knew how Peyton might be piecing together this conversation.

A short pause ensued before Lauren answered, "You're going to be single forever, aren't you?"

"Now you sound like Mom." A quick glance at Peyton's quivering smile proved her amusement. Time to shut down the conversation. "Check in on her while I'm gone. Take her to Finnegan's one night, or maybe for Sunday brunch. You know, fill in for me."

"She's not a baby." Her exasperated tone summed up the relationship between his mom and sister.

"She's lonely." His mother had never quite recovered from all the fallout from his dad's death. "Please do it for me, okay?"

"Okay. For *you*, Mitch."

"Thank you." He stopped short of another lecture about how their mom had always done her best by them. Lauren could never put herself in their mom's shoes. Nor did she have the life experience to consider how unprepared their mom had been to deal with being a young, broke widow left to raise two kids on her own. In contrast, his memories of their mom's early breakdowns were as sharp as the panic he felt boarding this plane.

"Okay. Gotta go now. Have fun." The line went dead.

Mitch rubbed his forehead and shrugged at Peyton. "Sorry. That was my sister. Had to take it."

"I understand. Logan is the same with me." She winked. "It's sweet. First hint that you aren't a robot."

"A robot?" Clearly he'd overshot his attempts to be dull.

"All business." She stepped inside the plane with him, unaware of the spike in his heart rate as he crossed into the cabin. She looked up at him, a blush rising. "But that's good advice . . . about not mixing work and pleasure."

She strolled ahead to find their seats, leaving him to follow behind her while blood roared in his ears.

Chapter Three

She shouldn't have baited Mitch. Throughout the long ride to JFK, she'd told herself not to provoke him, or flirt, or do anything else that the old Peyton might have done for amusement or to further an agenda. Not when she wouldn't follow through.

She was here only to make her brother and publisher happy and help raise money for cancer research. Taunting and teasing Mitch weren't tactics likely to sell books.

But when she'd seen him waiting in the boarding line, he'd stood out from the massive crowd pressing to be first on the plane. Nervous energy had shimmered around him like fairy dust. His bone-colored linen blazer and blue button-down shirt dressed up his dark jeans. The chunky black watch on his left wrist had commandeered his attention. More proof that he'd been panicked about her "just in time" arrival.

Everything about him had looked sexy—a word she hadn't used in reference to any man in almost two years—causing something inside to break open. Something frothy and fun, like welcoming a long-lost friend back into the fold. She couldn't resist its pull, despite the memory of how, last time she'd dived into the sea of love, Todd had belched out her remains and left them to wash ashore.

Moreover, gorgeous men weren't often also reliable, kind men—her brother being an exception (luckily for Claire).

An unfortunate reality of life was that beautiful people didn't have to work as hard to attract attention. Unchecked, that could develop into a sense of entitlement. Having never suffered false modesty, she'd admit that, until she'd met Todd, she'd never sought more than no-strings fun.

Her private confession filled her with heat. Not the point, though. No . . . the point was that she'd thought she'd been prepared to resist Mitchell Mathis. Thought she'd had him all sized up.

But after eavesdropping on his conversation with his sister, her interest had only increased. Might he, too, be an exception? Not that it mattered. He could not have made his credo about separating work and pleasure any clearer.

A petite elderly Indian woman in stylish lightweight charcoal cashmere loungewear retracted the handle of her carry-on and bent to attempt to lift it up to the overhead bins. Mitch tossed his backpack on his seat and tapped her on the shoulder.

"Excuse me, ma'am. May I help you?"

When she smiled, one hundred happy lines around her eyes and mouth deepened with gratitude. "Thank you. Right up here, please."

"Do you need anything from the bag before I stow it?" His patient smile melted what was left of Peyton's heart.

"No, thank you. I have my book and Ambien in my purse." A devilish grin spread across her face as she patted her black quilted Chanel handbag.

"Ah. A seasoned pro." He raised her carry-on as if it weighed no more than a pillow and settled it in place in the overhead bin. "I'm across the aisle if you need anything."

"Thank you." The old woman then peered around him to look at Peyton. "You have a good one here."

Peyton nodded, letting the woman—and Mitch—enjoy her compliment. The guy might be a robot, but he respected women.

"Need help with yours, too?" He turned to Peyton as she retrieved her book from her carry-on.

Before cancer, the Globejotter (Peyton's Insta handle) had never asked for help. She'd *had* to do it all on her own. But chemo, a double mastectomy, and reconstruction surgeries had forced her to rely on others a lot. Humbling at first, but she didn't hate her softer side as much as she used to. "Sure."

Mitch heaved her bag up to the bin and then sat down and immediately buckled his seat belt. Once he settled beside her, she noted the slight sheen to his skin. Did she make him nervous? In a good way, or a bad way?

Oh, stop!

Packing three hundred passengers on an Airbus 330 in summer was like leaving a can of sardines in the sun. No wonder he was sweating.

"We'll be boarding for a while, so you don't need to buckle up yet," she teased.

He looked up, his fleeting gaze avoiding hers. "I don't mind."

"Suit yourself."

He retrieved the emergency instruction card and studied it like he was prepping for a quiz, occasionally looking around as if searching out the emergency exits. He then stuffed the laminated trifold pamphlet back in the seat pocket and tightened his seat belt. His knee bounced until he caught her staring.

"I assume you ate at the airport because dinner will suck?" He pulled a moue.

"Actually, I stopped at the bar to watch a bit of the Yankees game and downed some orange juice and a banana. Since treatment, I try to avoid preservatives and other carcinogens in processed foods. That said, Alitalia's first-class service can be pretty good. Pasta, fish, wine. It'll come early so you can eat and then get some sleep."

His brows rose, and that intense gaze bore straight through her. "A pleasant surprise."

Yet he looked ill, not happy.

"Are you feeling all right?" She almost touched his forehead to check his temperature, like she would've if he were Logan. If Mitch got sick, maybe he'd cancel one or two bits of the press tour and she'd spend less time as media prey. Not that she wished him ill, but the silver lining . . .

"Yes. I'm fine." He released the fists he'd balled on his thighs. "Would you like to talk about tomorrow afternoon's meeting? Run a mock Q and A?"

"Mock Q and A?" She wouldn't mind hearing about the list of reviewers, but practice questions? This wasn't the time or place to discuss body-racking pain, needles, barfing, and panic attacks. "I think I'm better off winging it. It'll be more authentic."

His silence suggested he disagreed.

"Authenticity is important, of course," he conceded. "But you don't want to be caught off guard."

Enzo the flight attendant interrupted them to ask if they wanted a beverage. Mitch looked surprised that first-class cabin service would keep everyone comfortable for the twenty or more minutes that the rest of the passengers boarded and the crew prepared for takeoff.

"Water, please," Peyton said. Hydration was important on long flights.

Mitch waved Enzo off. "Nothing for me, thanks."

"Oh, don't do that. You might as well get what you've paid for. Have some wine! It'll help you doze off." Peyton nudged him with her elbow.

He shrugged. "Okay. Red, please."

Enzo nodded and moved on to the next row.

Peyton leaned against the divider between her and Mitch. "If I'm too bossy, just say so. And if you don't like being direct, we can come up with a signal, like you could pinch your nose or affect a slight cough or tap my shoulder."

He pursed his lips with a smile in his eyes. "Should it worry me that you seem to have lots of practice dealing with this particular issue?"

When he spoke, she couldn't help but stare at those lips, which had now softened into a slight grin.

She forced her eyes up to meet his. "Only if you don't like assertive women."

Three silent seconds ticked by, their gazes locked together, energy passing back and forth in supercharged currents. Energy that hummed in her chest and then spread to her fingers and toes.

Enzo returned with a small plastic cup half-full of wine and a bottle of water. "Here you are."

"Thank you." Mitch took both and handed the bottle to Peyton. "To a productive, successful trip."

"Cheers." She clicked her bottle with his cup before taking a sip.

Mitch chugged his wine in one gulp and then twisted the empty cup around in his hands. He stretched his neck side to side and then in a circle, and drew a deep breath. Then he glanced at the book on her lap. "*Good Luck with That*, by Kristan Higgins. Is it good?"

"So far. I'm behind on my TBR pile, but this one came highly recommended." The story was about learning to love yourself as you are in order to be happy. A perfect book for Peyton after the amputations and reconstruction to her body and soul. "Did you bring anything to read?"

"Not for pleasure."

"See? Robot." She twisted her lips. "Maybe I should call you Optimus Prime instead of Mitch."

"I promise I'm human, although that comparison is somewhat of a compliment, I think. Moral, smart, strategic. I can live with that." For a second, a bit of levity lit up his eyes.

Peyton smiled and finished her water. "I guess we'll see how well you live up to your namesake, then."

Enzo came to collect the trash. "We'll be taking off soon."

Mitch nodded at him while handing over his cup, but his mouth tightened into a straight line.

Overhead, a heavily accented female voice began droning on about seat belts, oxygen masks, and the other basic flight-safety equipment. Peyton sighed, planning to read for a while, eat her sesame-covered almonds, and close her eyes by nine o'clock. Six or so hours of sleep would suffice to help her body sync with Rome's time zone.

The plane lurched from the gate and taxied to the runway. Peyton had flown so many times it never occurred to her to worry, but she diagnosed the fear imprinted on Mitch's face as it drained of color.

The cabin jiggled as the plane picked up speed. Mitch stared straight ahead, jaw clenched, neck tense and straight. At liftoff, he clutched the armrests in a death grip.

Without thinking, Peyton reached for his hand and squeezed it. He snapped his head toward her in surprise, but she simply smiled. "Don't worry. After going through what I have, it would be wicked unfair of God to kill me off in a plane. We'll be fine, I promise."

He chuckled before his gaze dropped to their hands. He didn't release hers until the plane leveled off. "Sorry."

She reluctantly settled her hand on her lap. "For what?"

"Being unprofessional." One shoulder lifted. "Being a sissy . . . very un-Optimus of me."

She laughed, glad to detect a hint of humor beneath all the buttoned-down parts of him. "We all have our flaws. That's what makes us human, right?"

"So my fear means I'm not a robot?" Those full lips twisted into a wry smile, prompting a delicious quiver in her stomach.

"Seems not." Absolutely not. Mitch was very much flesh and bone. Just her damn luck.

He'd tried. He'd really tried to relax enough to sleep. He might've drifted off for forty-five minutes once or twice . . . maybe. The wide, fully reclining seats had promised better rest. And the flight hadn't been as bumpy as the one he'd taken to LA last winter. All around him, most of the other passengers had slumbered like bears in hibernation. But panic's tight fist had his throat, leaving him to stew in his thoughts about the book tour and Peyton.

At least being awake had given him one advantage. Throughout the night, he'd turned on his side and stared at Peyton while she lightly snored. Well, it was more of a breathy little puff bursting from her lips than a snore.

Up close and personal, she didn't look anything like her book cover. Her skin was almost luminescent in the cabin's bluish light. A peaceful expression made her appear innocent and defenseless, unlike when she speared him with inquisitive gazes and snarky quips.

They'd only just met, but he already suspected she hated being vulnerable, which made her memoir all the more puzzling and courageous. Not for the first time, he pondered the origin of her mettle. Did being born with the safety net of extreme privilege make it easier to take risks, or was there something more to it?

A small smile lifted the corners of his mouth in anticipation of spending the coming weeks in her company. He'd planned this journey determined to succeed for his own selfish reasons. As night waned, he folded her needs into his goals, too. She deserved something good after all she'd overcome and everything she'd put herself through to bring this story to market. He wanted her to earn that bestseller label many authors craved more than he'd wanted it for any prior client.

He hadn't wakened her for breakfast service, knowing she'd need her rest whenever she could catch it. Plus, he doubted she'd eat the sausage, given her stance on a healthy diet. One would think the reminder of her fragile health would help him keep her at arm's length, yet it didn't seem to be working.

The pilot's accented, static-riddled announcement that they'd be landing in thirty minutes stirred all the sleepers.

Peyton stretched and raised her seat. "Good morning."

"Good morning." He sipped the last of his coffee and then pushed his yogurt cup, croissant, and cheese toward her. "I saved these for you."

She read the label of the plain yogurt. After peeling back the foil cover, she sniffed it. "Thank you."

"You're welcome."

Her grateful smile took a sudden turn into a frown. "You didn't sleep."

"I did." Were his eyes bloodshot on top of being itchy? "A bit, anyway."

She shook her head. "What time is our first appointment?"

The fact that she hadn't committed the schedule to memory shouldn't have come as a shock. She didn't seem like much of a planner. Not his preferred type of client, but he'd already made an exception for her. "Four o'clock. It's a simple meet and greet with the publisher. The real work begins first thing tomorrow morning."

"Well, normally I don't recommend napping, but I think you should try to catch an hour of sleep when we get to the hotel. Tonight, stay up until eleven or so. Get on the time zone as soon as you can."

"I can't nap. We need to prep for all the interviews tomorrow." *Winging it* would not be wise, so he pressed.

"I'd bet my bank account you've made outlines and notes on everyone we're meeting. Email the relevant ones to me and I'll review them on my own until you wake up." She touched her breastbone. "Trust me. I'm the best bullshitter around. I'll be fine."

"You can't bullshit through this, Peyton. You've written a memoir. A serious one about a serious topic. If you aren't authentic, you won't get the bloggers and reviewers on your side. You need to be real. Very real."

She paled, her voice dropping to a low pitch as she croaked, "Okay."

He touched her forearm. "Are you up to this?"

A stupid question because canceling wasn't a viable option.

She glanced at her lap before meeting his gaze. When she did, the devilish glint had returned to her eyes. "Let's just say it's a good thing Logan is halfway around the world right now or he'd be in serious danger."

And in an instant, she'd secured her armor again.

"Siblings can be a handful." Like with the many ways Lauren had tested his mom—and him.

"From what I could tell, your sister sounds younger. Do you have other siblings?"

"No. And it's just you and Logan, right?"

"He's enough. I'm lucky. We've always been close." She spooned some yogurt into her mouth. When she licked her lips, he had to look away.

Client. Client. Client.

"I figured, considering how you shared the experience of documenting your treatment and recovery." He could never manage that with Lauren.

"I guess people will be curious about that . . . about how I let him see me in every raw, intimate, vulnerable way possible. Maybe some will even find that uncomfortable." She averted her gaze for a moment, giving a little sigh. "But the truth is that I trust him more than anyone. He's never judged me, shamed or shunned me, or done anything but love me, accept me, and make me feel safe. I couldn't have let anyone else as close. It had to be him."

"And yet, now it sounds like you want to kill him," he teased to lighten the mood.

An impish grin appeared.

"Well, yeah. I can be irrational that way." She cocked a brow and pointed the spoon at him. "Watch out."

"Duly noted." He crossed his arms as she tore into the croissant without any apparent appreciation for the magnitude of what she'd done while facing down death. He'd spent the past decade working with a lot of different women, none of whom had Peyton's combination of strength and vulnerability. Or her smile. "If you get nervous, remember, working on your memoir while undergoing treatment was harder than anything you'll encounter in the next two weeks. You'll be fine."

She stilled for the briefest moment, her entire face tightening even as her gaze looked like it lost focus. He expected some backlash, but she snapped back from wherever she'd gone. With a shallow grin, she said, "Look at us—such a team already. I'll get you through the flights, and you'll talk me off the ledge before meetings."

"Yin and yang."

Her smile broadened. "We should get T-shirts made."

"We could design a whole line—Taoist Tees." He knew something of Taoism because it had been one of Lauren's many phases—along with bottle flipping, dubstepping, and frozen yogurt—and she'd shared her insights with their mom and him on a regular basis.

She narrowed her eyes. "Pick a saying. Maybe the one about contentedness: 'When you realize nothing is lacking, the whole world belongs to you.'"

Only people with way more than they needed could make that statement with a straight face. Anyone who'd duct-taped his torn sneakers for a few weeks so he could pay the electric bill on time or worn two layers of socks and clothing to bed to keep the heating bill down hadn't the luxury to consider, let alone comprehend, it. When things were that tough, no state-of-mind mantra inspired feelings of safety and happiness.

"How about 'Who knows what is good or bad?'" He could wrap his head around that debate, at least.

Her eyes twinkled with humor. "I would've never figured you'd be into this stuff."

"My sister made it a mission to educate me," he embellished, leaving out the failure part.

"Did it take?"

"Maybe some." He smiled at the memory of Lauren's attempts to bully him into going with the flow. After a lifetime together, she still didn't get him. Since fifteen, he'd been the man of the house. That role required discipline, not a "go with the flow" attitude. "You?"

"Well, I started reading some stuff during chemo. Tried meditating—epic fail on that—but I find I do appreciate the here and now more. I'm far from a Taoist, but I'm all about baby steps. Little goals are easily accomplished, and progress makes you feel good."

"There's a certain kind of logic to that." He nodded.

"Oh no." She tittered. "More admiration for logic. Back to being a robot, I guess."

He would've smiled, but the plane engine shifted and the tin bird took a decided dip. With a sharp inhale, he clutched his seat. Peyton remained annoyingly calm.

"Apparently not." He smirked. "Fear keeps me human, I'm told."

She chuckled, adding a little shake of her head.

"I like you, Mitch." She shoved the last bit of croissant into her mouth and washed it down with water. "This is not necessarily a good thing."

"Oh?" How should he take that? "Would it be better if you disliked me?"

"Better for me, anyway." She shrugged, wearing a slight smile. He fought the urge to reach out and touch her jaw. "Okay, now. Don't freak out, but we're going to touch down in a few seconds."

Reality crashed in on his daydream. He nodded and closed his eyes. When the plane bumped against the runway, the entire cabin shuddered like a dog shaking off water. The brakes' deafening screech filled his head, but he breathed deeply. They were on terra firma. All was right with the world. Once his tension ebbed, exhaustion hit him, making each eyelid seem ten pounds heavier. A giant yawn escaped before he could control it.

"Oh boy, you need some sleep." Peyton patted his thigh.

He came alive at her touch. *I like you, too.* He kept that to himself. Uttering those words would blur the line before this trip had even begun.

She was right. This budding affection wasn't a good thing.

Chapter Four

Peyton stepped out of the shower and reached for a towel, catching her reflection in the mirror. The steamy air that had collected on its surface softened the harsh truth normally revealed by the morning sun. From a distance, the dappled glass hid her breast scars. Her Vinnie Myers nipple tattoos looked so real she mindlessly brushed her fingertips over them.

Nope. Not real.

She'd picked such a pretty pink color, too.

Most people probably thought the fake boobs (a.k.a. "foobs") made everything better—or at least close to normal. *Wrong.* Hers were no simple augmentation—more like postamputation prosthetics. A poor substitute that would neither replace the sensation of the real things nor breastfeed a child.

In no way did the hard, nipple-less reconstructed breasts give her the same feeling about her body and sexuality as real breasts. A year later, she still fought tears when thinking too much about all she'd lost.

After drying herself, she slipped into the hotel's luxurious dual-layer microfiber robe—a cozy barrier between her and that mirror. With less than twenty minutes to dress and meet Mitch for a quick breakfast before they took off for a day of interviews, she hadn't time to mourn what once was.

Why she still used a wide-tooth comb for her now-short hair, she couldn't say. She tossed it on the vanity and tousled the damp waves with her fingers. Silver lining—no need for a hair dryer.

Moisture still fogged the mirror, so she went to dress. She thumbed through the few items she'd hung and steam-ironed, choosing the cream-colored sleeveless dress with a mock turtleneck. Classy and sedate except for the flirty three-inch slits on both sides of its skirt.

It had taken all year to fit back into this one, but this morning she tugged that zipper all the way up. She stepped back in front of the now-dry full-length mirror and opened her makeup case. A little shimmer powder dusted over her face, a swipe of raspberry lipstick on her lips, and after a dramatic sweep of black eyeliner, a bit of mascara for the big finish. Voilà.

A woman who looked like someone she barely remembered stared back at her. *Magic.* If not for the shorter hair and low-heeled shoes, she'd think herself a mirage.

Her phone pinged from the other room.

Mitch, no doubt. Optimus had been a hasty nickname. Butters—from *South Park*—would be more apt, given their shared penchant for anxiety.

She glanced at the text he'd sent.

Ready when you are.

What a polite way of asking where the heck she was. *Still . . .* She grinned while typing her reply.

Jumping into the shower now.

She counted one one thousand before dots exploded on her screen. To head him off, she sent a second text.

Kidding. See you in two minutes.

A pause. Then his reply.

Great.

Given the amount of time it'd taken to receive that short note, he must've deleted whatever he'd first planned to text before choosing to go monosyllabic.

When she got to the lobby, she found Mitch intently typing on his phone. Sister? Work related? A girlfriend, perhaps? He must have one . . . or more.

He looked up. "Why are you frowning?"

Oh man. As embarrassing moments went, this wasn't too bad. But she hadn't ever thought about whether he had a girlfriend, so the phantom woman had triggered an irrational sense of loss. *Don't you dare ask!*

"Am I?" She brushed the sting of envy off with a sultry laugh. In her experience, she could count on the laughter ploy to redirect any conversation with a man, especially when followed by a suggestion or segue. "Must be hunger. Shall we eat?"

"Of course. I scoped out the buffet while waiting for you. It's remarkable." Without pressing for an answer to his earlier question, he gestured toward the double doors that led to the dining room, confirming for her that her deflection skills were still intact.

She knew this buffet, of course, from her Globejotter days. It was one of the reasons she'd selected this hotel. He opened the door and held it for her.

The delightful tinkling sound of silverware, the whir and sputter of cappuccino foam, and the scent of salty cheese greeted them.

"Divine." She surveyed the choices of prosciutto, salami, and bresaola, the egg and waffle station, Macedonia and fresh sliced fruit, assorted pastries, and Taleggio and Parmesan cheeses, among others. "Divide and conquer? Meet you at the small table in the corner."

"Fine." He wandered toward the cheese spread.

She went to the egg station and ordered a spinach-and-tomato omelet before flagging down a waiter to order a *caffelatte*. A whole pot of coffee would be better, but she'd settle for a full cup. Thank God research had not declared *it* a carcinogen.

When she arrived at the table, Mitch stood and waited for her to take a seat before sitting again and spreading his napkin across his lap. She smothered another grin. So fastidious and polite, almost like he'd memorized an old Miss Manners manual.

He glanced at her omelet. "That looks good."

"Doesn't it?" The rich golden egg creation, topped with a dash of salt and chive, glistened with butter. In contrast, his plate contained fruit, yogurt, and a sampling of muffins and pastries. She smeared fresh butter on her croissant and took one glorious bite before Mitch ruined the perfect moment by speaking about work.

"So perhaps we should talk through some softball questions, like what inspired you to write this memoir?" He forked a neatly cut slice of cantaloupe into his mouth and waited.

Never a moment to relax with this one.

She'd succeeded in putting off practice yesterday. Mitch had been so exhausted she'd insisted that he go straight to bed when they'd returned to the hotel. She'd meandered the streets, grabbing a *gelato al bacio* and sitting on the edge of the Fontana della Barcaccia to people-watch.

There'd been moments during chemo when she'd closed her eyes and pictured herself in some of her favorite spots in Europe, praying for the chance to see them again. Basking under an Italian summer sun once more had made yesterday's afternoon gelato a particularly blissful start to this trip. To her surprise, the brief meet and greet with the Italian editorial and marketing team had also been less painful than anticipated.

It seemed that those experiences had lulled her into a false kind of complacency, if Mitch's "the 'real work' must begin" attitude foretold the days to come. His anxiety now increased hers.

"The cantaloupe in Italy is succulent, isn't it?" She smiled and ate more of the omelet before swigging a healthy gulp of coffee.

He nodded, then swallowed. "It's excellent."

She took another sip of coffee, waiting for the caffeine buzz to awaken her nerve endings and engage her mind. Stalling, she gestured toward the grand chandelier in the middle of the room. "That looks like Venetian glass, doesn't it?"

He scarcely looked, shrugging before dabbing the corner of his mouth with a napkin. "Have you thought more about what you'll say if you're asked about posing for your brother?"

"Would you like to try this croissant?" She forced another smile and thrust it toward him. "Super flaky."

His gaze dipped to the pastry and then lifted back to meet hers. "Peyton." He set his hands on the table. "You're deflecting. Why?"

She tossed her napkin aside, giving up pretenses. "I told you, I don't want to rehearse. It's stressing me out, and to be honest, there's only so much of my day that I want to spend thinking about this stuff. I think it'll be best if I show up and be myself."

His unnerving eyes stayed fixed on hers while he thought. She liked and hated this quality—his directness and comfort with taking his time to form thoughts and speak.

"I'd be more willing to agree with you if I were certain you'd given any thought to the potential questions—and prospective answers—before today."

"I don't need to. We're talking about me. My life. My experience. My feelings. I mean, I wasn't the greatest student, but I'm pretty sure I know this subject better than anyone. It's not a test I can fail." She snickered, as one does when being clever.

The grim line of his mouth suggested he was unamused. It didn't, however, prepare her for what came next. "I know this tour is about you and your work, but please don't forget I have a job to do, too. People to answer to, who expect me to perform to the best of my ability, and others who are counting on me to make my payroll. Therefore, I'd appreciate some cooperation, if you don't mind."

Peyton sat back in her chair. Albeit in that nice way he had of saying unpleasant things, he'd basically called her selfish. *Well, well.* Maybe those days weren't as far behind her as she'd believed.

He raised a fair point, of course. She understood the stakes for everyone involved, and the time and money invested in bringing the book to market. But she also resented how everyone else viewed her memoir as a product and treated her like a paid spokesmodel.

No one cared that she'd be subjected to the judgment of strangers as they picked through each passage, all of which were interlaced with the fear, hope, panic, and loss that had marked every second of every minute of every day for a year. To this day she still fought those feelings from time to time. How could Mitch, Logan, and others not get that it physically hurt her to remember the days in the oncology wing, or the people she'd met who hadn't survived, or the naked emotions Logan had captured in all those photographs?

She didn't even want to be on this book tour, yet here she was, going along, preparing to spend her day locked in a room, being grilled by strangers about her treatment and her feelings rather than revisiting the Pantheon or heading to the Amalfi Coast.

To the extent anything she'd written could help others, she'd do her best to promote it. She would show up to read, answer questions, and sign books. But hitting lists had never been her goal, nor would she accept that burden. She didn't want her life—or any measure of it—to be defined by the success of the memoir. So to her, everything about this tour was a form of sacrifice, *not* selfishness. If Mitch thought it okay to scold her, then she would have no problem being frank, either.

"You want the truth? Nothing *inspired* me to write this memoir. It was all Logan's idea. He pushed me into it. Convinced me that redirecting our emotions and distracting ourselves during the great unknown of my cancer treatment would help—help whom, I still don't know. Us? Others? He's always looking for meaning in everything instead of accepting things as they are." She paused long enough to motion for the waiter to bring more coffee. "And I already told you about the photo shoots. Again, I didn't love doing those, but I trusted him and his instincts. I knew—somewhere in my very foggy, messed-up brain—that it'd be better to go along and reserve the option not to publish any of it in the end than to regret not documenting it at all. Right now, I'm having second thoughts about that."

Mitch sat there, spine erect, arms crossed, gaze absorbed in thought. She waited for his reply to her fit of pique. After a minute, she huffed. "What?"

"The second part is good. Makes sense. Not sure about the starkness of the first, though." His calmness suggested that he was managing her with his tremendous self-control, like a warning that he would not be manipulated or deterred. He intended to push her to her limit where his job was concerned. Strangely, his battle of wills excited her. "If readers think you were bullied into this, or that it isn't authentically you on any level, it could hurt sales." He frowned while spreading a bit more orange marmalade on a croissant.

She hadn't expected that reply or considered that, while she might know all about the subject of her experience, she had no idea about publishing or anything else related to selling a book. It would not do to concede this battle so fast, though. And she would never confess the truth behind her reluctance.

"Are you asking me to lie in order to sell more books and line everyone's pockets, including yours?" She set down her silverware and stared at Mitch as he sank his teeth into his croissant. Had she let his handsome face and nice manners obscure the fact that he, like so many others before, was using her for her name and what she could do for his career?

"We are here to sell books, Peyton." Like a stone tossed at a mirror, his words shattered any hope she'd held that she'd been wrong to doubt him. "Believe it or not, most authors are excited by that prospect. But, no, I'm not asking you to *lie*. Perhaps you could reconsider how you deliver the message—admit that it was Logan's idea and it took some encouragement, but that you got on board and felt empowered or braver because of it. Something like that, which I suspect is all true."

His expression told her he needed that to be the truth.

Truth—a flexible concept based largely on one's perspective. In her case, spells of doubt didn't diminish her pride in what she and her brother had created. Nor did they devalue the way she and Logan had worked together through the most trying time of her life to produce something that might benefit others. "I see your point."

She picked up her fork and stabbed at the last bit of omelet, refusing to look at him in case he was the type to gloat over his victory while she accepted the reality of their relationship. "Any other practice questions?"

He tapped the face of his watch. "I wish, but now we're out of time. We need to be at Stampa Coraggiosa by nine thirty so we have time to set up before the bloggers and press start showing up to speak with you."

Her stomach clenched. Now the rich omelet seemed like the worst decision she'd made since writing the damn book. "Maybe we'll get lucky and end up in a fender bender with one of the world's craziest drivers. Then we'd have a legitimate excuse to miss the interviews."

"That's not funny." He rapped his knuckles against the wood table, his face paling like it had in the airplane.

"I'm sorry." She bit the inside of her cheek to keep from smiling at his superstition. "But prepare yourself. I bet you'll hate driving through this city more than you hate flying. It's certainly riskier."

He stared at her, frozen with what appeared to be indecision. Of course, he wouldn't cancel the interviews, much as she'd love him for the rest of her life if he would. She reached across the table to pat his hand. "Bring something to read and don't look out the windows. Maybe you won't notice."

His gaze dropped to her hand, lingering there a moment before he withdrew his own. He stretched his fingers, then grasped his coffee cup and swigged the hot drink down in one gulp. "Let's go."

Mitch squeezed into the back of the small car, his gaze passing blindly over the notes on his iPad. He suspected his heavy-handed approach had not been the best way to ensure her cooperation on this trip, nor had it been sympathetic. Self-reproach was only somewhat responsible for the nausea rolling through his gut now. The taxi's high-speed zig-zagging through traffic made up the rest. He started at the blast of the tenth—or twelfth—angry horn, then tensed when a Vespa passed within inches of his window.

Peyton was leaning against her door's armrest, chin in hand, staring at the city through her window. He envied the way her eyes scanned the scenery as if committing it all to memory. Closing his own, he then forced his chin up and faced his own window.

Ten seconds later, they blew by the Colosseum. Photos and movies had not prepared him for its magnificence. The mammoth, crumbling ruin rose amid a modern city—a testament to the best and worst of humanity, and to the humbling truth about time and his own insignificance.

An elbow poked his side. When he turned, Peyton was smiling at him. Her beautiful face was as entrancing as the ancient city around them. The fact he wished he could protect her as much as promote her work posed a major problem.

Like the gladiators of yesteryear, he needed a shield against that smile—and her acerbic wit—so he could do his job, for both their sakes.

"Pretty awesome, isn't it?" She grinned. "Too bad we won't have time to tour it." She sounded disappointed, although he knew she'd already visited it in the past.

"Maybe someday." A nonanswer of the variety he often made to clients. Safe conversation.

"Don't think you can out-deflect me, mister." Peyton's low chuckle tickled something inside his chest. "Maybe after all of these cities and flights, you'll risk another trip to return for pleasure. From what little I've gathered about you so far, you've spent too little time enjoying what the world has to offer."

That she saw him so well should've bothered him, but it had the opposite effect.

He could think of several things he'd like to enjoy right now, but none had to do with flying or touring. Yet he'd already slipped up with Peyton by wading into personal territory instead of treating her like a client he was counting on to help build his new business.

Luckily, the cab stopped in front of the publisher's modern multi-story glass-front building before he had to respond. Just as well, because he hadn't a quippy rejoinder. Cleverness was the realm of those raised like her—with privileges and trust funds and such. In a life driven by needs, he'd taken comfort in the routines established to set and meet goals. Throwing caution to the wind? Slowing down just because? He couldn't even pretend to imagine himself doing either.

The driver said something in Italian as he gestured toward the entrance.

"Well." Peyton paused, hand clasping the door handle. "Here goes nothing."

She opened the door and stepped onto the sunny sidewalk while he paid the fare. He caught up to her at the front door, where she stood, one hand shielding her eyes from the sun as she gazed up at the building.

"Dammit, Mitch." She grimaced. "I hate to admit it, but I'm a little petrified."

She didn't strike him as a woman who liked to be coddled, although in another circumstance, he would've enjoyed wrapping an arm around her shoulders.

"I promise you'll be fine. When you need a break, give one of those signals you talked about on the plane, like tugging your earlobe." He waited for her to nod her consent before he opened the door and ushered her into the lobby. Italians loved marble and gilt, and this space had no shortage of either.

She whipped out her phone and took a selfie while he signed them in, then they went to the elevator.

"Am I allowed to refuse to answer a question?" Her face remained a mask of calm, but he noted the artery at the base of her neck pulsing beneath her skin.

He dragged his gaze from that vulnerable spot, but that didn't help much when he was left staring at her pretty face. Everything about her made his job harder. "Is there something in particular you're worried about?"

"No." Her brows pulled together as she glanced at her feet before her expression morphed into a polite, plastic smile. "But I'd like to know the rules."

He didn't believe her. Perhaps his stomach wouldn't be twisting if he'd read the whole book instead of depending on Rebecca's summary. He might not have put it down for good if the snippet he'd first attempted hadn't touched on bitter memories like a rough towel on sunburned skin. "You can always refuse to answer, although in my experience, that usually makes reporters dig even deeper. My best advice is to pause and think of an answer you are willing to share."

That always worked for him, anyway.

"What if that doesn't work?"

He crossed his arms and tipped his head. The fact that this otherwise playful, confident woman was so wary set his mind racing. Neither of them could afford a PR catastrophe at this stage in the game. "Like I said before, give me some sign and I'll be the bad guy and shut it all down. Deal?"

"Thank you." She squeezed his forearm. Despite the sedate outfit, she'd painted her nails a vibrant plum color. For the briefest second, he imagined their soft scratch on his back and then hid the slight shiver his daydream had wrought.

"You're welcome." *Enough.* The last thing a woman in her situation would be thinking about now was men, especially a "robot" like him.

Within minutes of their reaching the reception area, Regina Barsotti, the acquiring editor they'd met the day before, greeted them and walked them to the conference room reserved for the day's events.

Regina couldn't be much older than his sister. Today a formfitting red dress hugged her generous curves as she strode down the hallway in spiky high heels. As with yesterday, he could feel Peyton watching him as if curious about his reaction to the overtly sexy editor. His sole interest in Regina was how hard she was pushing the marketing team to sell the book.

"Did you both get enough rest?" She tossed a waterfall of dark-brown curls over her shoulder.

"Enough. I think I'm ready." Peyton nodded, although the palm she placed on her stomach suggested otherwise.

"Good. Your work gives me—how do they say—all the feels." Regina smiled and squeezed Peyton's hand. "We are so proud to publish the Italian translation, and we want the media to feel as we do."

The two women made an odd pairing. Regina was short, brazenly sensual, and brimming with energy. Peyton, a statuesque, restrained, ethereal beauty.

Another woman, thin and cute with freckles and a warm smile, stepped forward. "Hello, I'm Valeria, your translator."

"Nice to meet you." Peyton looked at Mitch. "Won't the reporters and bloggers speak English?"

"Most will, but some might not, and others might be able to better clarify their questions or your answers with some aid." He should've prepared her better. He would've if not for his infatuation and sympathy.

"Okay." Peyton shrugged, her gaze wandering the room until it stopped at the far corner. "Is that a coffee bar?"

"Yes. Would you like a cappuccino?" Regina asked.

Peyton clasped her hands in front of her chest. "God yes."

Regina spoke to one of the assistants in Italian and then directed Peyton to a comfortable chair at the far end of the table. "Angelina will touch up your makeup to cover the shiny spots for any photographs, and then we can begin. Francesca from *Tutto Sui Libri* will be your first interview."

Mitch had already become familiar with some of Peyton's mannerisms, like the twitch of her lips that betrayed her nerves before she smiled. Another tidbit that proved he was too consumed with her and her expressions.

The assistant delivered the cup of coffee to Peyton, who now sat still while Angelina dusted her face with powder. Regina and Valeria entered into a rapid-fire conversation in Italian, leaving Mitch to himself. He scrolled through his notes, happy to reconfirm that they'd scheduled only one hardball journalist. Peyton would be warmed up by the time that round of questions arrived.

A text came through from his mother. This was not the first text she'd sent him during the wee hours. He'd accuse her of being a vampire—except that she didn't sleep during the day, either.

I need glaucoma surgery. When will you be home? I'll need some extra help for a couple of weeks afterward, and I want to get this scheduled soon.

Mitch sighed. Lauren would be little to no help. He'd rather move his mother to his place for a week than commute to work from hers, but she'd never go for that.

I'm working now. Will call later. I return on the 8th. Go back to bed!

He was about to put his iPad in its case when another message came through.

I'll make you meatloaf to welcome you home. After all that fancy European food, you'll be craving a home-cooked meal. Mustn't forget your roots just because you're becoming successful.

For reasons he couldn't understand, she often cast his ambition in a negative light. It made no sense to him, but when it came to his mom and her habits, some things were better left alone.

P.S. Tell your sister I said hello. I'm sure you'll hear from her before I do even though you're in Europe and she's less than five miles away.

He hadn't the time or inclination to engage in that conversation, especially not now. He set a reminder to text his sister later, then turned off his iPad as a woman about his age breezed into the conference room. She wore loose slacks and a snug top, her hair tied in a thick braid down her back.

"Ciao!" She smiled at Peyton before setting her notebook, a tabbed copy of the memoir, and her phone on the table and sticking out her hand. "I'm Francesca. Thanks for meeting with me to discuss your book. You look wonderful today. Much different from that." She chuckled, pointing at the cover.

Peyton didn't cringe, but he might have. Remarkably, he didn't pick up the book and thwack Francesca on the head.

"Well, I couldn't look much worse, could I?" Peyton's bright laughter echoed off the glass surfaces in the room. A compensating deflection, he suspected. Yet another of the many tricks she employed to hide her real feelings.

Given the topic at hand, he couldn't blame her for building the arsenal, but it made her tough to know.

Francesca waved off Peyton's joke, took her seat, turned on the voice recorder of her phone, and opened her notebook. Without any hesitation, she asked, "So tell me, what would your—*come si dice*—great-grandfather say about this memoir? Would he be proud?"

Peyton darted a quick glance at Mitch. He held his breath, having no idea what she might say. Closing his eyes, he prayed she wouldn't say anything that could be turned against her or the work.

"The truth? Duck—that's what my brother and I called him—died when I was six, so I didn't know him well enough to answer that. However, he was a gentle man who enjoyed all forms of art. Ironically, according to my dad, he never cared much about critical reviews. He 'wrote what he had to say' regardless of what someone else might think, so in that way, I suppose we're alike. Still, I'd like to think he'd be proud of Logan and me . . . not only for this book, but for everything we've created to date."

Mitch heaved a relieved sigh and made a note to ask her about the odd moniker.

"Duck?" Francesca turned to Valeria and asked something in Italian. They conversed a few seconds, and then Valeria asked Peyton, "You said 'duck,' like the waterfowl, correct?"

"Yes. It's a nickname. He used to speak to us in a Donald Duck voice."

Valeria relayed that information to Francesca, who scribbled something in her notebook.

Francesca tapped her pen on the table. "Were there any disagreements between your brother and you during this collaboration, and if so, who won?"

Peyton's face blanked for a moment before she quipped, "If Logan were here, he'd say he won because this project was his brainchild. But he and I don't disagree about much—or often—so this was a true collaboration, devoid of drama. Well, he wasn't a big fan of the tattoo . . ."

"You mean, after the reconstruction surgery?" Francesca circled the area of her nipple with her finger, and Mitch looked away until the heat in his face and elsewhere faded.

"No, he understood why I wanted those." Peyton didn't look at him while she spoke, although she wasn't blushing, either. He supposed after having so many doctors and needles and knives poking at her body, she'd learned to detach when discussing it. "But I also got another tat—an infant angel holding a cross—right here." She pointed in the vicinity of her right ovary. "Chemo sometimes causes early menopause, so . . . I don't know. I was feeling a bit morbid at the time, I suppose. He said I'd regret it. Maybe he was right. Don't print that, though. I never like him to know when he's right." She laughed again, but its brittle quality hurt Mitch's heart.

A bunch of inappropriate, irrelevant questions crowded his thoughts. The idea of this intelligent, vibrant woman in menopause by thirty-two saddened him. Not that he knew if it had happened, or if it was permanent. Perhaps she never even wanted children, although the tattoo suggested she did. The real question was why any of it mattered to *him*. He went a little numb as he projected ahead to how often he'd be listening to Peyton recount her ordeal in specific detail.

"His name comes up a lot in your book. More than your parents', friends', or other men's." Francesca leaned closer. "The two of you seemed to shut out everyone else while you went through this experience. Was that intentional? And if so, why?"

Mitch didn't hear Peyton's answer, thanks to a memory that surfaced against his will. He'd been sitting by his father's hospital bed, which hospice had put in the living room, reading aloud from one of his parents' longtime favorite books, *All I Really Need to Know I Learned in Kindergarten*. Those final days had been marked by his dad's frequent unresponsiveness, labored breathing, fevers, and dysphagia. Mitch would steal glances at him in between paragraphs, or touch his dad's hand, hoping for a twitch or, better yet, a squeeze. Lauren asleep on the sofa, his mom working the dinner shift . . .

He pressed his fingertips to his temple. Fifteen more days of this . . . When his phone buzzed, he took it as a sign. With a quick glance at Peyton and a reassuring nod, he left the conference room to handle some business that wouldn't make him cry in public.

Chapter Five

Peyton babbled another answer she could only hope made sense at this late point in the day. By the eighth reviewer, she barely heard the questions anymore. Her mind skipped around, reminding her of the brain fog she'd experienced during chemo. She went on blind faith of the translator's accuracy. Her own fluency with Italian was limited to the common phrases used at restaurants and hotels.

Tightness gripped her shoulders and neck. A dull ache pulsed behind her left eye.

She glanced at the clock on the wall. Only four? This had to end. Now. Couldn't Mitch see the strain behind her stupid plastic smile? No, of course not. Like throughout much of the day—if he was even in the room—he was typing on his phone.

She stared at him until he felt her gaze, and then she tugged on her ear.

With a sharp nod of acknowledgment, he put his phone away and interrupted. "Excuse me, Signorina Barbosa, but it's been a long day and you've been questioning Peyton for forty-five minutes. Let's make this the stopping point."

Everyone looked at Peyton for confirmation. Nodding, she rubbed her throat. Yes, it hurt that much from all the talking. Another combination of an apology and a thank-you tumbled from her lips while she stood and brought an end to the grueling experience.

As the Globejotter, she'd worked alone in the privacy of hotel rooms. Interactions with locals had been on her terms, when the mood struck. Her self-imposed exile during cancer treatment and recovery hadn't helped her be more social, either. Today proved something that would shock people who'd considered her an attention seeker since childhood. She did *not* enjoy being the center of attention. Not like this.

Could she mastermind covering the high school principal's car in tinfoil or jump onstage with some band to get a laugh or surprise folks? Sure. But having every thought and experience analyzed, picked at, and evaluated by journalists made her blister with discomfort worse than those damn mouth ulcers caused by chemo. There was no way around the truth of it—this job plain sucked.

Throughout treatment, she'd assumed that, if she survived, things would one day return to normal . . . or a new normal that would somehow be magically better than the old one because of the wisdom and gratitude she'd earned through her experience. Instead, her new life had become a series of deadlines and meetings and sales goals and oversharing. Only now did it occur to her that she might never get her life back—the old life. The one she used to fill with carefree laughter and joy and adventure.

Meanwhile, in the back of her mind, the constant worry about her upcoming checkup—the one that could send her right back to square one—ticked like a bomb.

Although she'd promised God she wouldn't be selfish if he spared her, a growing part of her craved self-protection and self-care. Surely Mitch could make room for a few activities that brought pleasure and meaning unrelated to this project.

In a haze, she shook hands and mumbled more goodbyes to a roomful of people she hoped not to see again. Mitch grabbed beneath her elbow on their way out of the conference room.

"Are you okay?" He leaned close, lending his support.

She let herself enjoy the solid warmth of his body. "Please get me out of here."

He nodded, pushing open the door. "Do you need food or just rest?"

"Rest," she croaked, her voice dry and thin. She transferred her weight against the elevator wall, shoulders slouching.

"Okay." He stared at her with some concern as he jabbed at the banks of buttons, although she assumed his worry was limited to how well she'd manage the rest of the tour.

They rode the elevator in silence. The faint hint of his cologne lingered all around her. Not a single stranger joined them to act as a buffer or ease her sudden sense of overexposure in the small space.

Even given his intermittent appearances during the interviews, Mitch had overheard enough to now know much, *much* more about her than she did about him. On those occasions when he wasn't on his phone, she'd caught him staring at her, his gaze alert and riveted. Now she flattened her hand against her breastbone as if it could hide some part of her heart. *Fool.*

When the elevator doors opened, she burst through them and into the lobby, gulping in air. The idea that she'd need to repeat this scenario over and over for two weeks made her shudder. Once they got into the car, she leaned against the door and closed her eyes. Anything to escape the new confines and elude answering a single question more.

"You did well." Mitch's voice resonated like a cello. "So well I was able to handle some issues with upcoming tour dates as well as a few matters related to other projects, so thank you."

She popped open one eye with a harrumph.

"I'm serious. You're something of a natural. Authentic yet clever, able to deflect when the need arises." He looked ahead, smiling to himself.

Despite her utter exhaustion, that little smile of his lit something deep within her—the candle Todd had snuffed when he'd left her to face a new reality on her own. If Mitch weren't so focused on his work, that spark might draw her into the warmth of his sturdy embrace. To seek the comfort of a gentle kiss on her temple and a solid shoulder on which she could rest her head.

But even in a best-case scenario, she couldn't imagine opening her heart again. She'd destroyed a lifelong friendship for Todd. The residual pain of his betrayal—and her mistake—remained lodged in her heart like a hornet's nest waiting to be kicked. Even if Mitch liked her company, she had to remember she was his meal ticket. Given all that, she shouldn't spin fantasies of heated kisses.

Fortunately, the thought of letting any man see her naked—literally or figuratively—made her cringe. Handsome and tempting as Mitch was, she was no longer as confident or bold a woman. Chemo and mutilating surgeries had killed most every sexual impulse.

"You're scowling." Mitch frowned.

People often scowled when they resented someone, and she sure resented him for stirring up fruitless emotions she'd learned to live without. Now she grieved anew what was so far from reach.

"I'm tired and need to be alone." She shrugged. "No offense."

"None taken." He rolled his shoulders back and adjusted his legs in the tight back seat. "I warned you that dinner plans were ambitious. Let's cancel. I'm fine eating in my room and working tonight. You can rest, soak in the tub, or do whatever else will help you recharge."

Peyton sighed. Thirty-two and already an old lady. Her handsome companion showed no sign of regret about ditching her for the evening. How very humbling to confirm her insecurities. But right now, a hot bath and fuzzy robe sounded like nirvana. The fact that Mitch wasn't flirting seemed like another sign from God to let it all lie. "Thanks. I think you're right."

"We'll be up early to catch our flight to Barcelona. Would you like to have breakfast together again, or would you rather meet in the lobby at seven thirty to grab a cab to the airport?"

"Lobby. I don't need another monster breakfast."

"Okay." When he glanced out his window then, she wondered if she'd hurt his feelings.

Mitch paid the fare and followed Peyton into the lobby, where he came to a stop. Something in his expression seemed haunted, although she couldn't guess why. "I hope you have a pleasant, restful evening. I'll see you in the morning."

"Aren't you taking the elevator, too?"

He shook his head. "I want to grab an espresso next door and take a short walk around the neighborhood to energize before I get back to work."

A short walk. She would've made some quip about his workaholism, but she sensed that something more drove his need for a diversion.

Their location at the top of the Spanish Steps made this a pedestrian-friendly part of the city. Not that he'd know this.

"Do you know where to go?" she asked.

"I'm fine meandering."

"Well, at the bottom of the steps is the Keats-Shelley House. Keats's bedroom is preserved as it was when he died in 1821. Within a mile in any direction, you can be at the Trevi Fountain, the Piazza Barberini, or the Villa Borghese. And you'll find luxury shopping all along the Via Condotti at the edge of the piazza below, if you want to pick up something for your mom, sister, or girlfriend." *Oops.*

He blinked but didn't respond to that last part—a question, really. "Thanks. Sweet dreams, Peyton."

He retrieved his wallet from inside his leather backpack before leaving that bag with the bell captain. As he passed through the hotel doors, the late-afternoon sun lit his dark silhouette like a solar eclipse. Then, in a blink, he was gone. With her eyelids shut, she could still see his outline.

The second Peyton closed her hotel room door, she whipped off her clothes and drew a hot bath. For ten minutes, she had no regrets about her decision to spend the evening alone. To sit in silence and forget about the bloggers' hungry eyes as they questioned her about her diagnosis, her treatment, her family, her brother, her checkups, her outlook, her love life, her future.

The future. That was something she couldn't take for granted, but neither could she focus on it. Making plans only led to hope—a dangerous state when she'd learned that, at any time, she could be handed bad news. She hadn't even reached a full year cancer-free. At this juncture, living day to day was a big enough challenge. Being present had been her one vow, although a new career and a need for fulfillment kept pressing on her.

She sank beneath the water, blowing bubbles with her eyes closed, wishing she could disappear. Two days in and already she dreaded keeping this pace. When she ran out of air, she burst through the surface and wiped the water from her face, heaving a sigh.

Resting her head against the back of the claw-foot tub, she stared at the marble wall. Its gray and tan veins were due to impurities like clay and silt. Those imperfections made it more beautiful, unlike hers.

That stone would outlast her lifetime and many others. How many thousands of guests visiting this city to celebrate or mourn or work had touched this wall before her? How many would follow?

Gah. If she stayed alone all evening, she'd drive herself insane.

She unplugged the drain before standing and reaching for a towel. Once dressed, she texted Mitch. After all, there were few moods a good amatriciana couldn't improve, and a little eye candy never hurt, either. And if they got to know each other better, he might loosen up, which would benefit them both.

Meet me at the restaurant, please. Unless you want to risk me missing tomorrow's flight because I've run off with Fabio.

He replied before she found her room key.

Several more events coming our way. You should relax, and I should work.

Not what she'd hoped, but she never begged.

I'm going. If you change your mind, you know where to find me.

Smiling to herself at the challenge she'd laid, she closed her door and headed toward the elevator, her heart beating with anticipation. He didn't trust her—that much she knew—so he'd probably cave and show up, if only to ensure she didn't make good on her threat about Fabio.

The taxi left her off along the Tiber River, a block or two from the crowded, narrow piazza where the restaurant was located. One of the silver linings about ditching spiky heels in favor of more comfortable shoes was that her wedges wouldn't get caught in the gaps of the ancient cobblestone roads. The lively chatter and busy people bustling around her lightened her mood.

As she neared the timeworn four-story golden stucco building that housed the trattoria, Mitch came into view. He stood outside the front door, glancing at his watch, of course.

She whistled, causing him to look up. For an instant, an unguarded grin split his face, making her feel taller and prettier than she had in too long. Then he reined in his emotions, grin faltering and falling to a polite smile as he clasped his hands in front of his waist and waited.

Oh well. Better to quit while I'm ahead, anyway.

The sight of Peyton caused Mitch's lungs to expand. A bright spot of joy at the end of the short exploration that had brought about many mixed feelings.

His dad's ghost had haunted him while Mitch strolled amid old ruins and buildings that had survived time and wars and so much more.

With each step, he'd recalled the dreamer who'd gone to work for that tech start-up, hopes soaring, and who'd come to the dinner table each night to discuss all the places their family would visit once he struck it rich.

Sadly, before that start-up could take flight, brain cancer went to work, eating away all the hopes and dreams his dad had ever had. His father never saw the glory of the setting sun's golden-peach light hitting centuries-old stucco. Never dodged scooters, or sampled fresh-baked cannoli, or listened to Italian, Spanish, German, Dutch, and Chinese being spoken all around him.

Nor did his dad stand outside a tiny restaurant that smelled like tomato and onion while waiting for a beautiful woman who looked like a classic movie star to emerge from the crowd.

"Good evening." He bowed, trying not to fixate on the long line of her neck or the way the pale-plum dress swayed when she walked.

"One of these days I swear I'll be waiting for you for a change." She looped her arm through his and headed for the door as if she hadn't lit his every nerve on fire with her touch. When she leaned so close that they were shoulder to shoulder, the sweet, clean scent of her hair gave sharp contrast to the savory aroma of pork coming from the front door. "But I'm curious. You looked a little sad all of a sudden. What were you thinking?"

"Did I?" He shrugged, avoiding the discussion. "Must've been the sun hitting my eyes."

She cocked an eyebrow but didn't push.

Once they were inside the restaurant, his gaze wandered. Whitewashed stucco walls met with ancient rough-hewn wood-beam ceilings. The layout was something of an underground labyrinth filled with farmhouse and tile tables and idle chatter in a musical language he wished he understood. Modern beams stuffed with thousands of wine corks framing the bar that sat several feet above the first set of dining tables left him wondering about all the celebrations that had taken place here.

They followed the maître d' down a small flight of stairs to a table for two.

"Benvenuto." An older gentleman stopped by the table. *"Ti porterò alcuni menù."*

"Grazie," Peyton replied.

Mitch waited for an explanation.

"He's bringing us menus, but I don't need one. I'm getting the amatriciana. If you like pasta, it's to die for."

In truth, pasta at the Mathis house had been served with jarred sauce. Nothing to brag about. His mother had never mastered much beyond basic meat-and-potatoes fare.

"Are you willing to trust my recommendation?" Peyton asked.

The waiter returned and set the menus in front of them, but Peyton continued staring at Mitch with a question in her eyes. He nodded, having no particular taste for something else at the moment anyway. Her responding smile was worth it, even if he didn't end up loving the meal.

She pushed the menus toward the waiter, face filled with animation. Such a contrast to the way he'd left her earlier. *"Due amatriciane, per favore. E una bottiglia di Quaranta Sessanta. Grazie."*

The waiter nodded, rather stone-faced, and took the menus when he left.

"This might not be a tourist hot spot, but the food is good, and I love the vibe in here. Cozy, real." Peyton sat back, wearing a pleased smile. "It feels good to be back. There were days when I doubted I'd see this city again . . ."

He sidestepped the reference to her illness, sensing they'd both had enough of that topic today. "I didn't know you speak Italian."

"I don't. Not really. I've picked up enough to read menus and order room service. Food was always my favorite part of traveling. I'd hire tour guides to help me when I went sightseeing and needed a history lesson.

Then I'd peel away and lose myself for hours, wandering off the beaten path, looking for something unusual or undiscovered."

Her face came alive—eyes twinkling, cheeks flushed with warmth, lips curved upward—when she spoke about her past, giving him a peek at the energy she must've had when she'd been healthier.

"Do you miss it?"

She unfolded her napkin and laid it across her lap, a slight smile lingering on her lips. "Not at the moment."

The flirtatious grin—if that was what he was seeing—almost made him forget that this was a client dinner, not a date. *Not. A. Date.*

"Perhaps we should talk a bit about what to expect in Barcelona. Your first bookstore event . . ."

"Are you trying to ruin my favorite meal?" She smiled, but he couldn't miss the warning in her eyes.

"Okay, no work. So then, tell me, is there any place you haven't traveled to that you'd like to see?" A safe topic. Now he had to make sure he didn't stare at her mouth while she spoke.

The waiter passed by, setting down a small basket of freshly baked rustic bread. Peyton snatched a thick slice. She blended olive oil, salt, and grated Parmesan on a plate and dipped a corner of her bread into the mixture. "I've been everywhere. Well, almost every country. Not every city."

She shoved a hunk of bread into her mouth. He readjusted his napkin as an excuse to look away. It figured that his first experience being thunderstruck would be with someone who was not only his high-profile client but who might also get deathly ill again in the not-distant future. That sobering thought formed a knot in his chest.

"So there's no place left on your bucket list?" If ever a forehead-slapping moment existed, this would be it. He blamed his need to distance himself from her for why he'd reintroduced the specter of death into their casual conversation.

If the topic upset her, she didn't show it. Could the bread be that good?

"Did I sound obnoxious?" she asked. "I have to admit, having traveled so extensively comforted me during the lowest points of my treatment. I'm lucky to have seen most of the world—and been paid for it—before I die."

He'd opened the door to the topic, but he didn't like her contemplating her death, even when she did so with aplomb. His face must've betrayed his thoughts, because she fluttered her hands. "Let's not talk about me or my cancer tonight. After today, I wish I didn't have to talk about it ever again. Let's talk about you."

"Me?" *Oh no.* His life would bore this woman. Hell, it bored him most days.

"Yes, you, Mitch Mathis, a.k.a. Optimus, a.k.a. Butters."

"Butters? That's not flattering." He reached for comfort food in the bread basket.

"Better than Cartman." She chuckled.

"Let's stick to Optimus." He dipped his bread in her concoction. "At least I can pretend to take it as a compliment."

"Okay, Mitch-by-many-other-names." She set her chin on her clasped hands, a glint in those gorgeous pale eyes. *What would those shining pools look like when flooded with desire?* "Tell me your secrets."

I want you.

The waiter returned and uncorked the wine, giving Mitch a moment to collect himself. After Peyton sampled the wine and the waiter poured them each a generous glass, he left them alone. If Mitch had hoped the interruption would deter Peyton, he'd been wrong.

"So . . . you were about to share a secret." She swirled her wineglass, watching the garnet-colored liquid circle the inside of its bowl before settling, its legs trickling down the glass like tears.

He hid his longing behind a sip from his own wineglass. "If I did, it'd no longer be a secret. How about we start with something simple, like my job?"

"Small talk is dull. Besides, you heard my most intimate experiences today." Her cheeks filled with color, making him aware of how well she'd hidden her discomfort earlier. "It's only fair that I learn something personal about you. Something like . . . what was your most embarrassing moment?"

She sat straighter, as if eager for his answer. He blinked in the face of her probing question. Most embarrassing moment . . .

"You're blushing!" She chuckled before sampling more wine. "This ought to be interesting."

"It's really not." His phone buzzed, so he peeked at it. An update from Rebecca. He slipped it back in his pocket.

"I'll be the judge."

He sighed at his lose-lose situation before capitulating. "When I was around thirteen, I walked in on my parents in bed . . . except they weren't beneath the covers. In fact, they were quite adventuresome."

She choked on her drink and then laughed, waving her hands. "Oh God, I don't even want to think about my parents in bed. If I'd walked in on them as a kid, it might've turned me off sex forever."

It sure hadn't fueled his sexual fantasies. Then again, soon thereafter, they'd all had more important things to think about, and fantasies had taken a back seat to prayers and fear and then anguish.

"There's that sad look again. Did I strike a nerve, or is talking about sex making you miss your girlfriend?" She slouched back, placing her hands in her lap.

He shouldn't go there, but he couldn't stop himself.

"That's the second time you've mentioned my imaginary girlfriend." He tried to meet and hold her gaze, but she won that game of chicken.

"Imaginary? That surprises me." In a good way, if that smile indicated her true feelings. Might she like him as he did her? Not that it mattered.

"Does it?" He toyed with his fork to keep from fanning himself. "Starting my own business this year hasn't left much time for romance."

"What about Tinder?" She laughed at him when he choked, then leaned forward. "Seriously, Mitch. Good-looking, ambitious men never have a shortage of willing partners. Did someone break your heart? Is that what's behind the occasional glum mood?"

"No one broke my heart." He frowned. "And I'm not glum."

"No one's *ever* broken your heart?"

He recalled Mary Stewart, who'd helped him through the earliest stages of grief after his father had died. Then he thought about Danielle—although that was regret more than lingering heartache.

"Aha! There *was* a girl." Peyton clapped her hands together, a smug smile proving her to be very pleased with herself.

"'Girl' being the appropriate word," he mumbled, reluctant to get deep into the weeds with this discussion. When Peyton didn't back off, he elaborated just enough to satisfy her curiosity. "Eleventh grade— Mary Stewart, my first sexual experience. But that spring she dumped me for Tom Sample, a senior with a football scholarship offer from Clemson."

Peyton shrugged. "Jocks are all the rage when we're young. But puppy love isn't real heartbreak, Mitch."

"No." He knew heartbreak, though his biggest heartache had had nothing to do with women or romance.

"So you must be a love 'em and leave 'em guy, then." An abrupt scowl seized her face until it melted into something more contemplative. "Or you've never let yourself get close enough to get hurt."

"You seem to enjoy spinning these tall tales. Perhaps you should write a romance novel next."

She narrowed her gaze, circling the index finger she'd pointed at him. "I see what you're about, turning this back on me. Uh-uh. That only tells me to go for the jugular. Is the reason you have such a hard rule about not dating work-related women because you had a bad experience doing that?"

He swallowed more wine.

"I'm right." She preened.

Had it not been for the zip of pleasure he derived from her sing-songy tone and cat-ate-the-cream expression, he wouldn't have said more. But if the most he could ever enjoy with Peyton involved this suppressed sort of flirtation, he'd seize the moments where he found them.

"Yes, I, Optimus, robot-around-town, made the massive mistake of getting involved with a coworker when I worked at Savant's mystery and thriller imprint, Rebus."

Her eyes went round as she leaned forward, hands stretching across the table as if she might grab his and shake them. His fingers itched for her touch, but she withdrew. "Who?"

"It doesn't matter." He knew at once she wouldn't let him off the hook with that response. "Suffice to say, when it ended, she made my life hell."

"Did she accuse you of something?"

"No. Ours was a consensual relationship. But when we were together, I'd made the mistake of confiding my complaints about our boss to her, and of sharing some of my more-creative ideas. Very, very stupid, I know. Once we broke up, she not only took credit for some of my work but also cozied up to our boss and 'let things slip' at a time when she and I were both up for a promotion."

"Wow. I'm sorry she betrayed you that way." Peyton paled.

He nodded, well aware of Danielle's deft manipulation of the situation. It'd taken him a year to restore his reputation at Savant. Making a play for its newest author while on this tour would be beyond stupid.

His phone rang. It had to be his mom or Lauren—everyone else texted. For once he welcomed the interruption, because it brought an end to that unpleasant topic. "I'm sorry. Family call. Do you mind if I make sure it's nothing urgent?"

"Of course not."

"Thanks." He answered the call, tucking his chin and whisper-talking. "Lauren, if you and Mom aren't bleeding out, I'll talk to you later."

"Wait! Mom's freaking on me. I can't help her bake for the church fair Saturday because I forgot about the stupid thing and made other plans. Besides, I'm not the baker, you are. Can you reason with her, please? Tell her it's okay to buy slice-and-bake dough this one time."

This type of "emergency" wasn't anything new or unexpected, but something about Peyton staring at him from across the table made him acutely aware of how ridiculous the interruption was. "Lauren, I'm with my client. This can wait."

"You know Mom starts getting weird when you aren't around. If you don't calm her down, she'll have a stroke."

His relentless sister would keep at him until he caved. Given their mom's temperament, that stroke comment wasn't too far off the mark, either.

"Fine. I'll call her in an hour. Goodbye." He hung up and slipped the phone in his pocket. "Sorry."

"Everything okay?"

He nodded, unwilling to relay the details of the absurd exchange. Of course, had he been home, he'd have been happy to bake with his mother. Baking was the only thing he'd ever found in life that gave him the exact result he expected, as long as he followed the rules. A soothing hobby in an otherwise unpredictable and often unsympathetic world.

An eager smile returned to her face. "So how did it all get resolved . . . with the coworker chick? Tell me she ended up the loser in the long run."

He felt the grimace take over his face before he could stop it. It seemed he would not get away with brushing Peyton off. "I got transferred to the Epistle imprint to work on nonfiction. Lots of biographies by old men. But I did work my way up to the head PR spot in that imprint, so it worked out. Danielle has continued crawling over others' backs to climb the ladder at Rebus."

She laughed, low and sultry, and her eyes glowed like liquid fire. "What a shame you didn't stick with Savant and get to make her life a misery by flaunting better girlfriends in her face. Or perhaps I should be glad. Otherwise I might be sitting here with someone else."

"Clearly, that would've been my loss." Even *he* heard the hunger in his tone.

Like when they'd been on the airplane, another charged silence gripped them. He wasn't so obtuse that he couldn't feel the mutual attraction hanging in the air, surrounding them like a thundercloud ready to burst. Temptation pulsed with each heartbeat.

Before either said more, the waiter appeared with two steaming plates of pasta that smelled nothing like bottled Ragú. *"Buon appetito."*

"Grazie," Peyton replied as she picked up her fork. She then shot Mitch a sassy look. "Prepare to lick every last bit of that sauce from your plate."

She expertly twirled a forkful of spaghetti and placed it in her mouth, closing her eyes while uttering a moan of approval that made his groin pulse. Seconds later, she opened her eyes and watched him as if eager to gauge his reaction.

He did his best to mimic her technique, unprepared for the tang of salty pork, acidic tomato, and sweet onion flavors awakening his taste buds. His brows knit in surprise and he nodded. "Mmm."

"Told you." She smiled, forking up more pasta. "At least when it comes to food, I can always be trusted."

He set down his fork and studied her. A tic in her cheek told him that she knew she'd slipped up. He should let it go, but he couldn't— not after he recalled her earlier concern about questions she might not want to answer. "That implies that you can't always be trusted. Now *I'm* curious . . ."

Chapter Six

Peyton didn't often slip up that way, which proved how out of practice with casual conversation she'd become. Now she'd have to offer Mitch some explanation. She'd been careful to cut passages about Claire and Todd from the memoir because she hadn't wanted to cause Claire additional pain or embarrassment by making their rift known beyond the boundaries of Sanctuary Sound.

"Sorry," Mitch said, apparently reading her discomfort with the same precision he did almost everything else. "I didn't mean to pry."

"It's fine." She couldn't quite say why she wanted to blurt the whole ugly mess except that maybe, in some way, if they were ever to become real friends, she wouldn't have to worry that she'd hidden a crucial piece of history from him. Honesty at the expense of her dignity—quite a trade-off. "I opened the door, didn't I?"

"Not intentionally." He tried and failed to twirl his pasta right, making her itch to teach him, except she doubted that he'd like that. In her experience, men didn't much appreciate lessons from a date—or, since this wasn't a date, from a woman.

She gulped her wine and set down the empty glass. "You might as well know the whole truth, in case someone else finds out and brings it up."

His mouth fell open and he sat back. "That bad?"

She nodded. "The supershort version is that I stole my best friend's boyfriend."

His jaw barely twitched. He masked his feelings so well it made him hard to read. That kind of man was hard to trust, except that everything else about him seemed earnest.

She fidgeted in her seat. "The happy ending is that Claire—the old friend—is now engaged to my brother, and she's happier than she would've ever been with Todd."

Saying Todd's name aloud always brought up a bit of bile. He'd bewitched her, which fact humiliated her now. That her buried pain could resurface as sharp and insistent as a slam to the funny bone made it all worse.

"How can you know that?" Mitch's flat, unsympathetic voice caused her a moment of regret about telling the sordid tale.

"She's had a crush on Logan since childhood, for starters. But mostly because Todd destroys hearts. Not that I shouldn't have known that from the way he dumped Claire, but still." She scowled, tapping the edge of her plate with her fingernail. *What's done is done.* "He would've let her down someday. In a way, you could argue I saved her from wasting years of her life."

At the cost of one or two of her own.

"You must've fallen hard for him to have been willing to hurt your friend so deeply." The intensity of Mitch's scrutiny pinned her to her seat while making her hot and restless. "How did he let *you* down?"

She closed her eyes and pictured Todd's face two days after her diagnosis, when she'd caught him pacing in his bedroom in front of the drawers containing her things and the open suitcase he'd laid on the floor. He'd turned to her with a pathetic shrug and guilty face. *"I'm sorry, but I can't deal with the uncertainty. The idea of watching you suffer and be so sick . . . I don't know what to say except I didn't sign up for this."*

She must've mumbled that last part aloud, because Mitch asked, "What?"

70

There'd be no avoiding the most humbling part of the story now. "He left me the minute I got diagnosed." Once she got the courage to look up, she caught Mitch's expression hardening. "Having now gone through chemo, I can say I hated dragging anyone through that suffering with me. But Todd was so weak and disloyal about it, like I was supposed to feel sorry for *him*. In the end I got what I deserved, though, given how I'd treated Claire."

Mitch didn't offer platitudes, not that she would've believed any. At the moment, he seemed lost in thought . . . almost spooked. She poured herself another glass of wine to try to wash down her self-disgust.

"Seems we've both been double-crossed by an ex." He pushed the pasta around with his fork like he was poking around his brain, searching for more words. "Logan must be quite adroit to have managed dating Claire while remaining so involved with you and this project."

"He tiptoed on a high wire for a while, no doubt, with him trying to help me mend fences with her. He never expected to fall in love, but he fell so fast and hard I still can't quite believe it."

"Claire must be very forgiving." Mitch's expression softened around a respectful smile, setting off a pang of envy in Peyton.

"Well, in my defense, the first time I met Todd, I didn't know he was *her* Todd. As soon as I learned the truth, I backed away. But then he dumped Claire and chased me down, made me feel completely and unconditionally wanted. I . . . well, I regret it all very much. As for Claire, she hasn't forgiven me easily. It's taken almost two years, and even still, there's a fragility to our new relationship. She might never trust me again, not that I blame her."

Mitch nodded. "I guess no one goes through life without regrets."

"Like yours with Danielle?" That regret, however, was an error of judgment, not one of betrayal on the scale she'd achieved. "Or is there something else you regret?"

Please, God, let there be something to put us on even footing.

He stared straight into her eyes, the assessing gaze sending heat racing through her. As each second ticked by without a new confession, she withered bit by bit. No doubt he pitied her, and she hated that almost as much as she hated what she'd done.

"I've no regrets that will make you feel better right now." He reached across the table and clasped her hand so she couldn't withdraw. His touch, warm and firm, made her heart leapfrog into her throat while she braced for whatever he might say next. "I'm not judging you, Peyton. The heart has a mind of its own. Relationships and love are complicated. I've certainly never figured them out."

"Me neither."

His thumb caressed the top of her hand, although she wasn't sure he was even aware of it. "If things had turned out differently—if Todd had been the true love of your life for the next fifty years—maybe it would've been worth the loss of a friend. Who can say?"

No one had made that suggestion yet. Even she hadn't considered it. What *if* Todd had been her happily ever after? Did the rarity of lasting love make it worth any sacrifice? No. Some costs are too high, some betrayals too great.

"I doubt that. It was beyond stupid to think I could be happy with love I'd stolen from my friend." She swallowed with effort.

Mitch frowned, now squeezing her hand. "Maybe it was misguided, but mistakes are part of life, and hopefully, we learn from them. Don't beat yourself up any more than you already have. It's done. You're a different person today than you were then. Just be who you are now. It's enough."

Is it? Thank God she had the awareness to keep that question to herself despite being distracted by the warmth of his touch. Then, as if he'd heard that thought, Mitch released her hand and poured himself a second glass of wine. Already light-headed, she begged off when he offered her more, too.

He set down the bottle and raised his glass to make a small toast. "To the next chapter."

When he took a healthy swallow, her heart tapped against her ribs like someone banging on a door, demanding attention. *This one! This one!*

Looked like she hadn't learned a thing from *her* past mistake. She couldn't afford to make another, though. That thought was all that kept her from reaching across the table to hold his hand again. And yet, sitting there, a part of her—a pretty big part—wanted to test the waters.

"You're a good man, Mitch." Too good for her. "I hope when you decide to follow *your* heart again, it brings you happiness."

"Thank you." He shifted in his seat, a rosy tint filling his handsome face. "And thank you for dragging me out tonight. I know you're exhausted, but I did enjoy this meal . . . and your company. Perhaps we should wrap things up and get back now. I've got to take advantage of the time-zone difference to catch up on work."

Tactful as always, but his desire to put distance between them couldn't be clearer than if he'd painted a thick red line across the table. At least her initial plan to soften him up had worked. Their tentative friendship seemed to mellow him a bit. He hadn't even suggested she prep with him tonight. Kind of cold comfort, but better than nothing.

"Of course." She wiped her mouth, wishing she had one bite of pasta left on her plate—something tasty and filling after having emptied her guts onto the table. "Off to Barcelona tomorrow."

"You sound sad about that, but I thought you loved to travel."

"What we're doing hardly qualifies as travel. What I love is getting lost in a city—meeting strangers with no agenda, exploring alleys and local shops, taking off on an unexpected adventure. No plan. No rules. Only an open mind and heart. After chemo I made a personal vow not to waste time doing things that didn't fulfill me, yet here I am, stuck in sales mode." She glanced at him in time to note his pale face. She dared push him a bit further. "Is it possible to revisit the schedule—maybe move things around a bit to make time for some minor detours?"

She'd love to revisit a few of her old favorites with him.

He stared at her, head tilted to one side, eyes filled with stormy emotion. She hadn't meant to make him feel like crap about doing his job. Before he responded, she changed the subject. "In any case, I wish I were multilingual. I don't love trusting a translator to get things right in these interviews."

Mitch flinched at the sudden change. He then eyed the waitstaff and made the universal motion for "Check, please."

"I'm sorry you're stuck on this book tour with me when you could be making other use of your time." His soft tone made it seem as if he were talking to himself. Then with a more confident tone, he assured her, "Don't worry about the translators, though. The editors screen the interviewers. Since your publishers' interests are aligned with yours, you can relax."

"Mitch, I didn't mean to imply that I don't enjoy *your* company . . ."

"It's fine." He waved away her comment without meeting her gaze. After Mitch signed the check, he tucked his wallet away. "Shall we share a taxi?"

"Of course." She stood, having no idea how to soothe his hurt feelings. He waited for her to lead them out of the restaurant. "Will you sleep tonight, or will you be worrying about the flight?"

"A little of both." He'd resumed his Optimus persona, no doubt thanks to her thoughtless remarks. "We have a handful of interviews at Voz Fresca late tomorrow morning, and then that live reading at La Central in the evening."

She shuddered. La Central was a prominent bookstore. One she'd visited as a tourist a few times, often witnessing large crowds. Going back as a debut author made her feel like a bull being led to the ring. "That's going to be so hard."

"With your charisma, you'll be terrific with a crowd." His smile might've convinced her if something sad in his eyes hadn't thrown her.

"Thank you." She searched for a taxi while trying not to panic about the reading. She'd tabbed a number of excerpts ranging from the lighthearted to the darkest, but while the darkest might be the most honest and raw, she doubted she had the courage to stand in front of a crowd and recite those. Besides, most people might not find them uplifting. Of course, trying to think of any part of her trauma as entertainment was rather surreal to begin with. "I can't decide which passage to read. Which parts of the book do you think would be best?"

He stumbled . . . or didn't he? She couldn't be sure, but his frown didn't boost her confidence. "A memoir is deeply personal, so my advice is to read what feels most relevant to you. I can't choose for you, although I will listen if you want to practice."

A taxi slowed to a stop, and Mitch opened the door for her. Despite all the nice manners, his vague response disappointed her. She wanted guidance, or at least another false compliment to bolster her courage.

Instead he waved her inside with a little bow at the waist. "Your carriage awaits."

Given what lay ahead, she didn't much feel like a queen . . . unless you counted Marie Antoinette on her way to the guillotine.

—⁓—

The next afternoon, Mitch pressed his forehead to the wall outside the conference room and cursed his assistant under his breath. "Sorry, Rebecca. My patience is thin."

Very thin, considering the restless night he'd spent replaying his dinner conversation with Peyton, the bumpy flight he'd endured that morning, and the fact that Peyton had been less than ebullient with the first two bloggers during this spate of interviews. "I've got five minutes to digest this, so start again and explain how you not only missed some key long-lead pitch deadlines for Kendra Khan's next release but also informed her that the *Boston Globe* was reviewing her book when, in fact, it is not."

"I'm sorry. I only realized yesterday that two were still sitting in my draft folder. There are so many emails every day—"

"But you assured me two weeks ago they'd all been sent." He pinched the bridge of his nose, drawing a breath to lower his blood pressure.

"I made a mistake."

A big one! He would fix it, but he wished he didn't need to spend his day doing so when Peyton seemed to be foundering.

"Which doesn't explain the mix-up with the *Globe*." He pushed off the wall as Peyton returned from the restroom. Her expression suggested she hadn't heard him snap at Rebecca. She glided past him and into the conference room, leaving him some privacy. "I'll call Kendra and the *Globe* reviewer to deal with that mess, but you must go back through everything else related to her upcoming release and triple-check it, then email me to confirm there aren't any more errors. After that, go one by one through the checklist I left you and send me a status report on those items, too."

"All today?"

"Yes, today. I'm thousands of miles away, and you've shaken my confidence in your ability to manage what I've left behind. Check each and every item to confirm that there are no more surprises coming my way. If there is anything else you need to tell me, please do it now. I'd like to get back inside before the next interview begins."

"That's all. Looks like I'm in for a long day and night." Her put-upon tone might've gotten her fired if he didn't need her help—unreliable as it was—while he was abroad.

"I'll be waiting for those reports." He hung up, not even a little sorry for his curtness. Her mistake would ding his reputation with Kendra and her publisher. He didn't need this distraction now, when Peyton seemed off her stride.

Following his call to the *Globe*, he entered the stuffy conference room to find Peyton pouring herself a fresh glass of water. Picking his way around a too-big credenza and the extra chairs lining the wall, he crossed to her. The old building's window AC unit barely pumped any cool air into the room. As an added "bonus," the hideous, sputtering hunk of metal blocked the view from the room's sole window. "All set?"

"As good as one can be in this prison." She shrugged with the same malaise with which she'd answered every question thus far.

Somehow, between yesterday and today, she'd lost her mojo. If given the choice, he, too, would rather tour Casa Batlló or walk along the beach, but they both had a job to do, and with Savant breathing down his neck, he couldn't ease up on her unless she was feeling sick. And considering how Rebecca had screwed up with his other new client, he needed Peyton to hit a home run.

"I'll grant you, this room isn't ideal, but you seem preoccupied today. Don't you feel well?" He remembered learning about the long-tail aftereffects of cancer treatment, although his dad had never gotten that far. Peyton might still be taking medication that could cause lethargy, among other things. Or maybe all that conversation about her ex-boyfriend last night had brought her down.

"I'm tired." She sipped some water, then chewed on an ice cube. "Nervous about tonight's reading, too."

"Oh." He could fix that—pump her up. Like always, he channeled his middle school baseball coach, Mr. Ruiz, a guy who could always find the right words to encourage and inspire. "I know you'd rather avoid the spotlight, and it must be tough to revisit these topics with strangers. But remember—no one in the audience is being forced to come listen. Everyone who shows up wants to hear your story and cheer you on. They're making you and your book a priority for their evening, so you need to show up for them. Focus on your mission and all the research that might get funded by your effort. Above all, remember that you've written a fine book. Have faith. I've no doubt you can make a great connection with the audience."

"Thanks." She nodded with a hint of a smile forming. "Good advice."

Would she, unlike most people, take good advice when offered? He got his answer within two seconds.

"If things go well tonight, can we make good use of the big chunk of free time we have the day we arrive in France? Visit a vineyard outside of Paris and do a champagne tasting?" Her eyes twinkled with enthusiasm. "It's so close we could easily get back in time for the evening publisher event."

He shook his head. "I'm sorry to be a buzzkill, but you just said you're tired. I think you need real downtime to build back up for the next events. If you squeeze in side trips, you'll be exhausted. Like it or not, we have to prioritize."

"This"—she gestured up and down his body—"is why you're super-stressed all the time." She placed her hand on his shoulder and squeezed the spot near his neck. If he'd been a cat, he would've arched against her hand. "Trust me. Sometimes a break from all this work can be more invigorating than rest. Come on, let me plan a tiny side trip."

She got called back to her seat before he could answer.

Just as well. She and her book—not him—had to remain at the center of attention in the coming weeks. She was, of course, his focus, although he couldn't lie to himself and pretend that it was for purely professional reasons. He could lie to her, though.

The writer from the *Barcelona Review* swaggered in and sat down. Medium height, trim, with coal-black hair worn a bit shaggy. The guy's eyes lit up when he got his first good look at Peyton's smile, making Mitch's gut tighten.

"Hello, Miss Prescott. I'm Javier Molina, but friends call me Javi." He reached across the table to shake her hand.

"Nice to meet you, Javi. Please call me Peyton."

The little knot in Mitch's stomach screwed tighter when he thought she was flirting. *She's only smiling, stupid.*

Javi set up his phone recorder and then slouched back, feet planted wide apart on the ground, pen in hand. That cocky bastard was trying to intimidate Peyton with his domineering position. "First, let me say I enjoyed the book, although I suspect some of the caustic humor was meant to keep us at a distance."

"Not exactly," she muttered.

Javi hesitated but would be disappointed if he expected his silence would force her to elaborate. Mitch had watched her operate with interviewers in Rome. She'd make an excellent trial witness, answering only those questions asked—nothing more or less. Even this spare utterance seemed to have slipped through her fortress wall.

A day or two ago, when his sole focus had been his job and goals, he might've faulted her for using a buffer to keep from digging into old wounds. But how could he fault her for that when he found any excuse to bolt from the room whenever her answers began to cut him up inside as they sent him back in time to his dad's losing battle?

Javi prodded again. "In certain cases, the photographs are more raw than the narrative, although they blend seamlessly together. All but the cover photo, which has no explanation or accompanying exposition. It's a spectacular, harsh image . . . Can you tell our readers what was going through your mind when it was taken?"

"You mean aside from 'I'm going to kill you, Logan'?" She chuckled, buying herself a precious moment to compose her thoughts, Mitch guessed.

Meanwhile, Javi raised his index finger with a sly nod, as if she'd proved the point he'd made a moment ago about her defense mechanism. Rather than venture another attempt to flirt his way past Peyton's defenses, Javi simply stared at her this time, waiting for a real answer.

Her gaze drifted, eyes cloudy. If she'd wanted to discuss whatever happened at the time of that photo, she would've put it in the memoir.

Mitch loosened his fist and wiggled his fingers. She needed to do this for herself, and it might be easier on her if he left the room. It would certainly be easier on him not to listen to the story behind the photo that had captivated yet haunted him for weeks.

He wrestled with his internal debate until she sighed.

Without looking at Javi, she picked up the pen and began doodling on the pad in front of her while she spoke. "Forty-five minutes before Logan shot that photo, I'd used the magic mouthwash to help with my mouth ulcers. After the waiting period, I went to the kitchen to get some water. It was predawn, so I'd assumed Logan was sleeping. I took a few sips and then wandered to the living room window. Outside, the street was already coming to life, all shadows and movement and secrets. Garbage men emptying bins, night-shift workers heading home, a stray woman dashing toward the subway on an obvious walk of shame . . . ordinary people living their lives. Probably worrying about the electric bill, or looking forward to a sporting event, or maybe daydreaming about a new love. Things that had once occupied my thoughts but, in that moment, meant less than nothing to me."

When she paused, Mitch stole a look at her notepad. Daisies?

Her expression shifted to something self-deprecating. "And yet I envied them and those small worries . . . envied their health. Their nonchalance about another new day. I was so separated from it all—and not only by the glass. I swallowed a scream because I knew they, like me before my diagnosis, were taking everything for granted. I watched them, resentment festering because I might not exist long enough to even see those people months later. Worse, they'd never know. Life everywhere would go on without me, and very, very few people would care. Just like that"—she snapped her fingers—"it hit me that my whole life never mattered much. No spouse. No children. No impressive legacy from my Globejotter days. What, of value, had I done with my time?"

The room remained silent while she resumed her doodling. "I don't know what woke Logan. All I remember is that I turned when I heard the camera click, and then he kept snapping." She finally looked at Javi and tapped the book jacket with the back end of her pen. "That was his favorite of the bunch."

Javi straightened his posture while finishing his notes. Peyton shot Mitch a quick glance punctuated by a half shrug. What a strange, intriguing woman. Drawing flowers while relaying her existential crisis to a total stranger.

Mitch offered a sharp nod of approval when what he wanted was to gather her in his arms like a bouquet of delicate flowers and tell her that he would care very much if she didn't exist tomorrow or the next day or the one after.

Although riveted by her and his own daydream, when Mitch's phone vibrated, he had to check it because of the other client troubles. *Rebecca.* He grimaced apologetically before excusing himself from the room.

Chapter Seven

Peyton sat on the serpentine bench of Park Güell's main terrace and tucked her phone away after another failed attempt to reach Logan, then hugged her knees to her chest. Beyond the rooftops of Barcelona—with the iconic Sagrada Família rising toward heaven in the distance—lay the sparkling Mediterranean, all of it bathed in the dusky-rose light of late afternoon. She searched the horizon for answers, as she did at home. And as at home, she came up empty.

Two hours. Two hours from now, a roomful of strangers would be staring at her, listening to and judging her words, asking who knew what kinds of questions. This time she'd need to relive it all in front of many people, not simply one blogger at a time. Her stomach lurched again. It might take an act of God to get her off this bench and to that venue tonight.

Mitch had to be frantic wondering where she'd gone, but she'd needed space. Air. Freedom. Privacy. The daisies he'd sent to her room to wish her luck tonight hadn't helped any more than the profuse apologies and vague references to some sort of emergency he'd uttered each time he'd ducked out of the earlier interviews.

She'd be sympathetic if she believed it to be a family thing, but she had the distinct impression that he was in the middle of a work-related crisis. Not that that wasn't important, too, but *she* was also in a work crisis, and his number-one job while here in Europe should be to hold her hand through it.

Of course, those flowers had been a sweet—almost romantic—surprise. He must've learned of her love for daisies from the memoir, although she couldn't call to mind a passage that mentioned them.

She practiced ujjayi breathing while admiring the fantastical construction of the park—yet another unique Gaudí creation rife with his signature fluid curves and mosaics. Stacked in layers, its hidden nooks and crannies begged for exploration by curious visitors, the drip castle–looking buildings with tiled pinnacles teased the imagination, and a scalloped main terrace with an intricate ceiling provided shade. People lingered on the benches and meandered the many pathways. Flowers—so many flowers—in every direction.

Life unfurling everywhere—beautiful and unhurried. A gift from a man of great vision. A legacy, like her great-grandfather's.

Her phone buzzed. Probably Mitch, his thumbs flying across his keyboard, typing out "Where are you?" yet again. *Sweat it out, buddy.* If he couldn't hang in there with her when she needed him, then he'd better get used to trusting that she'd get herself to her appointments on time. Drawing a deep breath through her nose, she took another moment to soak in the beauty around her, in this small way keeping that promise to herself.

The urge to back out of the rest of the tour swallowed her like an icy pond on a winter day. She rested her forehead on her knees and blew out that breath. She'd faced worse, of course, like when biting her sharp tongue to keep from taking out her stress on a poor nurse who'd needed to triple-check her patient bracelet. Or climbing the walls and pacing the floor while waiting and waiting and waiting for each and every test result.

By comparison, this book stuff should be easy, yet it wasn't. Any way she sliced it, she'd known chemo would end, one way or another. This—going public with her story in a digital age—would last forever.

Letting that book find its way to strangers had been one hurdle, but coming face-to-face with readers? The fact that her mother might have been right all along caused her to gently bang her forehead against her knees.

"Mare, vull més aigua." A young girl shook her empty water bottle at her mother as she plunked onto the bench a foot or so from Peyton.

The first thing Peyton noticed about the girl's dark-brown, shoulder-length wig—it wasn't real hair. The second—it didn't fit well. A hand-me-down from someone, perhaps? Then the kid's spotty eyebrows and lashes slingshot Peyton back to that dehumanizing time, causing a chill to tickle her spine despite the warm summer afternoon. Hairlessness makes one look like some sort of alien that no one—let alone a child—should have to become while praying for good news and better health.

"No hi ha més aigua. Has d'esperar que sortim," replied her mother, a gorgeous Catalonian in a white muslin dress with a bright-orange poppy print. The woman took the empty bottle before holding her daughter close and kissing her head.

"Però la vull ara." The girl grabbed at her throat, sticking her tongue out like she'd die without more water.

"Ho sento." The mother frowned apologetically. She looked to be Peyton's age, yet the weight of chronic worry tugged at the corners of her eyes, making them appear much older.

Peyton didn't need to know what they'd said to each other. She knew what wasn't being said. The suppressed resentment and alarm at life's injustice. The bone-deep pain each hid in order to let the other enjoy a good day. The uncertainty they wrestled to the point of complete madness.

Giving the people one loves a sense of optimism by covering one's own fears and doubts can create unparalleled loneliness. Countless times, Peyton had been stoic with Logan or her friend Steffi when all she'd wanted to do was dissolve into a puddle of tears and be held and promised that everything would be okay. But she wouldn't ask for promises they couldn't keep while also forcing them to witness her pain. Even now, she never shared her concerns about the upcoming tests or recounted the recurring nightmare about being chased by a monster she couldn't see.

It could happen. Right now, a cluster of cancer cells could be regrouping, planning another battle. She could be thrust back into treatment, fighting for her life again, like this poor young child. The tingling sensation of tears filled her nose.

Another glance at the mother-daughter duo gave her the jolt she'd needed to keep from losing it. She was Peyton Prescott—a strong, competent fighter. She would pick herself up off this bench and do what she'd come all this way to do, if for no other reason than because the two women beside her might hear her story and find hope.

She smiled at them before rising from her seat and brushing off her skirt. The mother's gaze lingered, and in that silent space of time, Peyton's body flushed and tightened with the desire to offer some assurance. Instead, she withdrew her last water bottle from her bag and handed it to the child, because no words in any language made dealing with cancer easier.

That was the ultimate irony of her memoir, and one big reason why she found selling it difficult. Writing it had helped *her* sort through her own life, but she still questioned whether she—a sometimes selfish, vain woman from Connecticut—could truly help anyone else. Maybe the best she'd be able to offer was showing that sickness had some silver linings, too.

With her warmest smile, she waved goodbye. "Enjoy the beautiful day."

Perhaps the silver lining for this young girl and her mom was the shared hug here in this sunny, fantastical park, rather than an afternoon spent fighting about an unmade bed or forgetting to load the dishwasher or any of the myriad other trivial complaints people lodge when they take their lives for granted.

—⁓—

La Central—originally a maternity hospital—retained a monastic feel with its vaulted ceilings and hardwood floors. Peyton took a short break to sip some water, her gaze wandering over everyone's heads to avoid latching on to that of another person.

She set the bottle back on the podium—the only buffer between herself and the audience.

Mitch appeared to be pleased with the turnout, but to her, the large crowd represented more people to judge her and her story. She turned the page to continue reading from a part of the book that didn't force her to get too personal in front of strangers.

"*Today, when Frank still hadn't returned to the hospital, I knew he'd stopped treatment, as he'd warned he would. The audacious, pale-eyed, dark-skinned fossil who'd made me laugh during the most humbling days of my life will no longer greet me with his lopsided smile in these sterile waiting rooms. Or enlighten me with outrageous accounts of his late wife's kitchen disasters and his grandkids' feeble attempts at rap. Or boost my spirits with his gratitude for God, love, and the life he'd been given, which had lasted so much longer than those of the youngest patients in our ward.*

"*We came from different worlds, yet were united in our humanity and our desire to survive. Now Frank was another loss I'd need to overcome, like each clump of hair tumbling into the sink bowl.*

"*Had I wasted our time together, passively listening to his stories and laughing? Frittered those precious hours when I should've told him that he'd leave an everlasting imprint on my life—for however long my life lasts, anyway.*

"And still I fail him with that knee-jerk deflection. My go-to for running away from anything too real for fear of what embracing the stark, terrible truths of my life might mean.

"I've tried to picture death's door—to imagine the look in Logan's eyes at our final goodbye, to accept never knowing what will become of my family and friends down the road, to wrap my head around the concept of no longer existing.

"Acceptance won't come. I get only close enough that my heart feels too big for my chest, so I shove the thoughts away, as if refusing to face them will somehow reduce reality to a bad dream that will disappear when I wake. Yet I know denial will never bring me peace. Even now, panic strikes a match at the edge of my consciousness, its flames licking at the hope I cling to.

"So again I allow the cool hand of reason to rescue my heart from having to be brave. From having to stand in this moment and feel my life slipping through my fingers.

"Death will come for me, as it will for everyone. On a fundamental, philosophical level, I accept that, even if I can't quite connect with it. Maybe that makes me weak. Or strong? Either way, I feel better only when I focus on what cancer gives me rather than what it steals.

"One silver lining of sitting here being force-fed poison is that I have time to plan for my death. To make amends and say my goodbyes. Another? I'm not leaving young children behind, although I might've liked to experience motherhood.

"Still, like a summer swarm of gnats in the woods near the Sound, the irritating truth buzzes round my head. None of my rationalizations will teach me how to make the most of my life today, tomorrow, and if I'm lucky, the next day.

"I imagine Frank winking at me now, telling me to trust him and let the darkness fall so that I can see those stars."

Peyton closed the book, sweat rolling down her spine, voice rough from the tightness that came whenever she remembered Frank. She avoided Mitch's gaze by staring at a blank spot in the back of the room while the audience clapped.

"Thank you all for coming. I'm happy to take a few questions now." Peyton forced a smile, praying no hand would shoot up. Three ascended simultaneously. Another prayer ignored.

"Yes?" She nodded at a slight woman with spiky purple hair.

"Did you let that darkness in?"

"Not willingly." Her sarcasm didn't yield a single chuckle. Now hotter than a Rolex on Canal Street, she gulped more water. "I doubt anyone can escape it altogether, despite our best efforts. There were moments . . ." She closed her eyes and shook her head. No way would she go there now in front of all these strangers. How much more did she owe these people? If they wanted to mine her most painful thoughts, they could buy the book and support the cause. "Some are revealed later in the book."

That reader didn't ask more, so Peyton moved on to another—a tall man toward the rear of the room. Something about the harsh angles of his face gave her pause, but she couldn't ignore him. "You, sir, near the back."

Again she smiled, although that flimsy shield didn't protect her from the bladelike sharpness of his expression.

He had his phone held near his chest like he was recording the event. "Does your memoir offer any new or different insight on life and death than the dozens of similar books?"

Her pulse picked up and she shot Mitch a questioning glance, but his face remained a blank page—one of the scarier things every writer faces. Like when sitting at the keyboard, she was on her own now. The stranger's unwavering gaze tightened around her like plastic wrap. "I couldn't say. I didn't read other cancer-patient memoirs because I didn't want to be influenced by them."

He grunted, scoffing. "Most writers read widely and often."

"As do I, just not patient memoirs. Regardless, this book is about my personal experience—for better or worse. Other patients may have very different experiences with and feelings about this illness."

Before she could move on to the next reader, he broke in again. "So your last name—not the work—helped you get a publishing contract? And the fund-raising . . . a way to push sales?"

Bodies shuffled in chairs, and whispered murmurs of "*Horrible*" and "*Silenci*" floated into the air. But more debilitating than the obvious pity fanning through the audience was how this man had speared the epicenter of her own self-doubt.

She blinked, trapped beneath the overhead lights like an entrée under a heat lamp. Then that part inside that resented this tour—white-hot and sharp—found release. "Only someone petty or jealous—or both—would care *how* I got a publishing contract, but I assume my last name didn't hurt. My donating half of the profits to research is a mission, not a sales ploy. I assume you understand the difference, or should I ask my translator to jump in?"

A quick glimpse of Mitch's disapproving expression told her the defensive edge in her tone wouldn't win her fans, but she didn't care. She could name a dozen celebrities who got bigger book deals than she had despite using a ghostwriter. At least she'd written her own book.

The man—who she now assumed must be a frustrated writer—opened his mouth again, but Mitch cut him off, though probably to save her from making another self-destructive remark more than to spare her that guy's nasty insinuations.

"Sir, this is moving away from a discussion about the book." Mitch stared at her from his position on the side of the small stage. "Peyton, I think the young woman in the blue dress has a question about your experience."

Inside, Peyton quaked. She would kick the podium to feel better, but her recent tirade had given Mitch enough to smooth over. Her gaze darted around, seeking her escape—some way to bolt off this stage to avoid any more questions.

Questions, questions, questions. For days she'd been probed. At the moment, she'd rather hide in the wall hatch where abandoned babies were once left for the orphanage than remain at the podium.

"Peyton?" Mitch nudged.

She fixated on the woman in the blue dress. "Miss?"

"Thank you for to be here tonight." Her warm smile helped to quiet the roaring in Peyton's ears. Then she launched into a question in her native tongue, which the translator passed along as "My sister was diagnosed with triple negative breast cancer. I want to help, but everything I do or say seems wrong. How can I help her . . . like your brother helped you, but I can't write and take pictures?"

Oh God. Peyton's chest burned like she'd run ten miles. A crystal-clear image of Logan's initial reaction to her diagnosis—the face drained of color, the strain in his eyes from holding it together—popped up as if it were happening again. His pain had made hers more crippling. The reflection of her worries in his eyes had been too much some days.

She blinked to stop the warm tears in her eyes from spilling, then cleared her throat. This woman, like her brother two years earlier, needed help. The absurdity of anyone believing that Peyton—the least emotionally equipped person in the room—could give help almost made her burst into a fit of inappropriate giggles.

"I'm so sorry for your family, and wish your sister the very best outcome. As to your question, it's hard to say. Every relationship has different boundaries. Cancer will break down most of them over time, but I know in the beginning I craved time alone to process my diagnosis, the treatment options, the realities of how it would affect my body, my work, my entire life. My brother wanted to carry all my fear and pain for me—that's how this project started, as a way to channel our energy into something productive. But you can't take away someone else's pain, so don't try. Don't cheerlead or give platitudes. It's enough to be a steady shoulder of support and be understanding with her moods. Right now she probably has very little patience for other people's ideas."

When the translator finished speaking, the woman took a seat and another woman asked a question, but Peyton didn't hear it. Her mind had slipped back to those earliest days in Logan's apartment, when she'd stared at the blank wall, cupping her breasts in her hands, cursing her body, wondering why she'd drawn the short straw when she had so many more things she wanted to do with her life.

Mitch touched her biceps and then handed her a tissue. He was speaking to the audience now, but she couldn't focus on his words, either. Not with the tears rolling down her cheeks.

"I'm sorry." Her meek mumbling went unheard due to the scraping sound of chairs being moved and people gathering their personal items. The rude man from earlier had disappeared from the edge of the crowd while the line for signed copies began to form.

Mitch turned to her. "Do you need a break? Take five minutes in the ladies' room. I'll refresh your water."

"No." She cracked her knuckles and rolled her shoulders to loosen the tension. "Let's get this done and get out of here. But what about that guy—the jerk who said my book sucked?"

"He didn't say your book sucked."

"Unoriginal . . . whatever. I think he was recording the whole exchange. Will it end up on some blog or YouTube or something?" *FML if Mom's most dire prediction becomes my reality.*

Mitch's brow shot up. "I don't know. I'll check with the manager to see if he recognized him."

"What if he's some big-time reviewer and he pans me, my reading, my book?" She dug her fingernails into her thighs.

"There's nothing we can do about that right now, but if he were that big, the publisher would've invited him to meet with you earlier today."

She thought she saw the man again speaking to someone on his cell phone. An editor? His boss? When the person turned to the side, it wasn't him.

Two large stacks of books landed on her left. She sighed and put that guy out of her mind. Time to earn her advance.

One look at the slope of Peyton's shoulders and the wrinkled lines on her forehead made Mitch want to pummel the asshat in the back of the room who'd blindsided her. He sent a quick text to Rebecca to scour YouTube and other sites for any video or live feed that might go up in the coming days, assured Savant that the reading went well, then reset his Google Alerts to add "La Central" and "Barcelona" to Peyton's name.

He caught himself looking at his watch a fifth time while waiting for the last reader to finish her conversation with Peyton. At least Peyton appeared to be engaged and comfortable in the one-on-one with the reader. After what seemed like twenty more minutes, he and Peyton made quick goodbyes to the bookstore manager and others involved in organizing this event.

Peyton reached around her chair for her purse. "I need to go."

"I know. We'll get something to eat." Nine o'clock—an hour ahead of the dinner crush at most restaurants in this city.

"I don't know." She frowned as she dragged herself through the bookstore, eyes forward, expression tight as a soldier's freshly made bed. "Right now I'm thinking of a warm bath followed by a soft pillow."

"That sounds great, but you need to keep your strength up." He clutched her arm to bring her to a standstill. "Let's grab a quick bite . . . maybe tapas or paella?"

On a deep inhale through her nose, she closed her eyes and nodded. A small victory for him, considering how ticked off she'd been earlier this afternoon.

"Any preference?" He searched for the nearest taxi stand, then laid his hand on her lower back to lead her in the right direction. She didn't shrink from him, so he let his hand linger longer than he should, even though stifled desire was helping neither of them.

"Not tonight."

He opened the taxi door for her and then scooted in beside her. "Let's go back to the hotel and hit up something nearby."

"Fine." She clasped her purse on her lap, looking at him like she didn't quite trust him. "So that jerk. What if he causes a problem? I mean, I know I shouldn't have shot off my mouth like that, but I couldn't help myself. I have no patience for bullshit these days."

"He had an ax to grind." This wasn't the time to criticize her response. Everyone knew these days that video could be edited to make things look much worse than the truth. He guessed that was what prompted the worry in her eyes. "Nothing has come across my Google Alerts yet. Honestly, that exchange—while not ideal—wasn't anything anyone should consider viral gold. It'll be fine." *Please, God, let it be fine.*

When his phone buzzed, he prayed that it wasn't an alert. He checked the screen. *Mom.* He typed, Yes, I've calendared the surgery date. Can't talk now.

Peyton stared out the window, her long neck twisting away from him, one earring glinting in the light of passing cars or streetlamps. With her forehead now pressed to the glass, she asked, "Is that text more of whatever it was that had you so preoccupied earlier today?"

"That was my mother." He closed his eyes and let his chin drop. "I'm sorry about earlier, though. I thought you were holding your own, and I was dealing with a bit of a crisis."

Her limpid blue eyes turned his way, beckoning him to spill more details.

"Not concerning you. My assistant made a mess of things with a new client." He felt his jaw clench at the memory of the tongue-lashing he'd given Rebecca. "I had to fall on one hundred swords today, but I promise, you'll have my complete attention now."

As if the cab driver read his secret desire to give her a hug, he made a hard left at a high speed, which threw Peyton against Mitch's side. Taking advantage of fate, Mitch gave her a gentle squeeze with the arm that had fallen around her shoulders.

"Sorry!" She pushed off him, making him pray for another hard left before they got to the hotel.

"Peyton, I know tonight was tough on you, but you did really well, especially for your first time. And the way you take time to speak with the readers afterward is special. Those personal connections will help spread the word so customers flock to the shelves." His heart throbbed when she hung her head.

She sighed then and pushed her hair back from her face. "Do you always take the high road, or is it your custom not to scold authors who insult audience members? I mean, I've yet to see a bad temper, not even when your family bugs you with petty calls. This whole perfection thing makes it hard to trust you."

"You don't trust me because I haven't lost my cool?" Her logic astounded him.

"Yes. It's inhuman."

"Well, I *am* Optimus, aren't I?" He sent up a quick prayer of thanks for the opportunity to lighten the mood.

"Touché!" She chuckled for the first time all day—at least the first time he'd seen. "But be serious. I want the truth."

"The truth is that I've too much at risk to indulge wishes or bad habits." He picked at his thumbnail and glanced out the window to stave off the temptation of showing her how very bad and inappropriate he could be if he could afford to make a second client blunder in a single day.

"All business." She shook her head.

Better she think that and keep her distance. "Seems so."

"Well, then, Mr. Business, did I choose the wrong passage to read? I mean, it's obvious that guy was not impressed." Her eyes beseeched him for an answer he couldn't give. "Did the rest of the crowd seem as underwhelmed?"

"Forget about him. He's one person. The rest of the audience enjoyed the introduction to you and your work. Bottom line—you'll have rabid fans and you'll have people who ding you with one-star reviews."

"Because my book sucks."

"No. Because no book fits every reader. We all filter what we read through our experiences and perspective. The goal is to find more readers who get you than who don't." Work at Savant had taught him how hard authors struggle to accept this concept. Each one wants to be universally beloved and see nothing but five-star reviews. But a quick spin on Goodreads would show that even *To Kill a Mockingbird* has one- and two-star ratings.

"This is one thing I've dreaded since Logan proposed this whole idea. I'm a travel writer, not an author. I never wanted to be like— or compared to—my great-grandfather. Or have my work judged by strangers."

"There's a memoir with your name on it that proves otherwise."

She shifted, fluffing the hem of her dress, neither accepting nor denying his remark. "Be honest. Did I read from the wrong part of my book? I mean, if I want to make sure no one else accuses me of riding on Duck's coattails, tell me which part of my book you think is the most fresh or unique."

He couldn't keep lying, although the pit in his stomach opened wider. Now another client would rightfully be pissed at him. He'd never let things go so wrong before, but unlike with Rebecca's screwup, he could blame only himself for this one. "I don't know."

Her brows pinched together, and then she slapped his thigh and laughed. "Oh, come on, I'm not that fragile. At least tell me your favorite section."

"I can't, Peyton." With a sigh of dread, he confessed. "I never read the entire book. My assistant gave me a detailed summary and talking points."

She withdrew, her expression silent dismay and disappointment. "You're joking."

"I wish I were." He'd never meant anything more.

The taxi pulled up to the hotel, so Mitch paid the fare while Peyton pulled herself together. When they got out, she didn't look at him. "I'm not hungry."

"Peyton."

She whirled around on him, arms raised overhead. "Don't 'Peyton' me. All this time you've been pushing me to prepare, yet you're my publicist and you didn't even *read* my book."

Her arms slapped against her sides.

"Rebecca read it. Despite her administrative failings, she's an excellent reader and helped craft the pitch and promo materials. I leveraged all of my contacts and planned the entire PR campaign, which resulted in multiple recommendations from big hitters and nice placement among very popular literary tastemakers." His excuses tumbled to the ground like unwanted pennies, so he stopped talking.

She had every right to be livid. Hell, she could fire him and no one would blame her. And he'd lost all hope of her recommending his firm to anyone in the future. Oddly, that was the least of his concerns at the moment.

"Why?" She thrust her hands out in question. "Why wasn't my book worth reading?"

"That's not it." He reached for her hand, but she'd already turned to storm toward the hotel entrance. "Peyton! Let me explain."

"No," she called over her shoulder. "No more excuses, and I don't want to eat with you. Room service will do. And I'll find my own way to the airport tomorrow. I need some space from you and this whole tour."

"Please, just listen." He trotted to catch her, but her wide-eyed glare dared him to take another step. He stopped in the middle of the sidewalk.

She shook her head in disgust and pushed through the door, leaving him to deal with himself. He let his head fall back, gazed at the sky—smoky-gray clouds against a field of black—and cursed.

Bad enough he'd lost the confidence of two clients in one day. But the weight of Peyton's crestfallen look pressed on his heart for reasons that had nothing to do with his professional reputation. That, not the hit to his business, bothered him most of all.

She'd done him in. Captivated him with her irreverence and compassion. This yearning could not be more ill-timed, and yet its engine gained speed, urging him to consider that maybe something other than List Launch might be the key to his own happiness.

First he'd have to win back her trust.

Chapter Eight

"You'd better hide when I get home, because I won't be held responsible for any flying objects when I see you." Peyton flopped onto the bed while speaking with Logan. She reached overhead to nab the chocolate square from her pillow and unwrapped the foil. Dark-chocolate salted caramel—even better than a martini, although she could use one of those, too.

"I'm confused. Last we spoke you sounded rather upbeat. In fact, it almost sounded like you had a little crush on Mitch. You know I think it's time you get back on that horse, by the way."

She caught a glimpse of the daisies on the nightstand and groaned. "He's a fraud like all men but you. And even you have your moments now and then . . ."

God love him, but Logan did have a manipulative streak that he justified six ways to Sunday. She crumpled the foil and set it aside, then craned her neck to search for a second one. *Woot!*

"Hey now."

"Don't worry. I still love you, but right now I hate you a little." She propped herself up on her elbows and greedily devoured the candy, although even several pounds of chocolate wouldn't make this book tour any easier. "Reading for strangers is hard as hell."

And she hadn't even read from the raw parts of the book.

"I'm positive you were brilliant. Don't let that idiot who took a swipe at you sour the experience. He's a jealous bastard." Logan paused. "But let's get back to Mitch. What did *he* do to piss you off?"

She could tell Logan the truth, but he might then tell others, which would hurt Mitch's reputation. If Mitch never read *any* of his clients' books, his rep deserved the hit. But she sensed—from his tone, the pleading look in his eyes, and those damn daisies—that her book was the exception, not the rule. There must be some reason he chose not to read *hers*. That didn't make her feel better, but she wouldn't mess with his livelihood without knowing the full story. "I'd hoped for a different level of support now that we're in the thick of things, I guess."

"Then sit him down and tell him exactly what you need. I know you hate to ask for help, but there's no shame in it. It's not like you've ever done this before. And he can't read your mind. You put up a good show of strength when you want. Maybe he doesn't think you need him."

She rolled onto her stomach and then stuck one arm beneath her chest to raise her upper body off the mattress, still not comfortable with her full weight bearing down on the foobs. Always *some* reminder that nothing would ever be like before. "Let's talk about something pleasant. How's the engagement-party planning coming along?"

"Oh, Darla is handling it with the same fervor she does the annual literary fund-raiser." Logan often referred to their mom by her first name, especially when he was making fun of her.

"I'm glad. It's a big deal, and Claire might not admit it, but I bet she loves being made a fuss over."

"Well, then, she's in luck, because no one makes a bigger fuss than Mom." A warm snicker followed the statement, surprising Peyton. Perhaps this impending wedding would bring Logan closer to their parents. "Go make up with Mitch and then invite him to the party as your plus-one. I want to meet him."

"Get out of here." Although the idea didn't bounce off her armor like she might've hoped. Without any effort, an image of Mitch in a navy-blue blazer and pinstriped shirt sprang to mind. Cover-model material that made her heart flutter—God help her. The daydream was so vivid she could feel herself swaying to a classic love song on the patio with him, his hand on her lower back . . .

She shivered, then frowned at getting all tingly when she was still so pissed at him for being as phony as Todd. She couldn't be a fool for men twice!

"Well, if you don't bring your own date," Logan threatened, "I'll have to force one on you."

"Don't you dare!" He didn't have a single male friend that she liked. Jon—arrogant. Kyle—flighty. Sean—boozer.

"I don't want you sitting alone all night when your two closest friends are paired up. I know Todd hurt you, but you've survived so much since him. Next time will be different. I promise."

"You can't make that promise, Logan, although I love you for trying. But honestly, I don't feel sexy, let alone have the energy for romance yet." Maybe after her next checkup she also wouldn't worry as much about getting sick again. "It's too soon. I won't drag anyone new through recovery with me. Even I'm not *that* selfish."

"It's not selfish to want to be loved, for *however* long it lasts."

"Okay, we've gone into weird brother-sister territory here. If you're feeling a need to be mushy, go hang out with Claire. I'm going to sleep now."

"Fine. But on a serious note, talk to Mitch about this work stuff if for no other reason than so you can kick ass on the rest of the tour. You've put too much of yourself into this project not to give this your best shot."

She refused to agree with him or call him out on his own motives for wanting their book to succeed. "Good night."

"Sleep well."

After hanging up, she tossed her phone aside. Seconds ticked by as she swung her calves in little circles, thinking about Mitch's expression on the sidewalk. That gorgeous, stricken face of his that did all kinds of unwelcome things to her heart. Not to mention how aggravating it was—humiliating, even—to have to admit to herself that, despite her justifiable ire, she felt something more.

With a determined shove, she pushed off the mattress, slipped into her shoes, and stole down the hallway to his room for a showdown.

Room 204. She stared at the number, hand raised, ready to knock. Her heart seemed to be pumping itself up into her throat, but not from indignation or anger. From something much more dangerous, if the heat between her legs meant anything. Good to know she could still feel that, but it was not appropriate in these circumstances.

Stepping away from the door, she turned and trotted back to her room. Clearly she had yet to regain control of her brain and emotions, which had sped away like a twisting roller coaster two years ago and still hadn't pulled back into the station.

Tonight was not the time to talk—not when the idea of stepping into his hotel room aroused her to the point that she might now have to take the edge off by herself when she got to her room. Something she also hadn't done in ages because chemo had pretty much killed those urges along with the cancer.

Thank God she'd already rebooked herself on an earlier flight tomorrow.

Mitch groaned when he rolled over to turn off the alarm. His body had doubled in weight overnight, or so it seemed. Dread and exhaustion—a killer combo. With effort, he rubbed his dry eyes before peeling them open, then squinted at the daylight slipping through the slit between the blinds.

Bright white light. Despite the nagging sense that he had to shower and pack, he couldn't make himself move.

He scrubbed his hands over his face as if that would wash away the memory of Peyton's revulsion. Her memoir lay beneath his phone on the nightstand, where he'd set it down around four o'clock this morning. Given how he'd fucked up, he couldn't complain about the late night or the resulting nightmare he'd had of his dad crying out his name from behind a door Mitch couldn't open.

Regardless, he'd fix things with Peyton today. She couldn't avoid him on the plane. Telling her his story would suck almost as much as flying, but maybe, once she learned why he'd been unwilling to read the blow-by-blow details in her book, some sympathy would lessen her anger.

Pushing himself up against the headboard, he then grabbed his phone to clear out the in-box. It didn't shock him to see a text from his mother, but his eyes went straight to another note—from Peyton.

Mitch,

I switched my flight and took off before 6:30 this morning. I'm going to a tasting at Champagne Le Gallais today in Boursault, about ninety minutes outside of Paris, but I'll be back in time for tonight's party. I figured there was no need to prep since you never read the book. In truth, I'm grateful to you because now I've less guilt about my laissez-faire attitude. If you'd read my book, you'd know that the biggest lesson I've learned is that, at a minimum, people should choose to do with their lives what makes them happy. If all work and no play makes you happy, then you are living the dream. But as long as I'm in Europe, I'm going to make sure the agenda includes some things that make me happy.

P

He stared at his phone, frozen. A prank—surely—and not a pleasant one. Without thinking, he called her. Straight to voice mail.

"Peyton, it's Mitch. Is this a joke? It's not funny. Please call me."

He stared at the phone. When glaring at it didn't result in a return call, he tossed it on the bed and hit the shower. Hot water didn't help. The washcloth nearly tore his skin off from his scrubbing so hard and fast, then he nicked himself with the razor, too.

Still no call.

After confirming that she'd checked out, he hailed a taxi. On the way to the airport, he got her reply.

> Got your message. Checking in to our Paris hotel now. See you this evening. Happy to meet you in the lobby by 6. There is plenty to see in Paris. I recommend you don't waste your entire day working in your room.

It wasn't often he found himself speechless. It didn't matter that he had no one to talk to . . . he was sputtering anyhow.

"Sorry," he mumbled to the taxi driver, who glanced at him like he might be a little unstable.

Bit by bit, the layers of civility gave way to his building fury. Peyton was lucky there were still eight hours for him to cool down before he saw her.

—⁕—

This was not good. Peyton stood along a deserted stretch of D222, a two-lane country road that cut through Boursault, staring at the flat tire on her rental Passat. Four forty. Not quite enough time to get back to the hotel by six with this unexpected problem. She knelt down again, as if a second look would magically fix the flat.

As luck would have it, it had happened in a spot without cell service—not that she'd know whom to call for help without being able to access Google. Any other day, she'd have made the most of it and enjoyed counting the rows in each vineyard, which stretched as far as the eye could see in a patchwork quilt of golds, tans, and greens. Now she shook her head at the foolishness of taking the side roads for their beauty. There should be a town up ahead, but it could be a mile or farther away. It'd be faster to change the tire than to walk in search of help.

She knew little to no French, so she prayed that the manual would contain English instructions, too.

After reaching inside the glove compartment, she retrieved the manual, then popped the trunk to find the spare tire and jack.

As she sat on the road beside the flat, she breathed in the loamy air and recalled the excellent champagne she'd tasted earlier. A pretty damn magnificent set of silver linings to offset her current predicament.

She held her phone overhead once more, searching for any signal. Nada.

At least Mitch wouldn't be stressed quite yet. Not long ago, she'd texted him some photos of the vineyard and the Château de Boursault, a neo-Renaissance-style castle built in 1843 by Madame Clicquot Ponsardin (the Veuve Clicquot—or Clicquot widow) on a wooded hill summit, along with a selfie that included a flute of champagne, telling him she was on her way back to Paris. And, worst case, he'd know where to start the search for her remains if she ended up attacked by wildlife along the roadside.

She was on her knees, bracing the tire opposite the flat with a decent-size stone she'd found not far from the road, when she heard a bicycle approach from behind. *Help!* She spun around to find a preteen girl.

"Excusez-moi. Parlez vous anglais?"

"A little." The girl came to a stop.

Peyton was about to ask if the girl knew how to change a flat when she burst into a chuckle at how unlikely it was that she could translate that in any understandable way. She recounted the problem while gesturing to the tire and then her phone, but when the girl cocked her head, Peyton waved her off. "Never mind. Have a good day."

"Je vais vous envoyer mon père!" The girl pedaled away, leaving Peyton to figure it out for herself. *"Bonne chance."*

Several minutes later, hands now grimy and one nail chipped to the quick, she'd loosened the lug bolts. She was wiping her forehead with her forearm when the sound of a small engine buzzed through the air. Moments later, a man on a blue vintage Honda motorcycle appeared from the direction that the young girl had gone. He stopped in front of Peyton's car. Tan workmen's pants. A touch of silver glinting in his brown hair. He looked to be about forty.

"Bonjour." He toed his kickstand and approached her.

Her instincts—and the smile lines around his mouth—told her not to fear him. "Hi."

"My daughter sends me for to help." He pointed at his chest.

In that moment, she might've thrown up her hands to her new Lord and Savior. "Oh my gosh, yes! Please . . . and thank you."

He smiled at her, sun-kissed skin wrinkling the corners of his eyes, then motioned for her to make room before picking the jack up off the road and getting to work. Part of her wanted to lie back in the nearby grass and watch the clouds roll by for five minutes, but this experience had taught her she needed to learn how to change a flat.

She crouched beside him and watched as he placed the jack, raised the car high enough to replace the tire, then put the lug bolts back on, tightening them twice in a star pattern.

"Voilà!" He handed her the wrench and brushed his palms together as if that would clean them.

"Thank you! *Merci beaucoup!*" She fished around her purse and pulled out twenty euros, but he waved it off.

"Non!" He strolled back to his motorcycle and started it up, pointing at the spare tire on her car. "Must be slow. *Au revoir!*"

"Bye!" She watched him speed away, fantasizing for another moment about the quiet life he might live here in the French country-side. Perhaps employed by one of the nearby vineyards, or maybe he was a local teacher? He had a daughter, apparently. Did his wife pack picnics for them to enjoy—bread, cheese, wine . . . ?

Mitch! Going slow didn't exactly work well for her, but she wouldn't risk blowing out the tire and causing an accident.

She rolled the flat tire around the car and tossed it in the trunk along with the tool kit. Dirty hands, knees, and clothes. Not the best look for her publicity event, but she would scarcely have time to get to Paris and return the car, let alone make it to the hotel for a quick shower.

This side trip might have been a mistake, yet she couldn't regret it. Otto and Emma Müller—tourists from Berlin she'd met at the tasting—had given her several recommendations of trendy new eateries for when she got there next week. The divine double-blended Brie she'd sampled earlier had been buttery, and who could complain about tasting three different champagnes?

Until the tire blew, it'd been a banner day.

Her phone rang at 6:10, a full ten minutes past when she'd expected Mitch's frantic call. No doubt he was standing in the lobby, checking his watch every thirty seconds, calling up to her room, pacing around and going out of his mind.

"Hello, Mitch."

"Where are you?" His terse whisper-shout reminded her of when her dad had caught her sneaking into the house at 3:00 a.m. senior year, after she'd met Billy Baxter on his dad's sailboat for a little midnight fun.

"About twenty minutes outside of Paris."

"What!" he shouted, rather than asked. Now he'd probably stalked into some corner of the lobby where he wouldn't become a spectacle.

"Sorry. I got a flat tire in the middle of nowhere."

"Are you okay?" In that moment, he sounded concerned about her instead of the tour.

"I'm fine, and I learned how to change a tire. But I'll have to meet you at the party. I'll never make it back to the hotel before it starts. Given the tire incident, I'll have extra paperwork to deal with when I turn in the rental car."

She waited during an interminable pause. Finally, he asked, "Was this side trip really worth it?"

"As the pictures I sent prove, I had a terrific afternoon, met an interesting German couple, and learned about champagne. I'd say that is about ten times better than sitting around a hotel lobby discussing bloggers and cancer. So yes . . . totally worth it."

She heard what sounded like a muffled curse come through the line.

"You don't get to be pissy, Mitch," she reminded him, then drew a breath to beat back the anger rising at the memory of why she'd ditched him in the first place.

Instead of backing off, he doubled down. "I've never had anyone make my job as hard as you have. Most authors *want* their book to sell. They want to be prepared for questions and readings. They respect what I do and try to help me."

"And I suspect most publicists are well versed in the author's work, right?" Whenever cornered, she had her father's tendency to lash out. Mitch wasn't wrong to chastise her, though. She just couldn't admit that to him right now.

Silence. Almost half a kilometer's worth.

"I'll see you at the restaurant. Your editor booked a private room, and there will be at least a dozen bloggers waiting to meet you. I hope they aren't too offended by your attitude." He hung up without further pleasantries—an unusual breach of manners.

She'd pushed him past his limit. Instead of feeling a smug sense of satisfaction, her stomach turned over. That sick feeling only increased with each minute she spent in traffic. At 6:55, she was still forty minutes from the venue. She not only had caused him stress but now would embarrass herself, exactly as she had when she'd snapped at La Central.

When she burst through the doors of the private room, all eyes from the restless crowd clustered in small groups flew to her. She reached down to cover the quarter-size grease stain on her skirt, but nothing would hide the fact that she'd lost most of her makeup to roadside sweat.

She approached Mitch with more caution than she'd used to approach Claire in the immediate aftermath of the Todd debacle. "I'm very sorry."

He greeted her with a broad smile—a phony one, she knew, but he was a pro—gesturing to the woman on his left. "Peyton, this is Melissande."

Her French editor. *Smile and kiss some ass.*

"Melissande, lovely to meet you. I'm so sorry for the delay. I got a flat tire and—"

"It's fine, but now we begin?" Melissande's no-nonsense gaze grazed the length of Peyton's body. Down to business, like Mitch. Not that Peyton could blame her, given the situation. She'd effed this up for everyone, including herself. "Everyone is waiting."

"Of course."

"Good, I will make an introduction." Melissande nodded with the sort of aloofness many Americans still associated with the French, very unlike the stranger who'd rescued Peyton on the side of the road.

Peyton stood beside Mitch, impersonating a ventriloquist. "I know you're angry. I am very sorry I ran late. Believe me, though, I wasn't try-ing to be irresponsible. If I hadn't had the flat, all would've been well."

He stared straight ahead, his political-rally smile also on full display for the room. "When this event is over, I've already invited Melissande for drinks to smooth things over. I'd like you to suck up to her, but I can't force you. After that, it's best for both of us to have a cooling-off period. I've never failed before, so I'm still trying to decide how to fix our situation. Tomorrow morning at nine, you and I can meet in the hotel lobby to make some decisions about how we continue on this tour together. Savant will be expecting to hear from me within the next twenty-four hours anyway, and if we can't come to some workable arrangement, it won't be a pleasant conversation."

This didn't bode well for the rest of the tour, but she hadn't time to think of it now. Not after Melissande turned the room over to her.

About fifteen men and women stared at her, waiting for her to speak. *Screw it.* Sometimes the best way through an awkward situation is to jump right into its center.

"Good evening, everyone. Thank you for coming and for waiting. I apologize for being late. As you might have figured out from looking at me, I've just learned how to change a flat tire. Who knew breast cancer would one day lead me to a rural route near Boursault to learn that handy skill? But there was a silver lining. I enjoyed some excellent champagne and am looking forward to a much-needed warm bath. Until then, let me give you a little background about this project, and then you can ask me absolutely anything."

A few smiles soothed her nerves, so she shared how Logan had first approached her with the project idea, which he'd initially conceived as a work of installation art about the various costs of cancer—the emotional, physical, and financial. As the evening wore on, she kept trying to catch Mitch's eye, but his attention remained fixed on either Melissande or his phone.

In every way, he'd made it clear he was done with her, disappointed by her behavior, embarrassed for both of them. She'd made him and herself look bad in front of all these people, which had never been her intention.

Her worst fears about this tour were coming true, but she had no one to blame but herself. It was past time to pull herself together and do her job. Not only as a point of personal pride but also because now she could barely breathe at the thought of never seeing Mitch's soft smile again.

Chapter Nine

Mitch stepped out of the shower and towel dried quickly after another restless night. Last night over cocktails, Peyton had managed to charm Melissande, who promised to go back to the marketing team with some of Mitch's ideas for Peyton's book. A decent result given the wrong foot on which their evening had started.

As humiliated as he'd been standing in a roomful of impatient, insulted bloggers without his author, he couldn't lay all the blame on Peyton. He'd pushed her toward her tantrum. If she'd let him, he'd take a step toward making up for that today.

He tucked in his shirt, zipped up his khakis, and pulled on a belt, then grabbed his jacket and key before heading out the door. The boutique Hôtel Providence, a refurbished nineteenth-century townhouse hidden away on a street in the tenth arrondissement, was less than a half mile from one of the *boulangeries* Peyton had written about in her travel journals. Surprise pastries couldn't *hurt* his cause, and might help soften her up.

Mitch stepped inside the store and came to an abrupt stop—awestruck by the gilt and mirrors and murals, like something out of the Palace of Versailles. The dizzying and delicious aroma of butter, sugar, fruit, and chocolate filtered through the air. For a moment, he wished to change places with the bakers and spend his days working in a place like this. To focus on perfecting each item and seeing the look of pleasure in every patron's eyes. Now he scanned the dozens of breads and pastries lining the counters—too many choices. French-speaking patrons jostled him on their hurried way in and out of the store.

You would've loved this, Dad.

All those imagined vacations his father had described at the dinner table before any of them knew cancer was eating away at his brain.

Europe—an impossible dream at fifteen, now Mitch's reality. Maybe when his business was secure, he'd return with his mom and sister for pleasure to explore all the streets and shops and museums he'd been passing up to get to the next interview or reading. His dad would've wanted that for them. With Peyton's travelogues for guidance, it'd be easy to hit the best spots, although those journals wouldn't be any substitute for her company—at least her company when she wasn't ditching him.

"Alors, monsieur! Qu'est-ce que vous voulez?" The impatient woman behind the counter's expression told him everything he could not understand from her words.

He pointed out an assortment of croissants and then ordered two café au laits, which he transferred to the thermos he always carried in his backpack. He hid the entire stash of goodies there before jogging back to the hotel to meet Peyton in the lobby as planned.

Beautiful Peyton. Her loose curls bounced against her jaw as she approached him, and deep inside, a happy sigh lightened his heart as if yesterday had never happened. *Magic.*

Another sundress—the color of a ripe pomegranate—brushed the tops of her knees. For days now he'd admired her shapely calves. Imagined trailing his fingers up them. Was she ticklish? He gave himself a mental headshake.

"I told you one day I'd be waiting on you." She tipped her head expectantly. Her stiff posture suggested she was bracing for a lecture.

"I'll be impressed if it happens again." When he smiled, her shoulders relaxed. "Let's grab a taxi."

"Where are we going?" She crossed her arms.

He didn't want to spoil the surprise, which he hoped would prove that he wasn't the robot she believed him to be. After finishing her book, he couldn't dismiss her attitude about the importance of happiness, although in a life that had been about duty, he'd rarely prioritized joy. "I'd like us to consider a fresh start and had an idea you might enjoy—mostly, anyway."

"Mostly?"

He shrugged and gestured toward the door with his head.

"Very cloak-and-dagger of you." The glimmer of a smile tipped the corners of her mouth as she followed him outside. It seemed he'd broken through the tension. Now he had to get on with sharing his story and pray it'd be enough.

Their taxi dropped them alongside the Seine near the Pont Neuf. Mitch paid the fare, put on his sunglasses, and followed Peyton out of the cab.

"Last night I rattled a half-hearted apology, but I *am* sorry I put you in that uncomfortable situation," she said. "If you're going to read me the riot act, let's please get it over with."

"That's not why we're here." He pointed toward the bridge.

She stopped on the sidewalk and glanced around, her wrap dress fluttering in the breeze. The sunlight brightened her hair and practically glinted off her snowy-white teeth when she smiled. "Oh! Are we going where I think we're going?"

He lifted one shoulder. "Depends on where you think we're going."

Scanning the area, he took in the sight of Paris's oldest bridge, which spanned the Seine with a series of stone arches, all embellished with corbels, cornices, and other things—*1606*! He followed Peyton as she began to cross it, unable to comprehend the centuries between its construction and his being here.

Midway across, they came upon the bronze equestrian statue of Henri IV located in a small, rectangular parklike area. As Mitch got closer, he noticed a padlock affixed to the metal gate surrounding the statue. He held it for closer inspection. In red permanent marker, someone had written "A.C. + G.B." across its body. He frowned.

Peyton chuckled. "A love lock."

"What?" He let it fall back against the fence.

"Last spring, they removed forty tons of these from this area and made it illegal to put them here—the weight was dangerous for this old bridge. Someone recently took a big risk for love." Sighing wistfully, Peyton stroked it. "It's romantic. People inscribe them and then lock them as a symbol of unbreakable love."

"Teenagers?" Until this week, he had forgotten the intensity and dramatic emotion of that kind of infatuation. Then Peyton had blown into his life with her beauty and passion, and her constant challenges to him and his lifestyle.

"Oh, Optimus. There's no shelf life on romance. Adults fall in love, too." She shook her head and smiled. "You'll find these in many European cities."

Unbreakable love. His parents had had that until death sliced through it like a bolt cutter, but he rarely saw it elsewhere. Peyton hadn't found it with Todd, although the dreamy look on her face proved she still believed it existed somewhere.

Uncomfortable with the direction of his thoughts, he located the steep steps that led down to the Île de la Cité.

"Careful," he called over his shoulder as he started down to the little river island some called the beginning of Paris.

"Oh, I love this!" Her voice bubbled like a swift stream over rocks. "How do you know about the Square du Vert-Galant?"

"Your blog made it sound quaint. I wanted to see it for myself." With you, he thought, but kept that to himself.

A picnic. A romantic one, some might argue. He'd never been big on romance. Hadn't had much chance because there'd always been a more important demand on his time and his wallet.

Today he indulged the slightest breach of his rules. If asked why, he'd claim he'd win more cooperation if he stopped treating her solely like a client. But in truth, he could no longer stand Peyton viewing him as Optimus or Butters or anyone other than Mitch.

When they reached the bottom step, she skipped ahead wearing a giant grin. Free and easy, as she must've been often before her diagnosis.

"It's a perfect morning," he said while looking at the cloudless sky. They strolled into the small treed park, situated at the triangular tip of the river island, not far from the shadows of the Louvre. If he weren't so intent on why he was here, he might've been able to better appreciate what he was seeing. He stopped by an open bench and gestured for her to sit.

She eyed the bag he pulled out of his backpack. "Please tell me there are croissants in there."

"From Du Pain et des Idées, along with a thermos of coffee." His chest swelled when she clapped.

"This isn't what I expected. I admit, though, a little voice inside is freaking out, wondering if you've planned this nice break in order to take the sting out of bad news."

"You can relax. No bad news." He sat beside her. "This isn't about you or yesterday's misfortune. This is about me."

Her curious gaze had him sweating, but he owed her the truth. While she dug into the bag of croissants, he poured them each a cup of coffee.

"I try to minimize sugar now because it's known to feed cancer cells." She wrinkled her nose while picking through the bag and choosing a croissant layered with chocolate. "But in the spirit of living in the moment, I'm going to enjoy this. Thank you!"

Her animated personality made it easy to forget why they were here working together, so the reminder that she could get sick again threw him.

When she bit into the flaky crust, sugar-dusted pieces stuck to her face. Instinctively, he reached out to brush them away. The silky pillow of her lower lip sent a jolt through him, and she blinked, equally shocked by his unusual familiarity.

She licked her lips before pressing her fingertips to them. He had to remember to breathe while a pronounced silence stretched between them. Vaguely, he became aware of the distant sounds of traffic and pedestrians and boats passing by.

Steam curled into the air from her coffee cup. She sipped it and then said, "I'm all ears, Mitch. What do you want to say?"

No more stalling. He removed his sunglasses and stuffed them in his shirt pocket.

"I know your side trip yesterday was a reaction to your disappointment in me. I want to explain why I didn't want to read your book." He leaned forward, elbows on his knees, coffee in hand.

"We could've had that conversation at the hotel."

"True, but after reading your story these past two nights, I thought it better to step away from 'the office' and just . . . be."

She stared into her cup, wearing a wry expression. "I'm proud to have had a small effect on you, although the irony isn't lost on me."

"Irony?"

"Think about it." She screwed up her face. "Now, in the middle of the European book tour I'm flubbing, you're taking your foot off the gas to smell the roses—to mix a few metaphors."

"First, we'll fix the 'flubbing.' Second, this is a red light. Less—a stop sign. A little break so I can tell *my* story." He rubbed his forehead.

She straightened her spine and set down the half-eaten pastry. "Now you've got my attention."

"Don't expect much. I'm not *that* interesting." He paused, choked by the reality that his sob story didn't excuse his unprofessionalism. Nor was that the sole reason he wanted to share it with her.

She crossed her legs, shifting to face him head-on. Her eyes twinkled with a playful light. "If you're hoping I'll tell you not to bother, you'll be disappointed. After all the talking I've had to do, I'm ready to hear someone else's story for a change."

He set his cup on the ground. "Mine isn't worthy of a book deal."

"Lucky you," she deadpanned before sipping more coffee.

With a sigh, he confessed, "I didn't read your book because of my dad."

"He didn't like it?" She tipped her head.

"No. He didn't read it. I mean, he's dead." His phone buzzed in his pocket, drawing her attention, but he ignored it. No interruptions.

"I'm so sorry." Peyton seemed to be holding *her* breath, as if he might stop talking if she exhaled.

"Thanks, but it's been a long time. In fact, let me back up so you get the full picture. I grew up in Hoboken. My dad wanted so many things for our family—travel, college, adventure. He loved life." He smiled at her. "You remind me of him in some ways."

"So he was awesome?" She winked, making him chuckle.

"I thought so." He looked away, having revealed more with that statement than intended. "He convinced me I could be anything, despite the fact that we didn't have much of anything. Sadly, he never 'got ahead,' no matter how much he wished for and worked toward it. Funny, now, how I didn't see *that* irony at the time."

"We all take our parents at face value when we're young."

"I guess." A breeze rustled the leaves overhead, drawing attention to the fact that he was spilling his guts in a public park. He didn't remember ever sharing coffee in a park with a woman for any reason, nor could he recall the last time he'd talked about his family with anyone. "Anyway, for a little while—right after my sister was born—it looked like things were taking a turn for the better. My dad got a new accounting job with a tech start-up. Like many at that time, he accepted low pay in exchange for stock options. A gamble he believed he'd win. 'We'll be rich!' he'd sing."

Mitch recalled the burnt-almond torte his dad had brought to dinner that night to celebrate, its icing covered with sugared almond slivers, its layers filled with vanilla pudding. The joy in his parents' eyes. "Unfortunately, his dreams grew bigger and faster than the company, which never paid him much. My mom worked odd jobs to help make ends meet. Still, we were a happy family until he got diagnosed with stage-four glioblastoma multiforme."

"Oh!" Peyton laid her hand on his thigh, scattering his sad memories by making his body fill with such need it almost lifted him right off the bench. "I'm so sorry."

Mitch nodded, ignoring his phone for the second time. Peyton withdrew her hand, bringing him back down to earth and the tale he hadn't finished. "I was in high school at the time. The good and bad news was that death came within a year. But the medical bills piled up, and my mom was overwhelmed with a preschooler, a dying husband, and no safety net. She had to work two jobs, so I had to help take care of Lauren and also ended up being a caretaker for my dad."

"So young to deal with so much." Her gaze remained fixed on him.

He hardly heard her over the bubbling current of memories rushing through his head. He stared out at nothing, words now falling without thought or structure, bobbing along like fallen leaves on a river. "They call that type of brain tumor the terminator for good reason. I watched my dad die piece by piece. His speech slurred like a stroke victim until he couldn't speak at all. Gross motor functions became less and less controlled. But the worst were those last ten days. The doctors tried to combat his dehydration with a feeding tube shoved down his throat, and all speech was gone. He'd moan in pain because the tumor had grown so big it was pushing against the wall of his skull. His eyes would roll back, he'd convulse—more bloat from edema. It seemed almost a blessing when he would drift out of consciousness.

"The last time he was aware of me, I promised I'd take care of my mom and Lauren, hoping to give him the peace of mind he needed to let go. He struggled so hard to flick his wrist with a tiny thumbs-up . . . and that was it. The last thing he ever 'said' to me, basically, before he slipped into a coma. Those final hours—his skin blue and rumpled as his kidneys and other things shut down—I sat there holding his hand. Nothing is worse than listening to that awful death rattle. It sounds like a straw sucking the last bit of drink, except I knew the gurgle was the fluids pushing up and down his throat as his breathing slowed from four breaths per minute to three . . ." Closing his eyes didn't block the images. "In the end, I laid my head on his legs, counting down those final breaths until they stopped. Silence. Peace for him, but not for me." He pinched the bridge of his nose.

"Mitch . . ."

He shook his head, motioning with his hand. "His fight . . . That suffering affected me to this day. Back then, I had to stuff down my anger and grief to keep my promise. I quit everything after school and got a job to help my mom pay bills. At night I'd wake from panic attacks about what would happen to Lauren and me if my mom got sick."

Peyton squeezed his forearm. "You kept your word, and your dad would be so proud of what you've achieved."

Probably, although that hadn't been his sole motivation. "I needed to do whatever it took to make sure we weren't in that precarious situation again. Scholarships got me through Fordham without too much debt. I worked while in college to help pay for extras, and contribute to things like my sister's piano lessons. Once my career got going, I'd take my family to Rehoboth for a week each summer."

"I'm sorry I've teased you about being robotic." Closing her eyes, she hung her head. "I never meant it to be cruel. Or careless."

She reached for his hand and squeezed it, and somehow the painful memories he'd shared gently floated downstream.

"It's fine." He had to be honest. "Until recently, I've been grateful you've viewed me as dull."

She straightened, slowly removing her hand. "Why?"

He stared into her aquamarine eyes, transfixed by their pretty gold flecks. If she weren't his client, he might slide her up along his side, kiss her cheek, her temple, her lips . . . When he couldn't take that daydream another second, he glanced away. "Since Danielle, it's been easy to keep my professional boundaries . . . until you came along. I've been working overtime to keep my distance."

Having admitted the truth, he peeked up to gauge her reaction. When her cheeks turned pink, a satisfied hum vibrated in his chest. His heart beat fast at the hint of her feelings, urging him to seize the moment.

As if she were the center of all gravity, he tipped toward her, teetering on the edge of doing something out of character. His phone buzzed a third time, snapping him out of the haze. He should check it, but if he didn't finish his story now, he might never get through it all.

"Should you get that?" She pointed at his jacket pocket, where he kept his phone.

"In a minute."

"Okay." Her expression registered mild surprise. "So you're saying you avoided my book because you didn't want to revisit those memories."

"I thought opening that emotional baggage would interfere with my ability to work with you, so I passed the book off to Rebecca." He turned his body toward her. "Having now read it, I can assure you that Rebecca did an excellent job with her summary. I wouldn't change one thing we pitched or planned. Still, I've learned more about you from reading it, and had I done so from the start, I think our work together could've gone more smoothly. So for that, and all the other reasons, I'm very sorry."

Peyton didn't question him further. She seemed to escape into her own mind for a minute. He shifted on the bench, restless in the silence.

He looked up at the sky, envious of the birds overhead that soared above the chaos. "At the very least, I should've been forthright from the beginning. If you want to replace me, I understand. But please continue this tour regardless. I really want your book to succeed."

Peyton let out a long breath through her nose and stretched her legs, looking around the park before sharing her thoughts. "Don't be silly. I'm not firing you. But given what you've explained, can't you understand why the reliving of my experience for strangers is so hard for *me*?"

"I do. But don't you see that your courage is exactly what makes you special? It's why people want to come listen to you." Another flock of birds flew overhead, drawing his eyes up again, then he returned his attention to Peyton. "No matter what else has happened, and however Logan coaxed you into this project, *you* made the choice to publish. On some level, you want this mission to work, and you're so strong."

He stood and paced a few steps. "I understand why you'd rather make different use of your time now. But even if you aren't invested in how well the book sells, Savant cares very much. And now my credibility and reputation are tangled up with this project, too. As much as your feelings matter to me—and they do—I've still got a job to do. One I can't do as well without your full cooperation. Better yet, your enthusiasm. But now I'm stuck. I don't know how we both get what we need when I can't seem to treat you like every other client."

Peyton narrowed her eyes above a melancholy smile. "You're very much like my brother . . . walking me step-by-step toward the conclusion you want me to draw."

He raised his hands in a mea culpa. "I swear I didn't share everything to manipulate you. I brought you here—a place I knew you loved—to apologize and explain myself, and to give you a little break.

But I also want us to figure out how we go on from here, so I'm being as honest as I can."

"Oh, don't get me wrong, Mitch. I admire you . . . and the feelings behind all this." She grinned.

"Bottom line, we're on the same side here—or rather, we should be." His phone rang again. No doubt his mom, the vampire, at it again. Four calls in a row demanded his attention. He pulled it from his pocket, then frowned. It wasn't even 7:00 a.m. in New York. This couldn't be good. "Hello, Rebecca."

"Good morning. Did you get the link?"

"What link?" he muttered, turning away from Peyton so he didn't need to mask his expression.

"The YouTube link posted by the guy in Barcelona."

"No." He took a few steps away and swallowed a curse. "And?"

"Well, he trashed the book and posted the video of Peyton's response to him without supporting context. The good news is that he only has about three thousand subscribers and a bit more on Twitter. There aren't too many comments or retweets, so this shouldn't have a huge effect. It's strange that he hashtagged the foreign book title but didn't tag Peyton's or Logan's accounts."

Coward. "Thanks for the update."

"It might be better if it went viral. Controversy could help sell books."

In some cases, he might exploit a controversy, but he wouldn't put Peyton in the middle of a social media shitstorm. The mental setback would outweigh any benefit. Of course, his personal feelings might be clouding his judgment. Keeping his voice steady and low, he said, "No. Sounds like this will die out fast. Let me know if it starts to blow up, and then we'll revisit a new strategy."

He shoved the phone back into his pocket before turning to walk back toward Peyton.

"Everything okay?" Her pretty eyes filled with concern.

This news would kill any confidence she'd built up in the past twenty-four hours. With another set of interviews this afternoon and a bookstore event tonight, it'd be in her best interest to keep this from her, at least until after the reading. If she were any other client, he wouldn't even think twice about it. The job came first. Yet one look in her eyes made him feel like the world's biggest liar, bringing a definitive end to this lovely time-out.

"Mitch?" She pressed her teeth against her lower lip. "I know I've given you a hard time about dealing with other clients while we're here, but if you need to put out some other fire, I promise I won't flake on you. I'll be at every event on time. In fact, if you need to go handle something now, I wouldn't mind a little shopping spree. It is Paris, after all."

"No, it's not that . . ." He raked a hand through his hair. "Nice try with the shopping excuse, but we should prepare for the upcoming interviews. I'm happy to discuss different passages you might select for the reading tonight, too."

"After all you just told me? No thanks. I found my big-girl pants and will choose my own excerpts." Peyton stood to collect the empty bag and cups. "I get that I need a little attitude adjustment, but so do you. It's past time you learn to enjoy the moment. Take a breath and visit Paris while we're here."

"Isn't that what we're doing?" He gestured to the river, the trees, the remnants of their picnic.

"For a microsecond." She balled up the trash bag, tossing him that look. The one she gave him to let him know he wasn't fooling her. "If you insist on prep work, let's multitask and shop while we talk. The Paris fashion scene is hard to beat. We could even pick up something new for you."

He glanced at his attire, frowning. "Now I need a makeover, too?"

She pressed her fingertips to her lips while she surveyed him, forcing him to also reevaluate his khaki trousers, crisp white button-down, and charcoal blazer. "Last I read, new trends for men include pinstripes, oversize shoulders, and leather."

A sudden scowl seized his face so fast it almost knocked him over. Too-big tops and leather?

"No?" She laughed. With an approving smile on her face, she said, "To be honest, oversize clothing would be a shame on someone trim like you. We could insert a little more color into your wardrobe, though. Bring out the green and gold in your eyes. Play up that nice skin tone."

A flutter—yes, the word he'd rarely used before meeting her— tickled his chest. She liked his shape, his eyes, even his skin, of all things. If he let himself think about it, nothing would get done today.

"What's with the sour face? Is it that call?" She sighed, now looking at him like he was a lost cause. "There can't be any secrets left between us?"

He clasped his hands behind his back so she couldn't see them flexing. Damn that Barcelonan idiot to hell. "It's nothing urgent."

"Liar." She waved him off, then strode a few steps to the trash can.

"Only white ones once in a while." Close enough to the truth to quell some of the acid in his gut.

"A lie that won't hurt anyone." She kicked a stray stone with a huff. "Is there such a thing?"

He shrugged, staring past her to avoid her gaze, which caused her to glance over her shoulder to see what, if anything, he found so captivating about the Seine.

"At least tell me this. Is this 'white lie' business or personal?" She slung her purse over her shoulder.

He hesitated. Some relationships, like theirs, didn't fit neatly into either category, making her distinction irrelevant. "Does it matter?"

"I've told white lies to protect friends, and I've told them to avoid uncomfortable situations with coworkers. Of course, in neither case would *I* be happy to be duped." She laughed at herself more than anything else, he suspected. "How's that for a double standard!"

He treated her question as rhetorical and ignored it. His best option now was to distract her by moving them out of the park and on to a new topic. "Let's get going."

She twirled around one last time. "Take it all in, Mitch. The mineral scent of the river. The air laced with diesel fumes. The thrum of the boat engines and distant traffic. The centuries-old construction. Are you sure I can't tempt you to lose a couple of hours in the Louvre? Or to visit Oscar Wilde's tomb in Père Lachaise Cemetery? Or maybe you'd enjoy a stroll through the gritty, cool neighborhood of Belleville?"

Mitch glanced at his watch and shook his head, returning them both to the reality of their mission in Paris.

"No shopping, either?" She wrinkled her nose.

"We only have ninety minutes before the interviews."

"I'll be honest." She kept pace with him while they headed back toward the stairs. "I wish all the bloggers would be in the room at the same time, like a press conference, so I could answer each question just once."

He chuckled. "That would be efficient, but then no one would get an exclusive."

"None do anyway. They all ask the same things . . . all the boring stuff, too, about my family, my motivation, how I've changed, blah blah blah."

"It's a memoir." He reached for her hand to steer her around a pile of dog doo someone had failed to clean. She didn't try to wriggle her hand free, so he kept hold for an extra two seconds to memorize the warm, soft feel of it. When he let go, he cleared his throat. "What would you rather they ask?"

"Anything original." He studied her fine profile while they strolled across the bridge to the Left Bank. A sprig of bangs curled over one eye. Her forehead, the tip of her nose, and her chin aligned perfectly. Her porcelain skin begged to be stroked. She caught him staring. Flashing a quick smile, she continued with her other train of thought. "They could ask me about the worst person I met during treatment. Or how it felt to get the tattoos. Or if I ever had a crush on any of the doctors."

He stopped dead in his tracks. "Did you?"

"No. Well, maybe a girl crush on one kick-ass, no-BS female doctor. And I did love my Jamaican male nurse's wicked humor. Devan is three hundred pounds of happiness in scrubs."

He chuckled at that mental image and kept walking. "You mention him in your book. The one who brought in a guitar and sang with the kids."

"Yes! Oh Lord—his voice . . ." Then her smile receded. "But seriously, why is everyone bent on discussing my great-grandfather?"

"Your great-grandfather is a big deal."

"But he's got nothing to do with the book. Most who'll read it—Barcelona guy excepted—won't give one flying you-know-what about him."

Mitch winced at the mention of that reviewer, but Peyton didn't appear to notice. She seemed too consumed by her own argument to be paying attention to him now, thank God. "He's a point of interest. A starting place . . ."

"I don't want the comparison. And readers won't care, either. They want to know how to get through each day without giving up. They want a promise that, even in the middle of the very worst pain and fear, there can be grace and joy. They expect something real and accessible, not some Gatsby-esque history of my family. Duck's legacy is cool, and my last name *did* help me get a contract. That's why that guy's dig the other night hurt. But now *my* book is out . . . so I think the focus should be on it and me. And it should be a little fun. Humor is important, even—especially—when you're sick."

Mitch had hailed a cab while she spoke, all without meeting her gaze. The more she mentioned the Barcelonan, the worse he felt about keeping the vlog from her. "If that's what you want, then redirect the conversation. Take them where you want them to go."

"Says the man with mad manipulation skills." She scooted across the back seat. "I'm not like you and Logan. I react."

"I've seen you turn on the charm." His phone buzzed again. He looked at its screen, then closed his eyes, praying for patience. With an apologetic glance, he held up his finger to beg for silence and answered. "Mom, is everything okay?"

Peyton turned her face away and stared out the window. Hopefully she'd remain caught up in her own thoughts rather than listen to his end of this conversation.

"Oh, you're up. Good. I'm planning to cook and freeze some things this week so we have food while you watch me after my surgery. How do you feel about chicken potpie? I think I can freeze that."

"Potpie is fine, but let's talk later. I'm with my client now preparing for another round of interviews."

"Oh, sorry, honey. I keep forgetting about the time difference. I can't wait until you get home and things go back to normal."

He rubbed his temple. "I'll call you when I get a break."

"Are you having a good time?"

"We're working."

"From what I've read about her, she's sort of a good-time girl, isn't she?" The judgmental tone couldn't be missed. "Globejotter . . . she must want to sightsee."

"Yes, but like I said, we're both working hard." He hoped that would end the discussion.

"Oh, Mitchell, I recognize that tone. Don't get too infatuated—remember that mess with Danielle. And while this woman is pretty, she's from a whole different world. Different worlds complicate everything. You know, there are plenty of healthy, family-oriented women right here in Hoboken."

Since he'd hit his thirties a few years ago, his mother viewed every single woman he interacted with as potential wife material. "Mom, I'm hanging up now. We'll talk later—"

"Mitch!"

He closed his eyes a second time, but forced a smile and a pleasant lilt in his voice. "What?"

"Your sister called yesterday and invited me to dinner. Did you put her up to that? I don't want to go if you did."

He pinched his nose before saying, "I didn't pressure Lauren. If she invited you to dinner, go with it and be happy. Now, I'm sorry, but I do have to go, Mom. Love you."

He shoved his phone in his pocket.

"Another white lie?" Peyton grinned.

"Hm?" His heart sped up.

"You *did* put your sister up to that dinner. I heard you tell her to take your mom out earlier this week."

"Oh well . . ."

"It's sweet how you protect your mom's feelings. In that way, you're nothing like Logan." Her grin suggested she didn't hold that against her brother.

"If only my mother believed my white lies, she and Lauren would be better off," he scoffed.

"So would you."

"How do you mean?"

"She calls a lot . . . your mom."

"That's not normal?" he joked, seeking a way out of this conversation.

"Not in my world." She smoothed the fabric of her skirt, staring at her fingers, while his heart sank from how her words bore out his mother's warning. "My parents are at the other end of the spectrum and have pretty much been hands-off for as long as I can remember. The fact that you don't get any privacy might be why you're stuck with an 'imaginary' girlfriend."

A part of his heart snapped—a sharp little prick that made him snort. "I'm all my mom has. She spent her forties grieving and raising two kids, which didn't exactly attract eligible men. At sixty she doesn't see men banging down her door, either. And if I *were* hunting for a girlfriend, I wouldn't get involved with someone who couldn't make room for my relationship with my family."

He would've thought after everything Peyton had survived, she'd prioritize family, not brush them aside. But maybe her upbringing in a colder family meant she didn't view those bonds the same way he did.

"Of course you wouldn't." She looked out the window.

For days he'd shoved his feelings down, telling himself that harmless flirtation meant nothing. His current disappointment proved how much he'd been kidding himself. All this time, he'd subconsciously been looking forward to the day when she wouldn't be his client. Somewhere along the way he'd started to believe that maybe . . . *Fool.*

She swiveled suddenly, looking him dead in the eye. "But the right woman won't just make room for them. She'll share the burden so you aren't the only one trying to solve all their problems."

Now it was his turn to look away before she saw how much he wanted her to be that right woman. "Let's grab a café table near the publisher's office and talk about the interviews."

Chapter Ten

"It wasn't shopping, but it wasn't so bad." Peyton smiled as Mitch tucked his iPad away after spending the past hour bringing her up to speed about the various reviewers she'd be meeting next. The hard part had been staying focused on work while trying to process what she'd learned about Mitch this morning.

"You sound surprised, but I never set out to torment you." A lopsided grin punctuated his words.

It might not be his goal, but he tormented her nonetheless. Sitting close to her. The stormy intensity of his gaze. The casual way he'd dropped the bombshell about struggling to treat her like a regular client. And on top of all that, he'd revealed the inner strength of a boy turned man who'd given up his life, in part, to honor a promise to his dying father.

Her phone vibrated again.

"You'd better take that. It's the third or fourth notification in fifteen minutes." Mitch threw ten euros on the small café table that they'd commandeered for the past hour. In the sunlight streaming through the plate glass window at her back, his hazel eyes glowed like liquid gold. "Excuse me for a minute."

She drew in a deep breath. No jitters. No sour stomach. None of the other symptoms she'd experienced prior to interviews. Not even a desire to get up and run around the city to sightsee.

This must be what peace felt like. What she'd give to bask in the ambiance of the café longer to avoid reality and unanswered texts. But when Mitch disappeared behind the french-blue restroom door, Peyton took out her phone. Logan had sent all four texts. She scrolled back to read them in order.

1:14 p.m.

Hope you're okay. The guy's an ass who doesn't know shit about good writing.

1:21 p.m.

Are you ignoring me because you're pissed? I get it, but text me so I know you aren't flinging yourself off the Eiffel Tower.

1:25 p.m.

Peyton? Please answer. And remember, even bad PR is good PR.

1:34 p.m.

I'm worried and really wishing I'd been able to come with you now. Please call when you have a minute.

Peace vaporized and the croissants she'd devoured this morning now stewed in stomach acid, giving her cramps. The metal table jiggled from being knocked by her knee. She glanced around to make sure no one was watching, then texted Logan.

What are you talking about?

Within seconds, he replied.

Barcelona Bastard (my nickname for the douche). https://bit.ly/
Sh4$i0

Everything decelerated as if happening in slo-mo—the woman meandering to the table behind her, the worker wiping up a spill from the counter. Nausea soured the otherwise sweet aroma of the shop. She bolted from her seat and burst onto the sidewalk.

Each pore on her body began to sweat as she opened the link. There he was, the Bastard, alternating between his native tongue and English, calling her book insipid and then airing her mini rant without first playing the obnoxious questions that had prompted it.

At this point, the video had received eight comments, all in Spanish or Catalan. She didn't need Google Translate to guess that they were also unflattering. Avoiding *that* deep dive into pain, she toggled over to his Twitter handle. Fourteen retweets, five replies.

In the greater scheme of social media, this was a small blip. Almost less than nothing. Her own Twitter account had more followers than the Bastard's, and Logan's dwarfed them both. Not that the Bastard had bothered to tag her or her brother. Intentional or an oversight? She couldn't guess, but as long as she and Logan didn't reply, his video wouldn't blast to their followers, too. Maybe the guy had been wary of the backlash, especially from Logan's devoted fans, so he'd opted for a secretive sabotage.

The Bastard's negativity stung even more than she'd expected. Like it had that night, it dragged her self-doubt back up to the surface, where it now ate away at the confidence Mitch had helped her build.

She started when her phone rang.

"What?" she snapped at her brother.

"You watched?"

"Yes." She leaned against the building's brick wall, staring at the traffic. A trim young woman in fabulous red cat-eye sunglasses walked past with her papillon in tow, laughing at someone on the other end of her phone call. So carefree, enjoying the simple pleasure of gallivanting around Paris on a sunny summer day in gorgeous Manolos. The rosettes on the ankle straps taunted Peyton mercilessly.

"It's one opinion. From a *nobody*." Logan grunted. "*PW* and *Booklist* loved the book. Shake him and his jealousy off."

As with most things in life, that was easier said than done.

"Says the guy who doesn't have to be interviewed or read from the 'insipid' thing in front of a crowd again and again."

His heavy sigh practically heated her ear. "You're not going to focus on this one negative review and ignore all the good ones, are you?"

That incredulous tone made her feel more alone. She couldn't explain why any criticism always rang more true than any compliment. Could be vanity, or maybe self-doubt was easily stirred in everyone. Everyone but her brother, who seemed to breeze through the world with healthy confidence and an easy smile. This conversation supported her lifelong suspicion that he'd gotten all the really good genes and she'd been stuck with the leftovers.

Heaving a sigh, she said, "Screw it."

"What's that supposed to mean?"

"It means I give up."

"Give up? Are you quitting the tour?"

The urge to do exactly that bucked like a bull in the ring. If she ran this time, she'd have to go for good. Maybe even forfeit the advance. Find a way to make it up to the foundation when the donations weren't as healthy as predicted.

But she'd be free. Finally free after two years of battles and recovery and slaving away on a book that hadn't been her true passion. Free to live life on her terms every blessed minute she was given. Free to discover where her next steps should lead.

Logan's concerned tone broke her reverie. "Peyton, what's Mitch say?"

Ha! Mitch had danced around the subject like a true champ. This morning's white-lie conversation took on a different meaning in this new context. "Nothing."

"Nothing?"

While she'd been spinning mad fantasies about him, he'd been thinking her too weak to handle the truth. She'd be insulted and furious if her constant whining about every obligation of this tour hadn't in fact painted that unflattering portrait of herself.

As if summoned by her thoughts, Mitch came through the glass door. She forced a fake smile to buy herself time.

"All set?" he asked while putting his sunglasses on.

Her mind took off in different directions. Humiliation hogged center stage. He'd implied that he told white lies to protect the person from pain. But in truth, he'd also lied to her to protect his bread and butter so she'd perform well and further his goals.

Then the angel on her shoulder elbowed her way to the mic, reminding her that Mitch had a job to do. A job he counted on to take care of the people he actually loved. Peyton had never had that kind of worry or responsibility. Who might she be today if she'd been handed his deck of cards as a teen? Certainly not someone who'd traipsed the world without much thought to anyone but herself.

Her brother cleared his throat at the other end of the line.

"Logan, I've got to run. I'm fine. All is well." She dropped her phone back into her purse.

Confronting Mitch would be satisfying but unproductive. Yelling at him wouldn't reverse his pitiful impression of her, either. Nor would she respect herself much if she couldn't find the mettle to finish this damn tour and prove that Barcelonan jerk wrong.

"Shall we go?" When Mitch smiled, her heart softened. His ability to disarm her with ease should scare her, but she liked it. Honestly, she kind of craved it. "It's two blocks that way, according to Google Maps."

He'd been right to push back on her earlier. She *had* chosen to publish the book, take the money, fund-raise. At a minimum, she owed everyone involved her best, even if this tour wasn't how she'd otherwise choose to spend her time.

"Something wrong?" His brows gathered as he tipped his head to study her face.

"No." To force a smile, she recalled when Mitch had taken her hand earlier to steer her around a pile of trouble. That was him in a nutshell—a knight—and she could hardly stay pissed at that. "It's so pretty out I came to enjoy the fresh air before being grilled in a crowded room of strangers."

He shot her a wary look. "Are you ready?"

"Bring it on." She winked in the face of Mitch's surprised expression and then walked toward the publisher's building, leaving him trailing behind.

That evening, Mitch hustled with Peyton across the Rue de Rivoli on their way to the bookstore, expecting her to clutch her stomach or make a glib remark—do any of the things she'd done before prior reading events. Although she'd held her own during the earlier interviews, live reading events rattled her most. The imposing stone arches in front of Librairie Galignani—the continent's first English-language bookstore—could also give anyone pause. Of course, she'd visited and written about this store in her former life, which might explain her apparent lack of nerves when passing through the doors. And her failure to gawk in awe at its magnificent skylight, antique wood floors, and row after row of stuffed walnut bookcases.

After they met with the proprietor, who then introduced Peyton to the audience, Mitch scanned the crowd while she discussed background details about the memoir. Unlike in Barcelona, no one suspicious stood out in this crowd. At least not yet.

Another set of updates on *that* situation helped him to relax. Nine comments, eighteen retweets, no new activity in the past four hours. It wouldn't blow up now—yesterday's news and all that. Crisis averted.

His picnic idea had given them the clean slate they'd needed. Peyton cooperated with him and seemed almost ebullient in her determination tonight. Standing at the podium, she exuded humor and confidence. A marked difference from the first two cities on the tour. The only trouble was that it made her even more appealing, and he was already over the line when it came to his feelings about this woman.

She set the memoir in front of her and opened it to a marked page. He'd tried more than once to discuss what she planned to read, but she'd shot him down each time. He guessed she'd been protecting him from reliving his own bad memories, but since sharing those old ghosts with her—whose history with cancer made her eminently sympathetic—they no longer seemed quite as chilling.

As Peyton adjusted the mic, he uncrossed his arms and stretched his neck left and right, his heart beating hard with hope for her to make a good connection with the audience.

"I guess I'll dive right in." She nodded and began.

"A Small Price to Pay.

"I hopped around the waiting room on one leg, flapping my arms while humming the chicken-dance song to make Amelia laugh. For ten seconds, I had my life back—my precancer life. The one that involved my famous—or infamous—attention-grabbing antics, usually undertaken to make someone else happy.

"These past few months, I've forgotten what the impulse to be silly felt like. For all intents and purposes, that instinct died the day the doctor set a stopwatch on my life. One that incessantly ticked in my mind, night and day, warning me not to waste time on games while dealing with life-and-death stakes.

"*Fortunately, Amelia's eighth birthday offered a reason to play. Permission—no, a command—to hit 'Pause' on my problems for her benefit. I couldn't have picked a more grateful audience. She clapped, face flushed with happiness, even as she chided me for the many ways I'd messed up the dance. We were both giggling when, without a whiff of self-consciousness, she asked me to pose with her for a birthday selfie.*

"*My first bald selfie.*

"*I froze—uncertain—but I couldn't decline. She'd shown no discomfort about her own hairless face and scalp. I wouldn't risk allowing my issues to cause her to doubt her confident body image.*

"*I adjusted my scarf and crouched beside her, then she snapped the picture.*

"*While I squatted there looking at the photo of us and our 'frameless' eyes, Amelia noticed one of the gold four-leaf-clover earrings a friend had given me after learning of my diagnosis. Her cool, small fingers flicked it. 'These are pretty!'*

"*'Thank you. They're from a friend, for good luck with all of this.' I gestured around the waiting room, where it sometimes felt like we'd been abandoned. 'She beat her cancer, so she passed them on to me.'*

"*Amelia's eyes went round. 'So they really work?'*

"*'It seems so.' I saw the small holes in her earlobes.*

"*'Maybe my mom can get me a pair.' She glanced toward the hallway, where her mom had gone to use the restroom. Or, as I suspected, to cry in private, because no mother wants to celebrate her child's birthday in the cancer ward. Either way, I knew she'd return to Amelia's side with a reassuring smile.*

"*Still, the desperate hope in Amelia's pale-blue eyes when she glanced back at my earrings kicked me in the chest. I might be too young to die, but at least I'd had a first crush, a first kiss, a college graduation, and several thousands of miles of travel in my rearview mirror. Amelia still slept with stuffed animals.*

"Without thinking, I took out my left earring and set it in her palm. 'Take this and we'll share the luck.'

"'Is there enough for both of us?' Her knitted brows, all sincerity and concern, made it hard for me not to cry in front of her. This sweet, unselfish child should not have to endure such anxiety.

"Somehow I managed to speak past the lump in my throat. 'Yes! In fact, I think luck doubles when you pass it on.'

"'That makes four lucks because your friend passed it to you, so that is two, and now you passed it to me, which makes four! Now we both have double the luck.' Amelia smiled with pride at her somewhat dizzying mathematics. Obviously quick-witted, yet still so willing to cling to any hope for a cure. She put the earring in her ear and then took another selfie so she could see how it looked. 'Are you sure your friend won't be mad at you?'

"I gently squeezed her thin thigh. 'I'm positive she'd wish she'd been able to give a pair to you, too.'

"My chemo sessions ended before Amelia's. The last time I saw her, I gave her the other earring and a tight hug. I don't know if they worked for her, or for how long my luck will hold, but I can't discount the value of the joy they brought us both.

"No matter the ultimate outcome, those gold earrings were a small price to pay for the gift of Amelia's happiness and the reminder that, for however long we are on this earth, love and hope will always remain the most important ways we can fill any day."

The audience erupted with a round of applause.

Mitch dabbed the inside corner of his eye before he clapped. If he hadn't been at Peyton's side for most of the past twenty-four hours, he'd swear the woman he just watched charm the bookstore audience was an impostor. Confident. A little irreverent. Sexy. Much like the woman he suspected she'd been before her diagnosis.

This moment—her courage and bright, bright smile—sealed his fate.

Smitten. Not a masculine word, but apt. He couldn't keep his eyes off her. His heart skipped an extra beat whenever she glanced his way.

His chest stretched to the point of exploding because of her triumph here.

Even if the audience hadn't responded well, it would've still been a victory over her self-doubts.

Thank *God* he hadn't told her about that Barcelonan tool.

He followed her to the table that had been stocked with books to sign.

"You're on fire tonight." He gripped the back of her chair and leaned close, seeking her body heat. Despite right and wrong, he wanted her. Want didn't come close to it, actually. He vibrated with need—to touch her, to kiss those lips, to make this woman want to moan his name.

"Mmm." She nodded before pulling her pink pen from her purse and smiling at the first woman in line without sparing him a glance. "Thank you so much for coming."

She was working. Nothing personal. That's what he'd told himself more than once since they'd left the coffee shop.

A bookshop employee handed Peyton a sticky note with the correct spelling of the patron's name. This routine continued for thirty minutes, during which time Mitch stepped back and let her work.

Following two rounds of texts with his mother, seventeen emails, and a review of Rebecca's latest update with Savant, he put his phone in his bag and studied Peyton.

Today they'd been a true team for the first time. Her successful run of interviews had masked the absence of teasing, nicknames, and lingering looks that had previously mottled their interactions. The professional rapport he'd wanted from the beginning now left him cold and his chest hollow.

When he got her alone in the cab, he prodded her. "That was fantastic. Let's grab a drink at the hotel bar to celebrate."

"I don't know. I'm pretty tired." She slouched against the seat, her iridescent silver skirt billowing around her like a satin sheet.

"Oh. Well, I don't want to wear you out." He looked away. Through the window, the City of Light twinkled all around them. If he hoped to reach his room without making an ass of himself, he had to focus on anything but Peyton. His hand ached from the desire to reach across the seat and grab hold of hers.

"There are so many things you should've seen while in Paris." The wistful tone of her voice filled him with regret. "I wish we had more time to explore."

"We'll always have the park." A memory he treasured, even if it meant less to her.

The reminder wrought a smile from her, but it was too dark to see if she was blushing. "An amuse-bouche—to borrow a food term."

"Hm?" he uttered distractedly.

"The tiny sampler served at many restaurants . . . like a glimpse of all to come. A taste. Literally, a mouth amuser." She kissed her fingers as one does to signify something delicious.

Whatever she said next, he didn't hear. He couldn't concentrate on anything but her mouth. Her lips, smeared with petal-pink gloss. Hardly amusing . . . more like succulent. He didn't even want to resist the helpless sense of tumbling out of control or, in this case, toward her, despite his rules and the lessons he'd learned with Danielle or the fact that this vibrant woman still had a few hurdles to cross before being declared cancer-free. It gutted him to think of her relapsing or worse, and they weren't even lovers. Could he survive that if they evolved into more than colleagues?

Dragging his gaze away from Peyton's mouth, he returned his attention to the city lights until they arrived at the hotel. A few guests sat outside chatting in classic Parisian café chairs. He might've liked to enjoy their last night here that way, but she'd already shot him down. With so little pride left, he wouldn't risk another rejection.

When they entered the lobby, he started toward the elevator, but she stopped beside the giant potted fern and toyed with a frond. "On second thought, perhaps a Pépa would be a nice way to end the night."

"A Pépa?"

"A cognac-and-vodka cocktail."

A surging sense of victory tempted him to spring across the lobby to ring the large silver bell on the check-in desk. Instead, he gestured toward the restaurant and bar area. The sensual space, with its continuation of dark wood floors and walls, brass and silver accents, and bold floral wallpaper set against a field of black, hinted at something mysterious and a bit daring. A warning of what could come of crossing a line with Peyton, yet his restraint faltered with each second.

In one corner, he spied an old couple. The bald man, dressed in a jacket and tie, leaned forward to taste something sweet the elegant woman with a silver bun wanted to share. They were holding hands across the table, and she cackled at something he said. Their obvious affection—borne of decades of commitment, Mitch imagined—produced such a pang in his chest Mitch had to look away. Might his parents have been like them? He liked to think he'd had a good example of what love and commitment could look like, even if it hadn't lasted long enough.

He waited for Peyton to take her seat at the bar before he did. When he ordered a brandy, she asked for her fancier version. She interlocked her ankles while hooking a heel against the low part of the stool, giving him another glimpse of her delicate calves.

"What's going on in there?" She pointed at his temple. "You're acting strange."

"I was thinking the same of you." His words emerged with more bite than he'd planned.

"Are you upset with me?" She placed her elbow on the bar, laying her cheek against her palm, giving very few clues about her own mood.

His heart thudded as he probed her gaze, ultimately choosing not to elaborate. "No."

"Good." She flashed the bartender her gorgeous smile when he pushed her drink in front of her. Before taking a taste, she sent Mitch a vexed look. "If anyone has the right to be irked, it's me."

"You?" He swigged his brandy, letting it burn its way down his throat. Wherever this conversation was heading, he sensed nothing would be the same when it ended.

"Yes. Me." Her tone gave nothing away, although her half smile almost seemed flirtatious.

"How do you figure?" He'd bet his tense posture made him look more constipated than sexy. Hell, maybe he *was* a robot. He swigged more brandy, which intensified the hot, tingly feelings in his stomach.

She drummed her fingers on the bar top as if waiting for some kind of confession. "You didn't tell me about the Barcelonan's YouTube video."

He choked on his drink, then grabbed a napkin to wipe his chin. "You knew?"

Her face fell along with her shoulders before she flicked his biceps with surprising snap. "Darn it, Mitch. A little part of me held out hope that you hadn't heard about it yet."

His chest deflated under the weight of her disappointment. He almost never let down the women he cared about, and he cared about her. After knocking back the rest of his drink, he unbuttoned the top button of his shirt to cool off. His answer wouldn't flatter—that much he knew—but honesty seemed like his only way out. "If it had been a bigger deal, I would've told you. But it wasn't, so I kept quiet. In truth, I also worried that if you knew, you'd back out of the reading and maybe even the tour."

"So you think I'm a coward."

"Not at all. Compared with me—a guy who couldn't even *read* your work—you're incredibly brave." He signaled for the bartender to bring him a second drink, although there wasn't enough booze in the joint to wash his own weakness from memory. "But you're unpredictable, and I wasn't convinced you had the confidence to continue in the face of that criticism."

"I figured as much. It's why I had to turn this whole thing around. I won't have you or anyone else mistaking my distaste for self-promotion as an inability to hack this tour." She stared into her glass before taking another sip.

While the bartender slid a second drink in front of him, Mitch held out to see if Peyton would go on to chew him out, which he would've allowed. When she didn't, he asked, "How'd you find out about the video?"

"Logan." She licked the fancy stirrer before laying it aside. It took a second for him to stop thinking about the way her tongue had curled around that plastic. "He was the one texting me this morning. He called while you were in the restroom at that café."

"Ah." Mitch shouldn't envy her relationship with her brother, but he did. He wanted her to trust in *him* as her confidant. To rely on him like she did her brother, although Mitch's fondness for Peyton was far from familial. But this second strike of his would make it even harder for her to trust him.

Conversation died as she nibbled on some nuts and he remained too stuck in his head to say anything. She downed her drink in one long swallow. "Time for bed."

The lack of flirtation in her tone or eyes proved she hadn't meant that in the way he'd prefer.

So be it. He could not afford to make yet another wrong move. He folded his jacket over his forearm to hide the evidence of his infatuation, then stood and waited for her to leave, following behind once she did.

"Good night, Peyton," he said when they arrived at her room.

She paused after opening her door. "Despite the rocky start, Paris has been good. Thank you for sharing your story with me, and for giving me a little kick in the pants. Tonight wouldn't have gone so well without it."

"I'm sorry I didn't warn you about the video. You deserved more credit." The effect of his drinks had kicked in now. He could practically feel his inhibitions drifting away.

"I haven't given you much reason to believe in me before, so let's put it behind us." She then leaned forward, one foot bracing her door open, and leaned in to kiss him on the cheek.

Her soft lips worked like a match to a powder keg. In a flash, he'd caught her by the arms to keep her close. She didn't wrench free. Eyes closed, heart pounding, he kissed the pouty mouth that had tempted him for days. The gentle nip at her lower lip tasted of sweet fruit and a spark of citrus. A fevered urge to make love to her gripped him. He would've wrapped his arms around her and carried her off if he hadn't heard her sharp inhale.

When he opened his eyes, hers were aglow and round as quarters. They lingered in the hallway, their lips mere centimeters from another kiss. He stood, breath held, awkwardly clutching her elbows while refraining from walking her backward into her room without a clear invitation.

"Good night, Mitch." She eased her arms free, pausing to squeeze his hands, before stepping into her room and closing the door.

He stared at that door, wanting to believe in the light he'd seen in her eyes rather than in her quiet salutation. The pros and cons of knocking scrolled through his head like a ticker tape.

Pros: joy, orgasms, and peace. Cons: his unsolicited kiss might've already made their upcoming trips to Brussels, Berlin, Amsterdam, Edinburgh, Dublin, and London more than a little awkward. Not to mention the US launch, which Savant was emailing him about each day. Everything—his identity, his savings, his future—was tied to List Launch's ability to produce a string of success stories with its first clients. The cons were too big to ignore.

Tucking his chin, he retreated. She'd been clear, if kind, in literally and metaphorically closing the door he'd tried to open. Now he *would* regroup and get through the rest of the tour on his best behavior.

His room's midnight-blue walls and coverlet mirrored his dark mood. He tossed his jacket on the empty bed, followed by his shirt, slacks, and boxers, and then headed straight for the shower. Gritting his teeth, he stepped inside and turned the knob to *"Froid."*

———

Mitch woke with a start at the alarm, having fallen asleep a mere ninety minutes earlier. He'd spent half the night replaying that kiss and the other half rehearsing the apology he would have to make this morning.

He'd crossed the line he swore he'd never cross again . . . and once more, he'd met an unpleasant end. He stared at the ceiling, wishing for more time to regroup. For the privacy to work through his discomfort and disappointment. If he'd been at home, he could've spent hours baking an intricate confection. Creating something extraordinary from otherwise ordinary ingredients usually reassured him that someday he'd replicate that outside the kitchen.

But not today.

Not unless Peyton intimated regret about shooting him down.

Twelve more days together. Two hundred eighty-eight hours of the pleasure and pain of her company, and of the simultaneous wishes that it would speed by yet never end.

There was no point in dragging his feet. He showered, dressed, packed, and descended the elevator, practicing his apology one last time.

He rounded the bend to the lobby, heart in his throat, but Peyton had not yet come down from her room. Any other day he wouldn't think much of her tardiness. This morning, however, he guessed she dreaded seeing him. Had she, like him, spent the night practicing a speech—some kind words of rejection to hit reset yet again?

He didn't have to wait long for her arrival. Wearing an orange-and-yellow summer dress, she looked like the sunshine after a rainfall. He guessed she could see exhaustion stamped across his face, so he didn't even try to mask it.

"Good morning." She met his gaze for a second before letting hers drift.

"Good morning." He cleared his throat, hesitating. Holding out hope that she might surprise him with a hint of flirtation.

She tucked some hair behind her ear before raising her gaze to meet his. "Mitch, about last night—"

Damn. He held up one hand, his gaze now seeking a distant spot beyond her shoulder. "I'm sorry I put you in an awkward situation. I've no excuse for my behavior but promise you it will *not* happen again."

"Oh." Something soft in her voice snagged his attention, so he looked at her, but she waved him off with a half smile. "It's fine. Really. You'd had a few drinks. Who hasn't gotten swept up in a celebration now and then? To be honest, I'm rather proud of my effect on you, Optimus. By the time we get back to the States, you might lose your robot status altogether."

How like her to deflect with jokes.

His face burned. "Thank you for making this easier. We still have a lot of work ahead, and I would hate to have done anything to hurt our momentum."

"Please, stop." She reached out to touch his arm, and for a shining second, he thought she might tell him she wasn't sorry about the kiss. She might even confess to having liked it. "It's no big deal. Consider it forgotten."

He should have been relieved that he hadn't ruined everything, but her words punctured his already-battered heart. That kiss had been a *huge* deal to him while meaning less than nothing to her. Whatever attraction he'd believed had been mutual must've been imagined.

No matter what came next, he could not let her see his disappointment, so he smiled. "Done."

Her responding smile wasn't as bright as normal. "Well, let's grab a quick coffee for the cab ride. We could both use a little caffeine, I think."

"Good idea."

She cocked her head, eyes now twinkling. "It's rare, but I've been known to have one from time to time."

Another joke. He gestured for her to lead and then followed behind. A pattern he should have been used to by now.

This marked the end of the fantasies he'd spun about her. She'd opened no door for the future. No possibility of what might be after the tour ended. No indication that she'd seen past all his ordinariness to the potential for something more.

He'd ruined everything by turning the heat up too fast—something even amateurs in the kitchen know not to do.

Chapter Eleven

By the time the black cab stopped in front of Twenty Nevern Square, the London drizzle had subsided, although the lingering humidity would quickly turn Peyton's postchemo waves into a riotous mop of frizz. She stepped onto the sidewalk and caught her first whiff of the grassy, shaded park's earthy fragrance—a dank aroma common in parts of this city.

Mitch dealt with the cab driver, who'd set the luggage on the sidewalk. She rolled her shoulders, noticing a strange pulling sensation under her right arm. She'd dropped a few pounds since the trip had begun, too. Either thing could be due to all the work and restlessness of the past weeks, but she couldn't ignore the niggling fear that they could be symptoms of something more. That her upcoming checkup might bring unwelcome news.

As the driver pulled away from the curb, Mitch scanned the row of restored brick Victorian townhouses with a narrowed gaze.

"Ta-da!" She pointed toward the entry portico of the boutique inn, camouflaged amid the residences. The central yet tranquil location in Earl's Court put the inn at the top of her preferred hotels when visiting London.

"Doesn't look like a hotel." His brows shot up.

"One of many reasons why I love it."

He grinned. "You do seem rather upbeat."

"I *am*. This is it! A few interviews and a reading followed by a publisher party all in one day. I can't wait to go home tomorrow." She heaved a happy sigh, thinking about her bed in Connecticut, with its view of Long Island Sound.

"I'm sorry this trip has been such a chore." His light tone didn't match the withdrawal that had intensified every day since their last night in Paris, settling thickly between them like the misty air.

Her body still warmed at every recollection of the unexpected kiss that had sent her running in fear—of her own feelings, of trusting anyone after Todd, of dragging a lover into her still-fragile health crisis. In that moment, she'd thought she'd rather lose all her hair than undress in front of him. Then she'd spent the night alone in bed, hot with yearning. Frustrated by her overthinking. Wondering if maybe there wasn't a middle ground, much like her light relationships before Todd. The kind of romance where no one invests enough to get hurt.

There'd been a moment in that lobby the next morning when she'd found the courage to share her feelings—to tell him that it was her own insecurities that made her run. But he'd cut her off with an apology and firm promise that proved he'd thought it all a grand mistake. Despite her vow to put the kiss behind them, they had yet to manage the rapport they'd shared before that night.

"I didn't mean it that way." She reached out to touch him, but he moved to raise the handle of her suitcase. It had been this way for twelve days. She'd constantly put her foot in her mouth, and he'd steadily pulled away. Their now fine-tuned professional relationship made her miss the personal moments they'd enjoyed in that Parisian park and Rome and elsewhere prior to that night. "I'm just a little drained at this point."

He reached for his suitcase with his free hand. "Weren't you always on the road with your old job?"

"Yes, but I worked alone, so I didn't have to talk to people unless I chose to." When he grunted under his breath, she added, "Not that I haven't enjoyed talking with you."

He barked a short laugh. The fleeting twinkle in his eyes struck her heart like flint. "Too late. I know where I rank."

She should've laughed at his little joke, but she didn't. The man had no idea where he ranked because she'd diligently concealed the number of times she imagined what it would be like to walk hand in hand, or kiss him in a taxi, or fall asleep listening to the sound of his breath.

She'd expected to feel better with a number of successful events now under her belt, but she hadn't counted on missing his undivided attention. In fact, there'd been moments when she'd almost resented him for that kiss she couldn't forget.

Silver lining—the slow separation should make their goodbyes easier. The Manhattan launch party could be the last time she'd see him. He couldn't go with her to Chicago, Dallas, Miami, and San Francisco because he had commitments for other clients' soon-to-be-released books. Eager clients who wouldn't waste time fighting him, or pretend to dismiss a furtive kiss.

Yet his earnestness and gentleness kept calling to her, making the distance between them prickle. She no longer felt certain that she'd made the best decision by hiding her true feelings.

His quick smile had already faded.

"You're frowning again. Is it because my book didn't hit *Der Spiegel*'s nonfiction bestseller list?" Fifteen thousand copies during release week had sounded good to her, but based on the phone conversations she'd overheard, it wasn't good enough for Savant.

"I'm not frowning, although I am sorry I failed you on that count. But don't stress about lists. You did your job, which was to write a good book, promote it on your sites, and come on this tour. The rest is your publishers' and my job to figure out."

"I'm not stressed. If it weren't for the fund-raising goals, I couldn't care less if we hit any lists." She did, however, care that Savant was applying even more pressure on Mitch for the upcoming US launch. And while she didn't know all the details, she'd overheard enough to know that his assistant had made some other small bungle, and his mother and sister had argued about something. She could only imagine how exhausted he must be.

"Well, there's still time." He shot her an attempt at a reassuring smile. "We've picked up momentum this past week, and I'm optimistic about the US launch next week. Preorders are strong."

She stroked his arm. "Whatever happens, I appreciate everything you've done, Mitch, and I'll be recommending you to any authors I know. I hope you know that."

He held still, blushing. "Thanks."

He turned and started up the short flight of front steps with their bags in tow. She trailed behind him and through the archway and hotel entrance. Inside its tiny lobby, a pink potted orchid stretched forward from the registration desk like a delicate handshake.

"Excuse me." She stepped around Mitch when he paused to take in the hotel's mix of European and Oriental influences. Smiling to herself about the surprise she'd planned, she handed the receptionist her passport and credit card. Peyton glanced back at Mitch, hoping he wouldn't fight the upgrade. "I've moved you to a deluxe four-poster room. You'll feel like a king!"

He deserved that much after dealing with her initial reluctance to cooperate and everything that had followed on this tour.

"Hmm." The unusual squatty vermilion antique velvet chairs in the lobby now held his attention. That was for the best. He might've refused the gesture if he had been listening.

She signed the paperwork, pleased to pamper him, and then handed Mitch his key. "I wish the publisher party was this morning instead of this evening. There are a million better things we could do with a night in London than sitting in a pub, listening to the team blow smoke about my book."

Mitch shrugged. "At least you won't need a translator. I know how much you've hated that."

"True." She couldn't help but smile. Ever since he'd read her memoir, she'd noticed him identifying silver linings. It might be the first time she could claim to be a good influence on anyone. Maybe she should revisit the idea of a more personal relationship with him. At the very least, they deserved another brief escape from the work of this tour. A chance to simply be Mitch and Peyton, like they'd had in Paris. "Can we meet back here at one thirty?"

"Why?" He stopped, head cocked. "We're not expected until four."

"I know of a nearby detour I'd like to show you. It's nothing big, but it's special." She held her breath while hitting the elevator button.

"Well, then, I can hardly wait." When he grinned, the corners of his eyes crinkled. All she could think about was how nice it would be to wake up to that warmth. "I'll see you then. I've got some things to take care of first, so I'm off."

They parted ways in the hallway. Inside her room, she set her suitcase down to navigate the narrow space between the foot of the bed and the wall to get to the french doors that opened to the sizable private terrace. She flung them open before flopping onto her bed.

The guest rooms were spare, although her massive headboard and red bedding made a statement. She smiled, imagining Mitch's expression as he entered his own grand room with its four-poster bed, and looked forward to a romantic stroll in the Kynance Mews. Even if her last-ditch effort to suss out his feelings failed, she'd have one final private memory she could replay when she missed him in the coming months.

She sat up and unzipped her bag to sort through her things. Time to do her best Charlize Theron imitation so he wouldn't forget her easily.

—⁓—

Peyton opted against spiky heels, which would get caught in the cobblestone at the mews. She twirled in front of the mirror, the paisley boho dress swooshing as she spun. Her foobs looked surprisingly realistic through the dress's deep keyhole neckline. Bell sleeves added another hint of flirtation, as did the short skirt. She paired it with a square-heeled ankle boot and thick oval gold-and-pearl hoop earrings. But the most surprising accessory was a genuine smile, something she hadn't seen much of lately when looking in the mirror.

This outfit was something she'd wear on a date with Mitch if he invited her on one. Which he hadn't and might not ever—even if she summoned the courage to be bold enough for romance.

Her phone rang, surprising her. *Steffi?*

"Hey, Steffi. What's up?" She sat on the edge of the mattress and finger combed her hair. Steffi had been the other third of their childhood triumvirate, the Lilac Lane League, and one of the first people Peyton had told about her diagnosis.

"Up since dawn to take Emmy to swim team before I head to the lumberyard. We saw Logan and Claire last night, so I thought I'd check in and see how you're holding up."

"Pretty good. Ready to sleep in my own bed, though."

"Really? You used to hate to come home."

"I used to have more energy. And after all I've been through, as much as I still enjoy exploring new places or revisiting old favorites, I keep feeling like there is something more I should be doing with myself. I need downtime to figure out what that is."

"Who are you and what have you done with my friend?" Steffi chuckled.

"Ha ha."

"Kidding. I hear you, though. Trauma can make you see things in a new light. Look at what I did after the attack. Quit my job, moved home, started my own business . . . but the biggest risk I took was with

Ryan. That's the final piece that changed my life for the better and gave me the most fulfillment."

"And I'm thrilled for you that it all worked out. You and Claire both seem so settled and happy."

"Claire is floating around like a helium balloon these days."

"You have no idea how ecstatic that makes me." Peyton clutched a fist to her heart, eyes closed in prayer. "Thank God she found love after Todd."

"Thank God Todd is out of the picture for both of you." Steffi's hatred for him hardened her voice.

Peyton closed her eyes. She understood why everyone hated Todd and assumed she had grown to hate him, too. Yet despite her revulsion, a little grief lingered, probably because she'd handled his rejection in silence, knowing she'd get no sympathy after how she and Todd had hurt Claire. "Yes, that too."

After a slight hesitation, Steffi said, "Logan hinted at something brewing between you and your PR guy. I think you owe me the scoop after how you grilled me about Ryan when I first moved back home."

Oh Lord. Her brother kept thinking he could snap his fingers and manipulate her in order to fix the parts of her life *he* thought were broken. "There's no scoop."

"Peyton, maybe you can lie to yourself, but you can't lie to *me*."

"Fine." Steffi was the least gossipy woman Peyton knew, and it might do some good to release the pressure that had built up from bottling all her feelings. "Mitch is nothing like any guy I've ever been attracted to before. He's all business. I swear, a woman could run naked in front of him at an event, but he'd miss seeing her because he's so focused on his job." She laughed. "He takes his time considering every response. His mother and sister run roughshod over him, but he remains kind and gentle. And when he smiles, everything inside me turns soft. Then that face . . . My God, those eyes bore right through me." Without thinking, she skimmed her hand across her breast and down her stomach, as if he were touching her.

"Wow. I think Logan's onto something." When Steffi chuckled, Peyton made a sign of the cross, thankful that she'd kept the kiss a secret. "So then the real question is, does he feel the same about you?"

She winced, uncertain herself because of his mixed signals, like that kiss. In any case, a white lie would be best to keep Steffi and Logan from digging deeper. "There have been little hints . . . but he's got a rule against dating clients and colleagues because some coworker burned him years ago."

"Hm. If you worked for him, I could see that point, but his role with your book ends soon. It's not insurmountable. Logan thinks you're bringing him to the engagement party."

"Logan is crazy." Her whole body flushed in rebellion. "I'm not bringing Mitch to that party."

"Why not?"

Good question. Going to the party alone wouldn't be as fun, and she would love to spend time with him that had nothing to do with her book. But introducing him to the family would be a big step, and he might not even want to go. "I don't know."

"You're not still hung up on Todd, are you?"

"No!" Peyton scowled so hard it hurt her face. But she might be a little hung up on avoiding being burned again. She'd mistaken Todd's intense infatuation with her for love, and still didn't trust herself to know the difference.

"I thought running from love was always my thing, not yours."

Peyton bit her lip. "You wouldn't understand."

"I think I understand fear of vulnerability better than most, Peyton. Try me."

She glanced in the mirror again at the mirage of a whole woman. "I'm no longer comfortable in my own skin. My scars . . ." Not to mention the uncertainty of her future health.

"You're still a beautiful woman, but love has nothing to do with the way we look."

Peyton had been raised by a dad who'd constantly called her his little beauty and a mother who emphasized appearances, so it wasn't so easy to dismiss that conditioning.

"My brain knows that, but I've never been with a man and *not* felt sexy before. It's new and scary." Peyton envied the resilient patients who bounced back and embraced their bodies and second chances. Who didn't look in the mirror and still "see" their hollowed chests after the bilateral mastectomy. She could still picture the sickened look on Todd's face after her diagnosis, like he was watching the cancer cells eat at her from the inside out. "Besides, I'm far from the survivor milestone. Stray cells could be storming my lymph nodes as we speak. It doesn't seem fair to start a relationship with someone when my future is so uncertain."

With this much indecision, perhaps she should rethink the mews.

"It's not like you to let insecurity hold you back."

"I'm not who I used to be. In fact, I might not ever be that person again. I'm still searching for my new normal."

"That's fine as long as the new normal doesn't involve punishing yourself for past mistakes, or refusing to let yourself be happy."

"I'm not a masochist, but I won't go after happiness again at someone else's expense." If Peyton let Mitch get close and then she got sick, she'd rob him of happiness and time, and he'd already lost too much of both. She should remind herself of that every time she looked at Mitch, but all she could think now was *This is our last night alone!* "Listen, I know you mean well, but let's change the subject."

"As long as you promise to think about one thing."

"What's that?"

"The party is one date, and Mitch knows your health status. He can make decisions for himself. Bring him and see what happens."

Keeping it light, as she'd been considering. Before she realized it, she was smiling. Then her alarm dinged. "I've got to run, Steffi. Give me a day to unwind at home, then we'll grab lunch. Kisses to Ryan and Emmy."

"Nice dodge, Pey. See you soon."

Peyton pressed her palm to her stomach, then stuffed the phone in her bag and left the room with Steffi's words rolling around inside her head like a spilled jar of marbles. She arrived at the lobby, expecting Mitch to be waiting as usual. When he wasn't, she paced, fanning herself. She checked the time: 1:34? That walking Swiss watch never ran late. Had he slipped in the shower? Had a stroke?

Right when she began to get concerned, he rounded the corner and came to an abrupt stop upon seeing her. Each hair on her body fluttered as his gaze skimmed her from head to toe.

"You look terrific." With a pronounced blink, he cleared his throat.

"Thanks. So do you." There was nothing special about his classic caramel-colored linen blazer paired with a crisp white shirt and charcoal slacks except that he was the one wearing them. He'd make anything look attractive. "You're late. Trouble?"

"A call ran long. Rebecca . . ." He stopped himself and smiled, waving his hand to end the inquiry. "Not your problem."

"I'm happy to listen if it'd help."

He cocked his head as if no one had ever offered him help before. "Thank you, but let's not put a damper on whatever plans you've made."

His evasiveness tickled her senses. "Does this problem have something to do with my book?"

"No." He stared straight into her eyes. "I swore I wouldn't withhold anything from you—anything about your book, I mean. Just—never mind. I'm a bit fried. Sorry."

No matter what he said, he was withholding *something*, but then again, so was she. Feelings were tricky that way. "Okay."

A relieved smile appeared. "Where *are* we going?"

"Follow me." She led him outside, along the edge of Nevern Square, for the one-mile walk. They strolled through South Kensington along

Lexham Gardens and then on to Cornwall Gardens. The quintessentially British neighborhoods consisted of lengthy blocks lined with multistory Georgian-style townhomes rising on either side of the road like white canyon walls with windows and porticos.

"Things look different in London." Mitch glanced around for the tenth time. "More elegant . . . formal. Nothing like Hoboken."

"If you like this, just wait." She smiled because they were about to enter the mews through the arches at Launceston Place. They meandered onto the narrow cobblestone lane and stepped back in time, surrounded on both sides by brick-and-wood residences remodeled from former horse stables—some painted white, yellow, or blue—most embellished with outdoor potted planters and wild wisteria. An intimate pedestrian-friendly area that seemed miles and light-years apart from a major metropolitan city.

"Well?" Peyton spread her arms wide and spun around, heart filled with the contentedness this neighborhood always inspired.

Mitch looked up and down the picturesque residential lane, tucking his hands under his armpits and grinning. "What is this place?"

"The Kynance Mews. These buildings date back to the eighteen hundreds and first served as stabling for the Cornwall Gardens development." She clasped her hands behind her back with a slight bow. "Isn't this *the* classic example of quaint?"

He nodded, smiling broadly. "Do you know someone who lives here?"

"No." She headed west.

He followed. "So why are we here?"

"We've been pushing so hard I thought it would be nice to do one last thing together that didn't involve my book. Sort of like we did in Paris." She craned her neck to try to peer inside a window, one of her favorite pastimes. She imagined adorable hearths and old beams and someone sitting in a comfy chair, sipping rose tea, eating biscuits, and fiddling with a basket of yarn on the floor. Of course, she could never get a good look inside any of the homes. "Besides, it's pretty and historic. A lovely place to stroll."

He slowed to a standstill. "So we came here to *stroll*?"

"Well, yes. To relax and enjoy each other's company." She looped her arm through his with exaggerated purpose, then refused to release him. His cologne emitted a pleasing hint of spice. "To slow down and appreciate something you can't find in New York—not that you probably get out to see much of New York, either."

"Meaning?"

"Meaning you live in one of the greatest cities in the world, but I bet you never explore it without some goal in mind. In fact, I bet you spend all of your time at your computer, on the phone, or with your mother in Jersey."

"Careful." He said that so quietly she wished he'd shouted instead.

"I'm sorry. I don't mean to criticize. I admire your ambition and your dedication to your family. But I wish you'd take care of yourself as well as you take care of everyone else. So please indulge me this one hour, take a deep breath, and play."

"Play?"

She shrugged, still linked arm in arm, hopeful that he wouldn't wriggle free. "Imagine walking these same cobblestones one hundred and fifty years ago as a groom, caring for the Cleveland bays and phaetons or broughams in these stables. Or picture yourself living here now, in one of these small but pricey homes—maybe as an artist or perhaps a barrister—taking tea, riding your bike to work, stopping at the local pub on your way home. It can be anything that takes you outside yourself, your life, your problems. There's no right or wrong, no benchmark to meet. It's only for fun."

His gaze remained near his feet as they walked. "Is this what you do when you travel alone?"

"Often!" She tugged on his arm to get him to look up. "I love to get lost and let my imagination wander. Like now, we could pretend that we live in that pretty yellow house—my personal favorite." She pointed ahead to a home with expansive mullioned windows, two wrought iron Juliet balconies overflowing with red geraniums, and a bright-green door flanked by potted shrubs. Such a cheerful house that the people who lived there *must* be happy. "Maybe we're arguing about the new copper planters I want to install but can't afford. Maybe we hate the neighbor on the right because she's a big flirt who is always causing trouble. Or the one on the left whose kid practices the violin at six a.m."

"So we're roommates in this fantasy?" A sexy smile broke through his carefully arranged expression.

She welcomed the heat fanning through her body. "We can be anything. Anyone. I don't have to be Peyton Prescott, great-granddaughter of William Prescott, cancer patient turned reluctant author who can't go back to her old life and doesn't quite know where to go with her new one, and you don't have to be Mitch Mathis, man with the weight of three worlds on his shoulders."

They passed a half barrel filled with pink begonias. Mitch remained quiet, making Peyton wonder if she'd insulted him again. Coin toss on whether that would be preferable to him homing in on her slipup about her life in limbo.

"Make-believe and escapes don't make anything better. They just let you avoid dealing with problems. Your responsibilities are still there when you return to reality. And conjuring some false utopia makes reality a real letdown."

She should've known he'd heard every word she'd said. Still, she shook her head. "A mental escape can trigger creativity. Help you see a problem from a new angle. And even when you don't find a solution, at the very least, it gives you a break from your problems."

"Has it helped you answer the question of what you'll do after the book tour ends?"

"Not yet . . . but I have faith."

"Faith." He flashed a weak smile. "May I make a suggestion?"

"Of course."

"Think about what you need to be happy—a core need—and then figure out if you can build something around that. Like your brother has done with his photography giving him a public platform to be heard."

Logan *did* need to be heard, and loved to tell stories with pictures. She frowned when thinking of herself. "What if I have no idea what I need?"

"If you focus on it, it will come to you." Mitch peered up at the rooflines.

She admired his handsome face while he studied the mews. "What's yours?"

"Security." He grimaced, almost apologetically.

She laughed. "I wouldn't think that publishing is very secure."

"Not on the surface, but there will always be books in one form or another, and no shortage of authors looking for visibility. As long as I continue to work hard and be creative, I should always have a job."

"Hm. I suppose you're right. I guess I'll have to give some thought to my needs, but not here and now."

They came to the dead end, so they turned to go the other direction, toward Gloucester, where she knew of a nice wine store. Her plan—such as it was—had failed. It seemed he'd rather think about work and careers than play along with her.

He cleared his throat, looping an arm through hers again. "I'd rather invest in Le Creuset bakeware than those copper planters."

"Bakeware?" Her smile rose along with her hope. "Do you expect me to cook?"

"No." He stared ahead, a whisper of a grin on his face. "They're for me."

"You bake?" She chuckled.

He nodded. "I do."

"And cook?" She pictured him standing at the stove—no doubt in an apron to keep his clothes neat—searing some tuna or preparing some other meal to share with her while discussing their day. She'd be sipping wine and searching for the right playlist to set the mood.

"A bit, but I don't enjoy it as much. Cooking is more of an art form, whereas baking is about precision." He emphasized his preference with a single raised brow.

She chuckled. "Well then, you must be amazing."

He shrugged, too modest to brag, but not so humble as to deny it.

"What's your best dish?" she asked.

"Hmm . . . I make a great chocolate soufflé and a mean French macaron."

"I love macarons." When she ate sugar, anyway. Interesting that a man who didn't like to travel favored foreign desserts. Perhaps baking was his way to travel, or to escape reality. He just didn't know it. "What else?"

He gazed upward, thinking. "I'm good with pie crust."

"No, I mean what other secrets have you been keeping from me?"

"Secrets?"

"Talents." She rolled her hand over a couple of times while saying, "Habits, hobbies, tidbits I don't know."

He kicked a stray pebble, his expression pinched in thought. "I used to build models." That didn't surprise her. Another hobby that required his hallmark traits—patience and precision. "Starting at around ten, I'd get one or two new kits for the houses and things you place around a train set. My dad and I would work on them together. We'd planned an elaborate Christmas village, but we never finished . . ."

She squeezed his arm in empathy. "Do you have any pictures of what you did?"

"My mom must have some somewhere."

"I'd love to see what you looked like as a kid." She'd bet his eyes had been lit with curiosity before tragedy struck his family. He'd probably laughed plenty, too. Mitch was right about one thing—no imaginary games would bring back his dad or give him back the childhood he'd lost.

"Do you have hobbies?" he asked.

She wrinkled her nose, thinking back on her many phases. Unlike Logan, who took deep dives into art and photography, she bored easily and was satisfied to skim across the surface of new languages, musical instruments, dance classes, and such.

"I never had your persistence . . . unless you count pranking people. I was very good at that." She laughed.

"Not shocking." He smiled at her, then looked at the row of houses again. "Maybe we move to the blue one, there."

"Why?"

"It already has copper planters, so I can get my bakeware. Plus it looks a little bigger, and the wisteria across the street would make a pretty view."

"Fair points." As they neared the end of the mews, she reconsidered Mitch's opinion about how the trip from utopia to reality could be crushing. "In all seriousness, before I got sick, I used to daydream about renting a flat here. I love this street so much. It's like something from a fairy tale . . . a place for happy endings."

"Happy endings . . ." He snorted with a naughty glint in his eye, which made her laugh because it marked the first time he'd ever been remotely off-color.

She slowed her steps when they reached Gloucester, a busy thoroughfare. The end of utopia. A stubborn, selfish little voice in her head whispered, *Turn your fantasy into reality.* She'd always found that devil on her shoulder hard to resist. "There's a fantastic wine shop a few blocks that way. Shall we get a bottle to drop at the hotel before dinner? We can drink it tonight to celebrate the end of the trip."

"If you'd like to celebrate the end, then we will." He nodded, but he didn't sound very festive.

In truth, the part of her that would rather stay with him in the mews than return to New York didn't much want to celebrate, either. Those words filled her mouth, but she swallowed them for fear of ruining what little time she had left with Mitch.

———

Mitch gripped his pint at the bar in the Wenlock Arms while burning a colossal hole through the back of Harry Davies's head. If Peyton's editor gave her one more drink tonight, Mitch might reach overhead for one of the hundred heavy bar glasses and toss it at that bald spot. Clearly, that guy didn't have rules about separating business from pleasure. Neither did Harry appear to have any compunction about plying women with alcohol.

The pathetic loser had to be ten years Peyton's senior, if not more. Couldn't he see he was making an ass of himself?

Mitch rubbed his temples to stave off the headache springing from pretending to be interested in the dozens of casks and keg options at the bar while surreptitiously keeping an eye on every move Harry made.

Two things would slow down any rescue attempt he could make if Peyton got into a bind. First, he'd have to go over or around the massive square bar between them. Second, he'd need to part all the drunk people obscuring his view, which wouldn't be easy.

He swigged his ale. The pub's blackened wood floors and dark painted brick might as well have been a mood ring. Only nine o'clock? That couldn't be right. He would've guessed they'd already been there at least five hours.

Maybe that third pint of Dark Star Sunburst hadn't been a great idea, but even the hangover Mitch expected tomorrow wouldn't suck as much as his return to reality after pretending to be Peyton's boyfriend this afternoon. He'd known that game would come back to bite him in the ass.

Either way, this night marked the end of their tour together. He'd spent the past twelve days suppressing his feelings. Making excuses to slip away in order not to compromise himself or her. Now he wanted those days back. Anything for a bit more time. For a chance at that elusive happiness she seemed determined to seek at every turn.

He chugged the rest of his beer to drown his self-pity. Another glance across the bar caught her laughing, which prompted a smile despite the fact that he wasn't sharing it with her. She might not be his, but he'd make sure she didn't end up with Harry or anyone else in this pub, either.

"Sounds like you and Peyton got around the Continent these past weeks." Wes Smith, Naughton House's in-house senior PR guru, slapped Mitch on the shoulder as he wedged beside him at the bar.

Wes ordered another ale, then must've noted Mitch staring across the bar to where Peyton remained cloistered by Harry.

"She's a posh one, like I thought. But I still like her in spite of it!" Wes laughed at his own joke. "My wife's friend had breast cancer. Terrible thing. She thought she was fine for a spell, but then it came back in her brain. Wrecked her husband. Left two kids behind." Wes sipped his beer as if his story hadn't squeezed Mitch's heart to a dead stop.

His gaze flew to Peyton. It could happen to her. He knew it. He'd always known it, he supposed, although he hadn't let himself overthink it. His dad's hollow cheeks and anguished cries came rushing back. If Peyton *were* his . . . could he deal with losing her that way—would he survive suffering that kind of pain and loss all over again?

Wes leaned forward on the bar, oblivious to Mitch's thoughts, craning his neck left and right. "I'm hungry. Any toasties left?"

"I don't know." Between the ale that filled his stomach like a water balloon and the thought of Peyton's cancer returning, Mitch had no appetite.

Wes wiped a bit of foam from his lip. "So back to America? Wish you luck, mate. Sales and all that."

"Thanks, Wes." Mitch threw ten pounds on the bar, needing to get away from Wes, as if distance would erase the worry he'd planted in Mitch's head. "If you'll excuse me, Peyton and I've got an early flight," he lied.

"Ah, yeah. Don't want to get too pissed before a flight. Safe travels." Wes shook his hand before wandering two stools down to barge in on another colleague's discussion.

"Thanks," Mitch called after him before circumnavigating a dozen or more of the loud drunks to reach Peyton.

The blaring TV overhead and yammering crowd intensified the pounding in his head.

When he arrived, Peyton greeted him with a warm smile, reaching out for his hand, which made his heart beat out *mine, mine, mine* despite everything that should have kept him away from her. "Mitch!"

Then she hiccuped.

"This woman is brilliant," Harry slurred while encroaching on her personal space in a very un-British show of manners. Mitch wanted to punch the guy when his eyes dipped to that peephole in her dress.

"Brilliant!" she echoed, her voice tinkling with laughter. "Let's never leave London. I like it here."

Let's, she'd said, suggesting she viewed them as a pair. His heart rose inside his chest.

"We like you here, too," Harry murmured, emphasizing his remark with a quirk of his bushy eyebrows.

Mitch squeezed her hand. "Peyton, it's time to go."

"Oh pooh." She pouted. "Is the party over?"

"It is for us," he said before Harry could offer her an alternative.

"Okay." She blew kisses at Harry. "Thank you for all your hard work and the great party."

Harry tossed Mitch a perturbed look but relented. "Let's hope to see your memoir in the *Sunday Times* next week."

Peyton laughed. Poor Harry had no idea of her lack of interest in hitting a list. Of course, Mitch and Harry couldn't share that attitude and keep their jobs.

She leaned on Mitch, one arm draped across his back. He could almost taste the cider on her breath. Her head fell against his shoulder when she said, in a low voice, "We still have a party waiting for us at home."

"Do we?" He wrapped his arm around her waist, not at all put out that she sought assistance walking out of the bar. Her body felt warm and soft beneath his hand. Want flowed through him more briskly than ale poured from any cask in the pub.

"Mm-hmm. That wine we bought today. My room has a terrace. Perfect for a nightcap." They tumbled out to the sidewalk. Neither of them needed a nightcap. Her hair brushed his cheek when she looked up at the sky. "And look, it isn't raining. *Brilliant!*"

The dictionary definition of "bad idea" was a private party with Peyton. Yet ten minutes later, Mitch found himself in her room, sitting at the little café table on the turf-covered rooftop terrace, sharing a bottle of pinot noir.

Distant horns, a breeze, the faint sound of music coming through someone's open window. These things swirled around, making him dizzy, but nothing kept him more off-balance than Peyton. So full of life it seemed hard to believe she'd ever had cancer. He wanted—needed—to bask in her light and be carried away from duty and off to adventure, even if only in his imagination. Maybe she'd won that debate after all, or else he was now into self-flagellation.

"What will you remember most from these past weeks?" she asked, her legs stretched out, shoes kicked off, pink toenails stretched toward the sky as she flexed her feet. Those calves . . .

"I don't know. It's been a blur," he said, covering, knowing that his strongest memories were things he couldn't say, like the way she'd spent twenty minutes talking to one survivor in Amsterdam after the signing when he knew she was exhausted, or the dreamy look in her eyes when she'd eaten that pasta in Rome. Or that kiss . . . "How about you?"

"Square du Vert-Galant," she said without hesitation. "I love that *you* planned it for us. A little escape."

It'd been freeing to discuss his dad with her. Maybe he would be willing to risk living through that kind of hell again if it meant he'd get to look into her eyes every day from now until whenever. Would she welcome him reaching across the table to pull her onto his lap or reject him again? He was too buzzed to know.

He should go. This situation wasn't smart for either of them.

Before he spoke up, she raised her glass. "To us."

Then she waved her free hand like she was erasing her words. "Actually, to *you*! Thanks for giving up weeks of your life to walk me through my first—and last—European book tour. For making me take responsibility for this work when all I wanted to do was run from it. I might not ever write another book as long as I live, but somehow doing all this has made me feel a little stronger than when we started. More like a survivor than a victim. You've made this experience memorable, Mitch." She fell quiet and leaned across the table, staring into his eyes and licking her lips. "I've always loved Europe, but what I'll miss most when we get home is seeing you every day."

And then she blinked like someone waking from a daze. Her crimson cheeks glowed like embers. She stood, clutching her wine-glass, and moved to the brick railing to stare into the windows of other townhouses.

He finished his wine. Warm, humid air made it twice as hard to catch his breath. She'd miss him. His heart pounded so hard his chest pulsed. Now he stared at her from behind, the full moon above casting her in soft light. This entire scene seemed clipped from a movie.

He jumped from his seat when she pitched forward to get a better look at something below that had snagged her attention. In her unsteady state, she could have gone over the railing.

When he touched her arm, she looked up with those round blue eyes and smiled. "Don't you love this? A private garden—we can spy on all these people."

"Not so private." He then ran his hand along the metal railing to block her from leaning forward again. "If you can see them, they can see you."

"You're right," she whispered, now inches from him, and nodded as if she hadn't considered that. He was memorizing the shape and exact colors of her eyes when her hand landed on his chest.

He didn't dare move because he liked her hand there covering his heart. The scent of her skin and hair in the breeze filled the sliver of space between them. Without thinking, he closed his eyes to concentrate on it. Seconds later, her hand brushed upward. He opened his eyes, heart now thudding in his ears.

The air between them charged with the energy of an oncoming thunderstorm. *Careful. Careful. Careful.*

"Let's give them something to look at." She splayed her fingers through his hair, one hand and then the other, sending tingles fanning over his scalp and down his back. Twice, thrice . . . sweet torture. She watched her hands comb through his hair. "I've wanted to do this since the first time I saw you at JFK."

He settled his hands on her hips, barely breathing. He should push her away. "Peyton, you're drunk."

"Not too drunk. Just enough to be braver than in Paris." She placed one finger on his lips. "Let's not talk about the rules. I don't *care* about rules. Life isn't about rules . . . It's about living. It's about heart." She let her hand fall from his mouth and set it back on the center of his chest. "I only have one question: Does yours feel anything for me?"

She swayed a bit—a reminder that neither of them was sober. The ground beneath him dropped away as he nodded. "A lot, actually."

His words brought the prettiest smile to her face, so he could hardly regret saying them. It wasn't taking advantage. Not when he meant every word.

While he got lost in his own moral dilemma, she cupped his face and kissed him.

A tentative kiss that tasted of cider and wine and something warm and sweet. A second chance at the kiss that had haunted his dreams.

Gravity and weakened knees left him pinned against the railing with her body pressed against his. He feasted on her lips. Savored the heat of her tongue as he deepened their kiss. The sound of her breath, the beat of his heart, the rush of blood that raced to his groin, pulsing, pulsing, pulsing to the point of pain. He ran his hands along her waist and wound them around her back until he'd locked her in a tight embrace.

He wanted more of her mouth. More of the heat flowing through his limbs. The tingling in his feet. The breathlessness of it all . . .

She circled her arms around his neck, flattening herself against his torso. The soft hum in her chest reverberated, pushing him to kiss her more urgently and touch her like he would never stop.

The silky threads of her wild hair brushed against his hands, teasing other parts of his body. With his temperature rising faster than mercury on a sweltering summer day, he might combust right there on the terrace.

This woman could kiss with a seductive rhythm that promised pure delight. He lifted her into his arms, strode through the terrace doors into her room—one dominated by a double bed and its ornate headboard padded with velvet. They fell onto the mattress. She was panting, restless with want, which made him even hotter. He couldn't catch his breath, but even in his frenzied state, he didn't leap on top of her.

Stretching out beside her, he pulled her in for another kiss. When she melted into his arms, another surge of desire coursed through him, forming a single-minded purpose—to taste every inch of her skin. He kissed his way along her jaw and down the sensitive skin of her neck, encouraged by the way she shivered. With one hand, he tried to unbutton the little peephole that had tantalized him all night, eager to explore the trail through that valley and down her torso to her belly button.

A fatal mistake.

The wash of lust had shut down all reasoning, so it took an extra second for him to register her sudden stiffness. Then she wedged her hands between them and crossed her arms in front of her breasts as she turned her face away. He rolled onto his back, confused until he remembered why they were even *in* London and all that she and her body had been through.

"I'm sorry." He turned on his side and brushed her hair away from her face.

She closed her eyes. A tremor seized her shoulders as a tear rolled down her cheek. His blood drained, leaving his skin damp and cold.

Should he touch her, hold her, jump off the bed and apologize? "Peyton?"

She opened her eyes, held his gaze, chin quivering. "I'm sorry. I can't. I just . . . I'm not ready."

Chapter Twelve

"Please don't cry." Mitch's distraught expression completed her humiliation. "I'm sorry. God, I swear I thought—"

"You thought right." She curled onto her side, tucking one of the red crushed-velvet pillows under her head before pulling her knees close, like she could make herself invisible. "You didn't do anything wrong. I did."

"No. *I* broke my rule. I came in here knowing we were both too buzzed to make good decisions. Knowing this could happen—hell, I wanted it so much I couldn't stop myself." He sat up and shook his head, wearing an expression of self-hatred. The same kind she donned anytime she thought about how much she'd hurt Claire.

"Mitch, look at me." She waited to see the molten-gold shimmer in his hazel eyes. "I asked you here. I kissed you first. *I* orchestrated all this, starting earlier today when—stone-cold sober—I bought the wine. So don't act like I'm your victim. You're *mine.*"

His eyes widened. He didn't say a word, but she noticed his lips twitch. A smile in hiding, perhaps?

"That's right." She pushed up with one arm, lying on her hip. "You're my victim."

"Willing victim." He let that smile loose like a boy who'd got caught stealing the last piece of cake but knew he wasn't really in trouble.

The band of anxiety around her chest eased, allowing some air to fill her lungs. "That's nice."

"Trust me, where I was headed involved a lot of things, none of them remotely 'nice.'"

"Now you're being a tease." She fell back on the bed and closed her eyes. A few seconds later, she peeked at him. "I'm so messed up."

He stared into space while rubbing his thigh. "I should go."

"Wait." If he could read her mind, he'd know she didn't want him to go. Yet asking him to stay to cuddle would make her look more ridiculous than she already did. "I don't want you to think that I was playing you."

"I don't, Peyton." He leaned back on one elbow and grabbed her hand. "It's been a long couple of weeks, and you've had only me to lean on. That can muddy things. Make you think there's more to it."

"I'm not confused. I've been thinking about this for a while, even before Paris. But this got so hot so fast it scared me." She covered her face for a second, calling out to her old self. *That* woman would've dived into bed with Mitch and kept him there all night. "Not proud of that, but at least I'm being honest."

His eyes got that distant look he had when analyzing his options and things he could say. Optimus mode. She fought her smile because it seemed inappropriate in the moment, despite how much this trait of his intrigued her.

"If you want to take it slow, I can do that." He trailed a finger along her hip. "Nice and slow."

His touch moved through her until she felt it everywhere. She needed it so much she almost cried again. Her selfish nature begged to drag him into her uncertain world, in which her moods blew hot and cold and the future might not be so very long. She covered his hand with hers. "It's not that simple. I'm conflicted between what I want, what I'm ready to handle, and what you deserve. I don't understand myself anymore, and my body . . . Whatever you think you see in me, you aren't seeing clearly."

"It's simple to me. Maybe you feel a little lost now and then, but everything will work out. You're a fighter, Peyton. I see you clearly, and I like what I see."

Beautiful words, soothing as ointment on an open wound, but he couldn't have thought this through.

"You only see me from a distance. Trust me when I say that's the best view these days." She looked away, ashamed of her own vanity.

He took her chin in hand and turned her face back in his direction. "I prefer you up close, where I can smell your perfume, touch your hair, and look in your eyes."

"Other parts don't look so good."

"I've seen all the photos, and to me you're still one of the sexiest women I've ever met. I won't like you less because of a couple of scars." He rested his hand on her thigh, soothing her. "I've fought my feelings this entire trip, but I have to say, I'm not sorry I gave up that battle. It feels damn good to be honest with you. You know me well enough to know that I don't break my rules lightly. Doesn't the fact that I'm lying here tell you all you need to know?"

"Mitch, it's not only that." She didn't want to talk about her upcoming appointment, so she dodged. "Your life is complicated enough without taking on my baggage. Wouldn't you be better off with someone fun and breezy who can make you smile, instead of another person to support through recovery?" Or worse . . .

"You've been pushing me to throw caution aside since we met, and to live in the moment. To chase happiness. What's changed? Is there something else you're not telling me?"

She wouldn't discuss her concerns about the dryness down there or how the lack of nipple sensation might affect her enjoyment, or share how she hated her body for making her so afraid of grabbing hold of happiness when she couldn't trust that she might have to give it all up. Everything inside screamed to push him away rather than end up devastated by yet another loss. "It's been so long since I . . . you know." She gestured at the bed. "Since before I was sick . . . since Todd. I . . . I'm not ready to handle too much yet . . ."

If she could disappear, she would try.

When embarrassment and shame caused her to sniffle again, he reached out for her, tucking her against his chest like a spoon.

"I'm sorry that guy hurt you." He paused as if weighing whether to ask a question, then frowned like he'd decided against it. "I know you've been through a lot, and I'd never push. But I also can't leave you here alone and crying. How about we turn off the lights and get some sleep and see what the morning brings?"

Falling asleep in his arms with no obligation to disrobe sounded about as close to heaven as a sinner like her would ever get. She lay there listening to the sound of his breath, noticing his blunt, neatly trimmed fingernails, and staring at the stray dark hairs that peeked out from his shirtsleeve.

Cuddling had been much overlooked in her "before cancer" love life. This definitely qualified as a silver lining. "Thank you."

"For what?" His muscular body wrapped her in warmth and security.

She clasped one of his hands in hers and brought it to her lips. "For being a good guy."

He hugged her tighter to him and kissed the back of her head. "If being a decent human is your idea of a good guy, we need to reset your expectations."

Rolling over in his arms, she then planted one last kiss good night on his lips. "No matter what happens, I think you might be my very best worst mistake."

He kissed her forehead and fell onto his back, dragging her with him until she was nestled in the crook of his arm and her head lay against his shoulder.

Following three focused, calming breaths, she closed her eyes and drifted into a fitful sleep.

At dawn, Mitch woke her when he accidentally bumped into the luggage rack while trying to navigate his way out of her bathroom without turning on any lights.

"Are you okay?" she asked, rubbing her eyes as they adjusted to the dim room.

"I'm fine." He repositioned her suitcase on the rack. "Sorry I woke you, but I need to pack and shower before we head to the airport."

"Oh, of course." She pushed herself upright, glancing down at the wrinkled mess of her dress turned nightgown. Apparently she'd removed her bra sometime during the night. "I should get moving, too."

He came to the side of the bed—freshly washed face, minty breath, perfect hair—and leaned down to kiss her good morning. "If we hurry, we could grab a decent breakfast before we go."

She nodded, although her hangover-induced queasiness intensified at the thought of digesting anything other than water or juice.

Mitch stared at her before letting his gaze roam the bed, the pillow on the floor, the open terrace door. "The only silver lining about leaving today is knowing this is my last flight for a while."

"I'll get you through it." She smiled at him.

He winked and then grabbed his jacket on his way out the door.

Once he left the room, she set her feet on the cold wood floor before dragging her unwilling, achy body from the bed. Her pounding head demanded aspirin and water. She flicked on the bathroom's bright light, which made her squint. When she caught her reflection in the mirror, she gasped. Hair matted on one side while shooting out the other like a scene from *There's Something About Mary*. Mascara streaks beneath her eyes. Pasty skin.

No wonder Mitch had bolted from her room.

Bottles of medication and vitamins that she'd take for years to come littered the vanity. Mitch couldn't have missed seeing the stark reminder of how unwell—how literally toxic—she was, either. Strike two.

She growled and swept them aside, sending them to bounce off the floor.

He'd said he didn't care about her scars and her cancer, yet how could she trust that heroic claim? And what had she, a selfish woman who'd betrayed her friend for a man who left her at the first sign of trouble, done to deserve him?

She knelt to collect the bottles off the cold marble floor. After lining them up on the sink like toy soldiers—the battalion keeping her alive—she took her morning doses with an aspirin and water.

One by one, snatches of memories from last night replayed like yesteryear's erratic Vine videos. She dropped her chin and covered her face with both hands, desperate to hide from the images. She'd thrown herself at him and then dissolved in tears, yammering about her body and her fears. An unattractive and pathetic display that only a person with a savior complex would find attractive. *That* made sense. He'd rescued his mom, his sister, his clients, and now her. Peyton understood very little about healthy love, but this didn't seem like a good starting point.

—⁓—

For the first time ever, Mitch hardly thought about the fact that he was strapped in a chair thirty-six thousand feet above the earth, hurtling through space at five hundred miles per hour. *Ocean's Eight* hadn't held his attention. Planning for Kendra's upcoming release and updating his PR tracker for the curated lists that would promote Peyton's memoir had distracted him only a bit. But the main reason he'd been unconcerned about the flight was because he'd spent the majority of its eight hours trying to figure out what Peyton was thinking.

With the plane starting its descent, he'd almost run out of time to get an answer. He reached for her hand, threading his fingers through hers with a firm squeeze. Without taking his eyes off their hands, he said, "We've spent the whole day avoiding talking about what happened last night. Is this your way of letting me down easy?"

He risked a glance at her face.

She'd sucked her lips inward and stared at their hands. "I've been thinking about it." When she met his gaze, she was smiling. "I know, I—I rarely think things through before blurting opinions, but I've learned something from you these past weeks about the benefits of taking my time."

His chest tightened around his lungs. "So what have you concluded?"

"I really like and admire you—"

He groaned and released her hand. "It's okay. No need to continue the 'let's be friends' speech."

"It's not that, Mitch." She sighed. "Even at my best, I couldn't find a good guy, so I'm kinda leery that *this* version of me would appeal to anyone."

On the surface, he understood her point, but her distorted views about love were more layered than his most complex mille-feuille. "Do you think someone has to be perfect to be worthy of affection? If that's the case, I promise I'm not worthy. No one is."

She frowned. "Proving my point that I don't know anything about relationships. I spent my twenties footloose because I had too many adventures to experience. Then I met Todd and, bam, I was all in at all costs. I thought that thunderstruck feeling was love, but I got burned by its lightning."

"From what little I heard about Todd, he sounds nothing like me."

"True, but I've always jumped into things with both feet, and looking back, that's often led to pain. Leading with my heart again, after everything I've gone through to survive, seems much riskier now."

"Or maybe all those lessons led you here"—he gestured between them—"to a place where you can appreciate a steady, if sometimes less carefree, kind of man." He stared at her, and when she made no reply, he said, "Maybe whatever is between us won't last, but it won't be because I betray you or lead you on with false promises, Peyton. I can assure you of that much."

The heavy, bumpy thud of the plane touching down distracted him. He closed his eyes, gripping the armrests as the wheels screeched in response to the pilot's putting on the brakes.

Peyton touched his shoulder, bringing him back to their conversation. "I wish I'd met you before Todd and cancer. Before fear and selfishness tore me up. And when I say 'selfish,' I mean it. Hell, you've seen it on the tour. I'm struggling to find my way each day. How can my need to focus on getting myself together now be any good for you? You deserve someone in your life who can put *you* first for a change."

He remained quiet as the plane began to taxi to the gate, remembering his mother's warning that Peyton was not "their" kind of people. She'd grown up with choices instead of obligations. Her brush with death drove her to seek something larger-than-life while he'd be satisfied with something simple and grounded.

Yet he did understand her. In fact, he could even imagine feeling the need—the right—to be selfish. What would happen if he told his mother and sister that he wanted to focus on his own life instead of constantly managing theirs? That didn't mean any life he built for himself could be interesting enough for someone like Peyton, though.

The clatter of unbuckled seat belts drew him back from his musing. Passengers stood and started wresting bags from the overhead bins.

He turned to her while they remained captive in their seats. "I won't beg you when you're so uncertain. After the Strand, we won't have much contact, if any, unless you want it. When you leave here today, know that I think we could be exactly who the other needs. As you've pointed out, my life could use more laughter and adventure . . . more everything outside of my work and my family. If anything, you've convinced me it's okay to be a little selfish now and then. And I'd love to help you figure out what you need in the future."

She looked at him with a mixture of surprise and pride, but they deplaned before she could reply. While strolling toward customs, she slipped her arm through his. "Just when I think I have you figured out, you throw me for a loop, Mitch Mathis. Remind me not to play poker with you."

He smiled, sensing a softening. An opening. Enough room for hope.

They wound their way through the crowd filled with couples and families with parents scolding their kids for playing around the carousels. Happy, tired people returning from trips with more memories than they could fit in any luggage. Things that made life worth living, as Peyton would point out if she were paying attention.

She, however, seemed to be lost in her own thoughts, staring ahead at nothing at all. Anyone looking at her now would covet her patrician good looks; the tailored black-and-taupe floral cargo slacks, strappy sandals, and sleek black silk top; the Tory Burch tote bag. She looked like something out of a magazine or movie—*that* girl with the perfect life.

He grabbed her cherry-red Louis Vuitton bag, which had to cost more than his monthly rent, knowing what no one else could see. She was no better off than anyone—and, in fact, she might be in worse shape than many. He did want to help her find her way back to happiness, but it had to be her call.

After the final checkpoint, they spilled into the chaotic main terminal, walking past the chauffeurs with bored faces and whiteboard signs scrawled with client names.

"This is where we part." The prospect of saying goodbye without any answer filled his chest with sand. "Will you get an Uber?"

He hadn't quite finished his sentence when Peyton snapped her head toward a man who shouted her name. She let out an excited squeak. "Logan!"

Mitch stepped back as the siblings embraced. Logan lifted her off the ground for a second before setting her back down. Together they made quite a striking statement of beauty and privilege.

"Welcome home." Logan messed with Peyton's hair and then extended a hand to Mitch. "Hi, I'm Logan. You must be Mitchell."

"Mitch," he said, envying Logan's easy charm and warmth. "Nice to meet you. After these past weeks with your sister, I feel like I know you. And, of course, your work precedes you. The photographs in the book are remarkable."

"Thank you. And thanks for everything you've done to help promote our book."

"My pleasure." Mitch darted a look at Peyton, whose gaze bounced from her brother to him and back again.

"You two must be glad to be home after that endless dog and pony show." Logan bumped shoulders with his sister.

Not so glad, Mitch almost uttered. He studied the siblings again, both all smiles and comfort. Real friendship. He and Lauren didn't kid around that way. He'd been more paternal than friendly for most of her life. Could that dynamic change, or was it too late?

He said, "It'll be great when you join us at the Strand next week."

Mitch had a lengthy to-do list this coming week. Preorders looked good, but next Tuesday was launch day, and he wanted that Wednesday's event to be flawless because Savant staff would attend.

"Can't wait." Logan nodded. "First I have to get through the party this weekend. Mom's gone overboard."

When Mitch raised his brows in question, Peyton said, "The engagement party."

"Oh, yes." Mitch nodded. "Congratulations. Peyton's very happy for you both."

"I'm a lucky guy. But you'll see for yourself this weekend when you meet Claire. And of course, meeting the rest of the family will round out whatever you think you learned about the Prescotts from the memoir." He smiled, unaware that his assumption of Peyton having already extended an invitation was akin to a public fart.

Before Mitch could form an answer, Peyton weighed in. "Logan, could you wait for me outside? I'll be a minute."

"Sure." He grabbed the handle of her suitcase and waved at Mitch. "See you Saturday."

As soon as he was out of earshot, she looked at Mitch. "Sorry. I thought about inviting you but didn't want to put you on the spot."

"It's fine. I understand."

"I'm serious, Mitch. Until last night, I was merely a client and you had your rules. If I'd invited you, you might've felt like you couldn't say no. If this were weeks from now, after the end of our contract . . . But then last night and today. We still haven't made any decisions . . ."

He held up a finger, shaking his head. "*You* haven't. I know what I want."

She stared at him, hugging herself like a child standing on the high dive, staring at the water below. "If you could be happy starting slow and keeping it light, I would like to see you again . . . outside of work, I mean."

If she needed to start slow, he would agree. At least it gave him a chance. "I'd be very happy to see you outside of work."

"Would you like to come to the party? It'll be at Arcadia House with my family and friends—which I realize doesn't feel like a slow start. You should spend the night rather than make the two-hour drive home."

"Hmm. Spend the night with you at your family's fabled estate . . ." He reached for her hand. "I can't imagine anything I'd rather do."

"Only because you haven't met Darla and Harrison yet."

"Your parents?"

"Yep." She pulled a face.

He pointed at himself because she should know better. "I think I'm pretty good with difficult parents." That reminded him that his mother would be pissed about his plans because she'd be only five days out from her surgery by Saturday. For once, Lauren might have to step up.

"True." She smiled. "Why don't you plan to come up in the afternoon? The party begins at six."

A yes sat on the tip of his tongue, but her brother had trapped her into this invitation. "I'll come on one condition."

She waited with a curious look on her face.

"Be honest with me. Is this invitation what *you* want, or do you feel pressured because your brother put us on the spot?"

"I would very much like for you to come now that we're on the same page about expectations."

The crying babies, screeching luggage carousels, and overhead announcements faded as her words sank in. "Done. We'll talk tomorrow about next week's launch and reading, but you should go catch up with Logan now."

She glanced over her shoulder to the glass doors and then back. "I'd offer a ride, but we're going the other direction."

"It's fine, although I'd like to train Lauren to be as thoughtful as your brother." He leaned in to kiss her cheek.

She held him there for a hug before easing away.

"Maybe I can help with that, if I ever meet her." She winked and strolled toward the door, flashing her pretty smile one last time before she disappeared.

Having convinced her to give them a chance—however slight— he made some new vows: she would meet his family, their next event would go well, and her book would hit the *NYT* bestsellers list. When he put his mind to something, nothing could stop him, and this would be no different.

Chapter Thirteen

"Hello!" Peyton's voice echoed throughout the kitchen. She threw her purse on the counter while Logan rolled her luggage in through the back door. Neither of her parents replied from any corner of the house. No home-cooked meal was roasting in the oven. No celebratory cake was anywhere to be seen. No hugs. "Some homecoming."

Logan grimaced in an "are you really surprised" manner. He was right, of course. Peyton had long ago accepted that her parents' aloof nature had been passed down from the prior generation of Prescotts. They had their busy schedules, and they'd raised their kids to manage their own lives, too. Pretty much the opposite of Mitch's experience.

After setting her suitcase by the wall, Logan said, "Mom mentioned something about dinner at Lucia's."

"Shoot. I'm on London time. Not really up for going out on the town." Then again, Lucia's served awesome meatballs. "Are you staying dressed like that?"

"Oh, sorry. I've got plans with Claire."

She would love an invitation but knew he couldn't yet extend one without checking with Claire. Peyton wouldn't complain, though. Claire had come a long way toward mending fences, but some betrayals run too deep. Claire might not ever be able to love, or even like, her again. "What plans?"

"Anything but dinner at Lucia's." Logan snickered.

She slapped his chest. "Not nice."

"Gimme a break. I've dealt with Mom more these past few weeks than I have this entire year." He rubbed the back of his neck. "Trust me, she and I need a breather. I can't pretend to be interested in one more decision about figs with bacon and chile versus lobster toasts with avocado. In what world would I care whether the table linens are blush silk organza or white with gold trim? Thank God Claire and her parents get to plan the wedding."

Peyton smothered a giggle at the image of him sitting with their mom at the kitchen table, ticking through what could be a thirty-page party-planning checklist.

"Go then. Make your getaway." She opened the Big Chill retro refrigerator and found a pitcher of lemonade, so she poured herself a tall glass. "It's for the best, because if you stick around, I might put your head on a spit for interfering with Mitch and me."

"Liar. I wouldn't have jumped in if the sparks firing between you hadn't burned me. Thank me for the push and be done with the ruse."

He knew her too well, yet it would take more than sparks to bridge the things separating her and Mitch.

"You don't understand, Logan." She gulped the lemonade to cool down. "It's complicated."

"You think *I* don't understand complicated relationships?" He crossed his arms, brows raised so high she couldn't miss the incredulous expression. Yes, dating Claire when she'd hated Peyton had been incredibly complicated.

"Fine. I don't want to argue. I need a hot shower." She walked around the island and kissed him on the cheek. "It's good to be home, and you are wonderful to have come to greet me."

"That's more like it." He hugged her. "I'm excited for the domestic launch next week. It'll be great to finally do an event together."

It would be a nice change of pace to have a partner with her who could talk about the project and answer questions. Logan had always been better with a crowd that way. She nodded and patted his shoulder, then grabbed her suitcase.

"Want me to carry it up for you?" Logan reached for it, but she waved him off.

"I've got it. If you don't leave before Mom and Dad show up, you'll get stuck coming with us."

Logan gave an exaggerated shudder and then a quick wave. "Ciao!"

Peyton rolled her suitcase through the kitchen and across the foyer's oak floors—where she used to play a form of hopscotch on its stained harlequin pattern—to the grand curved staircase. Step by step, she started up the stairs to the childhood bedroom she'd reclaimed after giving up her apartment in the city when she got sick. Usually she bounded up and down, passing the photos on the wall without a glance. Today her homecoming put her in a nostalgic mood as she ran her hand along the hand-carved mahogany banister smoothed by decades of use.

She passed the black-and-white photos of Duck. Her gaze then caught her grandparents' image, reminding her of the awful fights she'd overheard between her dad and his profligate father. Ugly times, but her dad had seized control of the assets and saved the house and family from public embarrassment. Logan had never quite appreciated how that decade had shaped and hardened their dad like forged iron, but Mitch would.

Continuing her journey, she smiled at the gorgeous picture of her parents on their Italian honeymoon, then came to a stop at a sweet image of her and her brother hanging out the window of the old tree house on the property. The site of many Lilac Lane League secret meetings and sleepovers. Innocent young girls who'd never envisioned the kinds of heartbreak awaiting them outside this gated estate.

Her smiling face, with its missing tooth, stared back at her from a lifetime ago. That girl—the queen bee who'd run around town breaking hearts, mapping out dreams, looking for the next wild adventure—was long gone.

Originally she'd planned a temporary return home for her reconstruction surgery and recovery. Yet weeks had slipped into months, and
the months then stacked and burned like logs on a bonfire. Working on
the memoir with Logan, reconnecting with Steffi and, to a lesser extent,
Claire, learning to meditate—all excuses that allowed her to wallow in
limbo. For all the writing and speaking about seizing the moment and
appreciating the little things, in truth she'd done very little of that. She'd
become complacent, as if hiding at Arcadia could keep her safe. Another
glance at the tree-house photo reminded her of how foolish that was.

As she rolled her suitcase along the long hallway and over the nee-
dlepoint carpet to her room, she recalled Mitch's lusty expression in that
bedroom in London. Her heart beat a little faster, urging her to embrace
a new and better life with her second chance. When she reached her
room, she set her bag aside and flopped onto her mattress to close her
eyes for five seconds and simply breathe.

An hour later, her mother burst into her bedroom, waking her from
an unintended deep sleep.

"Oh, honey, you know better than to fall asleep after returning
from Europe. You've got to stay up to shorten the jet lag. I'm sorry
we weren't here to greet you, but I'm swamped with last-minute party
details and your dad's driven up to Mystic to check on some issue with
that hotel." She waved her manicured, diamond-laden hands with a
look on her face that proved she'd yet to get excited about the six or so
seaside inns he'd folded into the real estate portfolio. "Now hurry up
and get dressed. Dad and I made reservations at Lucia's."

"Go without me." Peyton sat up, stretching with a generous yawn.
"I'm not up for dining out."

"Don't be silly." Her mother walked to the windows to draw open
the curtains. Rosy summer evening light glinted off her blonde hair,
which she'd pinned in a French twist. After straightening the folds of
the floor-length drapes into a neat accordion pattern, she smoothed her

gray pencil skirt. "You need to eat, and your father and I want to hear about the trip."

"Then let's get takeout. I don't feel like getting dressed after my long travel day. Can't we chill?"

"Chill?" Her mother rolled her eyes and strode to Peyton's closet, picking through a few things until she settled on a simple blue dress. She laid it on the bed. "You know your father hates takeout because the steam overcooks the food and makes it soggy."

"Then you two enjoy a romantic meal and bring me back some spaghetti carbonara. We can talk later."

"Why am I getting a sick feeling, like you're trying to avoid telling us about this trip? Did something happen? I knew it. I knew this memoir was a terrible idea. Everyone—*everyone*—will be picking over the details of your life like crows on a carcass. And those photographs . . ." Her mother slapped one hand to her forehead. "I could strangle your brother. But, honey, the good news is that in six months or so, people will move on to the next thing. This will be the one and only occasion we'll be praying that a Prescott work doesn't hit a list or win an award. You can stay here, where people will respect your privacy, for the next few months and then leave once you're no longer being talked about."

On the surface, those words sounded almost cruel, but the genuine relief on her mom's face told Peyton she had no idea how the statement might've hurt someone with thinner skin.

"Sorry to disappoint you, but nothing bad happened, Mom." Well, that Barcelona Bastard hadn't been pleasant, but nothing terrible had happened. All in all, the trip had been good for her. She couldn't suppress the smile that flickered when she thought about Square du Vert-Galant and London. "In fact, something quite special happened. Something that could be life-changing in a positive way."

As soon as she let that slip, she gave herself a mental kick.

Her mother's gaze sharpened as she played with the lustrous strand of Tahitian pearls around her neck. "Well, don't keep me in suspense. What's the good news?"

"I have a date for Logan's party." She gulped at the thought of how Mitch might respond to her family, this house, her friends.

Her mother looked over her shoulder as if she could see down the hallway, then whipped her head back toward Peyton. "Is there some *European* in one of the guest rooms? Oh, you are so like your great-grandfather, gallivanting around, foisting strangers on Arcadia like it's one of your dad's new inns."

"Settle down, Mom. There's no one here now. My publicist, Mitch Mathis, is coming up on Saturday for the party. I invited him to stay the night so he wouldn't face that long drive home at midnight."

Her mom dropped her chin with a sigh. "You and your brother assume it's so easy to rearrange table seating. And really . . . your publicist? He doesn't even know Claire and has no personal relationship with Logan, so what is *he* hoping to get out of this? Does he plan to share insider pictures in order to boost your sales?"

It wasn't that Peyton didn't understand her mother's paranoia. Throughout the years, they'd all had run-ins with users who were more interested in associating with a Prescott than actually befriending one. Still, the fact her mother made no room for the possibility that Mitch might care about Peyton stung.

Peyton sat upright on the bed now, hugging her knees while smiling beatifically to offset her sarcastic tone. "Why, yes, Mother, it is a nice surprise to have a date to my brother's engagement party. And, yes, he's very nice and quite handsome. Smart, hardworking, loyal. A great guy. I feel very lucky to have met him."

"Don't be cute." Her mom crossed her arms. "Honey, really. Is this a good idea? I've worked with plenty of PR people. Don't let him lead you down a merry path only to drop you once his goal is met."

Peyton scowled and tossed a bolster pillow at her mother. "Why would you say something that awful?"

Her mom caught the pillow before it rolled off the bed.

"Don't throw this! You'll crack the mother-of-pearl shells." She laid it aside and then sat beside Peyton and squeezed her hand. "I'm sorry. I'm not trying to hurt you. I want to protect you. You've been through so much with that Todd and the whole thing—"

"By 'thing' you mean *breast cancer*." Peyton watched her mother wince.

"Yes." Her mother closed her eyes. "I don't know why you delight in tormenting me. I'm your mother. You have no idea how terrifying it is when your child has a life-threatening disease. Why is it shocking that I don't like to talk about it?"

Peyton had no reply. She had never yearned for kids but now wondered if she would like them and if she'd be any good at motherhood, or would she bumble through awkwardly like her own mother—well intentioned but so often wrong?

Mitch would be a fabulous father, though. He'd already had more than a decade of practice.

"Peyton, I worry. This man—Mitchell—he needs to sell you and your book. His reputation depends on how well he does that. I think it's a mistake to take him at face value."

"He's not using me."

One of her mother's brows arced. "You said the same thing about Todd when I warned you not to risk your friendship over him."

Low blow, but an absolute truth. Now that her mom had ripped open that scab, another pit of self-doubt oozed. "I don't need reminders, thanks. But you'll have to trust me. Mitch is not Todd. And it's just a date."

Her mom shrugged and threw up her hands. "Have it your way. And don't worry. When it turns out badly, you can come cry to me and I promise I won't say 'I told you so.'"

Peyton fell backward and covered her face, shaking her head. Logan might be right about Mom, after all. "Can you please make room for him at the table? And go have dinner with Dad. I've lost my appetite."

"Stubborn as ever. Why couldn't the *cancer* change *that*?" Her mom leaned forward as if they'd just traded cookie recipes and kissed her on the forehead. "I'll bring you back the carbonara. And some garlic sticks. I know you love those. Now, don't fall asleep again or you'll be up all night."

She turned and left the room, leaving a trail of Joy Parfum's powdery scent in her wake.

Mitch and his mother walked beneath the canopy of electrical and telephone wires and across Madison Street to his mom's apartment after her postsurgical checkup. Katherine Brafman, his mother's longtime friend and neighbor, was sweeping the stoop of her adjacent building, one of many apartment buildings lining the urban street where he'd grown up.

Mrs. Brafman stopped and held the end of her broomstick. "Mitch, so nice to see you."

"Hi, Mrs. Brafman. Nice to see you, too."

"What did the doctor say, Janey?" she asked his mom.

"The eye looks good. The blurry vision is mostly cleared up, too." His mom fished around in her purse for her keys. "Looks like I'll be back at work soon."

Mitch wished he had a way to help his mother retire soon so she wouldn't have to stand on her feet all day as a grocery store cashier. She'd worked so many different jobs for so long; she deserved a chance to relax.

"I'll stop over later tonight for a visit. Sadie brought me a whole cheesecake for my birthday yesterday." She clucked. "I need help to finish it."

His mom turned and patted Mitch on the chest. "You know my Mitchell is a wonderful baker, too."

"A man of many talents." Mrs. Brafman smiled and then turned to go inside as Mitch uttered thanks for the compliment.

While his mom unlocked her own door, he glanced around the aging brick building. His dad had been so proud when he'd bought the family's first home. Not a castle, but condo ownership had represented a piece of the American dream. While Mitch had since paid for a few upgrades to his mom's kitchen and master bathroom, the unit looked very much like it had when he was young. Same old furniture. Same chipping brick exterior. Same scent of vanilla candles and cooking oil wafting throughout its rooms.

He turned on the lights and helped his mom remove the light jacket she wore everywhere in summer as protection from overly air-conditioned offices and restaurants. "I'll do a load of laundry and cook a lasagna to get you through tomorrow night. I'll be back to check on you Sunday. In fact, I'll treat you to dinner if you'd like."

She hung her purse on the coatrack by the door and settled onto his dad's old leather BarcaLounger. Her glasses sat with the television remote on the small table beside the chair, but she didn't reach for them. "You promised you'd stay and take care of me after my trabeculectomy."

When she tossed out the big vocabulary words, she meant business. His full name might come next.

Mitch closed the door and held his breath for three seconds before replying. "I've been here all week, Mom, commuting to the city. The doctor gave you high marks. You can manage for thirty-six hours at this point. I've loaded the fridge, so you won't need to go anywhere, lift anything heavy, or do anything else. I'll even wash your hair for you today if you want to make sure you don't get water in your eyes."

"You know I appreciate all the help. It's just that I'll miss your company, honey. Can't you stay tonight since the party isn't until tomorrow? Or come home tomorrow night after the party?"

"I need to address a few things at my place tonight, and I'd like to have a few drinks tomorrow night without worrying about that long drive." Nor did he want to miss an opportunity to curl up with Peyton again, even if it was as chaste as their night in London.

His mother sighed and reached for the TV remote. "Guess I'd better hope that there are some good movies on tonight."

Mitch moved aside a stack of quilting magazines from the coffee table before taking a seat in front of his mother. "Mom, you've been encouraging me to meet someone for ages. I'd think you'd be happy now that I have."

She wrinkled her nose. "What's wrong with Katherine's daughter, Sadie? She's a sweetheart. She lives around the corner, helps her mom . . . If you moved back here, or even to Jersey City, you two could take the ferry or the PATH in to work. She works as an assistant to some bigwig banker, you know. She's smart. Why can't you date her?"

He recalled Sadie as a cheerful girl, five years his junior. He'd never given her a second thought as a teen, and couldn't remember the last time he'd seen her. "I'm sure Sadie is a nice woman, but Peyton—"

"Peyton. What kind of name is that? I mean, I'm sure she's very interesting, but she's not our people. Can you imagine her living here in Hoboken? You guys would have to be all the way down by Fourteenth." She punctuated her comment about the tonier part of town with an eye roll.

"*I* don't live here in Hoboken."

"Don't remind me." She pulled his dad's fraying afghan across her bare legs.

Mitch stood with a heavy sigh. "Aren't you being a little ridiculous? You don't even know Peyton."

"I know enough. Don't get me wrong—I feel sorry for what she's gone through." She made the sign of the cross. "Her book is good, and she's doing a wonderful thing with this charity stuff. But she grew up in Connecticut with a giant silver spoon. What will she have in common with me or your sister? With you? Will her parents even approve of us? And even if none of that is a problem, I worry she's going to change you to be more like her. I like you the way you are now."

He smiled at the compliment and the passionate, if pained, voice of her mini tirade. "You're jumping way ahead. This is a date, not a wedding. But she's surprisingly unaffected. I think you might like her. She's a dreamer, like Dad."

His mom shook her head, her eyes growing misty. "I'll never see you. You'll work in the city and move up there, and the next thing I know you'll have a sailboat or something!"

He lifted a bottle of pills and looked at the label. "I think the meds are making you a little goofy." He chuckled, although he couldn't deny the momentary allure of sailing with Peyton on the Sound. "You're talking crazy. I'm not going anywhere."

"Mitchell, there's a reason for that saying 'A son is a son 'til he marries his wife.'"

"By that logic, you should never want me to marry."

"At least if you married Sadie, you'd be here in our neighborhood, and Katherine and I could babysit our grandkids together." With a harrumph, she turned on the television and squinted while scrolling through the program guide. She stopped on the Hallmark Channel.

Mitch stood and kissed the top of her head. "I'll go start the laundry and lasagna."

She grabbed his shirt. "I love you, honey. I want you to be happy. In my experience, people from different worlds don't last, no matter how exciting it seems in the beginning. And after how I grieved losing your dad, I can't stand to think of you suffering that way if she gets sick again."

The roughness in her voice came from a place of pain. Neither of them had quite learned to shake those feelings. Maybe that was why they'd been so close, while Lauren seemed almost an outsider at times with her barely there memories of their father. She hadn't soldiered through that battle with Mitch and their mom.

He patted her hand. "None of us knows how long anything will last. Cancer patients can survive, while healthy people get killed by cars. I don't know if this date will lead to more or not, but I can't plan my life around variables, either. Besides, if you could go back knowing Dad would get sick, would you not have married him?"

Her eyes flashed with shock and anger. "I *loved* him."

"Maybe I'll fall in love, too. I can't know if I don't try. All I can tell you is that this woman makes me feel alive with possibility in a way I don't know that I've ever felt."

His mother frowned, and he couldn't help but be sad that she'd soured something he'd been looking forward to all week.

A picture of Lauren's first birthday party caught his eye. His father, a handsome man with piercing, intelligent eyes, stared him down. Mitch would never forget those eyes. Even at his sickest, Mitch's father's gaze had implored Mitch to be the man of the house and take care of his mom and sister. He'd kept that promise for years, but maybe it was time to reset the boundaries and get Lauren to step up. Surely his dad would've wanted Mitch to find the kind of love that his parents had shared?

He rose from the table, picturing Peyton's smile as he made his way to the kitchen. Within twenty minutes, he'd assembled the layers of lasagna noodles, marinara sauce, sautéed meatloaf mixed with garlic and parsley, and ricotta and mozzarella and was placing the pan in the oven. Ninety minutes later, he'd washed and folded most of his mother's clothes. Once the lasagna had cooled a bit, he cut it into small portions and saved them in Tupperware for easy reheating.

His mom had fallen asleep during a rerun of *A Country Wedding*. He wanted to make his getaway before Katherine came by with that cheesecake but hated to wake his mom. When he removed the remote from her lap and turned off the television, the silence woke her.

"Sneaking off?" she mumbled.

"Mom." He sighed, counting to five in his head. "You have my number—for emergencies only. Otherwise, Lauren will stop over at some point tomorrow morning to check in on you."

"We'll see," she muttered with doubt, then raked her hands through her hair and scratched her scalp.

"I love you, Mom, but I've spent more than half my life working and taking care of you and Lauren. I'm not your husband—I'm your son—and it's time I start looking ahead to something exciting that's all mine. Haven't I earned that without you making me feel like I'm letting you down?"

When he finished, her eyes were wide and her chin quivered. "I didn't *choose* for your father to die. I'm sorry I needed help to raise your sister and pay the bills because I didn't have an education and fancy job, but that's what families do—they help each other. You always thought so, too, until now. Seems this Peyton is already changing you, just like I thought."

Chapter Fourteen

Mitch rolled the window down while driving the Ford Focus Zipcar through the stone-and-wood front gate of Arcadia House. His heart sped up like that of a teen girl about to meet the royal family at Buckingham Palace as he crossed the estate's threshold.

He slowed to five miles per hour so he wouldn't miss a single detail. The welcoming sound of pea stone grinding beneath his tires as he wound along the lengthy driveway prompted a smile. When he drew nearer to the home, breezes carried the scent of briny air through his open window. Lush green grass and hearty shrubs bursting with purple hydrangea made him conscious of how mind-numbing Manhattan's monochromatic cement jungle could be.

Arcadia House sprawled proudly across the lawn, its magnificent shingle-style construction highlighted by a gabled roofline, multiple chimneys, white trim, balustrades, and a portico. His family home could fit inside its four-car garage with room to spare.

A handful of delivery vans, catering trucks, and workers gathered along the side of the house like ants at a picnic, no doubt delivering flowers, linens, and food for the party. It wouldn't shock him if a movie director stepped out from behind a tree and told him where to stand. He imagined his dad smiling down at his kid being a guest at the home of one of America's literary greats.

He shut his mind to the maudlin thoughts that often accompanied memories of his dad. And while the estate impressed Mitch, seeing Peyton was the real reason he came. He missed her intelligent blue eyes and smart-aleck smile. The casual grace of her stride. The sincerity that shone through even when she had her guard up higher and thicker than the Great Wall of China.

After grabbing the bouquet he'd picked up in town minutes earlier, he stepped out of the car and retrieved his duffel bag and the container of pale-pink macarons he'd made for her family. A perfect batch—smooth, shiny shells and small even feet. He was locking the door—probably an unnecessary step considering where he was—when he heard Peyton call his name. He turned in time to see her skip down the steps from the front door.

Her sunstruck hair shimmered as it bounced around her face, the sight of which filled him with light and heat. "You made it."

Her happy smile allayed any lingering concerns that he was here because of Logan's machinations.

He welcomed her quick kiss hello but couldn't hold on to her because his hands were full. "The drive wasn't too bad."

She made grabby hands for the flowers. "For me?"

He handed her the bouquet of pink gerbera daisies, orange lilies, yellow santini chrysanthemums—fresh and unpretentious, like her.

"I love them, thank you." She dipped her nose into the velvety heads, which looked beautiful next to her yellow shift dress, then nodded toward the container. "What's in there?"

"I made macarons for your mother for allowing me to be a last-minute addition." If life had taught him anything, it was that mothers never minded being remembered.

She clucked. "You're very wise, and I can't wait to try one of your signature treats. Now come on and I'll show you around."

A light breeze tousled her hair as she grabbed his sleeve and tugged him toward the front door.

"I'm probably not the first to say this, but your home looks like a movie set." His gaze drifted from the massive white door to sunlight glinting off the home's many windows.

"Let's just hope it doesn't turn into a horror flick tonight." She flashed a cheeky smile.

He came to a stop at the base of the front steps. "Is that typical of Prescott parties?"

"I guess you'll be the judge after you meet my crazy family. A closer look at my gene pool might convince you to catch the midnight train."

"They can't be that bad. They made you, after all."

"Ooh, pretty smooth, mister." She grinned before opening the door. "Let's stash your bag in my room first, then I'll give you the tour and introduce you."

"Sounds good." He stepped inside and then stopped again in the entry while he worked his way out of being awestruck. It smelled of hardwood and lemon oil and time and money. A stately residence filled with history and secrets. He could almost hear William Prescott's ghost pacing the hallways—floorboards squeaking—while reading his drafts aloud.

From the entry, he could see straight through a great room at the back of the house to a double set of french doors that presumably led to a patio and the sea beyond. To his left lay a formal reception room with a massive marble fireplace at the far end. A glass door beside the hearth appeared to lead to a paneled room that he couldn't see well. To his right, he surveyed an immense dining room with a door that also led elsewhere—perhaps a butler's pantry.

Peyton pointed straight ahead, then moved her finger clockwise. "Casual living area, dining room, parlor, and behind there is my dad's office, where we'll go later." Peyton then pointed up the curved staircase. "This way for now."

He readjusted his overnight bag on his shoulder and followed her up the stairs, zooming past the family pictures he would like to see. The second-floor hallway ran in two directions, like carpeted bowling alleys flanked by many doors. He followed her to the left.

She led him into a spacious, airy room with many windows, white beadboard wainscot, and cornflower-blue walls. A large window seat stuffed with bolster pillows offered a prime view of the Sound. Her room even had its own brick fireplace—painted white—at one end, and a bathroom en suite.

He set his bag and the cookies on the window seat's cushion and stared at the glittering sea. Nothing like the view of traffic and telephone poles on Madison Street, making it tough to shake his mother's voice from his head. Having lived this platinum-spoon life, perhaps Peyton couldn't be satisfied with less for long. "You woke up to this every day as a kid?"

"I'm lucky, I know. I didn't realize it as much at the time. This is what I knew—my normal. Don't be fooled, though. Life here wasn't as perfect as it seems."

"Or maybe your expectations of life are too high." He closed his eyes, wishing he hadn't voiced that.

She chuckled as if he'd been joking. "Anything's possible."

Rather than apologize and make a bigger deal out of what he'd said, he turned and glanced at her queen-size bed. In nanoseconds he imagined being wrapped up with her in its blue-and-white-checked quilt. First he had to endure the party.

She grasped his hand and he held fast. "Quick tour and then we'll get a vase for these flowers. My mother is either in the kitchen or out on the patio orchestrating everything."

"I don't want to disturb her."

"Don't worry. She'll brush us off in a matter of minutes, but we'll say a quick hello. My father keeps the good bourbon in his office—another reason that'll be our last stop." With a wink, she gestured toward the door.

He grabbed the cookies and followed her lead. "Whatever you want."

"Funny how that always works for me." She laughed.

They buzzed through the house at a dizzying pace, pausing briefly in the different rooms on their way to the kitchen, which was substantial and charmingly preserved in the period of the house despite its modern conveniences. Four chefs from All In Good Taste were already chopping, toasting, and roasting. He detected hints of rosemary, lemon, and sherry in the mix. In another life, he might've liked life as a pastry chef.

Through the windows, movement on the patio caught his eye. Dreamy white gauze curtains were blowing in the breeze. The disparity with which they lived their lives nearly made him laugh at the same time he had to tamp down some envy. He would love to treat his own family to something so grand.

Peyton stood in the center of the kitchen, arranging her flowers in a vase she pulled from a cabinet. When she finished, she spun on her heel, arms gesturing about. "My mom treated this affair like a small wedding, but it will be beautiful. The tent alone is worth the effort."

"But it isn't calling for rain."

"What she got wouldn't do squat in the rain. It's all about ambiance. Romantic, open—flowy." She pointed toward the door. "Let's go introduce you. She'll be nicest in front of strangers."

Peyton winked, but he wondered if there wasn't some truth to her remark. His own mother had complained that Peyton wasn't "their kind," so he couldn't begrudge Peyton's mother if she harbored similar doubts about him.

They walked out to the flagstone patio, where a long table was being set. Florists wearing red collared pullovers embellished with a "Smell the Roses" emblem were arranging fistfuls of white roses, hydrangea, and pale-pink peonies on a bed of willow that spilled across its length. He'd attended fancy parties in his career, but that spectacular centerpiece was made more resplendent by the crystal candelabras placed at every third chair. Some lady counted out square gold chargers, while another was doing something fancy with napkins. Mitch noted stacks of china and rows of stemware as well.

Mrs. Prescott looked up and then snapped a polite smile on her face. Dignified and elegant—like Peyton might look in twenty-five years if she didn't laugh enough between now and then—the woman bore a confidence that comes from being in charge. "You must be Mitchell."

"Yes. It's nice to meet you, Mrs. Prescott." Mitch returned her polite smile and extended the box of macarons. "Thank you for making room for me at the last minute. I hope it wasn't too much of an imposition."

She peeked inside, her expression inscrutable. "These look delicious, thank you. And please, call me Darla. Mrs. Prescott makes me feel old." Another smile, but not quite warm enough to dispel his awkward feelings about crashing her party. "Peyton speaks very highly of you. It sounds like you two had quite the trip."

"We did. Worked out all the kinks before our big event this coming week. I assume you and your husband will be at the Strand on Wednesday?"

"We'll see." A placating smile this time, accompanied by a shrug. "I'm sure Peyton has confided that I'm struggling with this memoir. I prefer to keep personal things private, not share them with the world."

"Mother." Peyton bugged her eyes.

"Should I lie?" Darla then turned to him. "Wouldn't you prefer I be honest with you?"

"Always." There was something refreshing in knowing where one stood, even if one stood under the heel of a woman like Darla Prescott.

Darla turned a self-satisfied expression on Peyton. "Now, let me go put these in the kitchen and then get back to making sure everything is set exactly as I asked. I swear, no matter how specific my instructions, the only way anything gets done correctly is if I manage it myself."

It unsettled him that he felt the same.

"We won't keep you." He tipped forward in a half bow, convinced she had no appreciation of the skill and time it had taken to make that gift. "Thanks again for having me."

She smiled and strolled inside, closing the door behind her as if to warn them not to follow.

Peyton looped her arm through his. "I'm sorry if my mother offended you. She's private. Well, sort of private. She loves to go public with good news—like this engagement."

"Don't let her get in your head. You did something extraordinary under trying conditions. It deserves to be shared and celebrated."

"Thank you." She touched her head to his shoulder for a moment. "I hope you don't end up sorry you came."

"How could I? I came to be with you." He looked into the eyes he'd hungered to see all week and wrapped an arm around her waist to keep her close. "All of the rest is unimportant."

She gazed at him, one hand on his chest, reminding him of that kiss on the terrace in London. Of course, she was sober now, which made the tender gesture better.

With her head tipped to the right, she said, "Let's make a pact to take a break from all work-related topics tonight and simply be Mitch and Peyton on a date in a natural environment."

"Sounds perfect." He meant that, although this was far from any natural environment he'd ever known.

"Are you ready to meet my dad?"

Mitch had done some research into the impressive business icon she called "Dad." "I wouldn't mind a bourbon."

"More proof of how smart you are."

They slipped through the house to the parlor, where Peyton knocked on the glass door beside the hearth. When she heard her dad's muffled

"Come in," she opened it. "Hey, Dad. Can you take a ten-minute break to meet my friend Mitchell?"

Mr. Prescott shut his laptop before standing and coming around the antique writing desk in the center of the stunning walnut-paneled office. Mitch kept his focus on Peyton's dad, although he would rather have inspected every book, award, and photograph in this hallowed room. The great William Herbert Prescott had written at that desk— yet Peyton had probably played in this space as if it were no big deal. "Mr. Prescott, very nice to meet you."

"Call me Harrison, please." He gave the firm handshake you'd expect of a guy who'd been born to money. Looked the part, too, with a bespoke shirt and tailored slacks, a full head of hair, and a strong jawline.

"I thought we'd break into your stash." Peyton nodded toward an antique beverage cart carrying a bottle of Michter's.

"The broken seal suggests you or Logan already have." Harrison shot her a knowing look before he checked his watch. "Guess I won't be getting much more done today, though. I've been hiding from your mother. You know how she gets right before an event."

"Unfortunately, yes." She made a wry face. "Mitch got a firsthand view of Mom in action."

Mitch darted a gaze between them both, a bit confused. "She seemed calm to me."

"She'll spare others the minutia, but if I go out there, I'll hear a litany of complaints. I wouldn't mind, but when I offer help, she never takes my suggestions." Harrison gestured toward the two worn leather chairs as he made his way to the bar cart. "Have a seat. I'll pour."

A minute later, he handed Mitch a tumbler with a three-finger pour. Mitch sipped it. Even his unsophisticated palate detected rich toffee undertones. "That's nice."

"I have my sources." Harrison tossed back a healthy swallow. With a pleased sigh, he asked, "So how are the European book sales going?"

Down to business. Mitch could respect that, although Peyton wouldn't enjoy the conversation. "Robust, although a hair shy of what was needed to hit any of the major European lists. But we're building great buzz here, and preorders are trending up. If we can hit the *New York Times*, we could see a bump abroad, too."

He stopped himself from going into more detail because he wanted to respect Peyton's wishes.

"You get paid no matter what happens, though, right?" Harrison's even tone almost hid the subtle hint of disdain.

Mitch's stomach tightened. "Yes."

"Pretty good gig there, like all my lawyers. Even when my deals implode, they get a fat check." Harrison took another swig, leaving Mitch uncertain about whether he'd been hit with a dig or a compliment.

"Literary PR's a bit of hustle and a bit of art—knowing how to position something as subjective as a book," Mitch said. "It's impossible to predict which debut authors will break out. In Peyton's case, however, we have a lot going for us. Accessible writing, powerful imagery, your family name—especially here in the US—and the charitable endeavor. We're leveraging all of the pluses and partnering with the foundation's PR team to cross-promote the launch. Peyton got comfortable in her role as author by the time we reached London. I think she'll hit a grand slam next week in the city."

Harrison winked at his daughter before finishing his drink. He smoothed his hand over the desk, then looked at Mitch. "Is your father in publishing, or are you like my son, off doing your own thing?"

"Dad—" Peyton interjected, but Mitch laid his hand on her chair to cut her off.

He shifted in his seat, feeling the weight of her gaze on him. "My father passed away when I was in high school."

"Oh. I'm sorry." Harrison looked genuinely uncomfortable. "That must've been difficult."

"It was. I missed him, of course. But, as Peyton might say, the silver lining was what I learned about responsibility. I doubt I'd own my own business now if my dad were still around and I'd enjoyed normal teenage freedoms and security."

"Well, that's something we have in common. My father lived longer, but he wasn't any kind of role model. Like you, I had to step in to keep all of this in the family."

"Daddy." Peyton squirmed, apparently uninterested in hearing a story she must've heard a hundred times.

Mitch had gleaned a lot from what he'd read about the Prescotts when he'd researched Peyton months ago. "Peyton and I were just talking about how no family is perfect."

"Cheers to that." Harrison raised his glass. "Now if we could get Logan to accept that so he doesn't end up disappointed in his marriage down the road."

"What are you talking about?" Peyton scowled as her hand came down hard on the arm of the chair.

"Nothing specific, but marriage isn't all romance and candles. It takes commitment and compromise, two things your brother has spent most of his life avoiding while chasing his art." Harrison raised a single brow as if it alone could defend any argument she might raise.

"I thought you two had come to respect each other more this year, Dad. If you can't be more supportive of him than this, maybe you should stay in this office tonight." Peyton set her empty glass on the table. "Not to mention how wrong you are about him. He's shown nothing but commitment and sacrifice for me since my diagnosis. And he's been blissfully happy with Claire despite making compromises for her, too. You shouldn't talk about him that way in front of someone you just met, either. Now I have to wonder what you say about me behind my back."

"Settle down, sweetheart. I don't mean anything by it. We were talking about imperfect families. It seemed relevant." He shot Mitch a look as if asking for some help, but Mitch wouldn't side with him against his daughter, especially not when he agreed with Peyton. "You know I adore Claire, but I worry about her holding your brother's attention for life. Nothing ever has before. Even *he* crows about his restless need to seek new stories."

"Logan's more at peace than he's ever been. I wish you could be happy for him instead of always picking him apart." Peyton stood, head shaking, and motioned for Mitch. "Mitch and I are going into town for an hour or so. I hope your attitude is better when we return. I swear, if you make one wisecrack tonight, I *will* find a way to make you pay."

Harrison didn't look perturbed. If anything, he looked proud of the spitfire who carried his genes. "Well, Mitchell, guess you can see what happens when you cross my beauty. Better be on your toes around this one."

Again, Mitch couldn't tell whether the man had praised or slammed his daughter. He polished off the last drops of bourbon. "I'll keep that in mind, sir. See you later."

They closed the office door behind them and then went out to the Zipcar.

Peyton grabbed her hair while making a strangled sound. "I don't even know what to say. I promise, Logan and I are not as freakish as our parents. They aren't always like this, either. Sometimes they're even kind of nice."

Mitch laughed. "Don't worry. If you ever meet my family, you won't think yours is so odd."

"If?" she repeated quietly while waiting for him to open the car door.

"Did I say 'if'?" He let her adjust her skirt so it wouldn't get caught in the door. "I meant 'when.'"

"Better."

He slipped behind the wheel. "So where to?"

"I need to stop to pick up a special gift I had made."

He snapped his gaze to her. "I thought you said no gifts."

"Don't panic. The invitation said no gifts. This is a small thing I did on the sly. I found some old photos that I had enlarged. When we get home, I'm going to slip them into a special album I bought. Claire likes keepsakes."

"You don't give up on that friendship, do you? It can't be easy to face your regrets and her rejection, but you keep at it. It's impressive."

"You're sweet to say so, but we both know I did something unfor-givable. I don't expect much. All I can do is keep hoping." She sighed, and he was happy to drop any subject that touched on her memories of Todd. "Anyhow, after we grab the pictures, I'll show you my favorite places. You'll like A Novel Idea. It's a combination bookstore, bakery, and gift shop. It's old and creaky, and the employees handwrite little reviews of the books and post them everywhere."

The outskirts of the small business district were coming into view—a collection of two- and three-story offices, restaurants, and retail outlets situated around a town green. Americana at its nostalgic best. "Why not do an event there?"

"No thanks. It's one thing to be in front of a roomful of strang-ers, but nothing will get me to stand in front of old teachers, ex-rivals, and other townsfolk who know me to discuss those photos or my own words. Now, no more business talk."

"Oh, right. Sorry. Bad habit." He hadn't realized how easily he lapsed into talking about work. Had he lost the art of conversation because his career had been his primary focus for so long? As he looked for a parking spot, he couldn't quite shake Harrison's wariness of Logan and Claire's opposites-attract relationship, which made *his* mother's warning harder to dismiss.

He glanced across the car at Peyton, who met his gaze with a smile. She looked happy and healthy and full of promise.

"I'm happy you're here." She ruffled his hair, melting the tension that had bunched up his shoulders.

Their parents knew nothing. If he could keep her smiling that way, everything would work out fine.

Chapter Fifteen

Twilight gasped its last breath before starlight and the golden sliver of the moon consumed the sky. Mitch was sitting beside Peyton. She doubted he noticed himself softly humming along to Cole Porter's "Let's Do It, Let's Fall in Love," which played in the background, thanks to the outdoor speakers her dad had installed a decade ago, but it made her smile.

She sat back to make room for the caterers to clear the dinner plates—which had been licked clean of the seared scallops with brown butter–and–lemon pan sauce—and to refill water and wineglasses.

Across the table, Peyton's mother spoke with Mrs. McKenna, no doubt about wedding plans. Logan was whispering something in Claire's ear, while her dad spoke with Mr. McKenna and Steffi's dad, Mr. Lockwood. To her left, Steffi laughed at something her brother must've said to her and Ryan. Farther down the table were other more distant friends and family, including Claire's beloved, if kooky, book group.

"I think it's time," Peyton murmured to Mitch, stomach tightening. Some might have advised her to hide in the shadows tonight rather than stand in the spotlight. "Wish me luck."

He rested a hand on her thigh with a smile. "You don't need luck. It's a beautiful gesture."

She pushed back her chair and stood, tapping a dessert fork against her wineglass. "Excuse me, everyone, but I don't want the night to pass without making time for a little surprise."

Wide-eyed gazes turned toward her, but she'd become numb to scrutiny after so many readings and interviews. She set her glass down and walked toward the far side of the patio, where she'd hidden a bag with the white silk-and-lace photo album she'd assembled.

When she returned to the table, she stood behind Claire and Logan to address all the guests. "I know we were under strict orders from my mother and the happy couple not to bring any gifts. But given how well everyone here knows me, I'm sure none of you expected *me* to follow the rules."

A ripple of chuckles fanned throughout the crowd. She glanced at Mitch, who nodded encouragingly.

"The first time I met Claire was at a sleepover Steffi had planned to welcome her to Lilac Lane. By morning, we had all become fast friends the way preteens do. Throughout the years, we spent many hours here at Arcadia. However, even back in the beginning, I knew—as did most everyone else—that *I* wasn't the only draw for Claire."

Logan winked at Claire and threw an arm around her shoulders. As usual, she blushed as others smiled at them and threw in a few "awwws" for good measure.

Peyton continued her speech. "Several weeks ago, Logan took me to look at some rings he'd been considering while working up to the proposal. To see him so excited and in love, so full of joy, and to know that a woman I've always loved and admired would be the person who'd share the rest of his days with him"—she paused to clear the tightness from her throat—"I can't describe what a gift that is. When I got home from Europe, I went to the attic—as one does when bored—to pick through the boxes of junk I'd stored up there from when I was young. Most of it was old journals and awards that would bore most everyone but me, but I also found a trove of photographs, including some of Claire and Logan." She handed the gift to Claire, whose hands trembled.

Peyton then looked at Steffi and Ryan, Steffi's brother Benny, and the McKennas. "None of us will be surprised to see that, whether on the dock or in my room or out in the tree house, whenever Logan joined us, Claire's cheeks glowed pink and her eyes shone. But what might surprise you is a pattern that I *hadn't* noticed before." She rested her hand on her brother's shoulder. "When you thumb through these images, you'll see Logan was often sitting near Claire, his smile in action, even when he was holding court with the rest of the group."

Logan shrugged. "I've always had an eye for beauty, what can I say?"

More "awwws" followed, so Peyton used that moment to return to her side of the table. "I thought you two would enjoy proof of your early mutual affection. I put it in the album hoping you might add pages as you build your life together."

"Thank you, Peyton." Claire opened the cover and started scanning the images, a smile spreading across her face.

Peyton raised her glass. "Duck would find the perfect words for this occasion. All I know is that, with life so fragile, we're all blessed to be here tonight, and to learn from these two how love can overcome all barriers and bring out the very best in anyone. To Logan and Claire— may you keep the feelings you have for each other today close at hand, and never take one precious moment together for granted. I love you both. Cheers!"

"Cheers!" Steffi chimed in and others followed.

Peyton took her seat after swigging some wine.

Claire whispered something to Logan, who then spoke with a voice roughened by emotion. "This is a beautiful gift, Peyton. As usual, I love that you never follow the rules, and hope that never changes."

A round of laughter followed his little joke, dispelling the sentimental ache taking up space in Peyton's chest and restoring the evening to its previous conviviality.

Mitch leaned close. "All that public speaking in Europe paid off."

"Good. I'd rather it pay off here than anywhere else." While the waitstaff began setting white-peach tarts on the table and pouring coffee, Peyton watched Claire and Logan pore over the pages she'd put together. "I think Claire likes it."

"I'm sure she does." Mitch held her hand beneath the table, turning Peyton's attention away from her continual effort to win Claire over.

His thumb stroked her palm, shooting tingles up her arm. She looked into his intent eyes, which appeared softer and dreamier tonight. Her chest filled with such warmth it made her yearn for more than a casual fling. Could she trust her heart this time?

Mrs. McKenna said, "Well, don't hog the album. Pass it around!"

Peyton's mom interrupted. "This seems like the perfect time to play a little game."

Logan groaned. "Game?"

"The Nearlywed Game." She made eye contact with one of the waitstaff, then made some hand gesture he apparently understood. "Now don't fuss, Logan. You know I don't enjoy inane games, but we had to do at least one activity to mark this as something other than a dinner party."

Peyton covered her mouth for a second, stunned. Her mother never did anything like this, not even when she'd thrown children's birthday parties.

"My family loves games." Claire beamed. "How do we play?"

The caterer returned with two book-size whiteboards and markers, then handed them to Claire and Logan.

"We all take turns asking the couple a question, and each of them has to answer *for the other* on the whiteboard. Then they'll share those answers and we'll see how well they know each other." Darla smiled at everyone.

Oooh. It felt a little like a trap to Peyton, but Claire smiled with confidence.

Logan downed a large swallow of coffee before grabbing the marker. "Best be on my toes."

"I'll start," their mom said. "Logan, if Claire were being served her last meal, what would she order?"

Logan barked a laugh and wrote his answer lickety-split. Claire tried to peek, but he turned his back to her. "No cheating. You know I need to win."

"Okay, Claire . . . what would you order?" Darla asked.

"Be honest," Logan warned Claire before she spoke.

She wrinkled her nose, then covered her eyes for a second, mumbling, "Something from the candy aisle at any grocery store."

Peyton's mother's eyes registered surprise, but those who knew Claire better nodded and chuckled. "Logan, let's see your board."

He turned it around wearing a cheshire grin. It read "The Sugar Factory's inventory."

Steffi broke in. "I don't know . . . I think you ought to be more specific. Reese's or brownies with walnuts top the list."

"I think Logan got close enough." Peyton clapped, thinking he got a softball question. She then leaned toward Mitch. "What's yours?"

He tapped his chin. "I'm not sure, but I can guess yours."

"Can you?" That caused an irrational bloom of pleasure to fill her lungs.

"That amatriciana in Rome."

She squeezed his hand. "Good answer!"

Steffi called out, "My turn, my turn!"

Darla sat and nodded, so Steffi turned to Claire. "Which of your physical attributes does Logan like best?"

"I know this!" Claire smiled while writing her guess.

"Too easy," Logan acknowledged.

"Okay, Logan, let's see if it's as easy as you think," Steffi challenged.

"Her eyes, of course. Beautiful, kind, and full of emotion." He kissed Claire's nose.

Claire reversed the board, which confirmed Logan's response.

"Want to know one of my favorite things about you?" Mitch whispered.

A little shiver went through Peyton, mostly because she still didn't quite like or trust her body these days. "Sure."

"Your calves."

"What?" She laughed.

"I've been obsessed with them from the beginning." He reached down and traced a finger along the back of one, sending a flurry of sparks up her legs.

Her heart beat faster from his touch and seeing him loosen up. "I like you buzzed on bourbon and wine."

He raised his wineglass at her before downing its contents. The irreverent yet intense way he looked at her now made every part of her body shiver with anticipation.

"My turn." Mrs. McKenna joined the game. "And this is an important question."

Everyone fell silent because of her solemn tone. "Claire, how many babies does Logan want?"

"Whoa!" barked Benny. "That didn't take long."

While everyone else laughed, Peyton reached down to place her hand above her angel tattoo.

Mitch whispered, "You're frowning."

Peyton forced a smile at the same time Claire twisted her lips in thought and wrote down an answer.

"Logan?" Mrs. McKenna asked.

He'd been drumming the table with his fingers, so he rolled his hand over with a shrug. "Four, maybe five."

Everyone gasped. Even Claire's eyes bulged as if his hair had changed color.

"Claire, you'd better get cracking soon so you and Steffi can commiserate," Ryan teased, before Steffi smacked him in the chest.

Claire and Peyton both stared at their friend while blurting some version of "Are you pregnant?"

Steffi elbowed her husband before conceding. "We weren't planning to say anything until tomorrow. This is *your* celebration." She gestured to Claire.

"Sorry." Ryan grimaced. "I forgot no one knew. Too much wine."

But Claire was all smiles. "This is happy news. I'm glad it came out tonight." She then looked at Logan and revealed her board, which read "two." "I love you . . . but five?"

"I'm sure we can find a compromise, as long as we keep practicing."

"Logan." Their mom rolled her eyes.

Peyton knew she should feel nothing but joy for her friends. She did, mostly. But being fun Aunt Peyton seemed like a distant second place, assuming she'd even be around to watch Logan's children grow.

"Oh, Darla, won't it be wonderful to have little grandchildren soon?" Mrs. McKenna's voice vibrated with glee.

Peyton closed her eyes when Mitch leaned close, half expecting him to continue playing his private version of the game with her. If he, like Logan, wanted a big family, it'd be yet another thing she might not be able to give him, even if she got the all clear to try after another year or two cancer-free.

"Are you feeling okay?" Mitch asked.

"Mm-hm," she lied. "But I'll be right back . . ."

Peyton wanted to slip away without being noticed, but her chair scraped against the stone, drawing Logan's attention. He knew. She saw it in the apology in his eyes. That made it worse because the very last thing she wanted was to cause him any regret or guilt about looking forward to his future.

"Peyton?" her mom called.

"Carry on!" Peyton didn't look back when she waved a hand in the air. "I'll be right back."

—ᴧᴧ—

Peyton had been missing for a while—her dessert untouched—yet no one but Mitch seemed concerned. He was standing on the outskirts of the crowd, staring across the lawn at the water, when Claire approached him from behind, her mahogany cane in tow. Her diminutive size belied the strength it must've taken to rebuild her life after the gunshot wound that permanently injured her hip, and to have forgiven Peyton enough to be planning a life with Logan.

"How are you enjoying your first Prescott party?" When Claire smiled, he understood why Logan loved her blue eyes.

"It's like something from a movie." He reached up and fingered part of the gauzy drape blowing in the breeze. "Very different from my normal life."

Her gaze swept from the tableful of flowers to the sea. "It can be quite intoxicating."

"Just like Peyton." He grinned at the sudden mental image of Peyton's smile.

Claire's bright eyes flickered with the barest hint of pain. "Yes, she can be that, although that's not always been a good thing for others."

"Or for her, from what I've heard." He trod lightly, but she'd opened the door. Maybe he could learn something that would help Peyton.

"This is true." Claire bit her lip. "So she's told you about Todd?"

"Only enough to express her regret about how she hurt you and ruined your friendship."

"Ah." Claire remained collected, her expression serene. "Well, life goes on and we all adjust the best we can."

He crossed his arms without saying much.

"You disagree?" Claire studied him like she was searching for Waldo in one of those busy drawings.

Obviously his expression had betrayed his thoughts. "Well, you make it sound static—like you get to a point and then decide, boom, that it's 'the best' it can be."

She glanced at her cane. "Sometimes we have to accept limitations."

"As long as we don't resign ourselves to saying we've done our best when the truth is that we're unwilling to risk going that extra step."

Judging by the flat set of her mouth, he might've said too much. He glanced over his shoulder toward the door Logan had gone through to check on his sister. Mitch wished they'd both come back to the party before he made things even worse for Peyton.

"Wondering what's keeping them?"

"Hm?" He returned his attention to Claire.

"Logan and Peyton?"

He hadn't heard the first part of her question, so he still didn't know what to say.

"They often get absorbed in their own little world. I'm an only child, so I can't quite relate to their relationship, but I think their special bond formed young because their parents were often embroiled in other things. This past year in particular, Logan's been desperate to help Peyton get her life back on track."

Mitch nodded. "She's been through a lot."

"She has, so I give lots of room to their relationship. If you have a serious interest in Peyton, you'll have to make room for Logan, too."

"Sounds crowded." Mitch finished the wine in his glass.

Claire smiled coyly. "Perhaps if she finds someone she can count on as much as Logan, she won't rely on him as much. I think he'd relax if he believed she was in good hands."

"It almost sounds like you're proposing an alliance." Mitch grinned.

"Ha!" She laughed. "Maybe that's not a bad idea, but I'd only consider it if you're a good guy. Are you . . . a good guy?"

"I think so." Despite her display of aloofness, her question told him she cared about what happened to Peyton. "Enough about me. Let's talk about the party. Did you like the photo album? I was with Peyton when she picked it up."

"It's beautiful—a very touching gesture. She's been full of them this past year." Claire hugged herself against the breeze. "I know she wants our old friendship back, but it can't be what it was."

"I think she knows you can't go back, like she knows she can't go back to who she was before cancer. But couldn't a new friendship end up stronger and more honest *because* of the pain you've worked through?"

Claire didn't get to answer, because Logan and Peyton returned to the party, at which point Logan tugged Claire to his side.

"I'm sorry. Didn't mean to be a party pooper," Peyton said to Claire. She turned to Mitch. "Or to leave you stranded."

"It's fine. Claire kept me company." He smiled at Claire, certain he'd made headway with his last remark.

"That makes you the lucky winner." Logan then kissed Claire's head. "But now I'm going to steal my girl back and start making our goodbyes so we can continue our celebration in private."

Claire elbowed him, but her smile suggested that she was as eager as Logan to put his plan in motion. He hugged Peyton goodbye and shook Mitch's hand.

Before they wandered away, Claire said, "Peyton, I really appreciate the thought behind the album. I look forward to filling it up, starting with pictures from this party."

Peyton's smile knocked Mitch's heart sideways like always. "I'm glad."

Claire nodded and then followed Logan toward their parents.

As soon as they were far enough away, Peyton whirled around on him, eyes narrowing. "Did you say something to Claire?"

"We were just talking."

"About what?"

"Life." He shrugged, eager to avoid getting into the details. A few couples were dancing at the end of the patio. "Should we dance, or take a walk?" Mitch gestured toward the dock that stretched into the Sound like a pointer finger.

"Maybe we should visit with Steffi, Ryan, and Ben. We didn't get much opportunity before dinner."

He'd be happy to get to know her friends some other time, but like Logan, he'd had enough of the group and wanted some time alone with Peyton. "If that's what you'd rather . . ."

She bit her lip, gaze zooming from the guests to the sea and back.

"I suppose no one would miss us for a while." She held his hand and followed him down the lawn.

They made their way to the built-in bench of the sturdy wooden dock. Water lapped against the pilings, the sea's surface reflecting diffused light from the house and the moon.

"Be honest, what did Claire say to you?" Peyton prodded.

He thought about the conversation and chose something that might cheer her up. "She was sizing me up to see if I'm good enough for you."

"Ha!" Peyton playfully slapped his chest. "She doesn't care enough to do that."

"I'm telling the truth. She wanted to know if I was a good guy, and she told me that, if we got serious, I'd need to make plenty of room for Logan in our life." Then he took a lesson from Logan's playbook and pulled her against his side. "I want you to know that *I* didn't follow you inside earlier because I thought you wanted to be alone. When Logan went after you, I wondered if maybe I thought wrong."

"I didn't mean to overreact, but the baby stuff blindsided me. I left the table because I didn't want to spoil everyone's excitement." She stared at the horizon. "Every time I think I've gotten past selfishness or envy, I catch myself reverting to old behavior."

Her hair blew about her face, so he tucked it behind her ear. "It's not selfish to feel sad or scared when you don't know what your future holds."

"It feels selfish when it interferes with my happiness for the people I love. And I do love Steffi, and Logan and Claire. I want them to have beautiful, healthy babies."

"I'm sure they know that, Peyton. You're very hard on yourself—expecting to be superhuman and never feel envy or grief."

She looked away. "Guess I'm a work in progress."

"Like the rest of us."

She shrugged, heaving a heavy sigh. "So did the party meet your expectations? Did you like my friends?"

"Everyone is very nice. Even your parents weren't as scary as you painted them. It must've been idyllic growing up in such a close-knit community."

"Yes, although it didn't prepare me well for the real world . . . or for hardship. Maybe that's why I'm struggling to figure out what comes next for me."

"For starters, you could stop putting yourself down. You fought a hard battle. You've written an acclaimed book. And now you've won the affection of this *amazing* guy who's really into you . . ." He chuckled, hoping to make her smile.

Instead, she looked him dead in the eye. "Are you? And don't answer too fast, Mitch. Starting any relationship is sort of terrifying to me, so please be honest."

The vulnerability in her expression made her more beautiful. He held her face in his hands so she couldn't avoid his gaze. "I've broken all of my rules to be here with you because I want to see where this could lead. To test whether our differences can bring out the best in each other. Or if we can reach a point where you'll turn to me when you're upset instead of your brother."

"Even though you know my . . . situation?"

Presumably she meant her uncertain health, although she never brought that up with him. He dropped his hands and squeezed hers. "*You* don't even 'know' your situation."

"But let's say this thing between us grows. I know I'm facing years of tests and can't even think about starting a family for a while, if ever. You seem like a guy who wants to be a dad."

He sat back, giving her point its due respect. "I've already been like a father for most of my life, so it isn't something I daydream about. For now, my baby is List Launch. If, someday, kids come into the picture, I'd welcome them, but I'm not yearning for them. And if I ever do, there are many ways to create a family and lots of kids who need a home. But why jump way ahead already? I could've sworn you spent the last several weeks preaching about living in the moment. Did we switch roles somewhere over the Atlantic?"

She acknowledged his point with a half-hearted smile. "I guess maybe part of me wants something steady to cling to right now because everything else feels unsettled."

"Who could be more steady than Optimus?"

"That's true." A grin lit her face before she threw herself into his arms and held tight.

He closed his eyes and let his breath rise and fall with the rhythm of the gentle waves rolling onto the shore a dozen yards away. Peyton was usually so strong that he could dismiss the fear she still lived with and would continue to feel for some time. He wouldn't allow his own thoughts to go to those dark places tonight.

Under the tent of a night sky strung with twinkling starlight, he put his faith in a fairy-tale ending.

Chapter Sixteen

"Well, that went well, didn't it?" Peyton's mother asked when she returned to the patio after seeing the last guests out.

"Very well done, dear," her dad replied, sipping another bourbon. "Now we can relax and let Claire and *her* family plan the wedding."

Peyton caught Mitch's eye while subtly shaking her head. The instant her mom opened her mouth to rebut, Mitch winked.

"I've already been asked to help with some of the plans." Her mom shot her dad a proud little stare.

He frowned. "Darla, they were probably being polite. Logan may be paying for the wedding, but if the McKennas are doing it, they can't afford your taste. Don't interfere."

"Nonsense. I can work within a budget, and I want a chance to get closer to Claire. She's going to be the mother of my grandchildren."

"Mom, Dad's right." Peyton leaned forward. "Let Claire and her mom make this their special journey. If they reach out, great, but don't push your way in."

Darla's ruby-red lips puckered while she toyed with a giant sapphire earring. "But you said you don't want a traditional wedding, which means I'll never get to plan one if I can't be involved with Logan's."

"I never said any such thing." Peyton scowled.

"Yes, when you and Todd were getting serious, I asked you if you'd want a wedding here or in some exotic destination, but you said you'd rather elope."

Peyton's entire body flushed. She couldn't look at Mitch. "That was because I knew I couldn't celebrate that relationship with anyone from around here."

"We all know you've never been one to do things the normal way. Even before Todd, you'd never wanted to settle down. I long ago gave up hope of shopping for dresses and tasting cake with you, dear." Her mom averted her eyes, but it was clear that comment was a warning shot fired at Mitch.

Peyton bugged her eyes at her mother, plotting her revenge—like faking food poisoning from the scallops or something.

"Darla, it's time for us to leave these two alone." Her dad stood with his empty bourbon glass and reached for his wife's hand. "Good night, sweetheart. Mitch. See you both in the morning."

Her parents closed the french doors, disappearing into the dark house.

As much as Peyton rejoiced over the end of the Todd conversation, she wasn't yet prepared for what would be coming next. The romantic night had set the stage for bed and all that *that* entailed. She stood and began straightening the chairs around the table.

"Can I ask something . . . ?" Mitch stared at his hands as he twined a napkin around his fingers.

"Sure." She gripped the back of a chair, keeping a smile in place.

"What your mom said about you and Todd . . . Were you two engaged?"

"No. We might've mused in that 'someday when we're married' way, but he never proposed. But because he was my first and only serious relationship, my mom prematurely went into planning mode." She shrugged with a light laugh. "You see how she gets carried away."

Mitch nodded, but his stone-faced expression told her he didn't find any of it funny. "And you haven't seen him since the breakup? He never once called to check on you?"

"I haven't seen or heard from him, although a few times I had a creepy feeling like he was watching me somehow. But I was on a lot of drugs." She leaned against the chair. "I told you, that's over. We don't need to give him another thought."

"I wouldn't have thought of him at all if your mom hadn't brought him up. I suppose I needed some closure on the subject."

That would be a miracle, considering that *she* didn't have closure and doubted she ever would. How could she when she'd never had the chance to confront him after she recovered? In her dreams, she'd bump into Todd on the street—he'd be laughing with some new woman—and he'd make some polite comment about how well she looked. Then she'd punch him in the face.

"Do I even want to know what spurred that evil look?" Mitch asked.

"I'm sure you've had plenty of revenge fantasies for that Danielle chick, haven't you?"

He nodded with a smile. "Say no more."

Time to change the subject. "Any favorite parts of the evening you'd like to share?"

"Being with you in a beautiful setting that didn't involve your book. Outstanding food. Keeping everyone's names straight has worn me out a bit, though." Mitch's gaze homed in on her as she finished straightening the empty chairs. "I'm more than ready to climb into bed."

She stumbled, her stomach a confused flutter of want and panic. Reaching across the table, she straightened the centerpiece that had been jostled when the caterers removed the candelabras. "Mm."

Mitch stood and stretched, cast in moonlight and shadows. Long and lean and slightly rumpled. She almost licked her lips from the look of him and grew hot from the memory of curling up beside all that muscle and warmth.

"Shall we?" He gestured toward the french doors.

She nodded and led him inside. "Maybe I should double-check the kitchen to make sure everything's put away. My mom hates coming down in the morning to a mess . . ."

Mitch caught her hand. "Will you relax if I tell you that I'm not expecting anything more than to spend the night like we did in London? At least not unless you want more."

Her heart took on a life of its own, flapping around in her chest like a bird trying to find its way out of a cage. She pitched forward, hiding her face by planting her forehead against his shoulder. "I'm so ridiculous . . . A woman my age shouldn't be this awkward."

"Peyton." He raised her chin. "I understand—even if I disagree with—your hang-ups."

He planted a gentle kiss on her nose, patiently allowing her to take a breath.

"Let me grab us some water." She crossed to the refrigerator and plucked two small bottles from the door. "All set."

On their way up the stairs, Mitch slowed in front of Duck's photo. "Can we hold up? I want to check these out."

She stood on the step two above his while he studied the pictures of generations of Prescotts.

"You don't mention your grandparents much." He peered at their image.

"Like my dad said earlier, he and his dad fought a lot. Grandfather pursued many artistic hobbies, thinking he'd be a great talent like his father, but he wasn't. He had no independent income yet spent money as if he were making tons, so he created a lot of chaos. My dad took control of the assets and had to sell a bunch of the property and stuff to pay debts and rebuild."

"Sounds brutal. No wonder you're so resilient. That's a lot to deal with as a kid."

She supposed she had been through a lot, although nothing like what he'd survived.

He then made his way farther up the stairwell until he came to the image of her and Logan. "Even back then you were striking."

When he smiled up at her, her entire chest filled with light.

"Thank you." She peered at the picture again. The innocence of it all left her with a bittersweet pang. "Seems like a million years ago."

They finished climbing the stairs. While meandering down the shadowy, silent hallway, he said, "I can see why you came home to recover. It's beautiful and peaceful, and you've got real friends here."

"For the most part, it let me step back from the world and reset." Only the memoir kept her tethered to any kind of obligation.

"So now that the book is out and you're coming to the end of the promotional tour, what's next? Will you stay in Connecticut?"

"I'm not sure." She opened her bedroom door and then closed it behind him. "After Todd and I broke up, I moved into Logan's apartment in Chelsea. Now he and Claire split time between here and there, so I can't crash there anymore. It'd help if I knew what my next career step would be . . ." She meandered to the dresser and picked through her pajamas, choosing a crimson silk nightgown. Wrapping both hands around it, she turned to Mitch. "Do you want to go brush your teeth first?"

His crooked smile appeared as he unzipped his overnight bag to retrieve a Dopp kit. "Sure."

While he remained sequestered in the bathroom, she set the nightgown on the bed and paced, shaking out her hands. Deep down, below the fear, she wanted to take this step. Wanted *him*.

He'd seen the photos. He knew what to expect.

She could do this.

She checked the nightstand drawer, as if the lube she'd bought this week might've somehow escaped on its own. Maybe she wouldn't need it, despite what she'd heard from other patients.

Oh God. She shut the drawer. Her nerves were more fried than when she'd lost her virginity to Matt Shepard.

The bathroom door opened, jarring her from her thoughts.

Mitch stepped aside and gestured toward the bathroom. "All yours."

"Thanks." She snatched her nightgown off the bed and slipped behind the safety of a closed door. She brushed her teeth for longer than usual, then washed and moisturized her face, brushed her hair, and finally undressed. The vanity's bright lights didn't do her any favors. No matter how hard Mitch tried to convince her she was desirable, scars and fake nipples didn't look sexy. Poking at a foob—something she rarely did—she wrinkled her nose. She couldn't fault the surgeon, but they didn't feel real.

She yanked the nightgown over her body and twirled in front of the mirror. Better, anyway. With a sigh, she opened the door and turned off the light.

Mitch—shirtless and stunning—had stretched out on her bed, wearing drawstring pajama pants. Her mouth went a little dry despite the abundance of mouthwash she'd swished around. His smooth skin appeared to be hand-painted over a ripple of muscle across his chest.

He said he'd wait for her to be ready, but this move proved him an expert at baiting a trap. He knew he looked hot. She'd be mad at him if she weren't throbbing with lust in a way that hinted she might not need that lube, after all.

"You look pretty." His gaze skimmed her from head to toe.

She raised one knee and twirled her foot. "I figured you'd prefer I keep my calves uncovered."

He chuckled, reaching out for her. "Yes, thank you."

After she turned off the overhead light, she crawled onto the bed. "Maybe we want to get under the covers?"

"Sure." When they repositioned themselves, he tucked her against his side. She was bracing for a kiss or a hand on the ass, but he surprised her with none of the above. "I've been thinking about how you keep saying you don't know what to do next, assuming you're not interested in writing more books."

"You got that right." She grazed his chest with her hand, leaving it to rest over his heart. Her muscles relaxed with each thump beneath her palm.

"I noticed how you spent a ton of time speaking with readers at every bookstore event since Paris, especially other patients and caregivers. It seemed like you enjoyed that interaction best."

She nodded, having never before given it that much thought.

He held her closer, laying one hand on top of hers. "What if you went back to school for a master's degree to work with chronically ill patients?"

"Wow," she blurted. "That's out of left field."

"Sometimes the best ideas are, but is that your way of saying no?"

She grimaced. "Your confidence is nice, but I'm not sure I could counsel anyone when I'm still such a mess myself."

"Don't underestimate your gift for making people open up, or your empathy for those facing what you've survived. Maybe the education would also help you come to grips with your own grieving process."

She looked up at him. "I've never considered such a grown-up job before."

"It was just a thought . . ."

"I know."

He rolled so they were face-to-face. "You don't want to talk about this now, do you?"

"Not really." She shook her head.

He kissed her shoulder and snuggled closer. "Do you want to talk about something else, or go to sleep?"

While wrapped in his arms, her body softened like chocolate in the sun. He smelled like sea air and mint and something uniquely Mitch. She didn't want to talk *or* sleep. She wanted to kiss those beautiful, full lips and bury her hands in that thick, shiny hair. She must've been staring at it, because he said, "You have a thing about my hair, don't you?"

She nodded.

"It's beautiful and it feels so good." She threaded her fingers through the front.

"Like you," he said right before he kissed her.

They weren't drunk this time, and she felt that kiss everywhere all at once. She kissed him back, gently sucking his lower lip before opening her mouth to let him inside. Heat and tingles and a surge of desire so strong she shivered, making her brain fuzzy.

Mitch shifted back. "You taste delicious."

She wound her arms around his neck to keep him close, stealing another kiss and another until she was on her back with the weight of him pinning her to the bed, his hands splayed through her hair, his hips beginning a tantalizing rhythmic grind against her pelvis.

"Peyton," he moaned, breaking the kiss and suckling her neck. His hand skimmed over her front and then down her thigh, which he then hiked over his hip. Confident yet pausing to give her time to slow him down or say no.

She throbbed like a woman who hadn't been touched in forever, which was pretty much the truth. The gentle ache below now demanded more of him and his kisses and his touch. Slowing down held no appeal.

His eyes shone with excitement. "I know you'd rather not talk, but I have to tell you that you're the most incredible woman I've ever met."

Her nose tingled, but she wouldn't let those joyful tears fall. She dragged her fingernails down his back, causing him to shudder.

He closed his eyes and kissed her again, his hand still holding her thigh in place. Another rumble in his chest and a more forceful thrust of his hips let her know that his body was racked with the same restless need as hers.

"Mitch," she panted breathlessly, throwing her head back to grant him access to her neck. Her back arched, her body hungry for more contact and friction.

He kissed his way down her neck, then released her leg and pulled up the hem of her nightgown inch by inch, stopping below her breasts. With a quick glance seeking permission, he then slid lower and planted a warm, wet kiss on her abdomen, then trailed his tongue lower while stroking his hands upward along her sides until he'd cupped her breasts.

The shock of being touched there by anyone other than her doctors made her go still, so he did, too . . . a heartbeat of a pause. When she didn't move his hands or stop him, he resumed his trail of kisses and gentle caresses until her body writhed beneath his with the most pleasurable kind of pain building in her core.

She reached her hands between them, to where he strained against his pajama pants, and untied the strings so they could push his bottoms off.

He looked at her as if he didn't trust that she meant what she'd done, so she grabbed him, stroking the length of his hot, hard penis. He crushed his mouth against hers, roughly kissing her now, all traces of delicacy and patience frayed.

He kissed her shoulder and she nipped his. His hands were everywhere, but he didn't remove her nightgown. She preferred that barrier for now, as she suspected he assumed.

When she thought she couldn't wait another second to feel all of him inside her, he reared back and reached for the condom he'd discreetly placed on the other nightstand, tore the packet, and rolled it into place.

Her heart raced so hard she struggled to catch her breath.

This was it. No turning back.

Mitch wanted nothing more than to channel the need coursing through his body into a hard thrust with his hips, but he didn't. "I want you, Peyton. So much . . ."

Desire had his body strung so taut he thought he might snap if he didn't get release.

"I want you, too," she muttered against his cheek, kissing his neck and then nipping at his earlobe.

He slid his hands beneath her top. "Can we take this off?"

She panted, wriggling her hips and legs, looking uncertain.

"You don't have to hide. We don't need this between us." He tugged at the silk, then waited.

She nodded, giving in to his plea. He smiled and began to yank it over her head, but she closed her eyes tight, like she couldn't bear to see his face when he caught sight of her scars.

Mitch tossed the nightgown aside. "Open your eyes, Peyton. I want to see them when I come inside."

She opened her eyes and they stared at each other, sharing the same breath. He could hardly believe they were here together after the stops and starts along the way.

"You take my breath away," he said before he slid into heaven, at which point his head fell forward onto her shoulder and his entire body shivered from the heat and pure ecstasy.

Momentum took over as they rolled their hips in a carnal rhythm, building in tempo and power. He lost track of time, of kisses, of her nails and moaning, and then his field of vision narrowed with his climax—it hit him so hard.

A little dazed, he rolled over, pulling her with him because he didn't want to lose the connection. She lay with her head on his shoulder while he dragged his thumbs from her hips along her waist to her shoulders and down again—over and over—neither speaking. The room felt like a sauna and smelled of sex and perfume and happiness. A sort of happiness he hadn't known before. The kind he didn't need to share with anyone but her.

The thought of it prompted him to wrap his arms around her and hug her so hard to his chest she coughed. "Sorry." He released her a bit and kissed her head.

"No apologies." She let loose a satisfied, slow sigh. "I feel so loose, like I couldn't control my limbs if I tried."

"Don't move. I like you right where you are." He rested his cheek against the top of her head and closed his eyes, needing another minute or so of this contentedness.

She pressed a kiss into the base of his neck and whispered, "That was so good."

Eyes still closed, he grinned and hugged her tighter. "Glad you thought so, but I think we can keep trying until we reach perfection."

She snickered. "Overachiever."

"Shh. I'm tired." He tapped her butt. "Let's get some sleep."

"Okay." She moved to pull away, but he locked his arms around her. "Where do you think you're going?"

"To get my nightgown."

He shook his head. "I'll keep you warm. Come on."

She glanced toward the spot where he'd thrown the flimsy thing, then nestled back into the crook of his arm. "You win."

After another minute of listening to her breathe, he said, "Thank you for inviting me here, Peyton. I've loved every minute of it."

She propped her chin on her fist, which she'd formed on his chest. "Thanks for not running away after meeting my parents."

A joke, her go-to deflection whenever he probed too close to an open sore. "You're not much like them . . . except that you can be hard to read sometimes, like your dad."

"Normally, what you see is what you get with me. When I feel like myself again, I won't be so hard to understand."

He kissed her again because those lips still looked kiss-swollen and sweet. "Let's stay locked in this room for a week. Pretend the world doesn't exist. Can we snap our fingers and have food appear when we get hungry?"

Her smile split her face. "I thought you didn't do make-believe?"

"Seems I'm making all kinds of exceptions where you're concerned." He reached up and brushed her hair away from her eyes. "I'll be glad when this launch isn't hanging over our heads."

"Me too, and not only because of this." She gestured between them.

"Soon." And with luck her book would be a success he could leverage to secure a pipeline of work from Savant.

She laid her head back down and tickled his chest. "No matter what happens with the book, one excellent thing came out of this whole author experience."

He smiled and rolled her onto her back, stealing another delicious kiss. "Best author experience I've ever had."

"Not a high bar when I'm the *only* one you broke your rules for." She stroked his jaw with one finger. "But I'm glad you survived my family without any bruises. Will I be as lucky?"

"Of course." His mom might not be any more welcoming than Darla, but Peyton had survived so much worse, so how bad could it be?

Chapter Seventeen

"What time are we meeting Logan at Ribalta?" Mitch called from his bathroom after brushing his teeth. For weeks they'd anticipated tonight's big event. He was counting on Peyton and Logan hitting it out of the park.

Peyton called back from his small living room, where he assumed she was still looking at pictures. "Five thirty."

Her calm voice proved how far she'd come since that first reading in Barcelona. He turned off the light and joined her, checking his watch. "We should get going soon."

She crossed to him, tugged at his collar, and then snuggled against his chest. "Thank you for everything you've done for my book and, more importantly, for me. I've felt hopeful since Saturday, like I can breathe again."

"Me too—like I have new life." He kissed her, lacking the more eloquent words that would impress a writer. The fact that food tasted better and colors were brighter would be much too clichéd, despite being true. Plus he'd promised to take things slow, so he simply held her tight with his eyes closed, something he could've done forever if his iPad hadn't started ringing.

"Your mom again, no doubt." Peyton eased away, wearing a playful smirk. "You should answer it this time."

He checked his watch again, then set the iPad in its stand on the coffee table and hit "Accept." "Hey, Mom."

When his mom's face appeared, her dimpled chin and neck consumed half the screen because she always held her phone at her chest instead of setting it in front of her. "I know you're busy. I only called to wish you luck tonight. I know this book is very important for your company."

"Thank you." He glanced up at Peyton, who was standing in front of him, looking very sweet in a black summer jumpsuit with white polka dots. "Peyton doesn't need luck, though. She's terrific with the crowd."

"So you've said—"

"She's standing here," he interrupted before his mother said something embarrassing, then gestured for Peyton to come say hello. As Peyton came to stand beside him, he sent a silent prayer that the virtual introduction wouldn't go sideways. "We're heading out to grab a quick bite before the event, but this is Peyton. Peyton, this is my mother, Jane."

His mother held her phone right up to her eyes as if that would give her a better look at Peyton. Instead, it offered Peyton and him a close-up of her nostrils. His mom flashed a smile no more sincere than the one Darla Prescott had given him on Saturday. "Hello, Peyton. I've heard so much about you. Congratulations on the book. Mitchell gave me a copy last month."

Mitch waited for a compliment of Peyton's work, which never came.

"Thank you." Peyton graciously stepped in. "I've heard so much about you, and Lauren as well. Perhaps when I'm finished with this tour, we can all go to dinner."

"Perhaps." A stilted tone iced the way his mom mimicked Peyton. The lack of enthusiasm and rolling out of the calendar to pick dates also spoke volumes to Mitch, and probably to Peyton, too. If he could make a face at his mother without Peyton seeing it, he would.

"Well"—Peyton hesitated, giving his mom one last chance to say something before she gave up and looked at Mitch—"why don't I use the restroom while you two finish up, then we can take off?"

When Mitch nodded, she turned back to the screen. "So glad to put a face to your name, Jane. I'll let you and Mitch work out the details of when we might meet in person."

"I hope you don't mind coming all the way to Hoboken." His mother's sweet voice belied the underlying challenge Mitch recognized in her reply.

"I don't mind at all." Peyton stepped offscreen, shot him a knowing smile, and retreated to the restroom.

Once he heard the door close, he speared his mother with a hard look. "I need a winter coat."

"What are you talking about?" his mother asked. "It's seventy-five degrees outside."

"You were chilly, don't you think?" He glanced over his shoulder, careful to keep his voice low. "I've seen you be kinder to homeless strangers."

"Honey, don't ask me to get invested in this already." Her free hand flapped all over the place. "You know I worry that she doesn't need you. If I'm wrong, then I'll admit it, but I think you'll be happier with a woman who can make you feel important."

He wasn't about to get into all the ways Peyton already made him feel important, or tell his mother how nice it was *not* to be needed for a change, so he shook his head and sighed.

"I'm sure she's a fine person, but this isn't one of my Hallmark movies where the fish out of water gets a happy ending. This is real life, and in real life, princesses don't leave the castle. Then there's how her health could affect you. We both know you never fully recover from that kind of loss."

Mitch swallowed the ball of anger now lodged in his throat. Unlike that shithead Todd, Mitch was tough enough to stick with Peyton if his mom's dire prophecy came to pass. He'd *want* to be there for her, too, but with Peyton mere yards away, this wasn't the time to debate it, so he said, "She's cancer-free."

"She's still got a ways to go to reach the five-year survival mark." With a sorrowful expression, she said, "I'm very worried for you."

There were plenty of survival stories out there. "If she gets sick again, I'll cross that bridge then."

Too late he noticed a shadow cross the screen. Peyton must've returned while the loud thoughts in his head prevented him from hearing her footsteps. How much had she overheard?

"Call me later."

"Bye." He hit "End Call" and the screen went dark.

"Ready?" Peyton asked.

A quick scan of her face revealed no obvious sign of having heard his mother's concerns, so he didn't make apologies for the appalling remarks. It hadn't been the auspicious introduction he would've preferred. Before he got them together in person, he'd need to lay some ground rules with his mother and sister.

"Yes." He welcomed the change of subject. "Are you? You never mentioned which passage you've selected."

In the past, she'd chosen entries that focused outward and involved people she'd met along the way. This week he'd approached her with the caution one would use to handle dynamite when suggesting she try something more personal with a more hometown crowd.

"You'll have to wait and be surprised like everyone else." She cocked a brow.

He grabbed her into a kiss. "No special privileges?"

"You get plenty of privileges, but not about this." She smiled, but the distant look in her eyes wasn't a happy one.

"Fine." He squeezed her tight before grabbing his keys and heading to the subway to meet up with Logan and Claire and the others. He'd privately reached out to her parents again this week and played up the Prescott optics to persuade them to come. But optics hadn't been his real motivation. He'd guessed, deep down, that Peyton could use her parents' support tonight. Hopefully, they'd show.

They boarded the train in silence and found two seats. Peyton remained preoccupied. Had she overheard his mother's dire warning? He leaned close and murmured, "You sure you're okay?"

"Yes." She stared at him, then let loose a big sigh. "It'll be different tonight, sharing the stage with Logan. Better, I think, although maybe a little part of me is afraid he'll outshine me."

Mitch slung his arm around her, relieved not to be discussing his mother. "Not possible. I don't care how popular he and his photography are, or how many women might swoon over him. This is your story. *Yours.*"

As they exited the station after the train deposited them, she admitted, "I'm also a little nervous to read in front of my friends. It's not like in Europe, where the hectic schedule and all the strangers made me numb."

"Haven't your friends read the book?"

"Maybe, but standing in front of them and reading aloud is different."

"But they're coming to support you, not to judge you."

"I suppose these jitters aren't anything a little wine won't cure." She smiled as he opened the door to the restaurant. At a table near the window, Logan and Claire sat with Mr. and Mrs. Prescott on one side, while Steffi; her husband, Ryan; and her brother Ben were on the other.

Peyton almost tripped, mumbling, "My parents came . . ."

"Of course they did." He kissed her temple, choosing not to share his role in their decision. Her genuine smile was reward enough. With playful sarcasm, he added, "Think I'll join you with that wine."

"Maybe we should split a bottle." She giggled, the sound of which worked its way through his muscles like a good masseuse's hands. "To be honest, I'm pleasantly surprised they made the effort."

"I'm glad." When they reached the table, he pulled out a chair for Peyton. His stomach growled from the aroma of pizza sauce and salty cheese.

She appeared to relax with the love of friends and family. And a bit of wine.

Tonight would be her best reading ever.

He just knew it.

Standing room only.

Peyton balled her hands into fists at her sides as they entered the cluttered Rare Book Room. Her head still hurt from trying to shove aside Jane Mathis's concerns about her cancer returning. That hadn't been what she'd needed to kick off her evening, and now that they'd arrived to this large crowd, performance anxiety began to rattle her, too.

Most of the patrons were milling around the makeshift buffet table overflowing with ricotta-filled squash blossoms, crab-and-avocado toasts, iced cookies, and plastic cups with prepoured white and red wine, while others began claiming seats in the many rows of metal folding chairs set up. Strands of white lights hung overhead, lending a festive atmosphere to the creaky old space.

Unlike Peyton, whose twitching made her look like she had some kind of tic, Mitch and Logan beamed. Their odd trio skirted the gathering crowd to meet up with the Strand events coordinator and Peyton's editor Krista. After a brief introduction to the moderator, Maura, and quick hug with Krista, Peyton stepped back to let Mitch handle the particulars.

"You okay?" Logan asked while Claire and the others took the front-row seats that had been reserved for them.

"I'll be fine once we start. It's just weird having people I know—people *we* know—here." This city had been her home base for almost a decade, after all. A few former "friends" had reached out by email when they saw posts about the event. She wouldn't even let herself scan the crowd for fear of making eye contact with one, although none had committed to coming.

"I know this is old hat for you, but I'm excited to finally talk about this project." Logan clapped his hands and then rubbed his palms together. "I'm proud of what we've created."

"I am, too." She touched his shoulder. "And I always give you credit for the idea."

Mitch arrived and interrupted them. "We need you both up at the podium. It's time to begin."

Maura made some introductory remarks about Peyton's and Logan's bios, and read the starred *Publishers Weekly* review before turning the room over to the pair. Peyton's skin tingled from Logan's ramped-up energy.

Sensing that she could use another minute to collect herself, she began by introducing Logan. "Welcome and thank you all for coming. Before I read from the book, I'm going to let Logan discuss the process of this project first, since it began as his brainchild. Then I'll read a short selection from the memoir, follow up with some of my own thoughts about how my experiences and this project have changed me, and we'll take questions at the end." Peyton gestured to her brother. "Take it away."

He flashed that smile that had won him admirers around the globe and then launched into a spiel about how he'd taken his experience with documentary photography to turn her journey into a story others might use to heal. While he spoke, she stared into space, imagining herself sitting in the sand at Arcadia House, scanning the horizon, searching for calm. She'd stepped back from the podium, so she practiced ujjayi breaths to find her center.

"In the end, the fact that my original idea of an installation art project turned into a memoir worked out for the best. Peyton bravely put her heart on every page, and I couldn't be more proud." When Logan finished, he touched her elbow. "And now for the main event, my sister and best friend . . ."

A round of applause forced her to take the mic. She glanced at Mitch, who winked and wore that broad smile that filled her with happiness.

Nodding, she faced the crowd and opened the book to the tabbed page.

"It's always hard to pick a single passage that represents the work, or is meaningful when taken out of context, so let me first give some background to the particular excerpt I've chosen tonight.

"A lot of what we read by or about cancer patients, whether in books or interviews or chat rooms, is riddled with what I call cheerleading. Being uplifting is very important, and while many of the passages in my book are about hope and small epiphanies I had along the way, I'm going the other direction tonight. I want to share the things no one likes to talk—or even think—about. The thoughts that don't make someone heroic or a 'good example' for others, but are nonetheless fundamentally human and real. I believe it's important to acknowledge painful, bitter moments as part of the process. Otherwise the sense of a 'failure' of optimism any patient inevitably has in those terrifying moments will only lead to more isolation, which isn't good for anyone.

"With that in mind, here we go . . .

"*I'm in the dark place now.*

"*Black and confining like a coffin with a peephole. As with any other peephole, the view of the outside world is somewhat distorted, but it's the only one I can see from in here.*

"*It's not the shoulder pain and stiffness, or the Frankenstein scars across my chest, or the fact that I'm still bloated enough that I doubt I'll ever get out of drawstring pants again. It's not that song 'Broken' that has triggered a full-body freeze ever since it was playing in the background when I got the original biopsy results. It's not even having to act brave and confident so the people who love me don't fall apart or smother me, although, dammit, that act can be exhausting. That's almost as taxing as trying not to complain about anything because I know—as everyone keeps reminding me—I'm 'lucky' to be alive.*

"Yes, of course, if you call what I'm doing now—how I'm feeling—living.

"But I don't always feel lucky. Not when fear burns inside me as if my bones have turned to dry ice.

"That awful question of 'What next?' scares even healthy people at least once in their lives. For me, it rains down like two tons of earth being poured on my head.

"I can't stop picturing stealthy occult cells swimming around in my tissue, looking for the ideal place to set up camp. A fold or nook or other foxhole where they can rebuild without being noticed. Logan and others encourage me to focus on the seventy-two percent five-year survival rate my doctor mentioned when I got my diagnosis. Maybe most think that sounds pretty good, but I hear a one-in-four chance of dying in the next five years.

"One-in-four chance of death.

"If anyone had those odds of winning the Mega Millions lottery, they'd start house hunting before the drawing even took place.

"And if I do survive, what does that look like?

"I'm so exhausted and achy and hormonally off-balance I can't envision cracking a real smile again. The wear and tear of my travel days is not an option, at least not yet. This project? I'm still not convinced it should ever see the light of day, where it will be picked over by others who'll thumb through its pages in search of optimism or insight they're unlikely to find. Love? That's a hole in my heart I don't want to examine too closely, but if I couldn't find real love when healthy, I can't imagine finding it when I'm this sick. Maybe that's for the best, though, because I couldn't take another goodbye.

"Not that I have many to say. Cancer weeds out the real friends from the false. It's sobering to learn how few true friends a person with thousands

of 'followers' and hundreds of acquaintances has. In one case, the fault is mine, but not so with the rest. It seems I sleepwalked through much of my healthy life, seeing what I wanted or remembering only what made me feel good. Perhaps my tombstone should read 'Peyton Prescott, Globejotter and Master of Self-Deception.'

"So now I lie in bed with the blinds drawn and swear to myself that, for however many days remain of my life, I will never again waste energy on hangers-on or insincere people. I will never say yes to things I don't want to do. I will forego being the life of the party and try harder to be a loyal friend. A person of substance. A woman with real purpose, even though purpose eludes me still.

"Logan thinks this project is my purpose—a way to transform something ugly into something pretty. He has always had an eye for the beauty in life and in people, and I know I haven't always made that easy for him, even though he doesn't complain. Before I die, I wish I could, for one second, be the person he thinks I am.

"But first I need to find the strength to drag myself out of this bed . . .

"Maybe tomorrow."

Peyton closed the book while the audience clapped. "Thank you. As I mentioned, it's important for caregivers and loved ones to let a patient experience the lows without feeling the need to respond with optimism and encouragement. The sentiment is appreciated, of course, but it can unintentionally invalidate the patient's feelings and fears, forcing them to keep those things to themselves. Silence is strangling to a person whose days might be numbered."

Jane Mathis's voice floated through her thoughts then, prompting her to add, "That said, there's always cause for hope and a time to push someone toward optimism. Toward making the most of whatever time exists. And while I've got a few years before I reach the five-year survival milestone, I feel more optimistic every day. In a strange way, I'm grateful for the new experiences and people my illness brought into my life, which I'm more determined to fill with the best people and goals.

"Thank you for coming tonight. Logan and I are happy to take all your questions now."

She risked a glance at that front row, and her throat ached when she saw her mother dabbing her eyes with a tissue. Seeing Darla Prescott, a woman who rarely—if ever—got emotional, do so in public meant more to Peyton than any bestseller list ever could.

A man near the front raised his hand.

"Yes, sir?" she asked.

"One of the things I loved about this book is the way it weaves the photographs with the journal entries, but I'm curious, did Logan ever consider writing entries from the caregiver perspective?"

"I'll let Logan take that one." She smiled and ceded the mic, always willing to step away from the spotlight.

"I'm not a wordsmith. I've always told stories with pictures, and while the subject is Peyton and the images capture her emotions, they also reflect my experience with her . . . my perception and day-to-day life as she and I met each challenge, setback, and triumph. Nothing I could've written would be more powerful than what I shot."

Logan stepped back and Peyton took another question, and another, and so it went for twenty or so minutes. Finally Maura, whose timekeeping skills rivaled Mitch's, shut down the Q and A. "Let's give Logan and Peyton a round of applause, and then a short bathroom break before they set up over there to sign books."

A minute later, Peyton excused herself to the restroom, which was located through another door and beyond some kind of storage area. Once she wound her way past piles of books and boxes to get there, she locked herself inside for two minutes of peace. *BreatheBreathe. In and out.*

She washed her hands and finger combed her hair. The event she'd most dreaded had concluded without a hitch, and she'd survived. Mitch should be pleased. Logan, too.

In a short while, she'd leave this bookstore and spend the night wrapped up in Mitch's arms, convincing herself and him that this relationship would not be the great folly his mom predicted.

She opened the door to head back to the Rare Book Room, but then literally fell back against the wall.

Todd?

She blinked as if he were a mirage. He seemed taller than she remembered, but just as slim. He removed his baseball cap, showing his wild brown curls, which he now wore in a somewhat longer style. His brown eyes—the ones she'd once thought so warm—turned her heart to stone instead of making her knees weak.

He'd tucked his hands in the pockets of a summer-weight jacket.

"Hi, Peyton." His weak smile worked like Novocain, numbing every inch of her body until she couldn't move. Couldn't speak. "I'm sorry to startle you, but I thought it would be best to catch you alone. You were incredible tonight."

The floor seemed to pitch like she was trying to stand on a raft in the ocean. Still, she could not make herself move. Surely someone would miss her soon.

"The book is great, and you look amazing." Todd gestured toward her hair, reminding her of how he used to love to wrap its long length around his hand like a lasso. She recoiled, which she supposed was better than the absence of any sensation. "The new style is becoming."

"Why are you here?" *Finally, words!* Her heart thumped so loud in her ears she couldn't hear anything else.

"I had to see you with my own eyes to know that you're okay."

Her arm twitched, itching to wipe that stupid grin off his face.

"Okay?" Sucking breath in and out so fast was burning her lungs. "Move away from me. I have nothing to say to you."

She sidestepped him and took long strides toward the other end of the storage room, which wasn't easy on shaky legs.

The prick followed her. "Please, wait. I have *so* much to say. To apologize for. I've thought of you so often. Worried. Wondered. You have no idea how many times I've picked up the phone but then chickened out because of how badly I treated you. I've missed you, Peyton. So much."

Although they'd crossed back through the door to the Rare Book Room and the crowd, she whirled on him, jabbing her finger at him. "Stop! You don't get to come here and say *that* to me."

"But it's true. Each page of your book tore up my heart. I was weak and afraid. Overwhelmed. I loved you so much I didn't think I could watch you suffer. I should've been stronger, but you were always stronger than me."

"Shut up. I mean it. Shut up!" She knew her voice was too high, but she'd lost control over her body the minute he appeared in front of that bathroom. From the corner of her eye, she saw Krista wince. "I'm not interested in you or what *you've* been going through."

All of a sudden, Logan and Mitch were at her side in a flurry of activity.

Mitch's arm came around her waist. "Come with me."

He didn't even wait for her consent before he started pulling her away from Todd.

Logan stood, arms crossed, feet planted, speaking to Todd through gritted teeth, while her parents and friends collected behind him. "You're not welcome, Todd. Leave now before you do any more damage."

Todd glanced at her, but she turned away from him and let Mitch lead her to the other corner of the room, where he shoved a bottle of water at her and kept others away. She didn't look back at Todd, so she had no idea what Logan did or said to get him to leave. The folks from Savant were probably displeased with her. Her parents, too.

When she found the courage to look up, she caught a glimpse of Claire's ashen face. Shame came rushing back, and she guessed all the progress she'd made had vanished in a heartbeat.

She could barely breathe. Why had Todd come when he couldn't believe she'd ever forgive him? As that thought struck, she almost fell backward from its blow. Of all the feelings circling her like a coil cinching her chest, this was the first time she'd actually grasped how Claire had first felt when confronted by *her*. Claire had too much class to walk over now and say, "I told you so," but she had to have been thinking to herself, *See how hard it is to forgive a betrayal?*

Warm tears spilled onto Peyton's hot cheeks.

"I'm so sorry." Mitch grabbed her into a hug. "What can I do?"

"Nothing," she said, coming back to her senses and daring a glance at the now-curious crowd. She eased away from Mitch and donned all her old armor. "I need to sign the books so I can get the hell out of here."

"We can take another minute." He reached for her hand, but she pulled away.

"The sooner I start, the sooner this ends. Maybe you can go smooth things over with my editor." She brushed back her hair, forced a smile, and walked to the signing table, where Logan was waiting. "Sorry for the interruption, everyone. There won't be any more ghosts from my past stirring up drama tonight."

Chapter Eighteen

"It's fine, Lauren." In fact, Mitch thanked God that his sister hadn't come to the event. Even if Todd hadn't crashed the party, the public venue wouldn't have been his choice for where and when to introduce her to Peyton. More to the point, Todd *had* crashed the party, and Peyton had mumbled fewer than a dozen words since leaving the Strand. "Thanks for calling, but I'm wiped out. Can I catch up with you tomorrow?"

"Sure. Just wanted you to know I got stuck working late for a closing. The good news is that my stepping in when Joe fell behind forced Gary to see the truth about that guy."

"Good for you. Can't wait to hear more about it next time we talk, but I have to go now. Bye!" He tucked his phone away and fished his keys out of his pocket, then opened his apartment door. Peyton went inside ahead of him. After he threw the dead bolt, he closed his eyes for two seconds. None of his attempts to pull her out of her funk had worked, and precisely zero fresh ideas sprang to mind.

"Would you like some water, or perhaps wine?" He tossed his keys on the kitchen peninsula.

She shook her head before crossing to the window to gaze at the nighttime cityscape. While his generic apartment couldn't compare with the grandeur of Arcadia House, the view through its window was equally spectacular, if also the opposite. Outside, the massive skyscrapers' thousands of lights twinkled all around her slight frame like low-hanging stars.

He flexed his hands as if groping for a way to turn back the clock to keep Todd from interrupting the event. Powerlessness clawed at him, making his amble across the living room feel like trudging through waist-deep mud.

Before he reached her, her phone rang. She dug it out of her purse and sighed. "Logan." She thrust it toward him. "Can you talk to him?"

He blinked. She *never* ignored Logan.

"Sure." He took the phone. "Logan, it's Mitch. Peyton can't come to the phone at the moment. Can I help you?"

"How is she?"

Good question. Mitch headed back to the kitchen for a bit of privacy. "Quiet."

"Claire, too. I can't believe Todd showed up after how much pain he caused those two." The ice in Logan's tone made Mitch shiver.

"I'm sorry he ruined everyone's evening." Mitch strained his neck to catch a glimpse of Peyton, but she remained turned away from him.

"It never occurred to me to look for him." Logan huffed. "Now I'm kicking myself I didn't see this coming."

"Don't bother going down that road. What's done is done."

"And what about Krista? Is she pissed?"

"No. I explained everything. She's just sad we didn't throw Todd to an angry crowd. You take care of Claire. I'm with your sister, so you don't have to worry. She'll call you tomorrow."

"Listen, Mitch, I don't know how much Peyton's told you, but I can't overestimate how deeply Todd hurt her." Logan paused. "She'd hate that I'm sharing that, but you need to understand the gravity of the situation. Peyton blew. Up. Her. *Life* for him because she'd believed he was 'the one.' And then she never got to mourn that relationship because we jumped straight into survival mode with the cancer treatment. My guess is that his surprise appearance will force her to sort through the Todd baggage. You should know—she's not great at letting people close when she's wrestling with her emotions. Be patient tonight and give her a wide berth."

Mitch drew a breath, letting the weight of Logan's words settle in his chest. "Thanks for the advice."

"Thanks for keeping an eye on her."

"My pleasure." He meant it, even if he had no idea how to help her.

He hung up, setting the phone aside before scrubbing his face with his hands. Leaving Peyton with her privacy, he stayed in the kitchen to steep the lavender tea he kept on hand. He stood at the counter for a few minutes—hands flattened on the granite, head hung low—inhaling the sweet scent of the tea-infused steam.

Mitch had only recently put Peyton's doubts to rest. He hadn't needed Todd to resurface and reopen all those questions. After removing the tea ball strainer, he poured two cups and then went back to the window where she stood—arms crossed—motionless as a statue.

"Try this." He extended one of the cups toward her.

She started as if she'd forgotten she wasn't alone, then sniffed the tea after taking it from him. "It smells good. Thanks."

Logan's warning beat against his conscience, but Mitch had never solved anything by backing off.

"Can we talk about what happened tonight?" he ventured.

"Must we?" She sighed.

"No." He sipped from his cup while trying to read her eyes. Gesturing to the sofa, he said, "Let's at least sit down and relax."

With one hand resting on her lower back, he steered her around the charcoal-gray chaise sectional he'd bought at West Elm not long ago. He'd been proud of the new look, which now seemed so trivial in the scheme of things that made life truly happy.

She set her cup on the coffee table and raked her hands through her hair, peering at him. "I'm sorry I lost control in front of everyone. I know I should've handled things better, but Todd shocked me. I hope no one videoed the confrontation, but at this point I can't care that much. God, how I want this *all* to be over."

Her expression melted into a frown so deep even her eyes appeared to droop.

"Peyton." Mitch took hold of her hand and kissed it, then covered it with both of his hands. "I'm not upset with how you handled things, nor am I worried about book sales right now. I *am* worried about you, though."

"I'm fine." She yanked her hand away and reached for her tea. The way she was gazing into the cup, one might think it held the answers to every question.

"You don't seem fine." Now it was his turn to cross his arms. "I know as 'Optimus' I might not be the most spontaneous, romantic man, but I care deeply about you. I'd do anything in my power to help you, including listening—without judgment—to whatever your feelings are for that man."

"I don't want to talk about Todd." She shuddered. "Why give him more power? He's been such a destructive force, and now he ruined tonight for Logan and Claire."

For Logan and Claire?

She covered her face with her hands, the agonized tone with which she'd emphasized Claire's name so visceral it shimmered around her like snowflakes in sunlight.

"I'm sorry." He rubbed her shoulder before prying her hands away from her face.

Tears pooled in her eyes. "Did you see Claire's expression tonight? I bet Todd's little performance sent me right back to square one with her. All the apologizing and effort I've put into mending that friendship erased in an instant." She snapped her fingers. "And who could blame her? I'm so stupid. I knew I'd hurt her, but until tonight, I never understood why it took her so, *so* long to hear me out, let alone accept my apology. But I can never forgive Todd for how he betrayed me, so what kind of hypocrite am I?"

"Peyton." He tried to rub her shoulder, but she shrugged him off.

"Seriously. If I can't do that for Todd, how can I beg for forgiveness again from Claire? I love her and I know it's important to Logan, but I'm fresh out of fight. I'm tired. So, so tired. Two years ago, my life got smashed into thousands of pieces. I've been going along, day by day, trying to put them back together—like if I complete the giant puzzle, everything will finally be normal again—except when I think I've got the pieces fitted together, it's like I'm looking at a Picasso version of myself."

When she closed her eyes, he waited, allowing her the solitude of her thoughts.

She opened her eyes a few seconds later. "I need to hit reset and figure out what will make me happy *now* so I can build a new life around that. And I'm sorry to say this to you after everything you've done, but this book is *not* that thing. I'd do anything to get out of the future tour dates so I can take time to get myself together without any obligation to anyone else."

He hadn't seen that coming. "I know the memoir began as a distraction for you, and the editing, publication, and promotion haven't been personally rewarding, but we're right in the thick of it now. The rankings are terrific so far, and drumming up more buzz with personal appearances could push it onto the lists and make it stick. After everything you've sacrificed and put into this project, can't you hang in there a few more weeks so you get all the rewards? After that, you'll be free to choose what comes next, whether that's going back to school or taking up your old job or anything else."

Peyton threw herself back against the sofa cushions, arms flung across her face, covering her eyes. "I want to scream so loud, you have no idea."

She dropped her arms and stared at the ceiling, eyes brimming with tears, her distress palpable.

His chest ached for her, and for himself. He'd pinned so much hope on her book when he got that call seven months ago. If he hadn't broken his rules, he wouldn't be here having this conversation or dealing with the mental and emotional conflict now giving him heartburn.

Despite his own goals and desires, he couldn't ignore the anguish etched on Peyton's face. "I'll cancel the tour dates tomorrow."

She sat upright, relief smoothing out all the creases in her forehead as she dabbed her eyes. "You will?"

He nodded. He had no idea how to do that without causing career suicide, but he'd worry about that in the morning. He'd known there'd be a price to pay for mixing business and pleasure, but he couldn't in good conscience push Peyton to continue on a journey that made her miserable. Especially not when he couldn't go with her to make sure she'd be okay.

Savant would be pissed at both of them now, and while Peyton might have no interest in publishing with that house again, he needed to figure some way to salvage his relationship with it. Kendra Khan was breathing down his neck now with her launch only four weeks away. He would need to focus on her and run down new client leads to hope to recover from this loss.

Peyton tipped her head, studying his face. "I couldn't care less that canceling will reflect poorly on me, but I *do* care about you and your reputation. I don't want to hurt you."

"Well, I don't want to hurt you, either, which puts us at an impasse." He turned his palms up and gestured as if his hands were a scale. "If I weigh my financial hit against your mental and physical health, there's no question about which is the right choice. We'll cancel the tour dates—or maybe Logan can go alone, although *you're* the author. I don't know. I'll think up some other way to create buzz . . . call the foundation and explore some alternative, given its vested interest in the book's success. Maybe we can get creative with Logan and find a new angle."

Instead of the smile and grateful hug he expected, Peyton stood and paced in front of the coffee table before stopping to shake her head. "Mitch, it means everything to me that you're willing to do all that, but I can't let you."

"You can't stop me."

"I'm serious. If I put my needs so far above yours, it's like the Claire thing all over, and I swore I'd never be that selfish again. Plus I'd be letting down readers who want to hear from me or ask me questions, and I know too much about the fresh hell some of them are already facing." She ran her hands through her hair once more, shaking her head. "It's been a shitty evening, but I'll bounce back tomorrow and finish the tour. Logan will be with me in Chicago, and Todd won't make any more surprise appearances. Besides, if I quit now, that jerk gets the best of me again, and I can't let that happen."

Mitch stood and hugged her, smoothing his hand over the back of her head. "I'm sorry Todd hurt you so much. But, honestly, there's a silver lining—or I think so, anyway. I'm grateful he turned out to be the wrong guy, otherwise you wouldn't be here with me now. We are just at the beginning of this, but I'm all in." He kissed her, but she cut it short. His heart absorbed the blow of her rejection even as he saw her eyes cloud with conflict.

"I love that you're looking for the silver lining. But look at what an effing mess I am. This is why I made you promise we'd take things slow." She cupped his cheek. "Please don't take this personally, but I think I should go home tonight. We'll celebrate when my head is clearer. If I hurry, I can catch a train—"

"That's crazy. You won't get home until after midnight, and you shouldn't be alone on a train for two hours right now. We don't have to talk any more tonight. If you're tired, let's go to sleep. See how you feel tomorrow."

"You have to get up early for work in the morning, so you don't need me keeping you awake all night with my tossing and turning." For an instant, her expression pinched. He had no idea what she'd thought about, but she didn't want to share it. "I've got things to do in Connecticut tomorrow, too, so let's call it a night and I'll come back Friday."

"You're leaving for Chicago on Friday morning."

"Oh, that's right." She was already on the move, reaching for the purse she'd left on the sofa table. She offered him a weak smile. "I'll come here straight from the airport on Saturday afternoon, and we'll do something fun. Maybe we can hit Union Square Greenmarket and then come here and cook a great meal."

No matter what she'd said, he could feel her slipping away. "I don't want to put you on a train at this hour."

"I'll order a car service." She pulled out her phone.

He approached her and clasped her arms. "That'll cost a fortune."

"That's not a problem."

He dropped his hands. "You really want to get away from me."

The instant that slipped out, he regretted it. He should've heeded Logan's warnings.

"This isn't about you, Mitch. I need to regroup, and I don't want to burden you with my crap when you've got enough on your plate." She slung her purse over her shoulder, determined.

"But I want to help you with your stuff, Peyton. Wouldn't you want to help me if our roles were reversed?"

"I doubt our roles will ever be reversed. You're always on top of everything with your goals and plans. You know exactly where you want to go. Please let me work out my stuff on my own so I can be your equal."

"You're already my equal."

255

She shrugged. "Well, I don't see myself that way . . . *That's* the point."

They stared at each other from a distance. His apartment seemed colder and darker than when they'd arrived.

"I can't argue anymore." He shook his head. "I wish you'd stay, but I won't trap you here."

"Thank you." She hugged him before grabbing his face and giving him a sweet kiss. "Thank you for trying so hard, and for being patient. I appreciate it more than you know."

Five minutes later, she was gone, and it was his turn to stand at his window, staring at the vast city, trying to mute his mother's voice in his head.

—◦◦◦—

When Peyton crept into Arcadia House through the back door at midnight, she didn't expect to bump into her father, who'd just closed the refrigerator door.

His eyes widened while he pulled the lid off a yogurt cup. "What are you doing home?"

"I decided to sleep here tonight." When he stared at her, waiting for a complete explanation, she hedged, offering part of one. "I have my checkup tomorrow afternoon and thought it'd be easier not to have to race back in the morning."

Her dad gave her that doubting look she hated. "I thought you and Mitch would be celebrating. Did you argue with or run from him because of Todd?"

She tossed her purse on the table. "Not the way you and Mitch think."

"What other way is there?" He spooned some yogurt into his mouth, leaning back against the counter.

He wanted answers, but how could she explain the jumbled thoughts in her head? Todd the wrecking ball had returned to knock down the life she'd reconstructed for herself. But even prior to that, her blood had run a little cold when she'd overheard Jane Mathis warn her son not to date the cancer patient. The one-two punch of those things seemed like a harbinger of doom. "Dad, I'm so tired. Can we talk tomorrow?"

"Sure, sweetheart. I'm sorry you're upset. I was very proud of you and Logan tonight. I think Duck would've been, too." He set his empty yogurt cup down and came around the island to give her a hug. "Get some sleep and don't give a second thought to Todd or tomorrow's appointment. You've always been a little warrior. Everything will be okay."

She inhaled the bergamot-scented cologne he'd worn forever, wishing she shared his confidence. Life had been so much easier when she'd been young and believed that he was always right about everything. Now she knew how often adults got it wrong.

Moments later, when she finally crawled beneath the covers, she pictured Mitch, alone in his bed, wondering what he'd done wrong. She'd hurt him by leaving, but she believed it for the best for now. That didn't mean her heart didn't ache, though. She picked up her phone and texted:

Got home safely. My cold pillow is a poor substitute for your warmth. Hope you are having sweet dreams. XO

———

Peyton sat on the exam table, fidgeting with the paper gown. She closed her eyes and sighed, rubbing her biceps to get rid of the goose bumps, although no amount of friction could overcome the icy temperature in the room. It seemed impossible that she couldn't see her own breath.

"Come in," she replied when someone knocked on the door.

Dr. Wang entered, staid as ever. She pulled out the circular stool on wheels and sat. "Hello, Peyton, how have you been?"

"Fine." Peyton smiled to no avail. Dr. Wang never smiled back. Not once in all the times they'd spoken had the woman smiled. Stiff bedside manner aside, the fact that she was one of the best oncologists in the hospital meant Peyton would put up with her cool demeanor. "A little anxious."

"Anxious? Have you been experiencing concerning symptoms?" Dr. Wang read through something in Peyton's file without making eye contact.

"Not really." She noticed her dangling feet fluttering, so she locked her ankles together. Her shoulders tensed. "Seems my new normal is living with a sort of general anxiety, like I'm always waiting for the other shoe to drop. Since I last saw you, I've lost some weight for no reason and haven't been sleeping great these past several weeks."

Dr. Wang looked up, wearing a concerned frown. "Have you been under particular stress, or has anything else happened that could cause those symptoms?"

"Well, I've been traveling around Europe. Of course, I used to do that all the time with no trouble. Then again, promoting my memoir has been very stressful. I suppose jet lag has affected my sleep." She left out the "should I or shouldn't I" melodrama with Mitch that had kept her up many nights last month, too.

Dr. Wang nodded. "Your blood work doesn't reveal any concerning levels, and your weight loss isn't a surprise given that schedule, but let's go ahead and finish the exam. Lie back and untie the gown."

While Peyton reclined, Dr. Wang set down her chart and washed her hands. Without any fanfare, the doctor began a thorough breast exam, her chilly, bony fingers starting on Peyton's left breast.

Peyton stared at the ceiling, having become quite accustomed to the clinical fondling of her foobs. She hummed to herself an old John

Denver song that she and Logan used to mock when they were little. They'd been so pleased by their own cleverness back then. The memory of Logan yelping those words as he flung himself off the dock at Arcadia brought a smile to her face.

That happiness vanished when Dr. Wang said, "Hm."

Was anything more terrifying than when a doctor muttered that sound?

The doctor's expression tightened as she fixated on a spot near the scar on Peyton's right breast.

"What is it?" Peyton had to work at lying still when all she wanted to do was leap off the table and scream.

"I'm not sure." Dr. Wang palpated the same spot again. "Do you do regular self- exams?"

Peyton shook her head. In fact, she'd avoided them, partly out of fear—which wasn't that uncommon, if her chat room friends were to be believed—and partly because she had no breast tissue left and had assumed any new cancer would show up elsewhere.

"So we don't know how long this has been here or if it's changed size." She pushed on the spot again.

"How long *what* has been there?" Peyton's hands were now fists at her side.

"There is a small lump. I don't want you to panic, though. It could be a bit of scar tissue, or the calcified soft-tissue remnant of a small seroma that got reabsorbed, or a lipoma, but let's get an MRI right away."

"No biopsy?"

"First we need an MRI to see it better, then we will take next steps."

Peyton gripped her stomach, her shallow breaths coming faster.

Dr. Wang touched her shoulder. "I know that sounds scary, but there is a very good chance that it is nothing threatening, so try not to panic."

"Easy for you to say," Peyton snapped, although she knew it wasn't Dr. Wang's fault. She should've been doing regular breast exams. What a stupid way she'd gone about her life, thinking that avoiding a problem would prevent it from happening. She'd teased Mitch for being like Optimus, but that beat being an ostrich like her.

Dr. Wang wrote out a prescription for the MRI. "Get this imaging done and then we'll regroup. If it isn't scar tissue, we'll need your surgeon to remove it and take a biopsy. I know it must sound like forever, but within a week to ten days we'll know whether or not we need to do anything further."

Peyton nodded, dabbing her tears.

Dr. Wang clasped Peyton's chart to her chest. "Peyton, stay positive and keep busy. Stress is not your friend when it comes to your health. I'll speak with you soon."

Peyton waited for Dr. Wang to exit the room before she bundled up her jeans, pressed them to her mouth, and screamed. Not once, but twice, and she didn't care if the pants didn't muffle her voice well.

She could not imagine going through chemo or radiation or any of the poking and prodding and sickness again. Last time she'd relied on Logan, but she didn't want to ruin his upcoming wedding. Could she hide it all from her family?

And then there was Mitch. He'd already gone through this and worse with his dad. It didn't matter that he'd sworn he wouldn't be like Todd; she couldn't ask him to be her person through treatment. To watch her suffer, lose her hair, and maybe this time not recover.

Her head ached from the panicked thoughts.

Trembling hands made getting dressed a struggle. Her temple seemed to be pulsing with her heart, and her field of vision narrowed. On her way out of the office, she ducked into a restroom and retched what little she'd eaten for breakfast.

After gargling cold water, she looked in the mirror. *Pull it together, girl.* She smoothed her hair and reapplied lip gloss. Before she reached her car, she'd scheduled an MRI for Monday. She sat behind the wheel, waiting for the last bits of adrenaline or whatever to ebb so she could get home safely. Once the shivers stopped, she turned over the ignition.

With little memory of the drive, all she could think about as the tires ground over the pea stone gravel was how thankful she was that neither of her parents' cars were anywhere on the property.

She leaped from her car, kicked off her shoes at the edge of the yard, and ran down the dry lawn to the dock.

BreatheBreathe. Breathe!

A gull flew overhead as summer breezes blew her hair around her face.

Why now? That thought looped through her mind, fastening itself there like an ugly black button. After everything she'd put into becoming a better person . . . Why now?

A surge of acid tore through her stomach. How could it be fair that Todd remained healthy enough to continue wrecking lives? Each time his image resurfaced in her memory, it reminded her of her own selfish stupidity.

A hoarse cry of frustration and self-pity burst from her throat, echoing off the Sound.

Depleted, she collapsed against the wooden bench where she and Mitch had sat last weekend. That already seemed like a lifetime ago, although her sheets still smelled a bit like him. What cruel twist of fate handed her a second chance at something like love only to then surprise her with yet another lump?

She should've fought her feelings for him instead of chasing silver linings and the fantasy of happily ever after. She caressed her right breast, but Dr. Wang's words didn't comfort her. Last time she'd remained hopeful—almost to the point of denial—until the pathology report slammed her against the wall. This time she *knew* to expect the worst.

Just once before she died, she had to be completely unselfish. Cutting Mitch loose would be the least selfish thing to do, even if it crushed her.

She wiped her eyes and dug her phone out of her purse before she lost her nerve.

"Hey." His voice pitched up like he was pleased to hear from her, making her heart twinge even more. "I was going to call soon. Are you feeling clearheaded?"

"Somewhat." She bit down on her lower lip and closed her eyes. Around her, the Sound looked muddy gray except for the tiny white-caps formed by the wind. *Breathe.*

"Why don't you come down tonight so you don't have to wake up as early to catch your morning flight? I'll cook something nice."

"Ever thoughtful and efficient, my dear Optimus." She smiled, picturing him in his apartment kitchen, wearing an apron and sautéing.

He chuckled, but she could hear the edge of nervousness through the line. Mitch wasn't stupid. He suspected he'd skated onto thin ice.

He'd fight to stay with her, so she had to throw him off in a way that he wouldn't want her anymore. She pinched the bridge of her nose to stave off the sniffles. If she thought this was hard, she'd have to work double time to hide her worries from Logan. Her brother's eyes caught everything, which made him a great photographer and a terrific snoop. "That sounds nice, but I don't think I should."

"Why not?"

She closed her eyes, her heart twisting in a knot. "I've been thinking . . ."

"Doesn't sound like I'm going to like what comes next." His voice sounded like it came from someplace deep in his chest.

"Probably not." A breeze whipped around her neck, making her shiver. She turned in to the corner of the bench, hugging her knees to her chest. "You have no idea how sorry I am to say this, but I think we jumped into an intimate relationship too soon. Not only because of the book stuff, but because I've still got so much baggage to unpack."

"I'll help you work through things if you'll let me."

"I know, and you're wonderful to offer, but I already explained why I need to do it on my own." *If I'm even around long enough to finish the job.*

"Peyton, hasn't everything been really good . . . until you saw Todd?"

"It has, but . . ." He'd handed her an out, and she had to take it. In Paris, Mitch had said white lies meant to protect others were okay, so she lied. "I've been thinking about how Claire allowed me to apologize, and maybe part of my work on myself is giving Todd a chance to make amends."

"The two situations aren't the same. Yes, you fell in love and hurt a friend, but *he* left you when you needed him most. Those betrayals don't warrant the same consideration."

She bit her lip hard. She considered telling him the truth, but then he'd feel duty bound to stick by her if only to prove he wasn't like Todd. "Even if Todd is undeserving, I still need closure—however that looks. How can I trust in love again if I don't work through all my feelings? And you deserve so much better than I can give you right now. I can't ask you to stick around waiting . . ." She covered her mouth with her hand to keep from letting the truth slip out.

"Peyton, I'll wait because I believe there's something between us worth fighting for."

"You've had to fight for so much your whole life. You shouldn't have to fight for love, too. Trust me, millions of women are so ready for someone like you to love them."

"I don't want those women."

"If I know you're waiting, I'll feel pressure to hurry up when what I need most is time to myself." Peyton tried not to imagine the bitter look that must now inhabit his eyes—exactly like she'd seen in Claire's eyes for years. She almost confessed the truth because she hated that his last impression of her would be one of selfishness when she was trying so hard to be selfless. But that disgust he had to feel was her best shot at pushing him away.

"I see," he said.

But he didn't see at all, because she wouldn't let him know how her heart now lay lifeless in her chest, her body as cold as the deepest water in the Sound. The numbness took over like morphine. "I'm sorry, Mitch."

"So am I."

Chapter Nineteen

"I have to thank you, Mitch. Things have been so much better at work since I started taking your advice." Lauren reached across the table for the butter, cutting another pat to mix into her mashed potatoes.

"Good." Mitch mindlessly forked his meatloaf. He shouldn't have come to Hoboken tonight. His mother's suffocating condo hadn't lifted his mood one bit.

"Lauren, that's too much butter." Their mom snatched the butter dish and set it on the counter behind her seat. "It's not good for your heart."

"You didn't say a word to Mitch when he showed up with three different homemade desserts." Lauren spooned a butter-drenched bite into her mouth. "Besides, I'm a fit twenty-three-year-old with no cholesterol problem."

"You'll get one if you don't start watching what you eat." His mom then thrust a hand toward him. "Tell her, Mitch. Tell her I'm right."

He drew a deep breath through his nose, having already arbitrated everything from how Lauren thought their mom should dye her grays to how his mother wanted Lauren to become a TRUE Mentor like Sadie. "Meatloaf and gravy aren't exactly a healthy menu item, either, Mom."

But thank God for the gravy, which saved the overcooked meatloaf from tasting like paste. He didn't offer a reason for why he'd been up all night baking.

His mom huffed, no doubt disappointed that he hadn't sided with her. He'd lost all patience for their insignificant, petty arguments after the way Peyton had spit him out like old gum.

When he'd hung up with her earlier this afternoon, he'd put Rebecca in charge of following up with After-Words in Chicago to make sure things were set for tomorrow's event. He'd then spent an hour on the phone with Kendra Khan, updating her on the rollout of her launch. At least there'd be no problem keeping the lines of *that* relationship clear. Kendra had even less humor and spontaneity than he did, but she'd written a damn fine—if dark—book.

"I thought it would be nice if we all drove down to see your uncle George on Saturday." His mom slurped some iced tea after that whopper of a non sequitur.

"Pass." Lauren ladled beef gravy over her mashed potatoes as if daring her mom to say something.

Thankfully, his mom remained too focused on her own goal to notice. "We haven't seen my brother in two months, and it's his birthday next week. He asks about you both all the time. I know he'd love to see us all. I think he's lonely since Addy died."

Aunt Addy had died seven years ago, and Uncle George had met a new companion not long afterward, but Mitch kept that mental note to himself.

Lauren groaned. "Please don't force me to make a four-hour round-trip to sit in Uncle George's little apartment, eating egg salad sandwiches while you two reminisce. He smells like mothballs."

"It's summer. He won't be wearing wool sweaters and the windows will be open." Their mother's grip on her silverware turned her knuckles white. "Why don't you ever want to do anything with our family, Lauren?"

"I do family stuff. I'm here now, aren't I?" She made a show of looking at her hands and then around the condo. "I'll send Uncle George a card and a gift, but after a long week at work, I want to sleep in and chill on Saturday."

"Mitchell?" His mother bugged her eyes, which was her preferred tactic for prompting him to join forces. "Jump in anytime."

He shook his head. "No thanks."

From the looks on both their faces, one might think he'd turned into a unicorn right there at the table.

"You okay?" Lauren shoved his shoulder. "You're acting weird and mopey tonight."

"I'm fine."

"Hm." She narrowed her eyes. "Are you pouting because I didn't make it to the Strand?"

"No." *He* didn't pout. That was their domain. "I'm preoccupied with another important launch."

"You're always busy dealing with book launches. Tonight is different." His mother sat back, arms crossed. "It's that Peyton, isn't it?"

He didn't meet her eyes.

"Did she break your heart already?" His mom clucked, fingers now drumming the table.

"Don't be ridiculous, Mom. Mitch doesn't mix work and pleasure," Lauren said, although she now eyed him with suspicion. He hadn't discussed his relationship with Peyton with her, and obviously his mother hadn't, either—a silver lining of their lack of communication, he supposed.

Mitch remained mute, pushing the dry meatloaf into a puddle of gravy.

Lauren laughed. "Oh my gosh, you *did* break your rule!"

"Oh, Mitch." His mom shook her head. "I warned you that different worlds always clash. But it's her loss, honey. You'll find someone else. Someone better suited . . . like Sadie."

He pushed away from the table—the legs of his chair scraping the floor—and took his dish to the sink. "I've got to go."

"Why? We haven't had dessert yet, and we have to finalize our plans for visiting George." His mom wiped her mouth with her napkin.

"I'm not going to see Uncle George this weekend, but I'll call him," Mitch said.

"Now *neither* of my kids cares about me and my brother? What did I do to deserve this cold shoulder?"

"Oy, the guilt trips, Mom. Why do we have to prove our love by doing everything you want?" Lauren asked.

Mitch was almost grateful for the Uncle George conversation because it kept Lauren from grilling him about Peyton.

"You hardly do *any*thing I want, let alone do *every*thing." Their mom rolled her eyes at her daughter.

Lauren plunked her forehead on the table. "Mitch, make her stop."

"Both of you, stop." His clipped tone caused them both to gape. He rinsed his dish and set it in the dishwasher, then filled the meatloaf pan with hot, soapy water. The women exchanged glances. "I mean it. I'm done with playing the Mathis family ref. Work out your relationship or don't, but this"—he gestured between them—"is not my relationship to fix. I've got my own problems, and you don't see me dumping them in your laps."

"Watch your tone. I didn't raise you to speak to me that way, Mitchell." His mom frowned.

"I'm sorry, Mom." He took a deep breath. "I don't mean any disrespect, although you were downright rude to and dismissive of Peyton. How do you think that made me feel, especially after I'd just spent a weekend at her family's house with her parents?"

"Did she complain about me?" His mom's indignant expression would've made him laugh if he weren't so pissed. "Is that what caused a rift?"

"No, *I'm* complaining about you. She has too much class to complain to me about my mother. But what if she'd overheard everything you said? Why would you bring up her health, or presume to tell me what I can and can't handle?"

"What did you say?" Lauren asked their mom, eyes bright with gossip-hungry interest. "And why am I the last to know anything?"

"If you came around more, you'd know more." His mom waved her hand at Lauren. "I wasn't impolite. I told your brother—in private—that he should be careful dating someone with her history because he's already been through that misery with your father. Any good mom would try to spare her child more pain."

"But I thought she was cured?" Lauren looked at him in confusion.

Before he answered, his mom interrupted. "She's only been cancer-free for one year. One! It could come back. You never know."

"No one ever *knows*," Mitch said. "We could all have cancer right now."

"Don't be smart. You *know* what I mean." His mother made the sign of the cross before setting her hands on her hips. "I won't feel guilty about trying to keep you from having your heart broken. If you'd stayed with me last weekend instead of going up to Connecticut, you wouldn't be brooding today."

He sat back, shaking his head. "You do realize that it's not up to you to decide who I date, right? You're so sure Peyton and I had nothing in common, but maybe that's because I've never been able to explore who I really am. Since Dad died, all of my decisions have been about what's best for the family. Never once have I felt the freedom to dream my own dreams."

"I didn't know you felt so burdened." His mother slumped in her seat.

"Neither did I." As soon as he said it, he closed his eyes. "I'm sorry. I don't mean that like it sounded. I don't resent you or regret where I am in my life, but there might be other things I'd like to do, too. Things that don't involve you, or paths you might not choose for me. Give me credit for being smart enough to know what I can handle and what I want."

"But look at what happened . . . It didn't work, like I suspected." His mom turned her palms up.

"And the world didn't end. I made a choice, and I'll live with the consequences. In any case, it'd be much kinder to say you're sorry that I'm hurt rather than saying 'I told you so.'"

"Good luck with that," Lauren mumbled.

"And you." He whirled on his sister. "Enough with the wisecracks. Instead of picking on Mom, go look in the mirror. When's the last time you did anything for her or me without being pressured? You've been coasting along as 'the baby' way too long. It's time to pitch in and give back, unless you're okay with us treating you the same way."

She looked at her mom while hitching a thumb at him. "If Peyton did this to him, I'm with you, Mom."

His mouth dropped open, but then Lauren reached for his hand. "I'm kidding, Mitch. Sorry. Very bad joke. I'll try to do better. I wish I'd made it to the reading, because now it looks like I'll never meet the Globejotter . . . or her hot brother."

Mitch shook his head. "Probably not."

Admitting that aloud made it all the more real and painful.

"Well, I guess this is a good reminder of why I should follow your rule," Lauren mused before licking the last bit of gravy from her spoon. "While I kinda like that *you* finally broke a rule, I'm sorry it backfired. What happened?"

He sighed. "Her ex showed up at the event. It's complicated. She says she needs time to process everything she's been through—with cancer, that breakup, the book stuff. I get that. She's been on a treadmill since her diagnosis and needs time to catch her breath."

"Makes sense." Lauren nodded.

"Not to me," his mom said.

"Only because you don't like to do anything by yourself," Lauren replied, then turned back to Mitch. "Give her some space. Maybe send her a note in a week or something, but don't be clingy. No woman likes a clingy man."

Their mom harrumphed, which caused Lauren to double down on her statement by bugging her eyes at him.

"Mom," he said, "let's not argue. I appreciate the dinner and know that you mean well. I'm sorry I brought my bad mood with me, and I'll go to see Uncle George on Saturday, okay? That said, next time I have a chance to be happy—however that looks to me—I'd like your support instead of a lecture."

"Fine." His mom raised her hands like he was holding her at gunpoint. "Far be it from me to be one of those mothers who doesn't know when to keep her mouth shut."

Laughter burst from Lauren, and even Mitch had to smother a chuckle. The pop of humor felt damn good at the end of his crappy day.

—⁓—

Jerry the Uber driver placed Peyton's suitcase in the trunk, giving her an extra moment to herself while in the back seat. The sickly-sweet aroma of the deodorizer dangling from the rearview mirror did nothing to stave off her nausea.

She snaked her hand beneath her wrap dress and across her right breast to feel the lump again. After a year of ignoring her foobs, she'd now massaged that spot a thousand times since yesterday, fishing for the baby pea-size bump beneath the ridge of her scar. Panic toyed with her head, making the lump feel a little different each time—bigger, smaller, oval, round, painful, numb.

As usual, the waiting was the worst part—or nearly the worst part—because anxiety made her as queasy as chemo did. Three days to go before the imaging tests, and then another few days for the results. Silver lining: she'd lose five more pounds before she got an answer, getting her back into *all* her precancer clothing. She scrunched a fistful of hair in her hands and pushed away the idea of losing it again.

When Jerry sank onto his seat and fired up the Ford Focus's small engine, she straightened her shoulders and pasted a smile on her face. "Thank you. We need to make a quick stop at 436 Forest Street first, and then we're heading to JFK."

"You got it, pretty lady." He returned her smile in the rearview mirror. His white hair, sunspots, and deep wrinkles proved him to be at least sixty-five, and she could always tell the difference between a harmless compliment and a come-on.

"Thanks." She then stared out the window for the three-minute ride to Claire's home, the familiar streets and houses blurring together. Peyton hadn't seen Claire since the Strand and didn't want to see her this morning. She'd texted Logan a minute ago, but he still hadn't responded by the time Jerry pulled up to the curb.

"Hang here for five minutes," Peyton told him. She exited the car and trotted up the steps to knock on the door, calling out, "Come on, Logan. Time to go."

The door opened, bringing her face-to-face with Claire, who was dressed in a boldly patterned Vineyard Vines dress and eating a double-chocolate-chip muffin. "Good morning."

"Good morning." The whole town knew that Claire devoured chocolate to cope with emotional upheaval. Peyton would bet anything that she'd been eating like a madwoman since Wednesday night. For a nanosecond, Peyton considered addressing the elephant on the porch, but then chose not to even whisper Todd's name. With a slight smile, she asked, "Is Logan ready?"

"Just about." Claire picked a chocolate chunk off the muffin top and popped it into her mouth. "He's brushing his teeth."

"Oh, okay." Peyton fumbled for a safe topic. "Cute dress. You're up and at 'em awfully early."

"I have an appointment with Fred Bastion at eight. He's redecorating his law office. Otherwise we would've stayed in the Chelsea apartment last night so Logan could sleep in longer." Claire tipped her head. "Why didn't you stay with Mitch?"

Claire, off on a fishing expedition with zero ability to play poker . . . or fish. Peyton could see straight through the attempt to discover how Todd's appearance had affected her. And yet, seeing her friend standing there gobbling a muffin, Peyton couldn't help but bite on the line she'd been thrown. "Mitch and I . . . That's over."

Claire's eyes went round, but Logan bounded down the stairs and interrupted them before she could ask more. He set his bag down to grab his fiancée into a hug while smiling at Peyton. "Hey, sis."

"Did you know that she and Mitch broke things off?" Claire asked before taking a giant bite of her muffin over the back of Logan's shoulder, which was a pretty cool party trick.

"What?" He released her, looking at Peyton with surprise. "Tell me this has nothing to do with that ass Todd."

Claire shoveled the final chunk of her muffin into her mouth.

"No." Peyton shook her head, her throat tightening like it did every time she thought about Mitch, and the real reason why she'd pushed him away. "But we don't have time to discuss this now. We've got a plane to catch."

As usual, Logan saw through her bravado. He gripped her arm. "Hang on. You're hiding something. What did Mitch do?"

"Nothing." She shrugged free of his grip.

"So what happened?" Logan hefted his bag up by the shoulder strap. "You two looked happy the other night at dinner."

She had been happy. Stupidly so.

"Bad timing." She shrugged, feigning nonchalance like a boss.

"Because of the book?" Logan quizzed.

"No."

"Peyton, you're stuck with me for twenty-four hours, so you might as well come out with it, because you can't hide from me for that long," he pressed.

She glanced at Claire and him. The worry pushed up from her chest, making her eyes and nose sting. Rather than dissolve into a puddle on the porch, she tensed every muscle and tapped into her strength. "Dr. Wang found a small lump during my exam yesterday. We don't know what's what, so I'm getting an MRI next week and I really don't want to talk about it or Mitch, okay?"

"Wait, what?" Logan's face went ashen.

Claire cut through his question with her own. "Did Mitch end things because you might be sick again?"

"*Are* you sick again?" Logan rasped.

Peyton couldn't deal with the third degree or soothing anyone else's emotions when she hadn't yet gotten her own under wraps. "I just said I don't want to talk about this now, and I mean it. So please, please, *please* drop it."

Before they could do or say another thing, she turned and jogged to the car, blinking nonstop. The confession had not been part of her plan, and now she'd be trapped in a car and on a plane with Logan.

Frak.

As she slid into the back seat for the second time, she caught a glimpse of Logan and Claire in an embrace. Claire dabbed the outer corner of his eye before they broke apart. He kissed her again, then came to the car.

When he joined Peyton in the back seat, he stared straight ahead without making eye contact. Neither spoke while the car wound through the quiet streets of Sanctuary Sound. She laid her head back against the seat and closed her eyes. Two minutes later, as Jerry gunned the engine to merge onto I-95 South, Logan grasped Peyton's hand and squeezed it.

The tears that she'd been holding inside began to leak from her eyes, but she couldn't look at her brother.

"I love you," he said, reaching over to wipe her stray tears.

"I love you, too."

"Should we cancel this trip? It feels like too much—"

"Absolutely not." She opened her eyes and looked at Logan. "Days ago I would've been happy to have the tour go away, but not now. Distractions helped me last time, so let's focus on the event and pretend like it's any other day."

He pulled a face. "I'd made plans for us to meet up with Johnny Murello after the event. He'd sold me on a new restaurant in the West Loop, but maybe I should cancel."

"No! I told you I need distractions. Let's assume the event will go well, in which case I'll be happy to catch up with him and have a good meal rather than sit alone in my room. Of course, if things go south . . ." She shrugged.

Logan bumped shoulders, making a brave stab at playfulness. "Any ex-boyfriends in Chicago you want to warn me about?"

She sniggered, which felt great. Maybe telling Logan her secret hadn't been the worst decision she'd made in the past twenty-four hours.

Her phone pinged a notification, so she glanced at it to find a direct message in her Facebook author account.

Ms. Prescott,

You won't remember me, but we met in Paris after your reading, where you kindly spent extra time talking to me about my wife. We've since been reading your book together. She's sorry she didn't meet you in person, especially after I told her of your compassion. Talking with you helped me feel stronger and able to help her better, so I wanted to thank you for helping so many people with your courage. We wish you well.

Sincerely,
Paul Boutell

"Good news?" Logan asked cautiously.

"Not from the doctor." She reached across the seat and grabbed his hand. "I know I've bitched a ton about all of this, but thank you for pushing me to do this book, Logan. Right now it and the people we meet are my salvation."

He pulled her to his side and, like a good brother who'd paid attention at the reading in New York, simply said, "I love you."

Chapter Twenty

After his publisher meeting, Mitch was dodging pedestrian traffic as he rounded the corner to his office—lunch bag in hand—when he pulled up short.

Claire's red hair and her cane, Rosie, would be hard to miss under normal circumstances. At the moment, her pink-and-green dress also stood out amid the gray and black clothing of other passersby. Pacing in a tight circle, she resembled a squirrel in search of food, and Rosie looked more like a weapon than a helpful apparatus.

"Claire?" he asked. "What are you doing here?"

He recalled that she and Logan kept a place in Chelsea, but that was more than a mile north of his Hudson Square office.

"Mitch?" Her head whipped up and her mouth fell open. "I, um, I didn't . . . I should . . . Oh, shoot."

He noted her red cheeks even as her eyes scanned his face like they were hunting for lost treasure.

"You seem upset." He gestured toward the door. "Would you like to come upstairs for some water or tea?"

She glanced around furtively, tightening her grip on Rosie. "Oh, no, thank you. I shouldn't bother you . . ."

The chance of this run-in being a pure coincidence seemed about nil to Mitch. She'd seek him out only for something to do with the Prescotts, although she appeared to be plagued by second thoughts.

Desperate for news about Peyton, he tried to keep her there.

"It's no bother. Come on in." He held the door for her, and then she followed him to the elevator for the one-story ride up to his office. When they entered the cramped but well-appointed office, he was grateful that Rebecca wasn't at her workstation. "Can I fix you a tea?"

"I don't need tea, Mitch." Her expression remained suspended halfway between a glower and that of a terrified rabbit.

"I assume you've come because of Logan or Peyton."

"Yes, I did, but I shouldn't have." She smoothed her skirt and fidgeted with her white-and-gold necklace.

He remained rooted in his spot. "Is this about the tour dates?"

"No." She bit her lip. "Honestly, none of this is my business."

"None of what?"

"Anything to do with Peyton." She shrugged, hanging her head.

His anxiety rose in direct proportion to Claire's obvious discomfort. "Rebecca should return soon. Let's go to my office for privacy."

She glanced back toward the main door while nibbling her lip before deciding to follow him. He closed his office door while she took a seat. After tossing his lunch on his desk, he leaned his hip against the desk's edge and crossed his arms. "You're obviously upset, so please tell me why you tracked me down."

She tapped her cheeks with her palms. "Believe me, the last thing I thought I'd be doing when I woke up this morning was storming your office."

"Does Peyton know you're here?" His erratic heartbeat made him light-headed. He should sit, but he couldn't move.

"Of course not! I haven't spoken to her or Logan since they left for the airport this morning, and I'm sure they have much bigger things on their minds right now than checking in with me." She widened her eyes in a way that suggested he knew what she meant by "bigger things."

Claire's emphatic tone seemed disproportionate to any concerns Logan or Peyton might've had about the Chicago event. His mind wandered. Had Peyton complained about him letting Rebecca handle the details? Had she secretly wanted him to go with her? No. Peyton had Logan, whom she always turned to for everything. So what had Claire so upset?

"Does this have anything to do with Todd?" he ventured, certain he'd scowled, as he did anytime he pictured that man's face.

Claire cleared her throat. "Isn't *his* reappearance rather ironic at this point in time?"

Ironic?

"He certainly threw a monkey wrench into everyone's evening." Worse, he'd crushed the bud of Mitch's new relationship beneath his heel on his way out the door. Never before had Mitch hated someone he didn't know. "But what's he have to do with your visit?"

When Claire shook her head, the disappointed gesture seemed aimed at him, not Todd. "Last weekend, I asked you point-blank if you were a good guy, and you promised me that you were."

Mitch shrugged, turning his palms up. "And?"

"And yet you're exactly like Todd," she spat. "With everything else Peyton's dealing with, and how it will affect Logan and the rest of the family, she deserved better from you."

Mitch rocked back against his desk. "Claire, I have no idea what you're talking about, but I resent your accusation. Trust me, I'm nothing like Todd."

She gripped her purse on her lap, looking at him with such a sorrowful, serious expression. "I *know*."

"Know what?"

"Why you and Peyton broke up."

Mitch pushed off his desk. "A breakup suggests we were actually a couple, which in hindsight might've been wishful thinking on my part."

"Is that what you're telling yourself now so you can walk away when she'll need support more than ever?" She tapped Rosie on the ground indignantly.

"First of all, I didn't walk away. She pushed me." Warning bells caused his skin to prickle as he replayed her words. "What do you mean by 'she'll need support more than ever'? Please tell me what's going on, because I'm in the dark."

Claire grew quiet, her eyes narrowed as if she were watching for some sign. "Wait . . . Peyton broke up with *you?*"

"Yes. She called me Thursday afternoon and said she needed closure with Todd. She must have unresolved feelings for him." As soon as he saw the horrified look on her face, he winced. "Sorry, I know he's a touchy topic."

Claire's head shook almost imperceptibly, but he caught it.

"It's not a touchy topic?" he asked.

"It's touchy, but I'm sure Peyton doesn't have feelings for Todd." Her cheeks were turning red.

"Well, she refuses to say much about him to me. After Wednesday's reading, she said that she felt like a hypocrite for refusing to let Todd apologize, considering the way you ultimately let her back into your life, so now she wants to try to 'get closure' with him."

Claire stood, hand clapped to her forehead. "I never thought things could get messier, and yet here we are." She looked at him. "I'm sure seeing Todd threw her, but trust me, her feelings for him are *not* the issue."

For a tense moment, they stared at each other.

Without more information, he had no idea what to say. "We're talking in circles. I'm still confused."

Claire turned ghostly pale. "I'm sorry I jumped to conclusions. I should go and let you two work things out, however that happens."

"Hang on!" He leaped from the desk before she reached the door. "You've got me worried now. Don't leave without giving me some peace of mind. I care about Peyton. If you think I can help her, tell me how."

She covered her face with her hands. "Oh, Mitch, I thought . . . but I shouldn't have assumed . . . and now . . . her privacy . . . It's not my news to tell . . ."

His heart was racing in his chest.

"Call her and *make* her talk to you." Claire touched his arm.

He shook his head. "I have to respect her request for space."

"She's stubborn, but she cares about you. Don't give up." Claire wrung her hands. "I'm sorry I interfered and got you worked up. It was so out of line."

And then everything came together in a crystal-clear epiphany. "Is she sick?"

Claire's face crumpled.

"Claire!" The word came out rougher than he meant it to.

She hung her head and kept her gaze on the ground. "She had an appointment yesterday . . . There's a new lump, but it might not be anything serious. She won't know for a week."

The floor fell out from under him, so he sank onto a chair. "Jesus."

"I'm sorry I don't know more. Logan and I only found out this morning. Logan looked so lost. I got so upset. I let the past lead me to assume you ended things once you found out. I'm so sorry."

He bent forward, forcing air into his lungs. Peyton, his father . . . Why did this keep happening? "She doesn't want me to know."

Claire covered her face with her hands. "I should've minded my own business. This was a huge mistake."

"Why *did* you come?" He stood and held her gaze once she lowered her hands. "I mean, from what Peyton's described, your friendship is based more on mutual love for Logan than anything else at this point, yet when you arrived, you seemed angry on her behalf."

"However our reconciliation began, she's going to be my sister-in-law and, with some luck, will be in Logan's and my life for years to come. I loved her for many more years than I hated her, and I know she regrets what she did . . . and not only because Todd wasn't worth it. I want her to be happy, and she seemed happy at the party last weekend." She sighed.

With some luck, she'd said. He couldn't wrap his head around this news or how Peyton must be feeling today.

"She'll kill me for telling you, and I can't blame her." Claire resumed her pacing. "Logan will be furious, too."

Mitch patted her shoulder. "I won't mention your visit."

"But I won't keep secrets from Logan. Hopefully, they'll forgive me because I meant well. But you know what they say about good intentions and the road to . . ." She pointed to the floor and fell silent while her gaze grew unfocused. "What will you do now?"

He ran his hands through his hair. "If I ask her about this before she's ready, it could be the absolute end for us."

"There's only one absolute end for any of us." She smoothed her hand along Rosie's ivory handle. "I can't tell you what to do—and my being here proves I don't always make the right choices—but last time, Peyton kept everyone at arm's length. I suspect she pushed you away now to protect you from having to go through it all with her."

Claire shouldn't be making more assumptions, but something about this one made inherent sense to him, especially considering some of his and Peyton's conversations in Europe. The one thing he now knew with certainty was that he wouldn't learn the answers sitting here in his office.

He glanced at his watch, then pulled out his phone to search for flights to Chicago.

"What are you doing?" Claire asked.

"Booking a flight to Chicago." He spared her a glance. "Want to come?"

"Oh, I don't think that's a good idea." She shook her head, eyes wide. "I hate to fly. Plus, I'm a little afraid to face Peyton and Logan so soon after what I've done."

"I detest flying, too, so we can commiserate. And no matter how mad Peyton might get, some part of her will be thrilled that you cared enough to confront me. Logan might be surprised, but I suspect he could use your support. He must be beside himself about his sister."

Claire bit her lip. "That's true."

"Should I book two tickets?" His thumbs hovered over the keyboard.

She grimaced before nodding. "Okay. I'll go throw a bag together and meet you at the airport."

"LaGuardia, four o'clock, nonstop flight on United. If all goes well, we could make it to the bookstore before the event begins."

"I'll see you at the gate." Claire stood, hesitating, her cheeks a bit flushed. "I'm glad that I was wrong about you."

"And I'm glad you were angry enough to let me know what's going on."

After she gave him her legal name, birthdate, and contact information and left his office, he finished booking the tickets and then zipped over to his apartment before grabbing an Uber to LaGuardia. On his way to the airport, he called his mother.

"Hi, Mitch."

"Mom, I'm sorry for the last-minute cancellation, but I can't make it to Uncle George's tomorrow. I'm on my way to the airport."

"Where are you going?"

"I need to go to Chicago."

"I thought you weren't doing that part of the book tour."

"I wasn't, but my plans changed."

"Is Peyton forcing you to go?" Her voice sounded hard.

"No, but I found out she got potential bad news from her doctor. I know you don't approve, but I need her to know that I'm here for her if she wants my support."

His mom didn't speak for a few seconds. "Well, then, I hope she appreciates you. And of course I hope that the news isn't as bad as you fear."

"Thank you." It wasn't a lot, but for his mother, that was progress. "I promise I'll take you to see Uncle George next weekend. Please send him my apologies, okay?"

"Call me later so I know you're okay. I'll call George and reschedule."

"Thanks, Mom." He tucked his phone away as the driver pulled up to the departures curb. The flurry of activity in the security line allowed him not to think too much about the lump in Peyton's breast until he found himself sitting alone at the gate.

Early as always, much like the first time he'd met Peyton in person. Since that day, he'd listened countless times to her describe the agony of waiting. He remembered that feeling from the past, but this felt different. He was no longer a frightened boy. He was a man with the strength to stand by her without crumbling. For him, the immediate concern was wondering how she'd react to seeing him again.

—⁓—

Peyton returned from the restroom without being accosted by an ex, so that was an improvement over her last event. She sat at the book-signing table beside her brother, sipped from her water glass, and then elbowed Logan. "You're pretty subdued tonight."

"Sorry." He straightened up and smiled at her, but she saw through the ruse to the pity and panic she'd wanted to avoid.

"Me too. I knew I shouldn't have said anything to you about the appointment, but now I need a promise from you."

"Anything." He leaned closer.

"If the worst case is true, don't you dare change one bit of your wedding plans or anything else. I mean it. I took too much from you last time. This time, I'll manage on my own. It won't be as hard, because now I know what to expect." Although that almost made it worse.

"Peyton, you don't have to pretend to be so strong for me." He squeezed her arm. "I know if I'm scared, you have to be terrified."

"Not helping." She looked away and signaled Roger, the employee who was lining up the readers, that they were ready to begin. Before the first reader came up, she muttered to Logan, "Time to sign. And if you can't buck up, I'm going to dinner with Johnny without you."

"Fine," he replied.

For a few minutes, Peyton fell into the groove of taking photos, signing books, and answering some personal questions. Things were humming along, and she somehow managed to put her little lump aside until Logan croaked, "Claire?"

Peyton snapped her gaze up, but instead of Claire, Mitch stepped into view. Her mouth fell open wide enough that people in line could probably see her fillings.

She exchanged a look with Claire and knew—*knew*—that Claire had told Mitch about the lump. Every cell in her body ignited, urging her to run from the room.

"This is a surprise." She struggled to meet Mitch's eyes. Yet there he was, in gorgeous 3-D, staring at her like there was nothing else on the planet. Her heart thumped so hard in her chest it might pound the stupid lump straight through her skin.

"A gate delay made us miss the reading. I assume it went fine?" He nodded an acknowledgment at Logan, who had already reached for Claire.

Peyton struggled to compute how Mitch and Claire both had ended up here together, and why . . .

"Of course." She would not fall apart in front of these readers, no matter how her desire to rush into Mitch's arms terrified her. "This isn't the best time to talk, though."

"I'll wait over there, with Claire." He collected Claire and wandered toward a stack of children's books.

Through her teeth, Peyton asked Logan, "Did you know they were coming?"

She scribbled her signature and smiled for a photo with a middle-aged woman.

"No," he answered before the next book came her way.

She grunted. "Claire told him about the lump. I'm sure of it. I can't believe she shared my personal medical information."

Before Logan could defend Claire—which would be impossible—a teenage girl interrupted them. "Hi. I'm Lelah, but I want you to sign this to my mom, Donna. She couldn't come tonight because she's sick, and"—Lelah cleared her throat—"well, I hope this will make her fight harder."

Peyton reached across the table and grabbed the young lady's hand. "I'm very sorry to hear about your mom. How are *you* holding up?"

She shrugged, her stoic expression never faltering. Peyton couldn't help but compare her to how she suspected Mitch must've handled facing the same fight at that age. "It's hard."

"I can imagine. Now I want you to listen to me, okay? It's super important that you remember that it's okay to still find some happiness in normal things. When I was sick, I didn't want my family to spend all their time worrying about me. If I saw them passing up things because of me or pretending not to be excited about things they were looking forward to, it made me feel worse, not better." She hoped Logan got that message, too.

She nodded again. "Thanks."

Peyton signed the book to Donna and handed it to the young girl. "Good luck."

It took another fifteen minutes or more to finish up with the audience. Peyton was running out of time to figure out what she'd say to Mitch . . . or Claire. After all the pleasantries had ended with the employees, she reluctantly joined Logan, Claire, and Mitch, who were waiting for her near the door. She averted her eyes while she worked through her thoughts about what Claire had done, and what Mitch planned to say.

Once they spilled onto the sidewalk, Claire immediately pulled at Peyton's arm, waving the men ahead. "Give us a second."

Mitch and Logan stood far enough away to allow Claire and Peyton some privacy.

"I know I crossed a major line and I'm *so* sorry. I thought you told Mitch about the lump and that he then broke things off like Todd. I went to his office but was about to turn around on the street outside and leave when we bumped into each other. By the time I realized he didn't know the truth, it was too late."

"Stop looking at me like I'm going to punch you. After what you've forgiven, I can't quite complain, can I?" Peyton blew out a breath. "That's not to say that I'm happy, because I'm not. I kept the truth from Mitch because I don't want to drag him through chemo and whatever else comes next."

"First of all, let's not jump to the worst-case scenario. But I don't think you'll have to drag him. He wants to be there for you."

Peyton slid a quick glance Mitch's way, catching her lower lip in her teeth. "He's already gone through this with his dad. It's not fair to ask him to be a caretaker, and I can't stand being pitied."

"His caring about you isn't pity, Peyton. It's love. I know how hard it is to trust a man after someone like Todd tears up your heart, but it's worth the risk. Don't let Todd keep you from finding happiness with Mitch or anyone else."

Love. It seemed too soon to throw that word around, and yet, at the same time, it didn't feel completely wrong, either.

Not as wrong as it felt to be standing on the sidewalk discussing Todd with Claire, anyway. But for the first time in years, she felt as if she had her old friend back. Claire had gone out of her way for Peyton today. If nothing else, that was a silver lining of massive importance.

"I can't believe you got involved and came all this way," Peyton said. "It kind of feels like old times."

"Maybe something like that." Claire's big blue eyes looked misty; then she surprised Peyton with a brief hug, which made Peyton's throat ache. Winning back Claire's friendship counted among her greatest achievements.

"Logan," Peyton called as Claire eased away. "Why don't you and Claire go meet Johnny? It seems Mitch and I have some things to discuss."

"Are you sure?" Logan's gaze darted between Claire and Peyton.

"Yes." Peyton nodded, managing a smile meant to coax Logan into letting go. "Show Claire around Chicago, and tell Johnny hi from me. I'll be in good hands."

Her brother hugged her and then grabbed Claire's hand. "I'll call you later."

Peyton shook her head. "Let's meet in the lobby tomorrow at nine to share a ride to the airport."

He kissed her forehead, then shook Mitch's hand. "Thanks for coming. Good luck."

Logan and Claire hailed a cab and disappeared, leaving Peyton alone with Mitch on the sidewalk, where she could no longer avoid him and those all-seeing eyes.

"Are you hungry?" she asked.

"No, but if you are, I'll take you somewhere to eat." He kept his hands locked behind his back while appearing to be watching her for any signal of her intention.

She shook her head, then met his gaze fully and sighed. "If it wouldn't kill my brother, I might've murdered Claire for involving you in this."

"Don't be angry with her for caring about you."

Peyton huffed, conceding that point, though it didn't mean she'd changed her mind about what was best for Mitch. "I appreciate the grand gesture here, Mitch, but it doesn't change the facts."

He narrowed his gaze. "What facts, exactly? The fact that you need to trust me to know what I want? The fact that you don't yet know what the lump is, but even if it is malignant, it doesn't change the way I feel about you?" He stepped closer, making her shiver. "Or the fact that you care about me? Because as hard as you're trying to push me away, I don't believe that's really what you want. And I know it isn't what you need."

"I've never pretended not to care about you. In fact, my caring for you is why I don't want to complicate your life, and I'm nothing if not complicated, even when I'm healthy." She'd raised her arms and then let them flop to her sides.

"I wouldn't know what to do with 'easy.'" He smiled at her with such warmth she wanted to smack some sense into him.

Instead she stomped a foot. "Don't you get it? I could die—"

Before she finished, he wrapped his arms around her. She made a half-hearted attempt to resist before she gave up and let her head nestle against his shoulder. He held her tight, murmuring in her ear, "If you're sick, I want to be there with you, no matter the outcome. Let *me* be the man you turn to this time. I promise I won't run away, and I won't love you less because you're sick or get bitter at times. You can trust me, Peyton."

"You love me?" As soon as the words slipped out, she buried her face against his chest.

He tipped up her chin. "I don't know all there is to know about you yet, but I love what I know. Your fire, your wit, your compassion and conscience, and your joy for life. You've helped me see what's been missing in my life. Give me the chance to learn more . . ."

"Asking you to stick by me if I'm sick feels wrong, Mitch. I swore I'd never hurt anyone *I* loved again."

"If you want to keep that promise, don't push me away, because that hurts as much as any other scenario you've got swimming around in your head." He smoothed her hair and then traced her jawline with his finger. "We're stronger as one because our differences compensate for each other's weaknesses. If we stick together, we can handle anything."

She looked into his beautiful topaz eyes and saw nothing but sincerity. With the first playful smirk she'd donned since seeing Dr. Wang, she said, "Since you broke your rules, jeopardized your career, *and* got on another plane for me, one could argue it'd be more selfish to deny your plea, couldn't one?"

"Absolutely." He kissed her, and his lips felt so right she forgot that they were in the middle of a city sidewalk.

Still, it was a lot to ask anyone, let alone a man in a new relationship. She broke the kiss. "Mitch, I need one promise."

"What's that?" He kept her wrapped in his arms.

"You suffered so much with your dad. If this lump isn't benign and things get too difficult for you, promise me you will feel free to cut and run."

"I'm not the boy I was back then, and the man I am now is wiser, thanks to you. Besides, this isn't a choice you make with your head. It's about heart, and mine wants to be with you today, tomorrow, and for however long it lasts, come what may. But let's not be so grim when there is reason to be optimistic. This lump might be nothing at all."

"That's what I told myself the last time." How blithe she'd been then, so invincible in her own mind until the weight of the truth fell on her head.

He squeezed her again. "Remember our flight to Rome, when you promised me that God wouldn't get you through cancer just to off you in a plane crash?"

She nodded, snickering.

"Well, I don't believe God will make me lose two people I love to cancer, either." He kissed the tip of her nose. "Let's not let fear override our faith."

Oddly, she felt better. "I have to say, I'm stunned that you got Claire on a plane. She hates airports and planes more than you do. I can picture you both triple-checking your seat belts and sweating it out the whole way."

"We managed." He kissed her again. "Anything is possible when you're fighting for love."

"If that's true, then maybe we have a chance, after all."

Epilogue

An orange evening sun ducked behind the buildings as Peyton and Mitch strolled the final block to Logan's apartment for the party he was hosting to celebrate their memoir hitting the *New York Times* hardcover nonfiction bestsellers list. The past ten days had been a whirlwind of flights and appointments and nail biting.

She'd been jumpy all day, awaiting a final call from Dr. Wang, but seeing that number pop up on her phone now made her heart stop. She halted outside Logan's building and gripped Mitch's arm before answering. "Hello."

"Peyton, it's Dr. Wang."

"Hi, Dr. Wang. I've been expecting your call." She stared into Mitch's reassuring eyes, thankful he was there for whatever news she got.

"I reviewed the pathology report, which confirms our suspicion that we removed a lipoma. I'm as happy to give you this good news as I assume you are to get it. There's nothing further to do at this point, but I urge you to do regular self-exams. Please schedule your next appointment for six months from now. Enjoy the rest of your summer."

A surge of relief made her knees feel weak.

"Oh, same to you. *Thank* you for calling." Peyton hung up the phone, heart pounding, now bouncing on her toes while wiping away the happiest tears she'd shed in some time. "It's a lump of fatty tissue. I'm still cancer-free."

Mitch pulled her into a hug. "I knew it!"

"It would seem we need to add ESP to your Optimus skill set."
He raised a brow.

"Dr. Wang sounded happy," Peyton continued. "If you'd ever met her, you'd know what a shock that is. She did, however, lecture me about self-exams."

"I'll gladly take over that duty." Mitch kissed her.

He'd been so unwavering in his support and affection she'd quickly let go of all insecurities about him seeing the foobs and scars and every other messy, imperfect thing about her. "You're hired."

He chuckled and then nodded hello to Logan's doorman before crossing the lobby to the elevator.

"The timing of that call couldn't be better." She heaved another sigh of relief. "This news lifts the cloud over our celebration tonight."

"We might need even more champagne." Mitch winked as Logan answered the door.

"Sis!" Logan grabbed her into a hug before shaking Mitch's hand. "We were wondering when you'd arrive."

In the kitchen, Claire was speaking with Peyton's parents, Steffi and Ryan stood by the island, and a few other friends were scattered around the living room. Silver balloons bumped against the ceiling, their streamers dangling in long curls. Logan had set some champagne on ice and ordered Thai takeout from their favorite place around the corner.

After she hugged and kissed everyone hello—cheerfully accepting congratulations on the book's success—she raised her hand for attention. "I'm sorry we're a little late, but I have good news. The lump is benign! I'm in the clear for another six months."

Her mother and father hugged each other as Logan swooped in to lift her off her feet. "Whoop! Now *that's* something to celebrate."

He poured her and Mitch each a glass of champagne and made a toast. "To my amazing sister, who lives life on her own terms, delivers zingers with a smile, and whose work has made us *New York Times* best-selling authors! Duck would be proud. We love you and are all relieved to learn you'll be healthy enough to keep us on our toes for a long time to come. Cheers!"

"Cheers!" The crowd toasted.

Before Peyton sipped from her glass, she held up her index finger. "I think we owe Mitch a nod for the effort he put into promoting the book. We wouldn't have gotten far without him. Most of you know how I vacillated about publishing and promoting this memoir, but Logan convinced me of its value. There were many days when I doubted my decision, and others when I wanted to kill my brother." She waited for the chuckles to peter out before she turned to face Mitch. "And while the bestseller status is a proud moment, it isn't close to being the best thing to come out of this process. Mitch, I can't imagine my life now without you."

"You don't have to." He leaned in and gave her a quick kiss while the guests all clapped.

The guests resumed their conversations while Peyton started tugging Mitch toward the buffet line. They'd almost made it there when Claire interrupted. "Peyton, can I steal you for a second?"

Mitch nodded and turned to speak with Logan and Ryan, while Peyton followed Claire into the bedroom, where Steffi was waiting.

"I have a little surprise." Claire closed the door and directed them to sit on the bed while she rummaged through the closet. A few seconds later, she returned with a familiar plaid binder in hand. "Our unofficial first publication."

"No way!" Steffi laughed.

Peyton blinked. "Is that the Lilac Lane League binder?"

Claire nodded. "I grabbed it from my mom's house earlier this week, knowing we'd all be together tonight. We've each had some real highs and lows these past two years, but I thought it might be fun to look back at where it all began."

Peyton reached out for the binder, and then the three of them lay, shoulder to shoulder, on their stomachs and began leafing through its pages.

Each one was filled with photographs—of them with paint-stained hands in the tree house, in matching bikinis on the dock at Arcadia House, at the prom with boys Peyton could barely remember (except Ryan, of course)—*Teen Beat* clippings of crushes, doodles, notes passed in class, wish lists, and one corny poem Peyton had authored in eighth grade.

"Ode to My Lilac Lane League"
I love my brother, 'tis true
But the sisters of my heart have been chosen
We've pledged our loyalty, too
As our friendship is one of devotion

I'd know them if I were blind
'Cause our bond cannot be broken
No better treasure will I find
And no truer words will be spoken

Peyton hung her head, groaning. "Oh God. How on earth did I go on to become a writer? You could blackmail me for my whole trust fund if you threatened to publish this."

"I think it's sweet." Claire smiled. "And not horrible . . . for middle school."

"Better than anything I could write," Steffi joked. She might not have a gift for words, but she could now build them a stellar "she shed."

Peyton reread the poem, frowning. "I didn't quite live up to the loyalty promise, though, did I?"

Claire smiled at Steffi. "We all split apart and walked our own paths for a while, making some mistakes along the way. Maybe we were broken for a bit, but we're here now and we've rebuilt into something stronger. That's what matters most."

Peyton closed the book and shared a group hug with her oldest, dearest friends.

A tap on the door forced them apart before Logan poked his head in. "Ladies, how about you save this reunion for a time when there aren't a bunch of people hanging around?"

They all wiped their eyes and uttered some version of "Okay."

When they rejoined the party, Mitch came to Peyton and snaked his arm around her waist. "Everything okay?"

"Everything's perfect."

He screwed up his face. "Think you'll feel the same way tomorrow when you meet my mom and sister?"

"I think I'll feel that way anytime I'm with you." She stroked her hand across his chest.

"Then maybe you should move back to the city." Mitch swigged some beer that he must've swapped with the champagne while she'd been MIA. "I have some empty drawers and closet space you could use."

"What exactly are you offering?"

"The book tour is over now. I know you're still weighing your next career move, but whatever you choose to do, move in and make your home base with me." His intense gaze still arrested her like it had from the get-go.

"You don't think we're moving too fast?"

Mitch shook his head. "We've both been around the block and learned from past mistakes. We're old enough to know when something is right, and too wise to waste time."

Given her health scares, she knew something about not wanting to waste a single minute. She wound her arms around his neck. "Well, this sure feels right to me."

"So you'll move in?"

With a quick kiss, she said, "I will. I've actually been considering surveying a class at NYU to see if I'd like going back for a master's, so it'd be nice to be in the city."

"Wow. What brought that decision on?"

"I've been mulling over what you said to me at Arcadia, and some recent fan mail has given me more confidence about the idea."

"Well, that's something else we can celebrate." He kissed her.

"When we leave this party, we'll steal some champagne and celebrate in private."

"Sounds like a plan." His broad smile had become her heart's home. She kissed his nose. "And I know how much you appreciate a plan."

ACKNOWLEDGMENTS

As always, I have many people to thank for helping me bring this book to all of you—not the least of whom are my family and friends for their continued love, encouragement, and support. My poor kids have had one too many take-out dinners lately.

Thanks, also, to my agent, Jill Marsal; as well as to my patient editors, Chris Werner and Krista Stroever; and the entire Montlake family for believing in me and working so hard on my behalf.

A special thanks to Ally Dunlap, who shared her experience with breast cancer with me, and to Carol Cofone-Hoffmann for sharing her false-positive postcancer checkup story with me. While each patient has his or her own journey and perspective with this disease, I know I couldn't have written Peyton's story without insight from these two women. And to my wonderful publicist, Crystal Patriarche, whose fascinating tale of starting her fabulous empire (BookSparks) and of its ups and downs inspired some of Mitch's experiences. My dear friend and amazing author Wendy Walker also shared the details of her European book tour to help me plan Peyton's journey, so I'm both jealous of and grateful for her experience. Also, thank you to Mary Frieberg for helping me with the bit of Catalan dialogue in this book, and to Krista Stroever for correcting my French! I also owe my gratitude to Sonali Dev and Liz Talley, who helped me untangle a plot knot that had me stuck mid-draft. And last but not least, my dear friend Jane Haertel (the "punniest" person I know), deserves credit for coming up with Peyton's Insta handle, Globejotter!

I couldn't produce any of my work without the MTBs, who help me plot and keep my spirits up when doubt grabs hold. And as noted in the dedication, my Fiction From The Heart sisters also inspire me on a daily basis.

And I can't leave out the wonderful members of my CTRWA chapter. Year after year, all the CTRWA members provide endless hours of support, feedback, and guidance. I love and thank them for that.

Finally, and most importantly, thank you, readers, for making my work worthwhile. Considering all your options, I'm honored by your choice to spend your time with me.

AN EXCERPT FROM
IF YOU MUST KNOW

EDITOR'S NOTE: THIS IS AN EARLY EXCERPT
AND MAY NOT REFLECT THE FINISHED BOOK.

Chapter One

AMANDA

There ought to be a warning anytime you wake up on a day that will forever change your life. Some harbinger—like a robin, lightning bolt, or black cat—so you don't find yourself blindsided. This morning's brilliant sunshine did not exactly scream, "Beware, today you'll discover that the most destructive lies are the ones you tell yourself."

If anything, the clear blue sky promised a perfect spring day. And so, blissfully ignorant, I stopped at Sugar Momma's on my way home from my routine three-mile walk along Chesapeake Bay. Normally, I'd never order a peanut butter–chocolate chunk cookie the size of a dessert plate and a decaffeinated salted-caramel latte with extra whipped cream at nine o'clock in the morning.

My husband, Lyle, wouldn't approve, especially not while I was pregnant. But he'd been away on business all week. While I wouldn't encourage anyone to lie to a spouse, in this case, what Lyle didn't know wouldn't hurt him.

If anything, I deserved this little—or not so little—cheat. Lately, my mostly charming husband had turned into a male version of Martha Stewart on steroids. It worried me to see how the pressure of putting together his new company's first real estate development deal was affecting him.

I'd done everything and anything to relieve his stress. Sex on demand. A gift certificate for a massage by Leslie Cooper, the best in town. Preparing his favorite meals. I even switched to lavender-scented cleaning products to create a soothing environment in our house. Thank God I had my mom to talk to because, on days when his mood blew cold, I would've been lost without her as my sounding board.

I broke off a section of the still-warm cookie and took a nibble. My eyelids drooped from the weight of cocoa-infused ecstasy. "Oh my goodness, Hannah. This is delicious."

Everything about her and her bakeshop intrigued me. They were my favorite discovery since moving into our new house a few blocks away back in December. The decor of her shop matched the bold colors she draped across her generous figure. Her ruby-red lips perfectly framed a larger-than-life smile and complemented her dark complexion. And she gathered all her braids into a single ponytail that was as thick as a fire hose.

I didn't know Hannah as well as I would have liked. We only spoke here, where her animated personality filled the shop with positive energy. My early attempts to forge a friendship failed when I sensed her keeping me in the "patron" box. Maybe she thought me too buttoned-up to be an interesting friend. Yet I often found myself wondering about her friends and family. Pictured her in a busy home kitchen, testing recipes. Imagined her knitting in her spare time—possibly because some of the shawls and vests she wore looked handmade. Most of all, I wondered what kind of partner could handle all her vivacity.

Not someone like Lyle. He preferred white tablecloths and efficient waiters to her and her eclectic shop—with its mismatched tables and chairs, folk art, and hipster music. I never argued the point, because it wasn't a hill worth dying on, but I found the whole vibe here warm and inviting. A friendly sort of place where you could exhale.

Hannah layered whipped cream on my coffee while winking at me. "Amanda, get yourself another cookie. You're eating for two."

I shook my head, begging off. "I need to watch myself."

"Where's the fun in that?" She tsked, then proceeded to squirt a liberal amount of liquid caramel atop the whipped cream.

"I promised Lyle I'd be good, for the baby's sake." When I rubbed my six-month bump, our daughter kicked my hand, thanks to the sugar rush. My heart always flipped a bit over the miracle happening inside my body, which shot my love for our growing family to a level beyond anything I'd ever dreamed. These past months I'd been exercising, sleeping plenty, and taking vitamins, while cutting way back on sugar and processed foods. "This morning's little detour has to stay our secret."

Hannah handed me the coffee, grinning. "That's exactly what he always says."

Wait, what?

"He does, does he?" Apprehension sank its nails into my spine. I chomped on the cookie to keep from saying something I might later regret.

I couldn't exactly be angry with Lyle when I was planning to keep *my* visit a secret. On the other hand, it wouldn't need to be a secret if he weren't so militant about my prenatal diet. It got on my nerves at times, but I knew he loved our daughter and me and wanted only the best for us. Still . . .

"Haven't seen Lyle all week. Where is he, anyway?" Hannah raised her brows while she waited.

I choked on the cookie. Did he really stop in that often? "Away on business. Big deal in the offing."

She must've been exaggerating. It was the only explanation that made any sense to me. Lately he'd been obsessed about diet and exercise.

Sugar Momma's heavy aroma of sugar and butter alone should make him run in the opposite direction.

"Mm, that man works hard. He always looks sharp in his jacket and tie. A man who means business, am I right?" Hannah chuckled, a rich, resonant sound that warmed the soul like my latte. "He keeps saying he can find me a better, cheaper space in town, but I like this location."

"Don't you dare move, Hannah. This shop is perfect for you." I hoped she couldn't see how shocked I was to be learning these things about my own husband.

ABOUT THE AUTHOR

Photo © 2016 Lorah Haskins

National bestselling author Jamie Beck's realistic and heartwarming stories have sold more than two million copies. She's a Booksellers' Best Award and National Readers' Choice Award finalist, and critics at *Kirkus*, *Publishers Weekly*, and *Booklist* have respectively called her work "smart," "uplifting," and "entertaining." In addition to writing, the author of the Cabot novels, the Sterling Canyon novels, and the St. James series enjoys dancing around the kitchen while cooking and hitting the slopes in Vermont and Utah. Above all, she is a grateful wife and mother to a very patient, supportive family.

Fans can learn more about her on her website, www.jamiebeck.com, which includes a fun "Extras" page with photos, videos, and playlists. She also loves interacting with everyone on Facebook at www.facebook.com/JamieBeckBooks.